Wedded Bliss

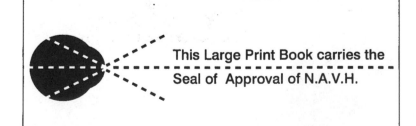

This Large Print Book carries the
Seal of Approval of N.A.V.H.

Wedded Bliss

Barbara Metzger

WHEELER
PUBLISHING

Published in 2004 by arrangement with NAL Signet, a member of Penguin Group (USA) Inc.

Wheeler Large Print Softcover.

The text of this Large Print edition is unabridged. Other aspects of the book may vary from the original edition.

Set in 16 pt. Plantin by Elena Picard.

Printed in the United States on permanent paper.

Library of Congress Cataloging-in-Publication Data

Metzger, Barbara.
    Wedded bliss / Barbara Metzger.
        p. cm.
    ISBN 1-58724-691-0 (lg. print : sc : alk. paper)
    1. Married women — Fiction. 2. Stepfamilies —
Fiction. 3. Nobility — Fiction. 4. Large type books.
I. Title.
PS3563.E86W43 2004
    813´.54—dc22   2004045970

A new beginning and a new baby.
This one is for Andrew David Siegal
with love

As the Founder/CEO of NAVH, the only national health agency solely devoted to those who, although not totally blind, have an eye disease which could lead to serious visual impairment, I am pleased to recognize Thorndike Press★ as one of the leading publishers in the large print field.

Founded in 1954 in San Francisco to prepare large print textbooks for partially seeing children, NAVH became the pioneer and standard setting agency in the preparation of large type.

Today, those publishers who meet our standards carry the prestigious "Seal of Approval" indicating high quality large print. We are delighted that Thorndike Press is one of the publishers whose titles meet these standards. We are also pleased to recognize the significant contribution Thorndike Press is making in this important and growing field.

Lorraine H. Marchi, L.H.D.
Founder/CEO
NAVH

★ Thorndike Press encompasses the following imprints: Thorndike, Wheeler, Walker and Large Pr int Press.

Chapter One

There ought to be a rule, Rockford decided. A gentleman who was busy saving the world should not be further burdened with querulous in-laws, criminal bailiffs, and capricious sisters. Robert, Earl of Rockford, quickly brought his twitching lips under firm control before his hovering secretary noticed, but he did have to laugh to himself, at himself. After all, despite his elevated title, his vast wealth, and his prestigious, although naturally unpaid position in official circles, he was no more than a jumped-up translator, or worse.

A gift for languages and a lifetime of training in the social arts made him the perfect diplomat, the ideal escort for visiting dignitaries and would-be allies. The prince regent valued Rockford's services — and his company — so much that the earl's request to join the military had been refused countless times. There was, of course, the earldom to be considered, with Rockford's heir still a minor. More important, from Prinny's view, was Rockford's knack for convincing foreign princes to cast their fates — and their marks, rubles, schillings, or kronas — into Britain's efforts to defeat the Corsican tyrant.

With his excellent memory and his ear for dialects, Rockford could almost tell which side of which mountain this princeling commanded, which plot of mineral-rich land that archduke controlled. With his reputation for scrupulous integrity and attention to detail, the earl had accomplished much on England's behalf. Soon, he felt, Bonaparte would be defeated and then he could think about accomplishing something more, although he knew not what, on his own behalf.

Right now he was involved, far more intimately than he wished, in convincing one of the visiting Austrians to pledge her brother's support for the war effort. Princess Helga Hafkesprinke of Ziftsweig would much rather pledge her hand to the wealthy, widowed Lord Rockford. Lud, the earl hoped Prinny never got the notion to trade Ziftsweig's allegiance for Rockford's ring on the plump princess's finger. He'd have to leave the country. Then again, perhaps Rockford's refusal to wed into a Teutonic dynasty could free him to join the army.

No, he was too old. At five and thirty the earl knew little of combat maneuvers, less of military discipline, and nothing whatsoever of rough camp life, field tents, or foraging. He adjusted one finely tailored cuff of his Bath superfine coat with his immaculate, well-manicured fingers. He'd stick with his translator's position.

Translator? Hell, right now he felt like a panderer, trading favors for fortunes. Surely his skills and experience could be put to better use than playing companion to the hefty Hafkesprinke heiress.

"My lord?" Rockford's secretary cleared his throat and anxiously gestured to the opened letters on the cherrywood desk. The first commandment of his employment was that the earl not be bothered with domestic matters, short of life and death. Poor Clifton was nervously awaiting judgment on the three letters he had brought to Rockford's attention.

Rockford turned his brown-eyed gaze back toward the offending correspondence. He supposed his dead wife's parents could not live forever, so that exonerated Clifton for plaguing him to read their whining. And the bailiff's absconding with Rock Hill funds was definitely a hanging offense, so that counted too. As for Rockford's spinster sister running off with the dastard, well, the earl would strangle her if he could. "You did well, Clifton."

Relieved, the man bowed and left, straightening a ledger on his way out of the dark-paneled office. Everything had to be precise and orderly for Robert Rothmore, Earl of Rockford.

Now nothing was, damn it.

He reread the letter from his former in-laws, knowing he would have to do something about their demands. He owed them a visit, at least. A jaunt north to Sheffield might even be to Rockford's advantage, his absence serving to cool Her Highness Helga's ardor.

Then he reread the other letter, from Rock Hill's aged butler, Claymore. Claymore carefully enumerated every item gone missing with the larcenous land steward, from silver candlestick to spinster sister. A copy had been sent to the local magistrate, but they were likely out of the country by now.

Rockford cursed, eloquently and in several languages. He supposed it was all his fault, being too busy to oversee the estate himself, being too trusting of a mere paid employee. Not that he cared about the money or the knickknacks, except for the stolen Rembrandt. Lud knew he had enough of both, except for Rembrandts, of course. He only had the one sister, though, no matter how distant their relationship had become.

Rockford poured himself a small glass of cognac, despite the fact that it was not yet noon and his customary hour for imbibing. If ever a man needed to bend his own rules, today was the day.

He should have insisted Eleanor reside with him in London, by Jupiter, no matter how much she protested. Hell, he should have married her off to the first available peer willing to take the outspoken, unfashionable female. Instead he had listened to his older sister's wishes, letting her stay at Rock Hill, stay unwed. A woman knowing what was right? Hah! He refilled his glass.

Jilted once, Eleanor hated men. Or so she had said, anyway. She also despised London society, with the insincerity as thick as the fog and the restrictive conventions as permeating as the constant dampness. The canons of polite behavior that Rockford lived by were nothing but codswallop to Eleanor. In one week, during her distant Season, she had offended every patroness of Almack's, swatted Prinny's wandering hands with her fan, and told Brummell he looked like a cyclopean frog with his quizzing glass held up to his eye. Rockford had gladly driven her back to Rock Hill in Leicester himself, with every expectation that she would stay there and manage his household. She'd managed to create a scandal and a criminal investigation and a deuced lot of trouble instead. Now he had to find a new estate manager.

Well, Eleanor would have to sleep in the bed she'd made. Be damned if they would see a farthing of her dowry, Rockford decided. They'd be lucky not to see the shores of Botany Bay. He had no intention of going after Eleanor, not even to recover the cherished Rembrandt Claymore listed as missing.

Worse than the money, worse than the masterpiece or his mutton-headed sister, worst of all, in fact, was what was missing from Claymore's list. The old butler never mentioned William, Rockford's young son. Usually there was word of the boy's health, brief news of his budding equestrian skills, some mention of his academic achievements. Surely the lad knew his times tables by now — so why was his name absent from the accounting? Had Rockford's sister taken a little boy with her to Gretna? Not even Eleanor could be so addled, Rockford hoped, but he would have to go check for himself. No servant, obviously, could be trusted with the task.

Within hours, the earl was in the saddle, headed north. When Lord Rockford gave orders, mountains moved . . . or carriages, baggage, and servants did, at any rate. Messengers delivered regrets for his social engagements. Grooms rode ahead to reserve rooms and horses and meals. His valet and his trunks, the four or five deemed necessary for a short visit to the country, would follow in the traveling coach. Rockford himself saw no reason to suffer through the trip in the slower, stuffy, confining carriage, not when he could ride cross-country and arrive that much sooner.

Rockford told himself concern was lending

urgency to the journey, not guilt. Why should he feel guilty about leaving the child alone? Heaven knew young William was being raised in the same fashion Rockford himself had been, seldom seeing his father. Like William, Rockford's mother had died in childbirth and, like William, he had been tended by hordes of caring servants until he was old enough for school. William, at least, had his aunt Eleanor, until she got some maggot in her brain about finding true love or some such rubbish.

The boy was fine, Rockford tried to convince himself as he urged his mount to greater speed, as if the hounds of hell were nipping at his heels. Nanny Dee and Claymore and Mrs. Cabot the housekeeper were likely spoiling the lad unmercifully, he was positive, and wasn't there a new tutor? The earl could not quite recall the fellow's name or credentials, but he had to be highly qualified to hold so important a post. His secretary would not have hired the man, otherwise. Or had idiotic Eleanor selected the tutor? Damnation. He should have interviewed the applicants himself.

He doubted his own father had ever concerned himself with tutors and such, being far too busy with his mistresses and his wagers. At least Rockford was busy with the Crown's business, not the hedonistic pleasure seeking his late, unlamented father had indulged in. He was a better father than the previous earl . . . wasn't he?

Rockford rode through half the night, having to put up at a second-rate inn instead of the suite reserved for him at the best hostelry along his route. The horse he was given was inferior too, which darkened his mood even further. So did the storm clouds that doused him with cold, bone-chilling rain. Hell and damnation, his own father would not have gone to half this effort or inconvenience.

Rockford might not have interviewed the tutor, but he had selected William's first pony himself, which was more than the previous earl had ever done. And while Rockford was not personally overseeing the boy's riding lessons, he did visit Rock Hill occasionally, for William's birthday when his secretary, Clifton, reminded him. One of the spring months, he thought now, although he had been in Austria last spring, and Brighton for the summer. Well, he had seen the child a few times before that. What more could anyone expect from a widower with diplomatic commitments, one who knew nothing of the nursery set?

The first time he had seen William was at his christening, following on the heels of William's mother's funeral. The babe had regurgitated sour milk all down Rockford's shirtfront. The second time, at his first birthday, the tot's nappy had leaked onto the earl's knee. On his second birthday, William had cleverly unfastened his own diaper, with even more disastrous results for Lord Rockford's linens. By the third anniversary of William's birth, the earl had grown wary, keeping his distance until the little chap proved his maturity. At Eleanor's urging, he had gone so far as to let William bring him a cup of tea. With the inevitable results for his wardrobe. He had not seen the boy since, Rockford realized.

By George, Eleanor must always have been daft, although Rockford had never recognized her condition. He pulled his beaver hat lower on his head in an effort to keep the rain from dripping down his collar, and swore at the weather, the rough-gaited horse, and the condition of the roads. He damned women in general and both his sister and William's mother in particular, for leaving the lad all alone. He cursed the butler for alarming him, and the bailiff for robbing him, and the regent for using him as bait. Mostly he railed against fate for making him responsible for a child he might not have fathered. There definitely ought to be a rule about that.

Rock Hill was just that: a heap of rocks on top of a hill. The house was a magnificent mélange of architecture, dating from the first stone fortress and added onto by successive titleholders. The huge gray dwelling with gray slate roofs overlooked acres of parkland and formal gardens, with geometric patterns of fields and farms laid out in the distance. All of it, as far as the eye could see and beyond, belonged to the Rockford earldom. Not just to Robert Rothmore, the current earl, but to his heirs and ancestors. Rockford felt the weight of those past and future generations on his damp shoulders as he rode up the long hill toward the vast ancient edifice that was his heritage, if not his home.

The place was nearly a palace, fit for state visits. Now it more often hosted gawking sightseers on public days. Still, the lawns were manicured, the shrubbery pruned to perfection. The scores of windows shone, even in the rain, and the brass fittings gleamed. Everything was proper, elegant, bespeaking great wealth, endless pride, and centuries of privilege, to say nothing of royal favor.

It was a dwelling well suited to Robert, Baron Roth and Rottingham, Viscount Rothmore, Earl of Rockford, etcetera, etcetera.

It was where he had been born, and where he would lie buried when he died.

It was where his heirs should be raised.

It was a blasted dungeon.

He rode around back, thinking to deliver the hired horse to the stables, then enter the house itself through the service doors rather than trail mud across the marbled front hall or the priceless Aubusson rugs that lined the corridors, unless Eleanor and her bailiff had carried off the carpets too.

An unfamiliar groom came to take his reins. "And you be?" the man asked insolently. "And what's your business?"

Rockford could not blame the fellow, since he must look no-account, dripping dirt and riding a poor specimen of a horse, without going to the front door.

"Rockford," was all he said. "I live here."

The man gulped, removed his cap, bobbed his head, and started to lead the tired animal away in a hurry.

Rockford stopped him with a question. "Where is Jake?"

Jake had been stable master for decades, putting Rockford on his first pony. The earl had been counting on the old horseman to do the same for William, or at least welcome him home.

"Gone to drive Mr. Claymore and Mrs. Cabot to the village to fetch supplies, m'lord," the groom replied, "and hire more help than what we keep on most times."

So no one was around to greet the prodigal son, not even the butler or the housekeeper.

The groom must have noted Rockford's frown, for he added, "We was expecting you tomorrow, else they would of been here. That's what the messenger said, leastways."

The slightly accusatory tone of the man's comment grated on Rockford's already fraying temper. "I do hope my arrival is not an inconvenience to my staff."

The groom shrugged. "You just might not find the place up to your standards, is all. Dinner 'specially. Bound to be potluck, with no time for fixing fancy dishes like you're used to in London. It's plain country fare here, most days."

Rockford could not imagine Claymore and Mrs. Cabot maintaining the Hill in anything less than pristine condition, nor its kitchens providing worse meals than he'd had on the road. The stables, from what he could see, were as neat and orderly as always, smelling of fresh straw and well-groomed horses, although there were few enough of them in the nearby stalls. He nodded. "And your name is . . . ?"

"Fred, m'lord," the groom answered, looking nervously toward the rear of the stables, as if wishing he could leave. "Fred Nivens. I were hired by Mr. Arkenstall, what left. But that don't mean I had any part in his thieving, like some hereabouts be hinting."

Still, he kept shifting his weight from foot to foot, and shifting his eyes from the horse to the earl to the back of the stables. Rockford would reserve judgment until he spoke to Jake and checked the ledgers for himself. Meantime, he walked with the groom and the hired horse toward the rear, glancing in the empty stalls. He did not notice any pony.

"Tell me, Fred, did my son ride along with Claymore and Mrs. Cabot into the village?"

Fred stopped short. "Master William?"

"Yes, that son." Rockford's patience was wearing decidedly thinner.

Fred scratched his head. "Why would you ask that?"

The earl tapped his muddy boots with his riding whip. He was not used to being interrogated by his own servants, and this one was either dense or deceitful. Either way, Fred's term of employment was growing shorter by the moment. "Because his mount is not here," Rockford said in slow and even tones that would have had his secretary shaking, "and Jake would never leave the pony out in the cold rain."

Now Fred looked at Rockford as if the earl were fit for Bedlam. "The nipper's been over to Mrs. Henning's for months now."

Months? His son had been gone for months and no one told him? Then again, perhaps Claymore had written, or Eleanor, but his secretary wouldn't have bothered him with such puny details as his five-year-old son leaving home for who knew where. Bloody hell, the lad could have joined the navy, for all anyone informed Rockford! And who the devil was Mrs. Henning, anyway?

"Tell me about this woman and why my son is at her house, wherever that might be, instead of here, where he belongs."

Fred Nivens began to brush down the wet horse, keeping as far away as possible from Rockford and that whip the earl kept rapping against his well-muscled leg. "As to the whys and wherefores," Fred said, "you'd have to ask Mr. Claymore, I 'spect. But Mrs. Henning, she's a widow what came here one day and said she was taking the nipper, to pack his clothes. Just like that, I heard tell."

Just like that? And Eleanor let this stranger take the boy? She must have been so ensorceled by her lover's blandishments that she could not keep her mind or her eye on what was important, namely Rockford's son. Damn her and that plaguesome bailiff; may they fall in a Scottish loch and get eaten by . . . by whatever creature of superstition lived in that benighted place. What if Mrs. Henning was an old witch who turned little boys into frogs, or a slave trader who sold them to chimney sweeps? Or a procuress who — Lud, it did not bear thinking on, so that was all, of course, that Rockford could imagine.

"Who is this female?" he demanded. "I have never heard of her."

Now Fred smirked. "You would have, if you'd visited more. Everyone knows her, by reputation, at least. She's Alissa Henning, what used to be Alissa Bourke, whose father was steward over at Fairmont. He got her educated way past her station, what gave her ambitions to better her lot."

Good grief, the woman sounded no better than she ought to be, and the groom's snide smile confirmed Rockford's suspicions. "Fairmont is Sir George Ganyon's place?" Rockford was already figuring how long it would take him to ride there if he cut across the home farm fields.

"Right, and Sir George has his eyes on her, they say. Lets her stay on in one of his cottages. Holding out for a ring, she is, I'd wager. Worked the first time, it did, when the doxy trapped some nobleman's son into marriage by claiming to be in the family way. His family don't recognize any jumped-up fortune hunter, naturally, so she's left to give lessons and hold other folks' children for ransom."

"She's holding William for ransom?" Rockford could not believe what he was hearing, or that his trusted retainers had let this abomination happen.

"Near as makes no difference. I spend half my time bringing food and fetching books. On the widow's orders." He neglected to say that the pretty widow refused to give him the time of day, but he did spit on the ground near the horse's feet, to show his opinion of the circumstances. "And Jake has to go give riding lessons over by Fairmont, to the young master and the widow's own brats."

She stole the pony too?

Chapter Two

Rules, hell. There were actual laws against kidnapping. Rockford had taken part in some of the parliamentary discussions about penalties, urging stricter enforcement. Otherwise no son of wealthy parents would be safe, be he from the nobility or the merchant class.

So much for safe if country bawds could get away with stealing an earl's son in broad daylight. Rockford threw his whip against the stable door. Not this time. He was the Earl of Rockford, and no one took what was his. Not ever.

"Can you drive?" he asked the groom, whose jaw was hanging slack at Rockford's reaction.

Fred nodded.

"Good. I cannot fetch the boy and his baggage home on horseback. Hitch up whatever coach is handiest. I shall meet you out front after I change into dry clothing."

"But, m'lord, your trunks ain't come yet."

Rockford was reaching for his saddlebags. "I always carry extra with me."

"But your valet . . ."

Rockford raised one dark eyebrow to show Fred Nivens he had gone far beyond the line. One could make only so much allowance for laxer country manners. "I do know how to dress myself, you know."

"A' course, m'lord," Fred said, staring at the pistol Rockford was also drawing out of his saddlebag. "Begging your pardon."

Rockford ran up the back stairwell, passing no one, but hearing some maids giggling behind parlor doors. No fire burned in his bedroom, naturally, with him not due to arrive for another day, but his anger kept him warm enough. He used his soiled shirt to dry his wavy dark hair, his limp neckcloth to wipe at his muddied boots. Despite his words to the overfamiliar groom, he could not easily remove the high-topped footwear without assistance, so was stuck with his uncomfortable, damply clinging buckskins. Nor was he used to tying his own cravat, so Rockford always carried a spotted silk cloth to wrap loosely at his throat. He'd do for a call on a loose-moraled adventuress, once he tucked the pistol in the waistband of his sodden breeches.

Fred was waiting in the carriage drive, that nasty smirk on his face. "I guess Widow Henning'll be getting her comeuppance, eh, m'lord?"

"You are not paid to guess," Rockford said

as he stepped into the lumbering old coach, realizing that Eleanor must have taken the family carriage. "Just to drive. Get on with it, man." When he saw that there were no hot bricks to warm his chilled feet, he'd thought of riding up with the groom instead of in the ancient equipage, since the rain had trickled to a mere drizzle. The man's insolent grin decided him otherwise. He'd have a word with Jake about his underling's impertinence later, after they had recovered William. There were codes of behavior to be followed, even in the country. Every Rockford employee met the earl's exacting standards or found himself dismissed — except, of course, for the ones who scampered off with the earl's belongings, in the earl's more comfortable carriage, before he noticed their transgressions.

Damn, how could he have left his estate, and his son, so long in the hands of others? Because he was busy, he answered himself, and he relied on his totty-headed sister. More fool he, for thinking a woman could act responsibly, especially a female in heat. Lud, he would have supposed Eleanor past such wanton cravings, with her fortieth birthday quickly approaching. That was a mistake, too, supposing he knew anything about women and their desires. What he did know, and cursed himself for forgetting, was that not a one of them was to be trusted.

Take this Mrs. Henning now. The devil

could take her to perdition, with Rockford's blessings, but he had to consider the wily widow before their encounter.

Henning, he recalled, was the family name of the Duke of Hysmith, so she had definitely married up, as they said. What she must not have considered before entrapping some green lad into leg shackles was that Hysmith had a clutch of sons, so disowning one would be no hardship. Now she was forced to live off Sir George Ganyon's generosity, which was another miscalculation on her part. The baronet had always been tightfisted, leaving his tenants' roofs leaking while he purchased another high-bred hunter. He had to be fifty by now, and still lusting after anything in skirts, if Fred Nivens could be believed. But no, the clever Mrs. Henning had chosen to take up kidnapping to make her fortune, instead of the uncertain future of a miser's mistress. Well, she would not see one more groat of Rothmore money, he swore. Not that she would have any use for it in jail. He adjusted the pistol at his waist. He'd never aimed a weapon at a female yet, but this conniving shrew deserved whatever justice he chose to mete out.

For now, Rockford's stomach roiled at the movement of the badly sprung carriage and the unaired, stale-smelling interior. No, he was queasy at the thought of poor William, he told himself. Heaven knew what the boy was suffering. Stolen from the only home he had ever known, torn from Nanny Dee's comforting bosom, abandoned by his aunt, and thrust among a female Captain Sharp, he must be wretched and afraid. Poor little tyke.

The poor little tyke was raking wet leaves in the fenced-in yard of a poorly thatched cottage. Lud, the woman had Rockford's son forced into manual labor! Things were worse than he'd supposed.

They'd driven past Sir George Ganyon's Fairmont, and Rockford had almost paused there, if only to get out of the cold, confining carriage for a bit. The baronet's home was made of the same stone and slate as Rock Hill, but appeared puny by comparison. Hell, Kensington Palace seemed puny by comparison to Rock Hill, but Ganyon's place looked dark and ill-kempt, with ivy growing over the windows and a shutter missing from one window. Rockford signaled Fred to drive on. Later he'd have words with his neighbor about harboring criminals, but now he wanted to get the boy and get out of the damned rocking coach.

Two boys were working in the widow's yard, he noted as he started to step down from the carriage, eager to put his chilled feet on solid ground. The one not raking was gathering acorns into a bushel — Zeus, had they taken to eating mashed acorns? He appeared taller and older, though, perhaps ten, Rockford thought, but what did he know of youngsters? Still, that must be William with the rake and the ugly brown knit cap over his ears. Rockford recalled the pristine white lace bonnet his infant son had worn, and felt another pang of remorse. Or else his stomach was giving one last protest to the coach's swaying as he got down.

The older boy told the younger, "Go tell Mother we have company, Willy," so there was no mistake. The dirty-faced urchin was Rockford's son, and they were calling him Willy, by George! The son of an earl was *not* called Willy.

The little boy ran into the house, but the older stood his ground, despite Rockford's glare. He glanced from the frowning stranger to the grinning Fred, and picked up the fallen rake, as if to defend his family from marauders.

"I mean you no harm, boy," the earl said, taking a tentative step toward the gate. "I am Rockford."

"No, the Earl of Rockford is handsome as the devil and dresses better than the prince himself. Everyone knows that."

Lud, Rockford hoped he dressed better than the corpulent regent! He reached up to adjust the loose knot at his neck, but the boy was going on: "And he rides like the wind. The Earl of Rockford would not be caught dead in that old rig where the pigeons used to roost."

So *that* was the noxious smell. Rockford cast a reproachful eye toward Fred, who was snickering. The earl wondered how long the groom would laugh when he was out of a job. He turned back toward the half-size gatekeeper. "I assure you, my boy, that I am indeed Rockford. I have come for my son."

"But you don't want —" the lad started, only to be interrupted by a woman's voice from the cottage doorway.

"That is enough, Kendall. You are being impolite to our guest."

"But he says he's —"

The woman noted what her son did not: the finely tailored coat, the rich leather boots, the arrogantly raised eyebrow, and the confident tilt to the chin. "Make your bows, Ken, and show the earl in."

"Yes'm," the boy answered, making a creditable bow and politely holding the gate for Rockford to pass through. "This way, my lord."

Rockford was surprised, and not just by the boy's good manners. The widow seemed younger than he'd thought, barely thirty, he'd guess. She was not as flamboyantly beautiful or full-breasted as he'd expected from an ambitious highflier, either. In fact, she seemed almost demure in her plain high-necked gray gown with the barest hint of ribbon for trim.

Gray was not the color he would pick for mistress material, nor did it suit Mrs. Henning's pale coloring and neatly coiled light brown hair. She ought to be wearing green, to match her truly fine eyes, or scarlet, to proclaim her profession.

Trying to keep his rekindled anger in check, Rockford gestured for Fred to walk the horses while he followed the widow through the doorway of her cottage. The first thing he noticed was the welcome warmth, then the smell of baking gingerbread. The small parlor was simply furnished but tidy, except for some piles of books. At least William was not being held prisoner in some foul hovel. In fact, he seemed fond of the woman, clinging to her skirts while he peered up at Rockford. The earl tried to smile for the boy's sake, as if to say, "I am here. You are safe. All will be well." William shyly smiled back, showing a gap where his front teeth should be. Rockford hoped that was normal.

"Will you be seated, my lord? Perhaps you would like some tea to take the chill from the day?" Mrs. Henning asked in carefully modulated tones, with no hint of an accent. But then Fred had said she was well educated.

"No, thank you," he replied, amazed that he could hold polite conversation with this vulture in dove's clothing. "I will not be staying and do not want to track mud onto your floor."

She smiled, making her seem even younger and prettier. Now Rockford could see how Hysmith's son had been caught, and why that old goat Ganyon was so moonstruck. "With boys and bad weather," she said, "a little dirt is inevitable. I do not mind, truly, if you make yourself comfortable."

Rockford had been around far too long to fall into that trap. He stayed by the door. She took up a stance by the mantel, tousling William's fair curls to dry them by the warmth of the fire. If he was jealous, Rockford told himself, it was for the fire's heat, not her gentle, seemingly loving touch. "My business will not take long," he said, more gruffly than he intended. "I want my son back."

"Of course you do. He is a fine boy. But are you sure . . . ? That is, have you made the proper arrangements? You do realize a boy cannot simply be left with servants, my lord. He needs —"

"I assure you, I am fully aware of what the son of an earl requires for a proper up-bringing." He raised his eyebrow at the tiny cottage. "I assure you, this is not it."

She gasped at his plain speaking. "I have done the best I could, my lord."

"Aye, the best you could to feather your own nest, I'll warrant."

She gasped again, and the older boy, Kendall, started forward, his small hands clenched into fists at his side. William cowered behind Mrs. Henning. She started to protest, to claim her innocence, Rockford supposed, despite all the evidence, but he held up his hand. "Enough. I want my boy, and I want him now. If you cause any trouble, I am prepared to go to the magistrate, or worse." He let his hand rest on the grip of his pistol at his waist, so she could not mistake his intentions.

Deathly pale now, she gathered both boys closer to her side, as if to protect them from a madman with a gun. "You may take your son, of course, because that is your right, no matter how bad a parent you might be. As soon as he is finished —"

"Now!" Rockford commanded. "I have been patient enough. I shall not negotiate for what is mine." Two long strides took him across the narrow room. He grabbed William's shoulder and pulled the boy to him, then took those same two strides back to the door, despite the child's objections. He ignored the shouts and the cries. He ignored everything until he heard the unmistakable sound of a hammer being cocked. That he could not ignore. He turned.

A lioness could not be more dangerous in defense of her cub. Mrs. Henning had taken a pearl-handled pistol from its pegs over the mantel and had it in her hand, aimed at his head. "I assure you, my husband's gun is loaded and I do know how to fire it. I will not hesitate an instant, sir, if you drag my son one more step out the door."

Her son?

"Your son?"

She nodded, but the barrel of the pistol did not waver from the center of his forehead, where she could not miss at this range and where she would not endanger the boy. William. Her son.

"Yours?" he repeated, as if, if he kept trying, he might get a more satisfactory answer.

"Mine. William Alexander Bourke Henning. Named after his father, William, and mine, Alexander Bourke. He has the same strawberry mark on his . . . posterior as his father and my other son, to prove it. Do you wish to see?"

"Mama!" both boys cried in protest.

Rockford looked down to see those same damnable green eyes. These were not spitting fire like the widow's, nor were they aimed at relieving him of what little gray matter he had between his ears. The boy's eyes were awash with tears, and his lower lip was trembling. "Yours," he repeated once more, carefully taking his hand away from the child's shoulder and gently brushing his fingers across the top of the lad's head before nudging him back across the room toward his mother. For the first time in memory, Rockford found himself speechless, faced with such loathing and disdain. And that was his own opinion. Mrs. Henning must think worse, for she never lowered the barrel, even when the boy reached her side.

What could he say to make amends for frightening an infant, for threatening to steal a woman's child? His mind could not think of the words, and his tongue could not have spoken them anyway. Blast, he was a diplomat. He was fluent in a score of languages. He was a first-class fool. "My . . . my son's name is William," was all he could stammer.

"So do you think you own the name, like you own half the county? The last I heard, not even earls had that right."

"Of course not. I just meant . . . That is, I had heard . . ."

She took her eyes off his head for an instant, to glance out the window to where Fred Nivens was turning the coach. "I can well imagine what you heard." Then she told her older son, "Go tell Billy to hurry with his bath, that his father is waiting."

With one look over his shoulder to make sure that his mother was well defended, Kendall hurried down a narrow corridor.

"Billy?" Rockford echoed after the boy left. That was worse than Willy. He started to say something about the respect due to the son of an earl, but thought better of it, since the widow still held her weapon, although the barrel was lowered, as if her arm was growing weary from the weight. He did say, "His name is William, after his mother's father."

She must have heard a hint of censure he could not keep from his voice, for the gun barrel rose again. "We already had one William, and since Billy is a good enough pet name for one of the king's own sons, we deemed it good enough for Billy."

Another profligate, scandal-ridden royal, just what Rockford wished his son named for. But he let it pass. The sooner he had William out of here, the sooner he could forget his blunder, and forget the silly-billy name. "You say he is at his bath? In the middle of the day?"

The little boy spoke up, braver now that he was back at his mother's side. "He fell in the mud when we were feeding Rosie."

"And Rosie is . . . ?"

"Our pig. We were bringing her acorns."

His son was throwing slop to pigs? Deuce take it, the child should be at lessons, learning to be a gentleman, not a hog farmer. Wisely, Rockford held his tongue. All that mattered was getting William back, and getting Mrs. Henning to put down that blasted pistol. He gestured toward the weapon. "Do you always keep it loaded? It seems an odd way of greeting guests."

She pointedly glanced toward the outline of the gun at his waist. "Do you? That seems an odd way to pay morning visits."

"But I do not have children in the house."

"And you might never have, if that pistol has a hair trigger." Then, to Rockford's amusement, Mrs. Henning blushed for speaking such warm thoughts out loud. He could not remember when he had last seen a mature woman — a widow, no less — color up. At his answering smile, she hurried on: "There is no danger anyway. The boys all know the rules, of course."

Since when did little boys follow rules? Rockford might not recall much of his own childhood, but he knew enough to question Mrs. Henning's confidence. Besides, the children were supposed to leave loaded weapons alone, but not stay away from ill-tempered and unpredictable swine? Her rules were absurd. Why, William could have been trampled or gored or —

"Papa!" The shout came from down the corridor, and was followed by rapid, running footsteps, and then a small dust storm blew into the room. Mrs. Henning stepped out of the way as a half-naked halfling, wrapped in a towel and a coat of mud, launched itself at Rockford's legs, almost staggering him. What the sudden onslaught did not accomplish, the stench nearly did.

Spindly arms reached up, and Rockford had no choice but to lift the boy to his chest. Now his entire set of clothing — his last set until his valet and his trunks arrived — would have to be destroyed, not just his breeches and his boots.

This one was William, all right.

Chapter Three

"I tried to catch him," a pretty young girl said from the doorway, clutching another towel to her.

Mrs. Henning was biting her lip to keep from laughing at the expression Rockford knew he must be wearing, along with a good measure of mud. "I know you did, Amy, dear," she said, while carefully hanging the pistol back on its high hooks. "Lord Rockford, may I introduce my sister, Miss Aminta Bourke. Amy, this is Billy's father, the Earl of Rockford."

The sister was about seventeen, sweet innocence personified in her sprigged muslin and ribbon-tied hair. She had Mrs. Henning's fair skin and green eyes, which she kept lowered to her toes. She made a polite curtsy, then offered her hand. When she noticed that her fingers were as filthy as the earl's son — and the earl — she raised her hand to her cheek in dismay, which left a smudge across her face. "Oh, no!" she cried, then dropped the towel and fled the room.

Mrs. Henning calmly retrieved the towel, smiled, and said, "You are her first earl, you see." She would have retrieved the monkey — surely that could not be a real child under the grime — clinging to Rockford's neck, but the boy did not let go.

At least he was not shy, Rockford noted. William did not appear the least daunted by his encounter with Rosie, nor by meeting the father he must barely recall. As for being intimidated by the eminence of the title or the dignity of the earl's bearing — hah! The lad showed as much respect as the pistol-wielding widow. Who appeared to be silently laughing at him. Well, he'd inform both of them about proper conduct toward their superiors, as soon as he could get a word in edgewise.

"Papa!" William was babbling. "I knew you would come! I just knew it! I told everyone my papa would come get me as soon as Claymore wrote you about Nanny's broken arm —"

Nanny had a broken arm?

"— and how Susie, that's the nursery maid, left after Aunt Eleanor found her and Mr. Arkenstall in the broom closet."

The bailiff in the broom closet?

"But then they made up, except that new tutor Mr. Arkenstall hired said he would help me get washed and dressed, only Nanny said it was wrong and wouldn't let him, that I could do it myself. Did you know water can go right through the floors?"

Onto the magnificent carved and painted ceilings? Or the priceless rugs?

"And so they sent Nanny off to her sister's, and he stayed, the tutor, but I did not like him, so I broke his birch rod —"

The tutor would never work again, if he could walk.

"— so I ran away. Only Aunt Lissie —"

Who the deuce was Aunt Lissie?

"— wouldn't let me stay because she said Aunt Eleanor would be worried. But Aunt Eleanor wanted to run away too, she said, and so she asked Aunt Lissie to keep me here. Isn't that fine?"

Aunt Lissie was Alissa Henning? *Fine* was not quite the word Rockford would have used, had he the chance before William started in again.

"So you did not really have to come, Papa, but I am glad you did, 'cause now you can meet Rosie. She's the biggest pig in the whole world, you know. Aunt Lissie said she was supposed to be d-i-n-e-r, but she is much too nice for that. You'll see. Oh, but now that you've come, maybe I won't have to go to lessons with Vicar?"

Not if he couldn't spell *dinner* correctly.

"But Kendall helps me. He's the smartest boy in the village. And Aunt Lissie teaches us to draw. Want to see the picture I made of Harold? That's my pony, but you know that. You sent him. And I told you his name in the thank-you letter I wrote. Aunt Eleanor helped, but she promised not to tell."

The boy smacked his lips against his father's cheek in a wet, noisy kiss anyway, just in case the earl forgot how grateful he was — or in case Rockford had one last clean spot.

"That's because Harold is the best pony in the world. And Jake lets us clean out his stall and brush him too. And we get to collect eggs, but Henny, she's the —"

"Biggest hen in the world?"

"No, Papa, she is the meanest, so we let Amy take her eggs 'cause she's a girl and Henny likes her better. So does Martin. He's the blacksmith's son, but we're never supposed to leave Amy alone when he's around 'cause he's got the biggest —"

Rockford put his hand over the boy's mouth. "Enough. You can tell me everything else later."

William nodded, but as soon as Rockford's hand moved he asked, "But I can stay here, can't I, Papa? Can't I? It's the best place in the whole world."

Mrs. Henning saved him by saying, "Why don't you go finish your bath, Billy, while your father and I talk? Ken, Willy, you can help. And ask Amy to check the gingerbread."

When the boys left, Rockford said, "Perhaps I will sit down after all, Mrs. Henning. Before I fall down."

She looked at her worn, chintz-covered sofa and the embroidered squares covering the bare spots on her stuffed chair, then she looked at the damp and dirty aristocrat. She shrugged, placed the towel Amy had dropped on the seat of a bare wooden chair, and indicated that was where he should sit.

The Earl of Rockford, consigned to the least comfortable chair in the house, sighed. He could not even blame her. For anything, it seemed. "I —" he began.

"Do not read your correspondence, I gather."

Rockford wiped his hand on his thigh, not that the fabric of his breeches was any cleaner. "My secretary . . ."

"Yes?"

"Will be boiled in oil." The earl found it amazing how, after a decade of never so much as issuing a challenge, he now felt like committing mayhem on at least a score of scoundrels. At least Mrs. Henning's lips almost curled into a smile at his words, which made his next words — a self-damning confession, actually — more painful. "He was only following my orders, however."

The would-be smile faded, as he knew it would. Rockford told himself her opinion did not matter. How could it? What did the respect of a poor country widow mean to the

Earl of Rockford? He sighed. More than he wished, when his own amour propre was at such low tide.

"Please," he began. "Will you tell me what happened here, how matters came to such a pass that my son is under your roof?"

"My badly thatched roof, you mean."

He could not deny that a Rock Hill scion deserved better than a tiny cottage, although Mrs. Henning's parlor was comfortable, except for his hard chair, and the fire was welcoming. He redirected his inquiry. "What happened to Nanny Dee, and do you know if she is all right? I would have . . ." He would have done a great many things differently, but it was not entirely too late. "Does she need anything?"

Mrs. Henning's expression seemed to lighten at his concern for the old nursemaid. "Her arm healed completely, thank goodness. According to Mr. Claymore, she is quite content at her sister's. It is over near Melton, I believe, where she has handfuls of nieces and nephews to fuss over her, as well as great-nieces and -nephews to coddle."

"That is all well and good, but if her broken arm did not bother her, why did she leave Rock Hill after so many years?"

"I think she took the accident as an omen to retire. In truth, I think she realized she could not keep up with your son."

"He does seem a bit, ah . . ."

"Energetic?" she supplied.

He was thinking *uncivilized,* actually, but he nodded politely. "And was there no one else at that entire estate to look after a little boy? I understand about the nursemaid, but surely there were others. Or a woman from the village."

"You must know that Rock Hill is not fully staffed. No, I suppose you do not. Most of the servants were dismissed, although I doubt their names were removed from the salary rolls. It appeared that Mr. Arkenstall was paying himself the wages of the unemployed workers, or that is what the vicar surmises."

"Surely Claymore would not stand for that. He has been butler to the family for ages. Why, he quite thinks of Rock Hill as his."

"Yes, but, like Nanny Dee, he grows old. He said he wrote, without receiving an answer. Without your agreement, of course, he held no authority over the steward, who kept the ledgers and claimed to be acting on your orders to economize. I doubt Mr. Claymore realized the depth of the fellow's knavery. No one did, especially Lady Eleanor."

"Ah, yes, my sister. How the deuce could she be taken in by such a rogue? I trusted her good sense."

"But she had no reason to doubt that Arkenstall was not merely obeying your commands. And the changes were slight, at first. A footman here, a dairymaid there." Mrs.

Henning folded her hands in her lap and looked away, not meeting his eyes. "And I think she feared that she too was growing old. She told me she wanted adventure in her life while she could still enjoy it. She wanted to have her one grand passion."

"She read too many rubbishing novels, that's what."

"No, she was reveling in the admiration of a dashing suitor. Mr. Arkenstall was a handsome man, with wavy blond hair and clear blue eyes. He did not look like a villain in the least. Why, all the women in the village used to sigh when he rode past, from the baker's niece to the vicar's wife. He had the manners of a gentleman and the facile tongue of a poet, knowing just how to flatter and cajole. He was very . . . persuasive."

Rockford could not like her description of the blackguard, the flowing locks and the flummery. He especially did not like the persuasive part. "Did he approach you too?"

She chuckled. "In such a . . . a coming way? Of course not. What could I offer a man of that ilk?"

If she did not know the answer to that question, Rockford thought, she had not looked in a mirror. "So you were not taken in by his false charm?"

"I did not say that. What woman does not like compliments? The whole parish was beguiled until he started raising rents and letting workers go. He blamed you, of course, maintaining his own goodwill as long as possible. He said your style of London living was too expensive for the estate to support the way it had been doing."

"I do not take a farthing from the estate! My personal investments provide more than amply for my needs."

"But he was your estate manager. Why should anyone doubt him?"

"So they believed I was a spendthrift, a wastrel, living the life of luxury while my dependents went hungry?"

She studied her hands again, without answering.

"I see." Despite his anger, Rockford also saw that the widow's were not the soft white hands of an idle lady, but strong and competent-looking. And calm. She was not wringing her hands the way her words were wringing at his soul.

"I believed I had competent employees."

"But you never came, never took an interest in Rock Hill. And then there were all those mentions of your name in the newspapers. Not that the whole village reads the gossip columns, but they hear things, even so far from London. Everyone knows how extravagant the prince regent is, how lavish his entertainments, how he and his friends spend fortunes on momentary pleasures."

"You should not believe everything you

hear." Although much of it was true. Rockford started to brush the mud off his sleeve, until he realized he'd be brushing it onto the widow's floor, and she likely had no maid to sweep up after him. Lud, what a coil. His reputation had a worse odor than his clothes, and he, Robert, Lord Rockford, was going to have to beg forgiveness from a countrywoman of no possible distinction except decency and green eyes. He took a deep breath. "And so you took William into your home?"

"I could not leave him there, could I?"

A less caring woman could have. The only worthwhile effort Eleanor had made in the boy's behalf was handing him to Mrs. Henning. "And the money?"

She did not pretend to misunderstand, but raised her chin. "My husband was taken from us two years ago, my lord, and I live in straitened circumstances, as you must be aware, supporting my household on meager funds and what I can earn giving drawing lessons. Lady Eleanor certainly was cognizant of my financial condition. We both agreed Billy would do better here anyway, with the boys to play with and lessons in the village, than on his own at Rock Hill. So yes, I accepted foodstuffs from Rock Hill, and money for Billy's clothes and schooling. More than was strictly necessary, I freely admit. I did not think you would begrudge classes for my sons with the vicar, or the occasional treat, not when you were likely spending more than all of it combined on a single pair of boots. I shall, of course, repay you for any —"

He held up his hand. "No, no, I never meant to imply that you had misappropriated funds from the estate."

"Of course you did. You came here armed, did you not? As if two women and two little boys were holding your son hostage, bleeding your coffers dry in exchange for his well-being."

Now it was Rockford's turn to study his fingers. "Perhaps at first," he admitted. "The gossip, you know."

She threw his words back at him: "You should not believe everything you hear."

He believed he needed a drink. And a bath.

Once again, Rockford was at a loss for words. There were no pat phrases he could mouth, no rules of proper conduct for such a blatant breach of common civility as he had shown to this woman.

Instead of waiting for him to flounder through an apology, as most other females would have, glorying in his grovels, Mrs. Henning asked, "So what shall you do now?"

After stringing that groom Fred Nivens up by his thumbs? "Why, I shall return to Rock Hill and straighten out the mess. Now that I am aware of the problem, everything will be addressed and corrected. Tenants will be recompensed, former retainers rehired, no matter the cost."

"No, I mean about Billy. Your son. Or have you forgotten about him again?"

The earl supposed he deserved the sharp edge of her tongue, but there were limits to what he would endure. "William" — he emphasized the boy's proper name — "is no longer your concern, madam. I shall see that he is properly reared, as befits my son. He is somewhat young for Eton, but I am certain there is a school that will take him."

"You would send a five-year-old child away from home, to live with strangers?"

Rockford might have said he was tossing the brat in the moat, by the look of horror on the widow's face. "No, I would have him educated properly among his peers, the same way I was."

He could tell she was biting her lip to keep from blurting an opinion of the results in front of her. Instead she asked, "Wouldn't Billy do better here in the country, among friends, learning about the land and people, the heritage he will inherit someday?" Again she refrained from stating the obvious, that perhaps the earl might have been a better landlord if he were more familiar with his holdings.

The earl heard what she did not say, nevertheless. He did swipe at his begrimed coat sleeve. To hell with her floors. He'd pay someone to come in to mop the damn things. Still inspecting his sleeve, he said, "I regret to inform you that *William* will not inherit Rock Hill. He is not my heir, not the firstborn son."

"You have another son?" She looked out the window, as if he were hiding the boy in the old carriage. "That is, I believe I heard it once mentioned that you had another son from an earlier marriage, but he was sickly. When I never heard of him again, and he never appeared, I suppose I assumed he had perished."

"In that case William would have become Viscount Rothmore," he said, iterating what any true lady of the *ton* would have learned along with her letters. "Instead my son Hugo holds the honorary title. He is twelve."

"And thriving?"

Thriving? How the deuce could he admit to not knowing? Rockford made a safe guess: "Hugo is doing as well as can be expected for a lad with a weak chest."

"Oh, I am so sorry he is afflicted. My husband died of a congestion of the lungs, you know."

He did not know that either. "My condolences."

She nodded. "And mine on the loss of your wife. Wives."

"Yes, well, my losses were some years ago."

Mrs. Henning seemed to expect more, so he continued. "Hugo's mother died in a carriage accident a year after his birth." He did not say that she was fleeing with her lover at the time. Nor did he say that she had not been a virgin on the eve of their arranged match. Hugo bore his name, which was all anyone had to know. "And William's mother" — whom Rockford had married to beget another, healthier heir, in light of Hugo's frailty — "died birthing him."

While calling out another man's name.

"How sad for you," Mrs. Henning said, a quaver in her voice.

Yes, it was, having to claim two sons possibly sired by other men. Rockford did not want the widow's sympathy, though, not for two unfaithful wives he'd never desired in the first place. "Yes, well, Hugo lives with his grandparents in Sheffield."

Before the widow's green eyes could turn from concerned to censorious again, he went on: "He was a sickly infant, under constant attendance by physicians there. What could I have done for him, widowed as I was, with no experience of children whatsoever? My wife's parents begged to be allowed to keep the boy, to assuage their grief over their beloved daughter."

And their guilt.

"But I mean to fetch him back now," Rockford went on, as if it were his idea.

51

"Like Nanny, Lord and Lady Chudleigh are getting on in years. He has the rheumatics and her sight is failing. I believe they wish to take up residence in Bath, for the waters, without a growing boy to look after. Now that I think of it, I will take William with me to gather Hugo. The two can become acquainted and keep each other company in the carriage while I take turns with the coachman."

"Oh, I do not think that is a good idea, my lord."

"What, my driving? I assure you, I am a competent whip."

"No, of course I did not mean to fault your driving. Billy is always telling us what a nonpareil with the ribbons you are, according to Jake, that is. But I really think you ought to leave Billy here while you make the trip."

"William is not remaining behind."

"It is a very long journey and, as you said, you are not used to children. Billy can be . . . somewhat difficult during lengthy rides."

"William will learn the proper way to behave. And not a moment too soon, it seems. He appears a robust lad, who could benefit from a firmer hand."

"But he —"

"Is my son. I am mindful of the debt of gratitude I owe you, Mrs. Henning, and am touched by the affection you obviously bear him, but the fact remains that William does not belong here. I am not going to leave my son to muck out stalls or be flattened by a pet pig."

"Or be reared in a humble cottage far beneath his station?"

"Exactly. I knew that a reasonable, capable woman such as yourself would understand."

"That Billy, your precious William, must not be mistaken for a peasant?"

"Now, that is not what I —"

"By his own father."

Chapter Four

"I find you offensive, sir."

Women rarely did. Fewer said so. Still, Rockford admitted, "I can understand where you might think so, from your point of view."

She wrinkled her nose. "No, I find the smell of Rosie about you offensive. I still have a few shirts and such of my husband's that I have not cut down for the boys yet. I think you and he were of a size. Would you like to borrow something for your return trip? You could change while I help Billy pack his things."

"I would be a hundredfold grateful, especially since my trunks will not arrive until tomorrow. But does your generosity and cooperation mean that you approve of my taking William? That you believe I am fit to have the care of my own son?"

"Approve? Not at all. It means, rather, that I believe you shall go your own way no matter what I or anyone else thinks. I doubt you ever let anyone's opinion sway you from your chosen course, no matter how misguided, so I shall save my breath. As you say, Billy is your son. As for the loan of a shirt, I merely wish to make Billy's ride in the confines of the carriage more bearable. If you will follow me, I'll show you where you might wash while I find the garments."

Rockford supposed he should be glad the woman's weapon of choice was a pistol, not a knife, or she'd carve out his liver. She was doing a good enough job with her razor-sharp tongue, and he could not even give the outspoken female the set-down she deserved, not when she had cared for his son and was offering him a clean shirt. This indebtedness was a humbling experience, one he would be careful to avoid in the future. Meantime, he followed Mrs. Henning down the hall, away from the merry sounds of giggles and splashing.

Being the connoisseur of art he was, he could not help assessing the watercolors that hung on the wall: better than the average amateur's, with a certain fresh charm. Mrs. Henning could not make her way in the world as an artist, he considered, but she could earn a fair living in London, teaching young females one more womanly skill.

Being also a connoisseur of womanhood, he could not help noticing the softly rounded curves of Mrs. Henning's figure, nor the wispy curls of hair that trailed down her neck, escaping the neat light brown coils. Yes, she could make a fair living in London with other skills, were the widow not so deucedly respectable. Her stride was purposeful, her back was rigid, and he knew without looking that her lips were pursed in disapproval. No, his hostess, his son's Aunt Lissie, was not to be considered as a barque of frailty. There was nothing frail about the female, from her confidence with the pistol to her refusal to bow to his authority.

"You do not like me, do you?" he asked when they reached a bedroom door.

"Why should I? I believe a man earns respect; he does not inherit it." She stood aside so he could enter. "There is water in the basin. I will be back in a moment with the clothes."

Definitely not bachelor fare, Mrs. Henning, Rockford repeated to himself. Any other woman would have tried to turn him up sweet, to tempt his interest, so see what he might offer in return for a bit of dalliance. Dally, hell. The widow left his presence as fast as her little sister had. Even her bedroom, almost the size of the parlor, reflected a steadfast character, being without frills or flowing draperies. The only hint that the woman might have a passionate nature was the size of the bed, nearly filling the room. He tried to picture her and the late Mr. Henning tangling the sheets there, and surprised himself by finding the image distasteful in the extreme. He was no voyeur, even of dead men's memories. On the other hand, he had no trouble envisioning himself unbraiding the widow's hair across those piles of pillows. Of course, the dead man had a better chance of enjoying the widow's favors.

As he removed his coat, his neckcloth, and his shirt yet again, Rockford wondered if the Hennings had been happy in their union. Had the late William felt trapped in his marriage if, as Fred had hinted, he had been forced into it? Or had he rejoiced in his pretty wife and growing family? Was it grief that had turned the widow waspish, or disappointment that her greedy ambitions had died with him? Rockford splashed water on his face and chest, then walked closer to the bed as he dried himself with the towel on the washstand. Perhaps she kept Henning's picture by her bedside, which would in itself satisfy some of his curiosity.

Instead of a miniature portrait, he found miniature soldiers, an army of metal warriors. The stack of books turned out to be a Latin primer, a volume of fairy tales for children, and a dog-eared *Robin Hood* he recognized from his own youth. On the night table he also found a pencil stub, a ball of string, a pennywhistle, and a rock of no great beauty or value that he could see. Mrs. Henning had given her chamber, with its large bed and lingering memories, to the boys. Never having had a brother, Rockford could not imagine what it might be like to share a bed with another boy, or two, if one counted William. Hell, he'd never shared a bedchamber with either of his wives. Not for more than an hour or so, at any rate.

As he roughly toweled his hair, the earl's thoughts returned to Alissa, Mrs. Henning, which they were doing altogether too often for his peace of mind and a piece of his anatomy. He was no rake, by George, trying to seduce every woman he met, and she was no wanton widow, no matter what the groom Fred had intimated. Likely Mrs. Henning had rebuffed the stable man, with good cause.

She was a good mother, he told himself, turning his back on that all too evocative bed, although he had as much experience with maternal feelings as he had with happy marriages. William seemed fond of her, and Eleanor, for what her opinions were now worth, had entrusted Mrs. Henning with the boy's care. Rockford would have to see about smoothing her path, later, when he returned to London. Perhaps he would offer to send her boys to the same school he found for William.

The more he thought of the idea, the better he liked it. William would have friends of his own, so Mrs. Henning could not accuse Rockford of abandoning the boy among strangers. At the same time, the earl would be repaying a debt — and have an excuse for seeing the widow now and again. Why, in view of his generosity, she might even come to see him in a better light.

Mrs. Henning was seeing him in good enough light, right then, in all his half-naked splendor. Standing in the doorway, an arm-load of clothes in her hands, she could not help but see him, to her dismay. Too late to leave, too late to screw her eyes shut, too late to wish she'd sent one of the boys.

Shocked, stunned, stupefied, she could only stand frozen in the doorway. And stare. How could she have thought he was of a size with her William? Lord Rockford was much broader in the chest, with well-defined, ridged muscles. No effete court dandy, this, but a man of action and exercise. He needed no padding either, with those strong, wide shoulders. Droplets of water glistened on a swath of dark hair that tapered to his narrow waistline, where, unless he'd stuffed the pistol down his — No, the gun was on the washstand. Good grief, William was never so . . . naked. Even when he was totally un-dressed, William was not this manly, this virile, this proud of himself for the reaction he'd caused. The black-haired devil flashed a wicked dimple. He was grinning at her dis-comfort, making no effort to retrieve the clothes that had fallen from her fingers, which had gone as senseless as the rest of her.

With her cheeks flaming scarlet, she stammered, "S-sorry. I should have knocked. But the door . . . the boys . . . the clothes."

"Think nothing of it, ma'am," he said, still wearing that grin and not much else.

He could at least hold the towel over his bare chest, she thought. Heavens, what if Amy came to gather Billy's belongings? Her poor sister would swoon. Alissa felt that she might, herself.

Then he said, "I assure you, Mrs. Henning, this is not the first time a lady has seen me at my bath."

It was his wink that let her indignation triumph over her embarrassment. Why, the rogue was enjoying her discomfort. He was flirting with her! First he thought her some kind of adventuress; now he considered her fair game for his lewd and evidently lusty attentions. She drew herself up to her full height — approximately at the level of his squared, slightly stubble-shaded jaw. She made sure she raised her eyes to his laughing brown ones, not his curved lips, his suntanned chest muscles, or his decently clothed but thoroughly indecent nether regions. "But I am not a lady, my lord, merely a respectable widow and mother. And . . . and this is not your bath."

"Quite right." He casually neared her,

bending to pick up the fallen clothes. He accidentally — or not, Alissa suspected — brushed his bare arm across hers as he leaned over. He held the shirt — her husband William's shirt — to his nose and breathed in the scent. "Ah, lavender. I was worried that the clothes might smell of mothballs. Anything would have been better than the stench of swine, but this is perfect. Thank you."

If the shirt was so perfect, Alissa wondered, why was he not putting it on? "I cannot provide trousers or boots, but I did find a waistcoat that might suit."

"Capital." He finally drew the shirt over his head and grinned as he started to tuck it into his breeches.

Alissa turned her back. "There is a neckcloth too, but it may be creased."

"It will be worse after I attempt to tie it. I do not suppose you would . . . ?"

That was enough, and more than enough. "I would sooner tie a noose around my own throat." She scooped up his discarded jacket and said, "I will try to sponge off some of the muck. You can explain to Billy, meanwhile, why you are so insistent on claiming him now, when he is content, when you have not bothered to come see him in two years."

The parting was a tearful one.
"But I don't want to go, Papa. I like it

here with Willy and Ken."

"You will have a brother of your own, William. You will like that just as much."

"I already have them, though. They're enough."

"They are not blood kin. It is not the same."

"But Hugo's only half a brother."

"He is a half brother, not half a brother. And that is more than the Hennings can claim."

"But they like me. Hugo might not."

"He will." Or Rockford would . . . How could he make two boys like each other? "He will. You'll see."

"But I will never get to see Willy or Ken again, nor Aunt Lissie or Amy," William wailed. "Just like Aunt Eleanor and Nanny Dee, who went away."

Rockford's borrowed shirt was growing damp, not from the boy's tears but from his own perspiration. Lud, he'd never managed weeping women successfully. How the devil was he to comfort a heartbroken child? And why had the blasted widow chosen now to stand aside? She had not hesitated to speak up before.

He knelt to the boy's level, then winced as he retrieved a metal soldier from under his knee. He put it, with the others, in the satchel at William's feet. "Nonsense. You can come visit to introduce them to Hugo. He'll want to meet them, and Rosie."

That was a bad decision, reminding the boy of the pet pig. "I'll never see Rosie again!" He kicked at the satchel, spilling the toy soldiers across the parlor floor. "I won't go!"

Rockford stood and glowered down at the small boy, who glowered right back at him. Rockford cleared his throat. So did William. Rockford crossed his arms over his chest. William used his sleeve to wipe at his runny nose.

Faugh. If that was an example of the boy's manners, Rockford decided, he belonged in this poor cottage, if not in Rosie's pen. Revolted, the fastidious earl almost decided to leave him here, dripping nose and all, but he could not. William bore his name, if nothing else. He fumbled in his pockets for the handkerchief his valet always placed there, then recalled he had no valet with him, no handkerchief. "Damn."

"That's a bad word."

And Rockford knew a lot worse, which the boy was likely to hear soon. Before he did, Mrs. Henning placed a linen square in his hand, and dabbed at William's nose with another, which she then carefully folded into his coat pocket. "Listen to your father, Billy," she said, having to retrieve the cloth to wipe her own cheeks. "I am sure he . . . he means well."

Means well? Damn it, Rockford swore, this time to himself, that was not the least help, measuring his incompetence against his intentions. He tersely thanked her for the handkerchief, then nearly shouted at the boy, "Now you listen to me, young sir. I am your father, and I know what is best for you. We shall have no more blubbering, do you hear? You are no infant to be causing scenes and throwing tantrums. You are a young man, a gentleman at that, a Rothmore of Rock Hill. Do you understand?"

William looked first to Mrs. Henning, who nodded in encouragement. He sniffed, then said, "Yes, sir."

"Very well. Now pick up your toys and make your farewells to the boys and Mrs. Henning."

William and the two other lads silently gathered the spilled soldiers while Rockford felt like a magistrate handing down a sentence of deportation. He could not even look at Mrs. Henning, but heard her blow her nose, then pat her crying sister on the back. "It is not forever, dash it," he finally said to the boy, but intending the others to hear him also. "There will be long vacations and holidays. Why, you and Hugo might spend Christmas here at Rock Hill, so you will see the Hennings in a few months."

"Truly, Papa?"

Well, he was not quite willing to make any

promises. And with the scrupulous Mrs. Henning looking on, he was not willing to lie, either. "We'll see."

The boy knew it for an evasion, and his lip started to quiver again.

Quickly, before William could unloose his tears — or the army from the carpetbag — Rockford hoisted him to his shoulder. "Come now. We must be off. The horses have stood too long as is."

As he made his bows to the widow, he could not help being affected by her tearstained cheeks. "I had not wanted to mention this yet, but perhaps your boys can attend the same school as William, once I have made the selection. At my expense, of course, in gratitude for your kindness."

She stopped crying on the instant. "What, it is not enough that you are stealing Billy away? You want to take my boys too? What kind of monster are you?"

Because she was overwrought Rockford chose to ignore her claim that he was stealing his own son. He did say, "We can speak of schooling later. My secretary —"

"Can go to the devil, carrying your check book."

He nodded and headed toward the door, William still in his arms. In Rockford's mind, the issue was not decided yet, for a gentleman always paid his debts, but he knew when to make a strategic retreat. "I wish you good day, then. And thank you."

William twisted his fists in Rockford's neckcloth. The wretched thing had been clean and neatly tied, after many efforts, for approximately twenty minutes. The earl halted.

"But," William whimpered, "but I never got any gingerbread. Aunt Lissie makes the best gingerbread in the whole world."

Now here was something Rockford could handle. "I am certain Mrs. Henning will pack us some for the road."

She shook her head. "I do not think it is ready yet."

Rockford loved gingerbread. He could not recall the last time he had had some, but the smell of it in the small cottage was making his mouth water. And he distinctly recalled her sending the sister to remove it from the oven. What, was the widow punishing the boy for his father's overstepping her private boundaries, whatever the deuce they were? "We could wait a few minutes while you check."

"I do not believe that would be a good idea, my lord."

"Surely you will not deny the boy a taste? If you are worried about ruining his dinner, we eat later at Rock Hill."

"But —"

"I will pay you for the blasted cake, madam. Or do you wish the poor boy to cry the whole way home?"

She left and returned with a basket, enough gingerbread for six hungry boys — or men — covered in a checkered cloth. She marched toward the waiting carriage and thrust the basket in the door while he followed with William and his satchel of toys. His small trunk of clothes was already strapped to the rear of the old carriage. "Here, my lord," Mrs. Henning said. "You may take this and your son. With my compliments."

Chapter Five

"Oh, dear, his lordship forgot his soiled shirt." Amy came up beside Alissa where she was standing in the doorway, watching the old coach lurch down the rutted drive that led to Sir George Ganyon's estate before joining the main road.

"Don't worry," Alissa said. "He will be back." She consulted the watch pinned to her gown. "I would wager on an hour at the most. Just put the shirt along with Billy's to be soaked."

Amy hesitated. "Lissie, Lord Rockford did not seem happy when he left, nor did you appear to wish his return."

"That is neither here nor there. The fact is that the boys are not the only ones in need of lessons."

"I do not understand."

Alissa took the pig-wallow shirt from her sister, but held it at arm's length. "No? Well, let us just say that his high-and-mighty earlship does not know quite as much about children as he arrogantly supposes. Nor is his every edict infallible. He is about to learn otherwise."

"I know it is not my place, Lissie, but, speaking of learning, do you think it wise to turn down his lordship's offer to pay for the boys' educations? I know you have been worried about making ends meet lately. And without the extras from Rock Hill for Billy . . ." The younger girl let her voice trail away, but frown lines stayed on her brow.

Alissa's brow matched, in shape and complexion and worry. "Do you think I don't know how our finances stand? I go over the accounts every night, counting pennies. And yes, Billy has been a godsend to us, both in the joy of having the little imp and the help they send over from Rock Hill. I honestly do not know how we will make up the shortfall, although we seemed to manage before."

Of course, that was before the boys needed more lessons than Alissa could give them, and the fees her father had set aside for Aminta's young ladies' seminary had run out, and Alissa's prize drawing student went off to London for her come-out. "We shall just have to economize further, that is all."

"Or I could seek a governess post, Lissie. You know I am well educated enough, even if I did not finish the term at Miss Plum's academy."

Alissa also knew her sister was too young and too pretty to find a position in a respectable household. Without experience and references, heaven only knew where she might land. Besides, their father had not meant either of his daughters to go into service. He had not paid for their excellent schooling so they might drudge in some other woman's household, but so they might make good marriages. How could Amy find a husband tucked away in some attic nursery? All her lovely young sister would find, Alissa worried, was improper advances and insult, like Lord Rockford and his sort usually offered unprotected females. Or widows.

"Fustian nonsense," Alissa said now. "You shall do no such thing as seeking employment with some harridan too spoiled to care for her own children. You shall find a fine young gentleman to marry and live happily ever after, with angels of your own to cherish."

Aminta sighed, a young girl's sigh of high hopes and daydreams, of air castles and knights on white chargers. "I do hope so." Then her feet touched the ground again, where her soles were thin and her stockings were darned. She pulled her knit shawl closer around her shoulders. "But I still do not understand why you refused his lordship's offer, and in so harsh a manner. Willy and Kendall need schooling if they are to amount to anything. You know that."

Alissa took one more look down the carriageway before shutting the door. "I do know they need an education, but I refused, you see, because that is not what the earl offered to pay for. He offered to send them to a school, a school of his choice. Not one I would select after meeting the headmaster and instructors and checking their credentials, not one close to home so I could visit frequently, not one that has boys from all stations in life, not just those with titles before their names. I would never send Willy and Ken somewhere they would be nothing except Lord Rockford's dependents, the poor waifs he supports out of charity. The other boys would know, and the teachers. Can you imagine how your nephews would be treated at such a place? What kind of instruction they would receive? Besides, Willy is far too young to be sent away. No, if His Arrogance wished to be helpful, he could have offered to pay for the lessons at Vicar's. That I could have accepted gladly."

Amy sighed again. "Lord Rockford might be arrogant, but his pride is not without cause, I swear. And not just because he has a title and wealth and that air of worldly experience about him. Why, his shoulders barely fit in through the doorway."

"Enough," Alissa said, the image of his lordship's bare shoulders doing somersaults in her skull. "He is merely a man, an overconfident, overbearing, over-indulged man, nothing more."

"Nothing more? Gracious, he is so handsome, I doubt I have ever seen a finer looking gentleman."

"At seventeen and country-bred, goose, you have seen few enough gentlemen to compare. I suppose Rockford is well enough in his way," Alissa added, lying through her teeth as she headed for the kitchen. "William was better-looking."

Amy looked at her older sister as if Alissa's eyes had clouded over, along with the sky.

"He was," Alissa insisted. "My William was an attractive man, without that hard edge of hauteur his lordship wears like an ermine mantle. I much prefer William's fair coloring to Rockford's dark looks, besides."

"Well, I found him stunning."

"I found him off-putting. Besides, handsome is as handsome does, and his lordship too often does whatever he wishes without care or consideration for others, contrary to the mark of a true gentleman, after all. My William would never ride roughshod over women and children, nor would he forget their very existence. No, I did not find Lord Rockford attractive in the least. Except in an academic kind of way, of course. He would make an excellent model for one of the Greek gods, perhaps. Or a fallen angel. Not that I would ever wish to spend enough time in his lordship's company to paint his portrait, of course."

"Of course not," her too-wise sister said with a smile. "So why are you fondling his dirty shirt?"

Alissa dropped the smelly garment into a bucket to soak. She would like to boil some of the starch out of Rockford, too, she told herself. For Billy's sake. The boy needed a father, not a distant dictator.

Alissa checked her watch again. She needed to fix her hair before he returned.

She sent her despondent sons out to groom Harold the pony, to give them something to do now that the gingerbread was gone. She did not tell them she thought Billy would be back, in case the earl was more stubborn than she thought. Or a bigger fool, if that were possible. The boys worried that someone would come from Rock Hill to fetch Harold before they had a chance to say good-bye, so they hurried off, with handfuls of carrots.

Amy went to see if Sir George's ground-keepers had missed any fallen apples from the bordering orchard, now that the rain had stopped. Usually there were enough apples for a pie and some preserves, after Rosie ate the wormy ones. Tarts would help the boys forget their sadness for a while, Alissa decided, as she went into the tiny bedchamber she shared with Amy. For once, she was glad for the solitude.

She sat on her narrow bed, the one nearest

the window and the draft, and stared at the nearby portrait she had painted of William when they first wed. In it, her late husband was laughing, looking not much older than Kendall, though far less serious than their sober eldest-born. William Henning never worried, never had a frown or a wrinkle from fretting over the future. Even when his father, the duke, disinherited him on his marriage, William was not concerned, nor when the boys arrived with more mouths to feed. They'd come about, he always said, and worked that much harder without complaint. He had not even complained while he lay dying, certain that he could overcome that too. They'd come about, he'd told her, with a smile on his fever-flushed face.

Sometimes she hated his memory, for the lies and the foolish surety that all would be well. All was not well.

Most times she recalled William fondly. The fact that a duke's son, albeit a useless third son, could cheerfully take up a post as assistant bailiff to her own father had always impressed Alissa, and impressed her more today, when she had faced the epitome of nobly born arrogance. William could bend. Not that he was in any way soft or unmanly, but he could sway, like a sturdy young tree, letting the wind blow past. Rockford was . . . well, he was like a rock, ignoring the wind, turning his rigid back on opposition. Nothing could move him, not when he ruled his universe.

What an impossible man.

So why was she recalling his bare chest and his raised eyebrow? Gracious, William would not have known how to lift one sandy eyebrow at a time, much less how to wear that superior attitude instead of a shirt. Was she being unfaithful to her dead husband's memory by comparing him to a London beau, a polished town buck, one of the first gentlemen of Europe's First Gentleman? William was just William. Rockford was a fixture in high society, a force of nature. And nothing to Alissa Henning.

She dabbed at her eyes with the handkerchief she'd meant to return to Billy. Now the poor little lamb had none. Lord, how she missed him already. And missed her husband, still, after two years. And she would sorely miss the money they both had provided, tomorrow. She was so tired of worrying, of missing what was gone and could not be recovered.

She was so wretchedly lonely.

Mostly, she thought as the tears kept falling, she missed mattering to a man.

Her marriage had been one of contentment, she supposed, after the first fierce, irresistible infatuation. They were only children when they met, barely Amy's age, fascinated by their new feelings. He was visiting a friend in the neighborhood; she was fresh out of girls' school. Innocents together, they explored both the physical countryside and their own budding physical sensations. That had ended with her pregnancy, their Gretna wedding, and his father's fury. William had been intended for the daughter of a marquis, not the daughter of a land steward. It did not matter to the Duke of Hysmith that Alissa's father was from a cadet branch of the Bourke barony, nor that her deceased mother was the daughter of a highly placed prelate. Her father labored for a living, and that was enough for His Grace.

When the duke cut his allowance, William stopped using the honorary lordship before his name, sought a position as assistant steward, and stopped believing Alissa was the most beautiful girl in England. Of course, she was big with child by then, weepy over her own father's shock and shame that led to his fatal illness. But William had always said he never regretted their marriage, and she believed him.

Was there anyone as foolish as young lovers?

Yes, widows who held on to dreams.

She was waiting near the door of that insufferably small cottage, blast her and her neat brown braids and spotless gray gown. Rockford knew she would be there, ready to say, "I told you so." Well, she had tried to tell him, so the entire debacle was on his head.

And on his coat, his boots, and the seats of the carriage. Gingerbread was not a good idea. The carriage ride was too long. Hah! Well, fiend take her and her forest-green eyes; she could have come out and said the boy suffered motion sickness. But not Mrs. Henning. Oh, no. She had to prove to him that he knew nothing about children, that she was the better parent, that once again he had acted without forethought.

Well, he hoped she was happy now. He suddenly knew more about small boys and badly sprung rigs than he ever wanted or needed. He knew the carriage would have to be reupholstered if not burned, and that he would never travel with the brat in a closed coach again.

Halfway to Rock Hill the earl had realized that William could never make the journey to Sheffield to fetch his half brother. Nor could the boy be left on his own at the place with no female to comfort him. Heaven knew the earl's attempts had succeeded only in discomfiting his own digestion.

There was no choice, really, other than drowning, but to return to Mrs. Henning's to seek the indulgence of a woman he would never have met under ordinary circumstances. In London he would not have given her a second glance, not in her plain gray gown and with her moralistic manners. He'd have taken her for a superior servant or a curate's wife, out of bounds, out of his circle, and uninteresting, to boot. Surrounded by children, she would have been less appealing than a bowl of gruel. Yet now he had to beg her pardon, and beg her for a favor.

Zeus, admitting he was wrong was getting to be like a plague of locusts, repulsive and recurrent. Once in seven years he could manage. Twice in one day? Unspeakable. Unfortunately he would have to speak, to ask Mrs. Henning to keep William until he could make other arrangements. First he'd nearly accused her of absconding with his son; now he had to apologize for not taking her advice, and for making the child miserable. He *had* meant well, for what that was worth.

It was worth nothing, obviously, by the scowl Mrs. Henning directed his way when she took William from his arms, wrapping the weeping child in the blanket she had ready. She held him close, despite the mess and the smell.

"Hush, lovey. Your father is not angry. No, he is not ashamed of you either. I am certain you are not the first Rothmore of Rock Hill to suffer travel sickness."

"No, Papa was sick too, only he got out of the carriage first."

"No, did he?"

Rockford decided he should have drowned

the boy when he had the chance. He had never admitted his condition to a soul, not in thirty-five years. What, the Earl of Rockford confess to a weak stomach? He'd never have heard the end of the laughter. Mrs. Henning was laughing now as she told the boy, "How clever. Perhaps he can teach you that wondrous trick."

Somehow the earl did not mind. Perhaps he could bear her humor because she had stopped the child's tears, because she hadn't said, "I told you so," because she handed him another of her husband's shirts, and because she looked so damn beautiful with his son in her arms.

How could he have thought her ordinary and insignificant? By London standards, of course, she was. By his own standards, she was so far beneath his notice as to be laughable. Why, then, was he thinking of her beneath him, and not laughing at all?

Fred Nivens, the groom, was laughing, though, making a slimy kind of snicker from atop the box. Rockford minded that very much.

"Walk the horses," he ordered with a jerk of his head, vowing to deal with the ignorant, insubordinate lumpkin later. He was ready to grovel if need be, but not in front of the loutish driver.

Reminded by eely Fred of who he was, and what he was, and what Mrs. Henning was not nor ever could be, Rockford drew himself up and took a deep breath. Before he could begin to beg, however, the widow went on, talking to William.

"And your father was even more clever to bring you back here, wasn't he? How do you think he knew I always keep those peppermint drops for when you are feeling ill?"

"He must be very smart, don't you think?"

"Very." She lovingly brushed damp tendrils of hair off his forehead and set him on his feet. "Now go on inside. Amy will fetch you those drops, and Kendall will help you with your clothes. I'll be in after I thank your father for letting us keep you with us a bit longer, all right?"

Was she some kind of saint, Rockford wondered, not belittling him to the boy when he so richly deserved her scorn? No woman could be so magnanimous. None ever had, in his experience, anyway. "That was generous of you, Mrs. Henning," he acknowledged. "And do not think I am ungrateful. For your kindness, and the unspoken offer to look after William until I return with his brother. You did mean that, did you not?"

She nodded, carefully folding the blanket that had been wrapped around the boy. Not meeting his eyes, she said, "I would keep him as long as you permit, my lord. He is a fine boy, just not a good traveler."

Rockford wanted to look at her eyes, to see

if they were as glade green as he recalled; he did not wish to speak of unfortunate illnesses. He needed, though, to speak of recompensing Mrs. Henning for the expense of having another mouth to feed. They would send food over from Rock Hill, of course, but his indebtedness went much further. And a gentleman always paid his debts.

After she had flown into the boughs over his offer to send her sons to school, however, he was leery of discussing money. He had not understood why she'd turned so prickly over the schooling, since he did not think her hen-wit enough to refuse out of pride. A woman in her circumstances could not afford pride, which she had to know. He was not bestowing charity, anyway, merely repaying a debt. Likely she did not understand about the rules of a gentleman. Either that, or she thought he had strings attached to the offer, as if he had to bribe women to become his mistresses. Diamonds or rubies were what they usually wanted, besides, not tuition fees, not that he was used to paying for a female's favors, of course. Nor would he ever consider the respectable Mrs. Henning for the position, except in idle speculation. She had to know that, too, the way she'd recombed her hair, with not a single soft brown curl trailing out of the neat, priggish arrangement.

No, she must have refused to let him pay for the boys' schooling simply because she was a doting mother who could not bear to part with her sons. Well, he could use her devotion to his advantage.

He removed a purse from his coat pocket and held it out to her. "This is for new clothes for William. I fear his are beyond claiming. What that child has against clean linens is a mystery for another day. For now, he would be embarrassed, I am certain, to have new apparel while his playmates did not, so please use the rest for Willy — that is, your son William — and Kendall. Winter is coming and they must need warmer garments." He would like to tell her to purchase herself a dress length in something other than the dowdy gray she wore, but he knew better than that. "And boots, if they are to ride with my William." He'd have two more ponies delivered tomorrow, and all the feed and fodder they required.

Of course, Alissa thought, Rockford did not want his son to be seen with ragamuffins. Bad enough the Honorable William Rothmore kept such low company, without them all looking like ragpicker's children. She was torn. She hated to take anything from the insufferable earl, as if hospitality had to be paid for, as if she did not love Billy like a son. But he did need a new, warmer outfit, as did her boys, and she could not pay for any of it. She reluctantly took the purse, with an even more reluctant curtsy, but said, "I will keep a proper accounting of how much is spent on my sons. You will be repaid." How, she did not know, but she knew she disliked being in this man's debt.

"Deuce take it, woman, this is not a loan. You are doing me a service that is going to cost you money, if my experience with the boy is anything to go by. In the week I will be gone, he could destroy your entire wardrobe, yes, and your sister's besides. I do not wish an accounting."

"Which is how Mr. Arkenstall cheated you so badly, I suppose."

"The devil you say! Arkenstall has nothing to do with this. Unless you are planning to run off to Scotland with my purse and my son."

"In a carriage? Billy?" Her lips quirked upward.

"William." He matched her smile. "So my son and my money are safe with you. If you need anything more, Claymore will have carte blanche. Just send to Rock Hill. And thank you for the gift."

"The gift? I did not give you anything but the loan of two shirts, a neckcloth, and a handkerchief that were sitting in a trunk, unused."

"No, not the clothes. The boy. You gave me my son. You see, bad traveler that he is, now I can imagine that William truly is my flesh and blood. Thank you."

Chapter Six

Rockford drove the old carriage back to Rock Hill. He made Fred sit inside, in return for that snicker. Once back at the stables, the earl spoke to Jake, his old head groom, then Claymore while the butler brought hot water, then the housekeeper over tea. He had known each of them nearly his entire life and depended on them to keep his household running. Jake might be missing a few more teeth, Claymore needed spectacles, and Mrs. Cabot forgot to put sugar on the tray, but Rockford trusted them. They were not to be faulted for the bailiff's crimes, nor for Rockford's sap-skulled sister's infatuation with the silver-tongued rogue. They'd tried to tell him, in letters his secretary must have considered too insignificant in comparison with the world events. On his orders. He sighed and asked for the brandy decanter, along with his tea.

His groom, butler, and housekeeper, every one of them, sang Mrs. Henning's praises. They were all relieved and delighted that she, not they, had the care of young Lord William. Not that the boy was any more of a hellion than his father had been, or his aunt, for that matter, but the servants were a great deal older. Five years old seemed a great deal younger, thirty years later. But at a mere twenty-seven, Mrs. Henning was well up to the challenge.

According to Rockford's loyal servitors, the widow was a fine young woman, an asset to the neighborhood, a regular attendee at church, and an excellent mother. She was a true lady, no matter her birth or what any nasty, spiteful, coarse-tongued churl might say.

So Rockford fired Fred. It was the most rewarding act of a thoroughly aggravating day.

"Dismissed? Me? But I does my job, m'lord, and none of those old dodderers can say different."

"None has. Your own words and deeds have proved unsatisfactory. If not for your lies and gossip about Mrs. Henning, I would not have raced to William's rescue, pistol primed and ready, like a Barbary pirate claiming his prize. You made me appear the fool, and created a dangerous situation, besides."

"The lad belongs here."

"When I have proper arrangements in hand for him. Until then he is safe and content at Mrs. Henning's, while you are out of a position for lying to me and besmirching the good name of a decent woman. The first rule for my employees is loyalty, and you broke it by caring more to defame Mrs. Henning's character than for my son's welfare. Why, if I were not in such a pleasant mood, I would take my whip to you for insulting a virtuous female."

Rockford knew he'd made the right decision when, after pocketing the coins he'd been given for severance, Fred sidled off, saying, "Don't know what has you in a good mood. You be no closer'n the rest of us to lifting the jade's skirts."

"Quiet!" Rockford yelled. "An insult to Mrs. Henning is an insult to my house. I consider her under my protection."

With nothing left to lose, Fred muttered, "Under your protection? Hah. In your dreams."

Fred did have more to lose: his front teeth.

"And good riddance, I say," the house-keeper said later, while she tried to find the earl a fresh shirt without bloodstains on it. The one she unearthed from the attics must have been his father's. It smelled of moth-balls. Rockford still smiled.

He did not smile during the next few days, while he waited for his valet to arrive. He went over the ledgers to see how badly Arkenstall had damaged the estate, and he transferred funds from his personal accounts into the Rock Hill coffers. He could easily absorb the loss, but it rankled that he had been so duped and his tenants so misused.

He rode out to visit each of the men who worked the fields, kept the herds, moved the flocks. He assured each of them that needed repairs would be made in the spring, if not before, that the rents would be adjusted, that an honest, fair man would be hired in Arkenstall's place. And he bought two ponies for the Henning boys so William did not have to ride alone. And two gentle mares for the widow and her sister, so the boys would be supervised on their outings. And a donkey with its cart so the Henning household did not have to walk to church when the weather was inclement.

Rockford told himself he was helping the tenants by paying them overvalued prices for the animals rather than offering them charity. He also bought their preserves and pickles, hand-woven yard goods and knitted caps. Mrs. Henning could find use for all of it, and she could not complain, for the farmers' wives needed the money. In fact, he wrote in the note he sent over with a wagonload of supplies, she was doing him a favor, allowing him to assist his dependents while not robbing them of pride. He could not recall the last time he considered anyone's pride but his own, but he felt good about it.

Riding his own lands felt good too. He rode daily in London, and at the frequent country house parties he attended, at hunt meets and races, of course, but this was different. He was alone, for one, without competition or conversation. No baying of hounds disturbed his peace, no braying of boastful riders, no babbling of the ladies he often escorted. He could go where he wished, for another, at whatever time he wanted, at any speed. He could follow the sun or follow a deer path, race a flock of ducks or a scudding cloud. He could stop riding altogether, to dismount to watch the leaves turn color and fall to the ground as the days grew cooler.

Most of all, he owned these acres.

A man could be content with such a life, the earl considered. Of course, he might also be bored within a fortnight with no convivial companions, no amusing entertainments, no delicate diplomacy to negotiate. The Earls of Rockford had always had their place at court, with influence extending across continents and kingships. That was *his* place, while Rock Hill belonged to posterity.

Before he left, however, Rockford vowed to make a difference here. And with his son.

He rode over to Mrs. Henning's, bypassing Sir George Ganyon's ugly house, to make sure that William suffered no ill effects from the carriage drive. The boy was fine and had a good seat on his pony, while the Henning children were slightly behind in their riding skills. Jake would make good horsemen out of all of them.

He was introduced to Rosie the pig, keeping his distance, as well as his hand on the collar of William's jacket when the boy leaned over the fence to make the introductions.

He employed all of his diplomatic skills, if not his ear for languages, to adjudicate the naming of the new donkey. If the regent could see him now, he thought with a smile, which faded as he recalled the latest London missive, demanding his escort at some fete in honor of the Ziftsweig delegation. Botheration.

And beyond botheration that the widow was not at home. She was in the village giving drawing lessons to the vicar's niece, Miss Aminta Bourke informed him, blushing and twisting the ribbon on her gown.

So Rockford decided to call on the vicar. He supposed Arkenstall had been as lax about supporting the local church as he had been about fixing the roads. That is, the monies Rockford had approved had gone into Arkenstall's pockets instead of where they might help the parish.

The vicar was delighted to see the earl, and to accept a donation to fix the church's ill-fitting windows. He also accepted lesson fees for William and the Henning boys until the Christmas holidays. After that, who knew where Rockford would find to send the boy, but it seemed foolish to start him at a new school with the term already begun and the vacation coming so soon anyway.

Rockford stayed as long as he could bear the vicar's enthusiasm for the new stained-glass windows, the roof repairs, and the new pews, all to be completed at Rockford's expense. Damn, if the widow did not come out soon, Rockford would be as poor as she was!

Perhaps she had already left and was doing errands or making visits in the village? Rockford could not ask the vicar, not without expressing an interest he had no intention of admitting, even to himself. He left and went to the local tavern for an ale. He sat in the public room, where he could look at the high street through the windows. None of the locals dared approach the dark-visaged, dark-tempered lord, not after Fred's garbled words about how handy he was with his fists, and how ready to go off half-cocked.

Rockford had another ale. Damn, if the female did not appear soon, he'd be as drunk as the smelly old sot slumped over at the bar.

This was totally inappropriate behavior for the Earl of Rockford, according to the precepts of the earl himself. Why, someone might think he was mooning over a common country widow, which he was not doing, of course. What he was doing, he told himself, was waiting to make sure Mrs. Henning had enough wherewithal for the proper care of his son before he left the vicinity. Now he would have to rely on the woman to handle her monies wisely until he returned. A female and funds? Hah! He might as well rely on the rain to hold off until he completed his journey.

He rode back to Rock Hill to make sure the packing was done for his next morning's departure for his in-laws' in Sheffield. This time he was taking his London traveling coach and driver, and his valet to care for the boy, although he had not informed his superior gentleman's gentleman of that fact. The fellow had reveled enough in his lofty position as valet to one of London's luminaries. Now he could earn the matching lofty salary. Rockford would ride alongside, of course.

As he left the village, the earl could not help looking around for a glimpse of Mrs. Henning. He spotted a female in gray skirts and almost fell off his horse twisting in the saddle to see her face. Confound it, that woman was seventy if she was a day, and snaggle-toothed. She gave him a grin, though, which Mrs. Henning never would have, so he tipped his hat and rode on.

He decided to leave more money with

Claymore in case the widow spent his purse on fripperies instead of necessities for William. Then he could put all thoughts of the woman and her money out of his head.

And concentrate instead on what kind of fripperies she might buy.

Alissa was indeed spending her money, her own, though, from her drawing lessons — not the earl's. Neither the vicar nor his wife saw anything wrong with her accepting recompense for caring for Billy, so Alissa stopped worrying about that and started doing mental calculations. She knew to a shilling how much remained of her late husband's inheritance from his grandmother, how much she needed for the rent on her cottage, and how much she could earn. The earl had been more than generous with food and funds for the boys' clothing so she could afford to spend a bit of her own hoarded coins on something she had wanted for ages, a new gown for her sister. Aminta was the one who watched the boys while Alissa was away giving lessons, and the one who helped cook and clean and tend the little garden patch. She deserved a reward — and a future.

A dress length of green silk would not stretch Alissa's budget too far, but would go a long way at the local fall assemblies. They could alter its appearance every week from the pile of trimmings they already had: scraps of lace, silk roses, gold braid, embroidered ribbons. They could even sew on sprigs of holly when Christmas drew nearer and the neighbors held dinners and caroling parties. Amy could look as fine as any of the other young ladies — no, better, for she was the prettiest girl around; everyone said so, not just her loving sister. With a fashionable new gown, though, she would shine. Surely she would catch the eye of some personable young man.

Alissa did not think Amy would do well as a farmer's wife. She managed with the vegetables and Rosie, but she was too delicate, too gentle for any rough-hewn rustic. Perhaps a clerk, a solicitor, or a banker, even, would notice her in the new gown and be smitten. He would not mind that she had no dowry, not when he discovered her sweet nature, her fine education, her polite manners. He'd be getting a charming, lovable helpmate, the perfect mother to his children — and he'd better appreciate Amy or he'd have Alissa to answer to.

Amy was young, but Alissa had fallen in love and wedded at that age, and was a mother not long after. Amy was inexperienced with large gatherings, but she danced like an angel, and if she was a tad shy and withdrawn in company, well, that would pass with more exposure to strangers, Alissa hoped. Besides, many a gentleman preferred a demure bride to a brash, selfish, and spoiled beauty who would make a demanding wife. A man who wanted a sophisticated social butterfly, a fashionable flirt, was not the man for Alissa's sister. Why, a man like Rockford . . . Heavens, a man like Rockford would eat gentle Amy alive, and spit out the green silk!

Alissa never aimed so high for her little sister, nor so low. She did not aspire to a title or a fortune or a grand marriage for Amy. Neither did she want an overbearing, overbred, upper-class rudesby who could ignore his family, not for Amy, not for any woman. Why, she pitied any female who thought for an instant that Rockford could make a decent husband.

He might make a good lover, though.

Alissa almost dropped the bolt of fabric she was inspecting. Heavens, the man was insidious, invading her very mind with evil intentions! He no more belonged in her thoughts than . . . than Rosie belonged in her parlor. She made her purchase and went home, her mind firmly focused on the future — Amy's future.

Yet a third person was thinking about Mrs. Henning and her money. That smelly old sot passed out at the bar was not just any smelly old sot; he was Fred Nivens, not so old, definitely smelly, and wide-awake now. He'd drunk the last of his severance pay and awakened outside the pub's back door with a headache and a thirst. Blue Ruin or revenge, he cared not which slaked his appetite.

It was all that widow's fault that he'd been fired, that he had no room, no board, that he had to chew on the side of his mouth. To be honest — if one such as Fred could be honest, even with himself — it was Rockford's fault, but he needed the rest of his teeth. Never for a moment did he blame himself, except for not taking Arkenstall's path with whatever the bailiff had left to steal.

He decided to pay a call on the widow — and on the pouch of money he had seen Rockford hand her.

"I want my share," he said with a slur through his missing teeth.

"Your . . . share?"

Alissa stood, but she did not put down the trowel she was holding. She was alone, tending the garden at the side of the cottage. The boys were at lessons in the village, and Aminta had gone with them, to see if the lending library had the latest *La Belle Assemblée* or Ackerman's *Repository*, so she might study the fashion plates before deciding on a style for her new gown.

The pistol was inside, and the surly groom from Rock Hill was outside, looking more like a ruffian than ever. Alissa had wondered why they kept the oafish man on after Arkenstall left, and wondered more now that the earl was in residence. At least that mystery was solved when he said, "That's right. I lost my post on account of you, and now I want what's due me."

"But I did not have anything to do with your being dismissed."

"Oh, no? You turned the earl against me, you did, hoping to keep all the booty for yourself."

"Booty? You are mistaken, Fred, if not foxed. I kept his boy, that's all. I think you had better leave now."

"Not without what I come for. I brung the pigeon for you to pluck, aye, and I fetched and carried for the brat too, taking orders from that old relic Jake, when Arkenstall promised I'd be stable master. Now I am out on my ear and you are sitting in clover."

No, those were the last of her cabbages. "I am sorry, but I cannot help you. I don't have the resources to hire a . . . a handyman." Not that she would consider Fred for the post of privy digger.

"No, but you do have that purse what his highness gave you. I saw him hand it over, I did. Now I want it."

The money for Billy's clothes? "I spent it."

"What, all of it?" he shouted, taking a threatening step closer to her, trampling a cabbage.

Alissa took a step back, closer to the house. She was not going to give this maggot a farthing of Rockford's money. "I had bills. I paid them, and my rent. There is nothing left but a few pence," she lied, "so you are wasting your time."

"A waste of time, is it? Then I might as well have my pleasure, iffen I can't have my money."

She understood his toothless leer all too well. "I would die sooner."

"What, too good for the likes of me? Well, you ain't good enough for his lordship, if that's what you're saving your favors for. His women are all soft, like silk, not dried up widows. They say he'll marry some foreign princess, even." He reached a filthy hand toward her shoulder.

Alissa struck at his hand with the trowel. "Get off my property this instant, Fred. You arc trespassing and I will not stand for it!"

He wrenched the trowel out of her hand and made a grab for her arm. "I don't intend you to be standing, I don't."

Alissa doubted she could get past him to the house and the pistol. She could scream, but who could hear? Panic rising in her throat, she pushed his hand away. "Don't do this, Fred. You will hang for sure."

"Only if they catch me. I'll be gone long before that."

Alissa turned to run, but he grasped a

handful of her skirt. She kicked out with her wooden-soled shoe.

"Bitch!" he shouted, letting go of the fabric to rub his shinbone, but not stopping his pursuit.

Alissa picked up the trowel and threw it at his head; then she started throwing the cabbages she'd collected. Panting, heart racing, she knew she could not hold him off for long. Then she heard hoofbeats.

Oh, Lord, she prayed, don't let it be the boys. Don't let this madman hurt the boys. Or Aminta. Heavens, the man must never catch sight of her little sister. She hoped it was Sir George, her dreadful landlord. He was mean and a miser, but he was acting as magistrate. "Help!" she screamed for all she was worth.

Fred had not heard the rider. He wiped dirt and cabbage leaves out of his eyes and kept coming — until he noticed that the widow was not fleeing. She was not screaming anymore either.

She was too busy watching the devil himself dismount.

Chapter Seven

This was not Amy's knight on a white charger, no fairy-tale Lancelot come to save the damsel in distress. This was elemental power, like a sudden dark squall descending from clear blue skies to destroy everything in its path. Vengeance on an ebony horse, he was, with a caped charcoal cloak billowing behind him. His black hair was windblown, his hat long gone, and he wore the darkest expression Alissa had ever seen on a man. He leaped from the back of his still-galloping mount straight onto Fred, knocking the former groom to the ground before Fred could finish "Bloody he—"

Hell. That was what it appeared to Alissa, watching her rescuer pound Fred's skull into the earth of her garden.

The ground was soft, though, and Fred's head was hard. Besides, he knew he was fighting for his life, so he struck out. His fist connected with the earl's eye. While Rockford blinked, Fred managed to roll on top of the slightly lighter man. He raised his muscular, laborer's arm high for a knockout blow.

Alissa snatched up the trowel and slashed at his fist before he could lower it. Fred yowled, but by then he was on the bottom again, and Rockford, no longer considering the ground as a weapon, used his well-trained right.

He kept pounding at the man even after Fred stopped resisting, using his right fist, then his left, for balance. Alissa feared he would kill the man. Not that Fred Nivens would be any great loss, but this would be murder, not justice.

"My lord, stop. He is unconscious."

Battle rage still coursing through him, the red haze of fury blinding him to the sight of blood, Rockford did not cease. So Alissa did what she usually did when the boys were playing too rough: she threw something at them. In this instance she had no towel or bucket of water, and the trowel could do more harm than good, so she threw a cabbage.

"What the . . . ?"

"He is unconscious," she repeated, once she had the earl's attention.

He stood up and wiped his hands on his coat. "And you are unharmed?"

"Yes." Alissa feared that, if she answered anything else, saying she was frightened out of her wits, or that she would have night-mares for the rest of her life, he would resume pummeling the former servant.

He took a step closer to her, mere inches away, in fact, and started swearing. Alissa could not translate most of the words, thank goodness, but she did understand that the earl had transferred his rage from Fred to herself.

"Then you are the stupidest, most idiotic female I have ever known," he shouted when he ran out of French, Italian, and German blasphemies and one particularly colorful Russian phrase about a bear and a Cossack and a bottle of vodka. "And I have known some truly featherheaded females. Hell, I was married to two of them. But you. You have to be the most jingle-brained of them all! Thinking you could defend yourself with a garden tool! What the deuce were you thinking, if you were thinking at all? Where was your damn pistol? Or do you only carry it when earls are expected?"

The pistol was inside, of course, but he did not give her an opportunity to answer that she was about to offer Fred money after all, admitting she had lied, in order to lure him into the parlor. She could not have run, but she might have had a chance with the weapon. She barely got her mouth open to speak before Rockford raged on.

"Where is your sister? Not that she could be much help, but how could you be out here by yourself when there are dastards like this on the loose? What if I had not decided to ride by on my way out of town? There are returning soldiers, dash it, out-of-work farmers, and who knows how many mangy curs roaming the woods looking for just such vulnerable widows. What possessed you to think you could live out here in near wilderness isolation by yourself?"

Alissa did not know where to start. How dared he shout at her when she was the one who had been attacked? Why, one might think it was her fault, that she had invited this muckworm lying among her earthworms out for tea! One might also recall that the out-of-work servant was *his* former employee, not hers. If he had not employed such baseborn scum, if he had made certain the man left the vicinity . . .

As for living alone with the boys, did the nodcock think she had a choice? Her husband was dead. So was the rest of her family, except for Aminta. Whom else was she supposed to live with? The ducal Henning relatives who did not acknowledge her existence, or her sons'? She'd found the least expensive rent where the boys could play, because that was all she could afford, by heaven. And it had been a thoroughly peaceful neighborhood, with little crime beyond the occasional drunken brawl or adolescent mischief — until he, the great Earl of Rockford, had arrived. She did not say any of it to the now silent, glaring lord, who was having a hard time keeping his aristocratic eyebrow raised when his eye was swelling shut beneath it. In fact, he did not look haughty at all. Angry, yes, and battered, but not half as arrogant as usual as he waited for her to wither in the face of his blistering accusations.

Alissa would not shrink away. She raised her own chin, looked him in the eyes — one eye, that is — and said, "Thank you."

The earl took a deep breath and started to brush leaves and dirt off his coat. His neck-cloth was untied and hanging down, so he pulled it loose and wrapped it around his cut knuckles. The action gave him time to regain his wind, and his composure. Lud, he could not remember the last time he had been so angry, the last time he actually wanted to kill a man. He might wish the occasional cow-handed driver to Hades, or the long-winded puff-guts at Parliament to perdition, and Arkenstall definitely ought to hang, but not at his own hands, by Harry. He had never even harbored such malice toward the man who had run off with his first wife, killing her in his carriage. Of course, the man had died too, but Rockford had not been half this angry.

What kind of diplomat showed such emotion? A poor one, who was quickly replaced by a cooler head. Rockford prided himself on his control, his aplomb, his dignity. There was not much dignity in rolling about among the cabbages, and he had shown no control whatsoever. And did not regret it in the least. What if he had not been coming to make his farewells? The thought of what might have happened made him shudder.

Alissa was thinking it too, now that the fighting and the shouting appeared over. She shuddered too.

He saw and held out his arms. That was all, no words, no superior, sardonic look. Alissa stepped into his embrace, just for the comfort, she told herself, because she had been so frightened. He held her with one hand and awkwardly stroked her hair, fallen out of its braids, with his wrapped hand while she cried.

"Hush. It is all right. He will never threaten you again. No one will. I will send someone over to keep watch. He can sleep in your stable, with the horses."

"No, I cannot afford —"

"You cannot afford not to. And I am not asking you to pay."

"But —"

"But nothing. My son's safety is involved too, you know, so stop being so deuced stubborn. That is, so independent." He handed her a lawn handkerchief that was embroidered with his crest.

Alissa wiped her eyes, then dabbed at the trickle of blood above Rockford's nearly closed eye.

And then the earl did a remarkably foolish thing for a man of his experience and prowess, an act so spontaneous as to be totally out of character. He kissed Mrs. Henning. Right there in the trampled garden.

Right after she had been pawed at by a disgruntled drunk.

Right after he'd shown the violent side to his nature.

Right after Fred had reminded her that she was not good enough for the Earl of Rockford.

Right. She slapped him. Hard. Then she said, "Thank you," again, for it was a good kiss — she could feel it to her toes — and a good lesson. This man would steal more than her money, and be just as heartless as the fallen groom, with less thought. After all, Fred had planned on robbing her. The earl was just passing by. "I will accept the watchman you mentioned, my lord. And I will keep the pistol more handy. I see now that no man is to be trusted, especially where supposedly vulnerable widows are involved. Good day."

That was it? He'd saved her virtue and perhaps her life, and she was dismissing him, the Earl of Rockford, as if he were a flunky? Granted, he ought not have stolen that kiss, but she had not kept her lips locked together, either. At his haughtiest, despite smelling like a cabbage and not seeing out of one eye, and his knuckles stinging like the devil, he drawled sarcasm: "I see your gratitude is boundless, madam." He bowed. "I shall not bother you again. Good day." He walked toward his well trained horse, who had wandered off, but not far.

"Wait."

Ah, he thought. The widow was not as outraged as she pretended. He would have raised his eyebrow, if he could. "Yes?"

"What about him?" She pointed toward the flattened greens.

Rockford looked at Fred, who had not stirred. "I doubt he will cause any further trouble."

"But you cannot leave him here, in the garden."

"You wished him brought into the house, perhaps?"

"Of course not!" Alissa wished she had slapped him harder; he was being so insufferable, simply because she had rebuffed his unwelcome — well, his unworthy — advances. "I wish him out of my sight!"

"I should bury him?" He studied his wrapped knuckles. "I think not."

"Nonsense. You should take him to Sir George Ganyon."

"Your landlord? Why? Does the baronet rent rooms to felons? I knew he was careful with his money, but that seems extreme."

Alissa almost stomped her foot. "Sir

George is acting as magistrate while the squire travels to Scotland."

"In chase of my errant bailiff, I suppose. I'd rather have my Rembrandt returned than Arkenstall."

"That is irrelevant. Sir George can see that this scoundrel is locked up."

"At his place, Fairmont?"

She nodded. "Until he can be sent away."

Rockford looked to his horse, who seemed to be content cropping the widow's herbs. She'd likely blame that on him, too.

"I cannot carry the dastard double, not without laming Mephisto, whom I aim to ride to Sheffield. Nor would the stallion carry Fred across the saddle, if I were inclined to walk alongside leading him."

A glance toward his tasseled Hessian boots indicated how disinclined he was.

"There is the cart," Alissa suggested. "You could tie your horse to the back."

So he drove off, the eminent Earl of Cabbage, behind a donkey, with a bloodied bully unconscious at his feet. Of the three, Lord Rockford wondered, which was the biggest jackass?

Rockford would have seen the former groom put on a boat, courtesy of His Majesty's navy, but he really had to catch up to his valet and his carriage. He would have to raise the valet's salary, of course, when the man saw his current state, but there was no help for it. So he drove into the courtyard of Fairmont, an ugly, squat stone dwelling. Ugly, squat Sir George came out to see for himself his noble neighbor driving a donkey cart.

Rockford delivered the now-groaning groom, and he delivered a scathing lecture on the rules concerning social responsibility, the care of dependents, and the maintenance of thatched roofs.

From a man who had not inspected his own estates in two years? Sir George guffawed. "Great joke, Rockford. Never knew you for a wit."

He could not start another melee, not in front of the baronet's gaping servants, so he nodded curtly, smiled slightly, and refused to come inside for a drink. He did get Sir George to agree to look after the widow's welfare, including returning the donkey cart, having his men watch for suspicious strangers, and putting a new roof on the cottage.

All of which cost money.

"So you see, ma'am," the large-nosed, short-legged man told Alissa, "I'll have to raise the rents, come the new year."

She had been forced to invite the baronet in for tea when he drove the cart back, leading his own mount, a brute as ill-natured as its owner. She'd sent the boys to the stable with the donkey, away from the curling lips and darting eyes of both the stallion and Sir George Ganyon. Sir George's ears were too big and full of hair to flatten back like the horse's, but they would have, when he noted that the donkey got a warmer welcome than he did.

Alissa put down her cup untasted. "But we agreed on a two-year lease, which is not up until next summer. I cannot afford any more."

"Tut, tut." He brushed crumbs off his protruding belly and smacked his fleshy lips as he reached for another macaroon. He nodded toward the plate of sandwiches and biscuits, which Alissa had prepared in case the earl returned with the donkey. "You are living well enough off his lordship's bounty."

"But that will end when he makes other arrangements for his sons."

Sir George lowered his head, revealing the bald spot in his mouse-brown hair. Sons were another sore spot. He had none, after burying two wives. The widow had two off that weakling Henning who'd died of a chill, the milksop. Rockford had two dead wives, too, but had two sons to show for it. One was supposed to be sickly, but the other seemed healthy enough, if a bit scrawny. Young Rothmore was a regular hellion, he'd heard, but the cub could sit a horse well, the hunt-mad baronet had noted.

He had no sons. That was simply not fair. He did not particularly like children, but that was not the point. He found the younger Henning boy shy and sissified. The sprig clung to his mother when she brought him by with the rent. The older one was distant and distrustful. Standoffish, just like the widow. He'd teach them all the proper regard, the baronet vowed, someday.

Meantime, here Sir George was, nearing the midcentury mark, with no sons to leave his lands — and no brawny lads to work them for free· until then. He did not even have a daughter to give him a son-in-law to help farm, or grandsons to inherit Fairmont. Rockford's visit had reminded him all over again. He'd also reminded the baronet of the drab young widow residing in that old run-down cottage no one wanted. If a nob like Rockford were interested, perhaps Sir George ought to take another look.

She was pretty, Ganyon supposed, in a delicate way, with her neat brown hair and her clear skin. He preferred his women lush and lusty, redheaded and warm-bodied, like Lucy down at the tavern. Mrs. Henning was slight, with barely enough meat on her bones to cushion a man. He couldn't like that bony chin, either, if it meant she'd be obstinate and argumentative, but she did fill out the top of her gray gown nicely enough. She wore plain, serviceable, obviously home-sewn clothes, which frugality he admired, but she wore the airs of a lady, too. Sitting straight like she had a poker up her behind. Bah! Everyone knew she was nobbut the daughter of Alexander Bourke, a land manager with no lands of his own. Despite that useless education Bourke had paid for, she was no better than she ought to be either, according to local history. Hadn't she run off to Gretna with that duke's son just in time to keep the first boy's birth legitimate? Henning's people never gave them tuppence, he'd heard, because it was such a misalliance.

Still, that was, what, ten years ago? He'd never heard of her playing fast and loose on young Henning, nor after the chawbacon stuck his spoon in the wall. Lucy at the Black Dog was available to any man with the coin. Mrs. Henning acted as if she was unavailable to any man, at any price. Until Rockford came. Well, the earl was never going to marry the jade. Sir George had a better offer to make her.

"My housekeeper just left," he put into the silence of Alissa's mental calculations of rents and interest rates.

He was offering her the post? Alissa could do it, she supposed, although she had no experience running a large household. Working for the old skint was not something she could look forward to with enthusiasm, either. Nor did she like the notion of her boys having Sir George Ganyon as a model of manhood. She had been to his house a few times, and it appeared to be as ramshackle as the baronet, with his food-stained shirtfront and gray-tinged neckcloth. His hunting dogs appeared to have the run of the house. The horses might have too, from its condition. Talk in the village was that the baronet refused to spend his money on repairs or sufficient servants, but Alissa was used to hard work.

She did more computations. Whatever Sir George paid — and it had to be more than she was earning now — she would be better off. With no rent to pay or food or coal or candles to buy, she might even be able to put some money away for a dowry for Aminta. Of course, she would no longer be able to take her sister to neighborhood gatherings. Alissa doubted she would be invited once she went into service. Perhaps the vicar's wife would agree to chaperon Amy to the local assemblies along with her niece. Amy would *not* become a servant, not while Alissa could draw breath.

Then she had an awful thought. What if the balding baronet did not mean for them to live at Fairmont with him? After all, if he were such a nipcheese, he might balk at feeding three extra mouths besides his new housekeeper. He might intend for her to come daily, leaving her boys with Amy, working in exchange for the rent on the cottage. Gracious, she would be in worse straits, with no time to give lessons, and no time for her sons.

She would not do it. They could all move into rooms in the village if they had to, above the butcher's shop or the lending library. The boys would miss the freedom of the cottage, but they would be closer to their lessons. Perhaps they could run errands to earn a few coins. Without the garden, they would need the extra income.

As if reading her thoughts, Sir George mentioned her sons. "I suppose I will have to pay for their schooling, when I don't need them for harvest or haying or sowing season, of course. And they'd have chores, naturally. Horses don't clean their own stalls, eh?"

He would pay for his housekeeper's children's education and let them ride his horses? Goodness, all the stories about his cheeseparing ways were wrong, and Alissa would make sure everyone knew it. She offered him the plate of pastries again. "Then you would have all of us live with you?" she asked, to be certain.

He took another macaroon. "Where else? I ain't paying for any pricey boarding school."

"And my sister?"

"How old's the chit now, seventeen?" When Alissa nodded, he stopped chewing, but did not stop speaking, so crumbs dribbled over his thick bottom lip onto his paunchy lap. "Old enough to marry her off, I suppose."

"That was my thought, too. I have great hopes for the winter assemblies."

"Right. Get her fired off before she gets notions in her head. Can't have m'wife's sister going for a servant. Wouldn't look good."

His . . . wife?

Chapter Eight

"Your . . . wife? I thought you said your housekeeper had left."

"Right, and I see no reason to hire another one. Never do a lick of work anyway, always complaining. Might as well have a wife, if I have to hear the whining. And I need a son. Two would be better, just in case. You're a proven breeder. Good hips." He waved the half-eaten macaroon at her lower body. Then he waved it in the air. "And a good cook. What more can a man ask, I say?"

He could ask if she wished to marry him. Alissa did not. Trying to be polite instead of paralyzed, she said, "But . . . but I had not thought to marry again."

"Naturally you hadn't. Who'd take a female with no particular consequence, no dowry, and a parcel of dependents? I thought long and hard about it myself, but don't want to spend the blunt to go up to London to find a chit to marry. All of 'em are empty-headed anyway, so you'll do."

"I don't —"

"Now don't go getting missish on me. A woman in your position can't be expecting bouquets of flowers and pretty words. Never wrote a poem in my life and don't intend to become one of those artistic idlers now. You've had all that romantical claptrap once already, anyway, and look where it got you. No, you're a widow with boys to raise; I need a wife. Simple enough. You can't afford to be picky."

She could not afford a raise in her rent either, but marriage? To Sir George? As awful as working for the baronet might be, the idea of wedding the boor was a great deal worse. He was using his fingernail to dislodge a bit of macaroon from his teeth.

"I appreciate the honor, Sir George, truly I do —"

"Yes, yes. I suppose that's what they taught you to say in that fancy academy your father sent you to. A waste of blunt, if you ask me. But get on with it. I have things to do, you know."

"I appreciate the honor, but I cannot —"

"Demme, you expect me to get on my knees? Bosh! I'd never get up again. I am too old for that fustian nonsense, and so are you. You're not too old to give me sons — I checked with the apothecary." He waggled his bushy eyebrows suggestively. "And I ain't too old to get them on you, never fear."

She'd fear choking on his unwashed odor

116

first. How could he think that she might . . . ? That they could . . . ? The baronet was more imaginative than any of those poets he so disdained. Before Alissa could reply, however, before she realized his intent — Heavens! She could never have anticipated his intent in a million years — he leaned over the low table and pressed his wet, fleshy, macaroon-strewn lips against her cheek.

She pushed him away and moved to the far end of the sofa, wiping her cheek with a napkin. "Sir, you forget yourself!"

"I haven't forgotten how to please a filly, if that's what has you in a pother. You can ask Lucy at the Black Dog. No, don't suppose you'd have any conversation with the likes of Lucy." He shrugged. "She does not have a lot of conversation, anyway. Besides, it's not such a bad thing, you acting the lady, for it's a ladyship you'll be. You must have thought you'd move up in the world, marrying young Henning. Too bad he was so far away from the succession, and got himself disowned to boot. Well, now you can have that title you always wanted."

"I never wanted a title. My father was a perfect gentleman, and he never had one. My mother was content being Mrs. Alexander Bourke, and I was content being Mrs. William Henning."

"Heh. You can't fool me. Every woman wants that 'Lady' in front of her name, wants to go into dinner ahead of the vicar's wife, and wants to sit in her own pew at church, too. That's all well and good, having a spouse who the neighbors curtsy to, but don't you go thinking of putting on those airs in my bedroom. It's sons I want, not vapors and smelling salts like my first wife, or headaches like my second, or nagging like my third."

"Third? I thought you had two wives?"

"The third one doesn't count. Never made it legal like. The housekeeper, don't you know. I said I'd marry her if she started breeding. Three years of listening to her complain and I still have no son. She's gone now, like I said, so you don't have to worry."

Worry about what? That he would toss her out if she did not produce the requisite heir, or that he'd be unfaithful once they were — No, Alissa could not bring herself to say the words.

She could clean his house and cook his meals, but share his bed? He most likely had fleas, like his dogs. And that was one of the baronet's more appealing traits.

"I am sorry, Sir George, but I cannot accept your, ah . . ." She dredged her mind for the proper word. Kind? Generous? He was none of those things. "Startling offer," she concluded.

He started to get red in the face, the thick eyebrows lowering to nearly cover his bloodshot eyes, just as the boys came running into the room, with Amy behind them.

"Here, now, what kind of rag manners are these?" the baronet said, glaring fiercely at Alissa.

She could not tell whether he meant her refusal of his offer or the children's hurried, noisy entrance to the parlor, until he went on: "This is an adult conversation, not a nursery party."

"But it is time for tea, Mama," Willy said in a low voice, coming to stand beside her. "And you promised."

Her older son, Kendall, stepped close to his brother and added, "We washed up special, after putting the donkey away."

Aminta stayed in the doorway, uncertain whether she was considered an adult by the angry old man.

Not the least bit shy of the blustering baronet, Billy noticed the nearly empty plate of pastries. "There are no macaroons left!" he complained loudly. "And they are my favorites! He ate them all?"

"Impertinent brats!" Sir George spit out, along with the last few crumbs. "Go on, get out. Your mother and I are not finished talking."

"Yes, we are, sir," Alissa said, getting to her feet and standing with an arm around each of her sons, after she affectionately patted Billy's head. "This is my house still, and these are my boys. I did promise them a special treat in honor of Billy — that is, the Honorable William Rothmore's return to us for an extended visit."

The baronet did not rise. "Demme, we haven't settled this yet."

Everything was settled, as far as Alissa was concerned, but she was not willing to make a scene in front of the children. "We can converse as I walk you out while the boys have their tea. Aminta, dear, please pour. And, Billy, there are more macaroons in the pantry. Why don't you go fetch them?" She headed toward the door, picking up her shawl as she went.

Sir George had no choice but to leave, unless he wanted to stay to fight the boys over the poppy-seed-cake slices. He lumbered to his feet and followed Alissa, ogling the younger sister as he passed.

Once outside, Alissa nervously eyed the restive horse tied at the gate, but she went closer, to lead Sir George farther out of hearing distance from the house. She could see four heads peering out the window.

"Now cease this foolishness, Mrs. Henning. I have made you a proper proposal. Could have made you an improper one, by Jupiter. Widow and all, you know."

She did not know. What, were widows fair game for every tomcat on the prowl? She was no man's prey. Alissa raised her chin, noting that she stood almost taller than her un-wanted guest. "Yes, sir, you made me an offer, and I have refused. I fear we would not suit."

"Not suit? What kind of cr— What kind of poppycock is that? I am a man, you are a woman. That is all that matters."

"Not to me, it is not."

"Demme, give me one good reason why we wouldn't suit, then. You owe me that."

One good reason? She could give him a score without stopping to think. The first one was that she considered him a repulsive toad, but good manners kept her from saying so. "Very well. I do not believe we could have a good relationship because of your despicable arrangement with your housekeeper."

"I told you, she's gone."

"And your dishonorable attitude toward our agreement concerning the lease on the cottage."

"We never had it in writing."

"Then there is the way you spoke to my boys."

"Spoiled brats."

"And I am not attracted to you."

"So what? None of my other wives were, either. You shut your eyes and think of the next day's menu. I wasn't that keen on bed-ding the sour-faced biddies, but I managed. You can too, to keep you and the brats out of the poorhouse. You can find yourself some young stallion — after I've got my son, of course."

"I would never break my vows!" she said. "But that is another thing, your, ah, other women. Like Lucy at the tavern."

"Faugh, every man has his separate interests. Your Henning might have been a saint, but you'll not find another. Rockford has a new mistress every month, they say. Sometimes two."

Two months or two mistresses at a time? Alissa wondered, but then she returned her attention to the baronet, who was trying to scratch his back with his riding crop. His horse took the opportunity to nip at his shoulder.

"Bloody hell!" Sir George cursed, then slapped at the horse with the whip. "Goddamn hayburner."

Alissa gasped. If she had been considering marrying the maggot even for an instant — which she had not — his violent temper would have convinced her otherwise, to say nothing of his foul language. She looked back toward the window, hoping the children had not heard. "Mind your tongue, sir."

He scowled at her. "You'll get used to it, woman." He went back to scratching his lower back with the crop. And lower still.

Alissa turned away. "I do not care for your manners."

"You'll care less for starving, when I throw

you out of this cottage."

"Are you threatening me?"

"I am saying that you have no choice, missy. Didn't Rockford say Fred Nivens was coming ugly with you? I fined him for disturbing the peace. Put him to work on the roads, in lieu of the cash. Clever, eh? The earl was complaining about their condition, too. Well, there's more than one groom gone bad. You need a protector. You need a house, for this one will fall down on your head before I put tuppence into it. You need someone to take those brats in hand and fire off that sister of yours. And you need money, because no one will let you teach their daughters how to scribble, after I tell them how you played the jilt, kissing me and then turning up your nose."

"I never —"

He ignored her protests. "In other words, you need a husband, and I am the only one offering. Your reasons why we shouldn't get hitched aren't worth a groat."

"But I do not like you!"

He snorted. Or perhaps that was the horse.

"I do not like your horse!" Alissa knew she was sounding desperate, but could not help herself. "And I hate dogs!"

He dropped the whip. He dropped his lower jaw. "Demme. You hate dogs? No one hates dogs."

Alissa crossed her arms over her chest,

pulling the shawl tighter. She had not intended to be out in the chill this long or she'd have worn her cape. "I do. They are filthy, vicious animals."

He closed his mouth and twisted it in a black-toothed smile. "That's all right, then. You can't have met my dogs. For a moment you had me scared, there. What good is a woman who doesn't like dogs? But mine are all fine animals. Nary a biter in the pack, unless they have cause, of course."

"I have met your ill-behaved hounds. They tear through my gardens, rip down my laundry line, and cause havoc with my chickens. And I have indeed seen them at Fairmont, a snarling pack of mange-ridden mongrels."

"Mange? Mongrels? I tell you, they are the best hunting pack in the shire, and I can trace their breeding back for more generations than my own."

"And I tell you they do not belong in a house, and they do not belong around children. As for training them to kill foxes . . ." She shook her head to get rid of the image she saw there.

The horse tossed its head too, slashing long yellow teeth. Sir George stepped back. "I know what it is. You had a fright once, eh? Or stumbled on a hunt, what? That's why it's ridiculous for females to go out with the pack. No stomach for it. Well, that's one thing I would never ask you to do. Don't believe in women riding hell for leather, I don't. So. We're agreed then?"

"We are agreed on nothing! I do not wish to marry you, sir!"

"What, do you think to force me to raise the ante? I already said I'd pay for your brats' schooling. I suppose I could fork over a few pounds to dower the little chit. Be worth it not to have to feed her for long. Now stop playing coy with me, missy, for I am getting sick of this, and my horse is tired of standing. He gets mean without a good run, he does. Here, we'll seal the bargain with a kiss. I know the brats are watching, so that will put the lock on it, eh? Wouldn't want them to think their mama was a loose woman, what, kissing a man who wasn't her intended?"

Alissa backed away, but he grabbed her wrists and started to pull her closer to his chest. She struggled, but he held fast, with arms used to controlling headstrong horses. She tried to kick out at his legs with her booted feet, but he nimbly skipped aside, cackling. "I like a filly with spunk in her. You surprise me, Mrs. Henning. Didn't know you had that much spirit. I wager I am going to enjoy our marriage a lot more than I figured, if you like to play these games."

This could not be happening, Alissa thought. Not again! Not in her own front yard. This time no avenging fury on a black steed was going to come to her rescue, either. She twisted as Sir George started to press his thick lips toward hers. She thought she might be sick if he actually kissed her on the mouth. He gave her wrists a hard jerk, making her lose her footing so she half fell against him, with the stench of his dirty linen in her nose.

"Now that's more like it. Games can only go so far, you know, missy."

Alissa regained her balance and came down hard with her boot on his toes, starting to say, "I am not playing any —"

But a voice came from the doorway of the cottage: "Let my mother go, or I will shoot."

Her boy, her firstborn son, Kendall, the quiet one who took his position as man of the house so seriously, was standing in the dirt path from the cottage with a pistol in his hand: the pistol he was never, ever supposed to touch. Willy stood behind him, fists raised in fighter's stance. Rockford's son brandished the fireplace poker, and was already covered in its soot. Amy was white-faced and trembling in the doorway, but she was gamely clutching a kitchen knife.

Sir George laughed. "You'll never shoot me, boy. Too much chance of hitting your mother."

"Yes, but I won't miss if I aim for your horse." Kendall brought the barrel of his father's gun around to the pawing stallion, one of the baronet's favorite studs.

Sir George let Alissa go, saying, "I see the brat has more bottom than I gave him credit for, too. Well, you'll learn better manners than that," he told Kendall, "before I am through with you. Your ma and I are getting leg-shackled. We were only playing."

Kendall looked uncertain, the gun wavering. The others cried out in protest.

Alissa backed away from the baronet, reassuring them. "No, I am not marrying anyone, least of all Sir George." When she reached the smaller boys, she gave them each a hug, and sent Aminta a confident smile, bringing a bit of color back to the young girl's cheeks.

To the troll who thought she would leap at his offer to share his cave, Alissa said, "I am not playing games and I am not playing hard to get. For the last time, sir, quite simply, no. No, I will not marry you. No, your addresses are not welcome. I will move to another village if I have to, but I will not turn my boys into lackeys, nor will I become your unpaid housekeeper and brood mare. I will report you and your unwanted attentions to Squire Winslow, as soon as the magistrate returns. And I will also tell him you are using Fred Nivens to work at what should be your expense. Now leave, before I take the gun from Ken's hands. I will not aim for the horse, and I will not miss, I swear. My rent is paid until the new year, so we have no further business. Good day."

Alissa cried herself to sleep that night, although she was not by nature a maudlin soul. She had learned ages ago that tears availed her nothing but reddened eyes, so she usually set herself to solving her problems, rather than merely dampening them. Tonight she could not hold back the tears.

She did not want to be afraid, but she was. Fred Nivens, and then Sir George, even Lord Rockford in his way, had shown her how very vulnerable she was. Nivens would be around, and Sir George would turn a blind eye to his actions, as long as the baronet could squeeze work out of the former groom without pay. She doubted she had seen the last of her pig-headed — although Rosie was prettier — landlord, either. And Rockford would be back in a week to take Billy away, and to bedevil her more. The world, it suddenly seemed, was not a safe place for an unprotected female.

She did not want to move. She had friends here, and she had carved out a niche where she was comfortable and accepted for what she was, not who her father or husband had been.

She did not want to uproot the boys again, to move into meaner accommodations, another village that might not have a school she could afford. What would become of them without education, once they grew up a bit? They would have to become common laborers, or indenture themselves to some skilled artisan to learn a trade. Worst of all, they might take the king's shilling and go for soldiers. Kendall was almost old enough to become a cabin boy in the navy. The very thought of her stalwart son taking ship for years at a time brought on a fresh wave of tears.

She did not want her sister to become a governess, going from one abusive household to another, withering into an old maid with no hope for a husband and babies of her own. Worst still, pretty Amy could be subject to the same assaults and insults Alissa had suffered. How could her fragile sister fend off the likes of Fred or Sir George, or an employer's lustful son, a butler with bad intentions? What if she were forced? There would be nothing left for her but a life on the streets. But how could Alissa provide a dowry for her sister when she could barely provide a roof — leaking in the eaves and inhabited by spiders as it was — over their heads?

She did not want to be forever pinching pennies, struggling to teach young ladies the rudiments of watercolors, or straining to make the poor soil yield up another crop, to get them through another winter.

She did not want to be so very, very alone.

So she cried.

Chapter Nine

Lord Rockford would cry too, if he knew how. Instead he was simply miserable, sitting up with the driver of his coach on another blasted rainy day. The weather was not making him wretched, nor the carriage ride, nor the fact that his horse had come up lame and had to be left at an inn some miles back. No, what had Rockford out of sorts was the sort of passenger he carried inside the coach.

Deuce take it, he thought, there ought to be a rule. People should do what they say they are going to do, by George. He was a man of his word. Everyone should be. The world would be a far better place.

For instance, when a set of in-laws said they would rear up a boy, they should do it, until he was full-grown and ready to take his place in the world. They should not suddenly decide their grandson took too much effort. They should not simply hand a twelve-year-old boy, a sickly one at that, over to any in-experienced, unknowledgeable, unenthusiastic stranger — like his father.

Lord and Lady Chudleigh were not getting too old to care for the boy. They were too lazy. They had little enough to do with Hugo, Viscount Rothmore, that the earl could see. In the few days he had spent at Chudleigh Hall, Rockford never once saw them take a meal with the boy, or a walk. He'd never seen them hold a conversation with the lad until they bade him a formal farewell. They might never see Hugo again, yet all they could do was shake his hand and tell him to be a good chap. What a contrast, Rockford thought, to how Mrs. Henning was always patting or hugging or kissing her sons and his own William. He would not think about her.

No, his former in-laws were not the ones growing too old; the boy's nursemaid was. Like his own Nanny Dee, Mrs. Doddsworth was serving her third generation of children, all in the same family. She still adored her latest baby, Hugo, when she did not confuse him with his mother, Judith, Rockford's first wife. She was too old to navigate the nursery stairs, when she did not get lost, so the boy never went on outings. If the whey-faced, spectacled lad ever saw sunshine, Rockford would be surprised. When he asked, Lady Chudleigh claimed the child was too prone to chills. Rockford would be sickly too, kept inside all the time.

The last tutor they had for him was a retired dean, a scholar. Rockford thought he might have suited the bookish child except, his valet learned from the other servants, Mr. Hemplewhite never left the library and his private research. Why, he'd been dead for two days, collapsed across his papers, before he was found — by poor Hugo, of all people.

So now Rockford had the boy. His heir. Lud, the sickly child could never be his own son. He could see something of Judith about Hugo, her eyes, the delicate bone structure, the fine blond hair. He saw nothing at all of his own dark looks.

He could conceive of having conceived the disaster-prone imp back at Mrs. Henning's, but never this withdrawn, solitary boy. The few times he had tried to engage him in conversation, the sprig was polite but distant, all too apparently more interested in the book he was reading than in his father. They had nothing in common, not horses or sports or politics, the usual masculine topics of conversation besides women. Rockford could not feign an interest in the book on botany Hugo was studying, Hemplewhite's last contribution to academia, and doubted the youth was interested in it either. Likely the boy was as skittish of Rockford as Rockford was of him, his lordship thought, retreating into his book the way Rockford retreated to the box of the coach. The earl could not tell. He could not read the child's expression behind the thick glasses, although his blue eyes appeared guileless. His mother's similar blue eyes had seemed similarly guileless, too, the whole time she was plotting her elopement. Hell, Arkenstall had looked honest enough when Rockford had interviewed the bastard.

The young viscount was a good traveler, at least, unlike William. He picked at his meals when they stopped, which was worrisome, but he claimed to enjoy the fare and be full, so Rockford stopped fearing for the interior of his coach. His valet, Petrie, did not mind riding with Hugo at all, which was saying a great deal. Petrie found the young master to be well mannered, undemanding, patient at the long wait while the lame horse was seen to, and not the least bit nauseated. Definitely not Rockford's son, the earl thought, on all counts.

Judith had not been a virgin when they wed in a match arranged by her parents and his father. The infant was born early. She was running off with her lover when she died. Those were facts. Added together, they made a damned good case, Rockford had always felt, for Hugo's being a cuckoo bird in the Rothmore nest. Still, he'd given his name to the puny infant that no one expected to survive. How could he not claim him, without bringing scandal to his name and the Chudleighs', shame to his career? No matter that a scant year later Judith's death created the very bumblebroth he had tried to avoid. They had covered up the circumstances so only rumor remained, which Rockford had countered by looking down his nose at anyone who dared mention his deceased wife. The baby had survived a perilous infancy.

Now, for better or worse, Hugo was Rockford's heir.

So what the devil was he going to do with him?

He could not send him off to school, not this pale-skinned, reed-thin, bespectacled boy wrapped in mufflers and blankets and mittens. Hugo was subject to sniffles and coughs and putrid sore throats, according to Mrs. Doddsworth. He needed possets and potions and mustard plasters. Rockford did not know whether to hire the boy a tutor or a private physician. He made his driver pull up at every inn they passed to replace the hot bricks at Hugo's feet. That, at least, he could do, keep him healthy — as healthy as could be — until they reached . . . where?

He could not simply set the young viscount down at Rock Hill. The servants there were as ancient as Mrs. Doddsworth and the dead tutor. What kind of life was that for a lad? It was the one Rockford had led as a boy, but he had not been frail; neither had the servants. He'd had Jake and the horses, the streams and his sister, then school. Hugo would have none of that. Rockford doubted the boy had been taught to ride, so swaddled in cotton wool had they kept him. He would have William for company, but what if that hellborn babe brought a contagion back from his rambles? Would Claymore know what to do? Without Nanny Dee, could any of the other servants nurse a child through a life-threatening illness?

Rockford did not even know if there was a competent doctor in the vicinity of Rock Hill, or a mere bloody-handed surgeon who'd likely bleed the boy to death.

He could hire younger, more experienced servants in London, but the air there was dangerous for anyone with dicey lungs. Everyone knew that, which was why so many invalids went abroad, or to Bath. The very idea of that fusty place made Rockford shake his head. He could not think of a worse situation for a child, with all those dodderers and wounded soldiers.

Rockford was certainly not going to take up residence in that city of sufferers. Besides, he traveled. He went to Brighton in the summer, to hunt country in the autumn, house parties for half the winter, abroad when his diplomatic services required and the war situation allowed. He could not very well leave the near-invalid Hugo with mere servants, new ones at that, no matter their credentials. Look what happened when he trusted Arkenstall's references.

Blast! He could not send the boy to school. He could not leave him at Rock Hill. He could not take him along to London. He could not count on his old servants, or trust new ones. That left . . . Mrs. Henning.

He clutched at her name like a falling man grasped the gnarled roots that protruded from the cliff face. He might not know how deep the roots went, or how sturdy the tree, but he held on with his bloodied fingertips until he found purchase for his feet, or help arrived, or the roots gave way.

Mrs. Henning knew children. She loved them, even troublesome William, as hard as that was to believe. They said she was a competent nurse, if one overlooked the fact that her last patient, her husband, had not survived. She kept a neat house, which to Rockford denoted an orderly mind. She had enough knowledge of society to instill some poise in her charges, and she was learned enough to oversee their education. Most of all, she was poor. She could not refuse his offer.

Rockford took his first easy breath since leaving Lord and Lady Chudleigh's home. There, a simple matter of careful thought brought about the ideal solution. Mrs. Henning could take charge of Hugo, and Rockford could get back to the business of charming an alliance out of the Austrian princess and her recalcitrant brother.

Of course, his heir was *not* going to reside in a hovel. Genteel poverty did not suit the future Earl of Rockford, nor the present one. But how could Rockford install the widow at Rock Hill? Her reputation would suffer if he were ever in residence, which he intended to be more frequently, to straighten out the mess Arkenstall had left.

Her reputation seemed to matter to Mrs. Henning, and her standing in the neighborhood. He could understand, for Rockford's good name mattered to him, too. Of course, her name was nothing, but she might balk at blemishing it, for her sons' sakes. He would hate to see her boys suffering bloodied noses and cut lips, trying to defend their mother's character.

If there was anything Mrs. Henning possessed, it was character. She was no raving beauty, certainly not an heiress or a well-connected society belle. Still, she had countenance. There was something about the stiff-backed female that intrigued Rockford, that put more than her reputation in jeopardy. He could not put his finger on it, but, Zeus, he would love to put his fingers on Mrs. Henning's soft skin. Having her under his roof would be more temptation than he thought he could resist.

He was not a man of ungoverned passions. The very idea of uncontrolled urges was abhorrent to him, actions practiced by debauchees and drunks, and at least one deceased wife. Give way to base instincts, illicit and unsavory hungers? Not the Earl of Rockford. Let his fellow peers act like stags in rut; Rockford had too much dignity. He had his own standards to maintain, his own rules of proper behavior for a nobleman.

And yet . . .

And yet he had kissed Mrs. Henning. Lud, she had tasted sweet for a moment, until she recalled herself and her surroundings and her would-be seducer. She'd smelled of flowers and gingerbread, and he might have taken her, there in her vegetable patch, if she had not slapped him. If having an affair had not been on his mind, it had definitely been in his breeches.

No, Mrs. Henning was not safe in his home, neither her reputation nor her virtue. Something about the aggravating female made him forget his lifelong tenets about soiling his own nest, about keeping to his own class, about seducing respectable women. She was respectable, innocent of carnal knowledge with anyone but her dead husband, chaste. He would swear by it. And he would destroy it all.

One way or the other, or both, Mrs. Henning would be ruined. And she was poor, so she had to accept his offer.

Lord Rockford felt sick, despite riding outside the carriage.

From the kitchen, Alissa heard the horses coming up the seldom-used drive, and the boys shouting, so she took off her apron and tried to push a stray curl back into place. Rockford was back, come to fetch Billy away unless she could change his mind. She did not have time to check for flour on her cheek or stains on her skirts. She would have to do, and hope for the best.

The best she could hope for, she had decided after another sleepless night, was the position of governess to Rockford's sons until he sent them away. She meant to ask him the moment he returned, before she lost her nerve or he hired someone else. Taking a post meant giving up any chance of taking Amy to parties and balls, but Alissa did not wish to go to social gatherings where she would have to face Sir George Ganyon. In addition, she did not think the baronet would threaten her if she were known to be in the earl's employ. He would not want a wife who had been in service; he would not want to anger his noble neighbor, a man with the ear of the prince and the eye of a marksman. After seeing the condition of Fred Nivens, only a fool would rile Lord Rockford. Sir George was an immoral maggot, but he was not a fool.

To be safer still, she would carry the loaded pistol when she traveled back and forth to Rock Hill, the way she had been carrying it since the baronet's visit.

On the other hand, the earl might wish her to live at his home, to be in constant attendance for the boys, and that would suit her also, if she could take her sons and her sister. Surely there was room at the vast manor house. Goodness, there was room to barrack half the peninsular troops. Rockford could not begrudge them the space, she prayed. The boys could share a chamber, the way they always had, and she could share with Amy. That way Amy could help with the children without being an actual servant, and Rockford would be getting two caregivers for one price. He simply had to see the advantages of such an arrangement, for Alissa surely did.

She could earn more money by being a governess than by teaching painting, she calculated, and perhaps the earl might keep her on permanently, or until Billy outgrew the need for a woman's attention. After all, the boys would return from school for holidays and such, if they became ill or misbehaved and got sent down, a distinct possibility in Billy's case, and someone should be at their home to greet them. Rockford would not want that burden.

And he would not be there often, thank goodness. Alissa could not like working for the hard-eyed, hard-to-please man, but he seldom visited Rock Hill. He was sure to return to his London life and the *ton*'s diversions soon. The quiet country life could hold no appeal for the earl, or he would have been here often.

She smoothed the skirts of her gray gown and straightened the scrap of lace she wore as a cap over her coiled braids. Yes, she looked like a proper governess. And Billy wanted to stay with her, if Rockford cared for a child's wishes. The vicar said he would add his recommendations, too. He also said that no one would think ill of her for taking the post, for the whole village knew how hard she was working, trying to keep her family together. The vicar lived in a world of faith, hope, and charity, though. Alissa lived in the real world. There would be talk, and there was nothing she could do about it except hope her friends did not believe any gossip.

At least she was not asking for charity. Nor, she would have to make clear, was she asking for any post other than that of governess, lest Rockford get ideas. Judging by that kiss, a libertine like Rockford always had those ideas. She believed he would never force himself on a woman, especially one in his employ, but she would carry the pistol anyway. To his credit, he had never looked at Amy with that swinish leer of Sir George; otherwise Alissa would never consider asking for the position. She would simply have started packing to leave, to go heaven knew where.

She wanted to stay, and she wanted the job. With so much — not just her future but that of her entire family — dependent on the earl's whim, she gave him a bright smile when he leaped down from the driver's bench of his coach. She might have smiled anyway, he looked so fine. The journey had added a golden tan to his cheeks, and she liked his dark hair mussed by the wind this way, instead of pomaded into some fashionable arrangement. It made him seem more ordinary, more approachable. Otherwise he could have stepped from a gentleman's fashion plate. His neckcloth was spotless and tied in some intricate knot, its stark white a gleaming contrast to his firm, slightly shadowed jaw. His midnight-blue coat stretched across the broad shoulders she would never forget, and York tan gloves covered his strong, masterful hands. Below strong, muscular thighs, his high boots gleamed, a tribute to his valet after such a long journey, and the golden tassels on them swayed with his graceful stride. He was altogether magnificent, like a champion Thoroughbred at the racetrack, perfectly groomed, perfectly conditioned, the finest specimen that money and breeding could create. And Rockford knew it.

It was a good thing he was seldom at Rock

Hill or Alissa would have lost her courage to ask him for the position. He'd most likely laugh at the pretensions of a lowly country widow.

Before she could speak, Rockford groaned. Lud, he thought, if the widow was going to turn charming on him, he was sunk. He'd been hoping to find Mrs. Henning still in the boughs, still angry over his manhandling her. That way he could restore his brain to the rule of order, with a chance to erase his wayward thoughts. That radiant smile just etched them permanently on his brain.

Hearing the earl's moan, Alissa ran back inside and fetched the tin of peppermints she kept handy. "Here, my lord," she said with another smile, "this should make you feel better."

Better than what, he wondered, a slug?

Chapter Ten

"I am fine, madam," he said brusquely, turning his back on her and her hopes. He went to let down the steps of the carriage, though, and opened the door. For a minute Alissa could forget about the arrogant earl and her need for his approval. She wanted his elder son's approval too.

Hugo stepped out of the carriage and blinked against the bright sunlight. He reached up to adjust his spectacles, and to push the warm cap off his head. She did not see much of the earl in the boy's much fairer looks and far slighter build, but his air of confidence proclaimed his paternity. Here he was, thrust among strangers, and the youngster did not appear the least bit disconcerted. He was Rockford's son, all right. He made her a polite bow, and then gave her the smile Rockford so seldom showed, and her heart went out to the poor motherless boy on the instant.

"Welcome, Lord Rothmore," she said when Rockford did not make the introductions. He was talking to the driver and ignoring her and the children. "I am Mrs. Henning, a neighbor, and I am delighted to meet you. I should like to introduce my sister, Miss Aminta Bourke, and my sons, Kendall and William Bourke. Children, please welcome Hugo, Lord Rothmore."

The last of her charges was nearly jumping up and down in excitement, his eyes beseeching her to hurry. "And this," she told Hugo with a smile, "is the Honorable William Rothmore. Your half brother, whom we call Billy."

The earl turned and frowned at that, but did not interrupt the introduction.

Billy rushed forward, then skidded to a stop inches from Hugo and made a half bow. "May I call you Hugo or do I have to use your title? Are you really sickly or just pretending so you don't have to go to school? Do you like strawberry tarts? Aunt Lissie — that's what I call Mrs. Henning; she said it was all right, so maybe you can, too — said most boys do, so I saved you one. They are the best in the world."

He reached into his pocket and pulled out a flattened, oozing pastry with one corner missing.

Hugo's brows raised as he inspected the unappetizing offering, and he shook his head. "We just stopped for a bite a few miles ago when the horses were changed, so I am not hungry. But thank you, and I should like to be called Hugo, I think."

A fastidious diplomat too, just like his father, Alissa thought, hoping he had not hurt Billy's feelings, after the younger boy had been so looking forward to his half brother's arrival.

She should not have worried. Billy crammed half the tart in his mouth, strawberry preserves dripping down his chin. Then he reached into the same pocket where he'd kept the pastry and pulled out a frog. "I saved this for you too."

Amy giggled, but Alissa was horrified. She started to step forward, but Hugo reached out first. He carefully transferred the amphibian from Billy's grubby hand onto his own gloved palm.

"Oh, capital! *Bufo calamita,* the Natterjack toad," he said happily. "It is quite rare, especially in this area, you know, so you were lucky to spot him, and clever to catch such a handsome specimen." He gently handed the creature back. "You'll have to release him soon so he can make his winter home, of course. In the same place you found him would be best. But thank you for the opportunity to see one up close."

Billy looked up at Alissa, strawberry-smeared lips spread in a wide grin. "I told you he'd be the best brother in the whole world!"

"So you did, Billy. So you did."

Alissa was relieved and impressed, and so was Rockford, as he came around the side of the carriage. He held up his hand to stop his younger son's enthusiastic greeting before William could transfer any of his mess onto Rockford's clothes. "Why don't you and the Hennings take Rothmore around to see the pig or the ponies?" Hugo had an honorary title and it should be used out of respect for the ancient lineage he represented, Rockford thought. No one ever called him by his given name, Robert, which was as it should be. The widow most likely had her own, more casual rules, which would have to change. He sighed at the task ahead. "I would like a few moments with Mrs. Henning."

Now that the opportunity had come, Alissa was not certain she wished to take it. He looked so large, towering over the children, and so disapproving, his dark eyes fixed on the dust of her pathway, the unraked leaves. "Amy, you can join us for —"

"Alone," was all he said.

"— tea later, if you wish," Alissa finished, while embarrassment tinged her sister's cheeks red. Amy fled with the boys, and Alissa was alone with the earl and her doubts. What choice had she but to ask him, though? Her hands nervously fussed with the knot of her shawl, but she squared her shoulders and led him into the parlor.

She did not look well, Rockford thought as he took the same hard chair he'd had before, across from Mrs. Henning's seat on the sofa. Now that he had a closer look at the widow without her sunshine smile, she appeared drabber than he recalled, her eyes older, more tired, her complexion the color of her ugly gray gown. Lud, she wasn't sickly, was she? That would never do at all. Even worse, she seemed agitated, high-strung. But then she took a deep breath — he watched the rise and fall of her breasts with appreciation — clasped her hands in her lap, and smiled. Good, she was steady and sure, in control of her emotions. His intuition was not entirely unreliable.

"Mrs. Henning —" he began, just as she said, "My lord."

They both smiled and both started over.

She said, "I have a proposition —"

While he said, "I have a proposal for you."

"Yes?" she asked, eager enough to let him go first.

"Yes, you will?"

Alissa's brow knit in confusion. "Yes, I will what? I have not heard your proposal yet."

"Yes, you did. I just made it."

She retraced the peculiar conversation in her mind. "A proposal of . . . ?"

"Marriage, of course. The usual thing."

First Sir George, now this. It was, indeed, getting to be the usual thing, Alissa thought, a nervous laugh rising like a bubble in her throat. "Marriage to . . . you?"

"Well, not to Hugo, that is, Lord Rothmore. Of course to me."

Of course. Earls marched through her doorway every day and asked for her hand — her work-roughened hand, at that — in marriage. The world had gone insane, the walls tipped on their sides, the floor risen to the ceiling, the — "Deuce take it, woman, you are not going to swoon, are you?"

She opened her eyes. "Of course not. I never faint."

He shoved her head down between her knees anyway. "Fiend seize it, I knew this was a bad idea!"

She pushed him away and raised herself from that undignified position. "No, it is not a bad idea, if you mean it."

He was still standing, pacing, actually, in the small room. "Of course I mean it. I am not in the habit of saying things I do not mean."

Alissa needed a moment to gather her wits, now that blood had returned to her brain. "Would you pour a cordial, please? There is a tray near the window."

He found the bottle of brambleberry wine, poured a glass, and drank it down in one swallow. When she coughed politely, he recalled himself, cleared his throat, and poured out another glass. He put it in her hand and said, "I am making a hash of this, aren't I? I had planned it better in my mind."

"Not at all, my lord. It is just so . . . so startling."

"But sensible. I have been thinking of it all the way from Sheffield, so do not worry that this is some sudden whim. Your sons deserve a better life. My sons deserve a mother's care. Our marriage can best accomplish both goals."

He meant it. Lord Rockford might have been discussing his next order of snuff, for all the warmth he showed, but he meant to offer for her, Alissa Bourke Henning, a widow of spotted past and uncertain future. "I need to think about it."

He raised that arrogant black eyebrow as if to ask what she had to think of, his wealth or her poverty. He pulled the chain on his fob watch and consulted the timepiece. "Five minutes ought to be enough, if you are the woman I take you to be. If not . . ." He shrugged. If she were so cork-brained as to turn him down, she would not be a fit mother to his sons anyway.

She did not need three minutes.

He was handsome, titled, and rich. On the other hand, he was too attractive to be faithful, too highly born for a commoner wife, and rich enough to buy a princess for a bride. An Austrian princess, to be exact. He was also arrogant, authoritative, and a possible rake. But he had not offered her the improper proposal she had feared, and he was not Sir George Ganyon.

"Yes, my lord. I am honored to accept your offer."

"Good. I will ride to Canterbury to fetch a special license. We can be married next week."

"Next week?" she said with a shriek, then adjusted her tone to a mere squawk. "So soon?"

He consulted his timepiece again. "We have not been betrothed for thirty seconds. Do not tell me you are getting cold feet already." In a way he was relieved. It had been an impossible notion, really.

Alissa had no feeling in her feet whatsoever. If they got up and ran away she would not have noticed — or blamed them. "No, it just seems rushed."

This time he took a quizzing glass out of another one of his pockets and surveyed the tiny room through its magnifying lens. He also cocked his head at a rustling sound from the thatch overhead. "Do you truly wish to live here a day longer than you have to?"

Still unsettled, she wondered if he would pull a toad from his pocket next, like Billy, but she had to shake her head, no.

He nodded. "Once I depart for Canterbury, you can remove to Rock Hill and plan the wedding from there without destroying

151

your reputation. Claymore will help, and I shall leave blank drafts on my bank."

"That is very logical, my lord, and generous. But . . . but what kind of wedding do you wish?"

Neither of his first wives had asked his opinion about the actual event, and he had never thought about it. He looked at his watch. If he were to have a decent meal and a long bath and a good night's sleep — his first since setting out with Hugo, what with worrying over the boy's health — before leaving for London in the morning, he had to be going soon. "A short one."

"A . . . short wedding."

"You know, no long speeches, no scores of attendants, no miles of receiving lines. Other than that, whatever you wish. I understand your first marriage was a hurried affair in Gretna. This one you can plan to your heart's content, in a week."

Which showed he knew nothing about weddings. Alissa wondered how much he knew about marriage. "Will there be a honeymoon?"

"What, go off and leave the cubs alone? What would be the point of getting wed at all if I wanted that?"

Alissa could see he was impatient to be on his way, but she was having doubts. Not enough for her to renege on her recent acceptance, but doubts all the same. She felt that since she was not having palpitations, she was entitled to a few qualms. "I have to ask, my lord, what kind of marriage are you intending?"

Not another short one, Rockford said to himself; that was for certain. He was not going to go through this again. But how many kinds of marriage were there, anyway? Good ones and bad. "I am intending us to have a good marriage, a convenient one."

"Which means?"

"Which means that you will be a countess, the highest-ranking female for miles. You will have unlimited wealth at your fingertips, and servants to see that those fingers never do an ounce of work."

Alissa hid her roughened hands under her skirts.

"It also means," Rockford went on, "that your sons will have the same advantages as my sons, the same education, the same opportunities. Except, of course, those that come with the Rothmore name and titles, or the prestige they carry. I cannot provide what their birth did not."

"My boys do not need the auspices of your title, my lord. They are the grandsons of a duke."

"Who never recognized their births, correct?" He went on without waiting for an answer: "Old Hysmith is dead now, but his heir, Morton, is just as much of a prig. Morton's wife was the worst of the lot, acting like an empress instead of a mere duchess, despite her father being a piddling baron. She died after giving his grace two sons, but of course you know that. Were you thinking that Kendall is in line for the duchy?"

"No, there was another brother between my husband and his eldest sibling. I believe they each have hopeful families."

"No matter. The fact that your sons are the wards of Rothmore will get them entry almost everywhere. Your sister too, of course."

That was almost everything she wished. "But what about you, my lord? It seems all the advantages of this marriage fall to my lot."

"Oh, no. I will no longer have to worry about being entrapped into matrimony by some conniving shrew or her matchmaking mother." Or a particular plump princess from Ziftsweig, Austria. "That is a great advantage."

"Enough to wed a stranger?"

"Added to the fact that I shall find it very convenient not to have to worry about the children, yes. That will be your function."

"You could have hired a housekeeper or a governess to fulfill that need. At much less expense."

"But finding good, loyal servants is not that easy. Besides, servants give notice, move on to other positions, retire to open board-inghouses and inns."

"Wives can leave too, you know."

He did not need the reminder. "Would *you* go off and leave your sons?"

"Never!"

"Fine, because once we are wed and they become my wards, you cannot take them. There, are you satisfied now? I need to be on my way."

If they were to spend a lifetime together, surely he could give her another minute or two. "What about you?"

"What, would I run off? Or do you mean to ask if I would have affairs?" Her blush answered his question. "If that is your concern, I shall never disgrace you. Beyond that, a jealous, prying, complaining wife would be inconvenient in the extreme."

The warning was plain. She was to keep his house, while he kept on with his bachelor life. A marriage of convenience, according to his rules. Alissa could not have expected more from the arrogant earl. Goodness, she never expected half this much, so why was she disappointed?

He was looking at her through his quizzing glass again, and could see distress in her downturned lips and the shadows in her green eyes. "Deuce take it, woman, do you expect me to profess my love, to vow eternal devotion?"

"Of course not. You barely know me."

"Precisely. I have been married twice before, and I hardly knew either of those young women. I did not love them, nor they me. That is the way it is done. The sensible, logical way. My marriages were not successful, but neither was yours, leaving you with almost nothing."

"Nothing?" she asked in affront. "I have my sons."

"As I have mine. But you chose to follow your schoolgirl's dream and ended here. Love in a cottage," he said with a sneer. "How sweet, how touching. How blasted buffle-headed! You and Henning threw everything away for love when you were young. Now you are practically starving. Would you throw away all that I have to offer, because I cannot promise such puerile pap?"

"The marriage you are proposing is so . . . cold."

"So is winter without coal to burn."

Nothing was colder, Alissa decided, than this arctic aristocrat who was in too much of a hurry to tell his betrothed that he liked her. She knew he lusted after her from that previous kiss, but he had never spoken of more children, or where they would live. Not one word of mutual respect or admiration passed his lips, no mention of how affection could grow. Of course not. Nothing grew on stony ground.

A short wedding and a convenient marriage were all he wanted — and all he was willing to give. Remuneration for services rendered. Alissa was not sure she liked him either.

"Think of your sons," he was saying in exasperation, putting his magnifier and his fob watch back in their pockets, an indication that he was more than ready to leave. "Think of your sister and what you can do for her. Did I mention that I will provide a dowry? Lud knows my own sister will never have the use of hers."

She was thinking of the rest of her life, but she could not afford to think of herself, could she? "Yes, of course. You are right. I am an adult now. There really is no choice, anyway, is there?"

"Not for a sane woman, no. There never was." For which he was liable to burn in hell, using her need to satisfy his own.

"Then once again, my lord, I accept. I will marry you."

He let out a breath of relief, then scowled at her air of resignation. "You do not have to act as if you are this year's sacrificial virgin, you know. Some people consider the Earl of Rockford quite a catch."

Especially the Earl of Rockford, Alissa suspected. Aloud, she said, "But they were considering the title, not the man. Marriage is to both."

"An intelligent woman. I knew we would

suit. But are we finally agreed, so I might go get the license?"

This time her answer would be forever. She made him wait an endless heartbeat, then said, "Yes."

"Excellent. I shall be off then."

"What about the boys?"

"I'll be damned — pardon, dashed — if I'll take them along."

"No, I mean telling them. Shouldn't you inform your sons about the marriage? And mine, while you are at it."

"You'll do better at that than I would."

"No, I think it should come from you. Besides, I need to sit here a bit and catch my breath."

"And worry that you made the right decision. You did, Mrs. Henning. Do not fret." He came over and kissed her briefly, on the forehead.

That was how he sealed an engagement? Alissa decided the man did not have one iota of romance in his soul. "Safe journey, my lord."

He bowed and left, then paused at the door. "My friends call me Rock."

He had friends?

Chapter Eleven

Rockford should have known his clothes could not survive an entire encounter with his youngest son. As soon as the earl announced the engagement — Great gods, he was going to be married, again — William leaped off the bale of hay he had been standing on, directly into Rockford's arms. Now bits of straw clung to the earl's coat, along with sticky bits of tart and other debris and odors he did not care to identify. Showing great restraint, he thought, the earl neither dropped the boy nor cursed at him. After the wedding, he decided, someone was going to have to teach the brat the proper decorum for an earl's child. And to stop jabbering like a magpie.

"That was my best wish, you know!" he was chattering now. "That you would marry Aunt Lissie. Can I call her 'Mama,' do you think?"

"You will have to ask Aunt Lissie, um, Mrs. Henning, Alissa, the lady." His countess. Oh, Lord, what had he done?

"Having a mother is much better than having an aunt, isn't it?" William wanted to know.

"I should think so." Rockford looked toward his other son. "What do you think, Rothmore?"

Hugo replied, "She seems nice. She did not kick up a dust about the toad either. Grandmother Chudleigh would have gone off in heart spasms. She never let me keep any of my specimens or collections. Perhaps Mrs. Henning will."

Still in Rockford's arms, William laughed and said, "Of course she will. Aunt Lissie is top of the trees, I told you. She lets me keep crickets and newts and that little snake I found and —"

In his pockets? Rockford set William down and turned toward William, Mrs. Henning's younger son. She was right: Having two Williams would prove confusing. "What about you, Will?" he asked, compromising. "Are you pleased to have a new father?"

Willy gave him a nod and a grin, then ducked back behind his brother.

"And you, Kendall. Do you approve?"

Kendall kicked a wisp of straw away with his toe, not looking at the earl. "You should have asked me first, my lord."

What, Rockford consult a ten-year-old about his marital affairs? That was absurd. He raised his brow at the very nerve of the

160

whelp, the gall . . . the courage. Kendall considered himself the man of the house, who by rights should have been asked permission to court one of the women in his care. Rockford had just trampled the widow's pride, he knew, giving her no choice but to accept his offer, on his terms, but could he do the same to this earnest boy who was trying to perform the duties of a man? No.

"You are right, Henning," he said, giving the lad the name and the respect due to him. "I should have stated my case for your approval. But it is not too late. I can withdraw my suit if my credentials do not meet your requirements." And pigs would fly first, he thought, but went through the motions. "I can provide well for her, and all of you."

"Can she buy a new dress?" Willy wanted to know. "Not a gray one?"

The idea of his bride wearing mourning for her dead husband did not please Rockford. "As many new dresses as she wishes, and for your sister, also. Definitely not gray. You may tell your mother that I insist on that."

Kendall nodded. The idea of the earl insisting on anything did not bother him the way it would have his mother, but he was a man. Or trying to be. "And you would never hurt her?"

The earl gave him a look that would have had half the members of White's recalling a previous engagement. "I am a gentleman,

161

Henning, and a gentleman *never* harms a woman." He glared into four pairs of eyes. Two pairs were Alissa green. One pair was blue behind the spectacles, and one pair was deep brown, like his own. "Is that understood?"

Four heads nodded, two sandy ones, one blond, and one dark, but not as dark as his own color.

"Fine. What else? I will provide your mother a guaranteed income, if I predecease her, and a home for her lifetime, and for all of you."

"Do I have to share a bed with Willy?" his youngest wanted to know. "He snores."

"Do not."

"Do too. But if you roll him over, he stops."

"No, you will be at Rock Hill, William. You know how many rooms we have. No one will need to share."

"I don't like to sleep alone," Willy protested.

Rockford ran his fingers through his hair. Lud, you'd think he was negotiating the end of the peninsular campaign. "We can decide all that later, after you have seen the place." He'd be gone. Mrs. Henning could handle the details. He did not want to think about where *she* would be sleeping.

Kendall was not finished. "You won't ever make my mama cry, will you?"

162

Now here was a poser. If Kendall thought Rockford could answer that, he had more faith in manhood than was warranted. "Women cry for different reasons. I cannot guarantee your mother will never become a watering pot, but I do swear not to make her unhappy on purpose. Now are you satisfied? I need to be on my way."

"One more question, my lord. Will you keep Mama safe from Sir George?"

"You mean Fred Nivens, don't you? He is gone."

"No, he is not. He is working on the roads. Him too, but I mean Sir George Ganyon at Fairmont, especially."

William piped up: "Ken had to fetch the pistol. You should have seen him, Papa; he was the bravest boy ever. Aunt Lissie said so."

The pistol?

"And Sir George made Aunt Lissie cry, too. We all heard her. You won't let him scare her anymore, will you, Papa?"

His trip to Canterbury was suddenly delayed. He'd set the stinking baronet out for crow bait first.

"No, Sir George will never frighten her again. I will see to it, and that I can promise you."

"Then I give my permission for you to marry my mother, sir. But what should Willy and I call you? Billy never had a mother and

Hugo never knew his, but we did have a father. It would not feel right to call you that or Papa."

Rockford was more concerned with finding out what Sir George had done than what the Henning boys should call him. "Why don't we think about it until the wedding? We can decide later, all right?"

Kendall nodded, then solemnly shook Rockford's hand, sealing their agreement. Then he pushed his brother forward. "Go on, Willy. You have to shake or it's not official and Mama can't marry him."

Will held out a hand that had been feeding pieces of apple to the donkey. Rockford sighed and shook it. It occurred to him for the first time, far too late, that he was not gaining a mother for his two sons. He was gaining two more blasted brats to raise.

Rockford informed Sir George of the coming nuptials, but he did not invite him to the wedding. He invited him, instead, to Gentleman Jackson's Boxing Parlor in London for a bout of fisticuffs.

Recalling the condition of Fred Nivens, Sir George declined. He also declined an invitation to join his lordship at Antoine's fencing academy, Manton's shooting gallery, or any local farm, field, or vacant lot suitable for a dawn engagement.

He did not get the wedding invitation, but

Sir George did get the point.

Rockford left, satisfied. As soon as his orders were carried out, Mrs. Henning and her brood would be under his protection, under his roof. Now if he could get her out from under his skin . . .

He was not satisfied, not at all.

It was easier to keep busy than to think. Alissa found it better to be consulting modistes and wine merchants than to be alone with her thoughts. She planned her wedding, a short one-day event, while trying to avoid considering her marriage, a lifelong commitment.

The wildly unequal match might raise eyebrows, but the ceremony, she vowed, would not embarrass Lord Rockford. With the advice of the vicar's wife and nearly every other lady in the village — and Claymore, Rock Hill's aged but efficient butler, of course — she planned a reception fit for a countess.

If anyone found the engagement offensive, they held their tongues, in Alissa's presence, at least. How could they do otherwise? Whether they approved or not, considering her the worst kind of fortune hunter, she was going to be Lady Rockford, countess of Rock Hill and all its dependents. No one wished to insult a lady of such grand possibilities.

The wedding breakfast would be lavish without being boastfully ostentatious. Most important to Alissa, the local people would be providing food, drink, and entertainment, new suits for the boys, new gowns for her and Amy. She was not sending to London, as so many did, not when the villagers needed the custom, and not when they were still her friends, she hoped. They were all invited to the party, too, with trestle tables set up in the barn for those who felt uncomfortable in the big house.

For the first time since her first marriage, Alissa was going to have a gown she did not sew herself. She did not have the time, for one thing, and she could afford to pay the MacElroy sisters to create a more intricate gown than she could, for another. Why, she could afford to order a dozen gowns! The MacElroys needed the income, she reasoned, still needing to justify the extravagance in her own mind. She ordered three, and three for her sister, to be ready for the wedding. And new bonnets and gloves and shoes and capes and nightclothes and fine, silky underwear for them both.

The boys were ecstatic about their new residence, especially the maze and the stables and, for Hugo, the large library, but Amy was in alt at her new clothes. She almost ruined one dress length, weeping in happiness. The boys almost ruined their new outfits, also. Billy discovered the tailor's chalk, and Hugo overturned the dish of pins while his spectacles were off. Willy would not stand still for the fitting, and Kendall seemed to grow between the first fitting and the final one. Still, they were all happy to have enough shirts and stockings so that they did not have to be as careful of their apparel.

Between fittings and meetings with the cook and Claymore, Alissa had to answer questions from Rockford's tenants. He had made promises to repair Arkenstall's mismanagement but he was not there, and the men needed to proceed before the winter. So Alissa gave approval for new roofs, new equipment, new crops and methods to try. She was not her father's daughter for nothing. Her husband had always discussed his work with her too, and taken her with him on his rounds. She knew about land, and the farmers were happy enough that someone listened to their concerns, even if she was only a woman. Mrs. Henning had a good head on her shoulders, the locals agreed. Too bad her father had no son.

Rock Hill itself also needed her attention. What was the point of serving the best wines and foodstuffs to the guests if the house was in disrepair? She hired extra servants to help the elderly staff, and oversaw their work herself. Lord Rockford had bargained for a chatelaine. She would see that he got his money's worth.

Every minute of every day was full, and

not half what she considered necessary was accomplished. Why, some brides took a year to plan their weddings, and she had a week, with four boys to keep out of trouble at the same time. The days were too busy for reflecting, but, ah, the nights.

Alissa fell into bed at night thinking she would fall into exhausted sleep instantly. She did not. For the first time since before Amy's birth, she had a bedchamber to herself, having shared one with her sister before her marriage to William and then after he died. Now she was alone for the first time in years, without Amy's chatter to keep her awake, without any rustling in the roof overhead. Sleep was still elusive. Worries were rampant. Panic was pending. How could she sleep?

She looked around her bedchamber, the countess's apartment that had long been vacant. It was almost as large as her entire cottage, but far more elegant, the blue velvet hangings faded a bit, but the rich Aubusson rug was as vibrantly colored as any she had seen. The hearth always had a fire burning, not just when she was in the room, and one of the maids had no other job but to wait on her here. The candles never smoked, the windows did not leak, the mattress had nary a lump. She had her own sitting room next door, a dressing room just for her clothes, and a tiled bathing room with water that was heated in the attic pipes, instead of having to be carried up all the stairs.

Amy's room was down the hall, and almost as lovely, decorated in rose and pink. She was, like the room, blooming. The boys had adjoining rooms in the nursery upstairs, with a footman to serve them, a valet-in-training to look after their clothes and help them dress, and one of Jake's undergrooms to accompany them about as they explored the huge estate.

Alissa never had to give another drawing lesson to another untalented, uninterested student. In fact, she had found an unused attic room with just the proper light for a studio. If she found the time, she intended to paint a scene of Rock Hill for his lordship's wedding present, so she did not have to use his money to purchase his gift. Besides, she enjoyed painting. As soon as the wedding was over, the house was in order, she found a proper tutor for the boys and an eligible match for Amy, she could paint to her heart's content.

She never had to count her pennies again, either. A quick glance at the open ledgers showed Rock Hill to be a hugely profitable estate, despite Arkenstall's depredations. She now had paid-up accounts at every store in the village, and access to what seemed unlimited funds in London. She did not feel the least guilty over spending Rockford's money on a few luxuries, like her elegant lawn nightgown with violets embroidered across the low neck and scattered along the hem.

Alissa rubbed the fabric between her fingers, delighting in the softness. Not only could she never have afforded such fine material, but its lack of warmth would have been an invitation to frostbite in her cottage, and its sheerness immodest, with the boys in the next room. Willy was just outgrowing nightmares and crawling into her bed. Now a footman slept in one of the nursery rooms.

She never had to wear flannel again, or worry about her baby crying in the night.

With all these luxuries, with all the blessings that had come her way, Alissa asked herself how she could dare to complain. What had she to worry about that was stealing her rest?

Only the fact that she had sold her soul to the devil, that was all. In return for security and comfort, she had given herself to a man she did not know, one who inhabited an entirely different sphere from hers. Why, she belonged in the beau monde as much as her painting would belong in the empty place where the stolen Rembrandt had hung. Worse, Rockford did not want her, Alissa Henning. He wanted only a glorified housekeeper. Oh, he wanted her body, she had no doubt, but the same way a stag used tree bark to rub his antlers: Rockford would be scratching an itch. Almost any tree would do, but a wife was handy. In less than a week she had to welcome the toplofty earl to this very room, admit him to her body . . . pay her debts.

How could she live with a man who had no heart, who saw nothing but practicality, who considered children a burden and a wife the solution to a pesky problem? How could she, the daughter of a bailiff, be welcome in his elevated circles?

She wanted her flannel nightgown back, her sister in the next bed, her boys in the next room.

A few days before the week had passed, Rockford sent a note — to his butler, not his bride. Claymore adjusted his spectacles and announced that his lordship had acquired the necessary license. He would return on Wednesday night. The wedding could go forward Thursday, as planned.

As ordered, more like, Alissa fumed. She had no idea if he was bringing guests, if he had relatives she should invite, if he wanted lobster patties instead of breaded oysters. Rockford could be bringing his friend the prince regent, for all she knew. She had no idea of his wants and wishes, and her head ached from all the decisions she had been forced to make. Her patience was wearing thinner with each sleepless night.

It was his wedding too, she thought. He

might show some interest — in it or in her. Now he was returning, he said, the very evening before the ceremony. They had no time to speak, and Alissa would have no chance to air her concerns. He had most likely planned things that way on purpose.

Claymore cleared his throat. His lordship also sent orders, he iterated, looking somewhere past her left shoulder, that she was to select an engagement ring and a wedding band from the vault, along with whatever jewelry she wished to wear.

"The Rockford collection, you know. A great deal of it belongs to the current countess." When he finally noticed her blank stare, he added, "That is you, madam."

Alissa had never heard of the Rockford collection; nor had she ever heard of a groom who did not select his bride's ring. Even if there was a traditional engagement ring, handed down for centuries, he should have handed it to her himself.

Claymore went back to looking beyond her and her displeasure. "The last Lady Rockford had the sapphire set. His lordship's first wife wore the Rothmore ruby. I daresay his lordship thought you might wish a different set, and he did not know your taste well enough to make the selection."

"He was in too much of a hurry, you mean. The man does not have a romantic bone in his body."

Loyal Claymore bowed, wisely refusing to comment on his employer's bones, his business in London, or Mrs. Henning's bridal nerves.

As she followed the butler to the vault, Alissa clutched at the one sign of hope she could find: Rockford had remembered she needed a ring.

Or Claymore had.

Chapter Twelve

He was drunk for his first wedding. Suffering the morning after for his second. Now Rockford was simply suffering. Another blasted wedding.

By pushing himself and his horses to their limits, he had obtained the special license, seen his solicitor about the settlements and guardianships, sent notices to the papers, and attended the fete in honor of Princess Helga and her brother. He'd thought it his duty to tell her highness about the coming nuptials before she read about it. He should have recalled that she could not speak English — or read it.

Luckily his excellent valet was able to cover up the bruise on his cheek from the wineglass she threw. Since they had been in a crowded ballroom, surrounded by the elite of the polite world, and the glass was full, there was no way to cover up the scene.

Now he stood in the Rock Hill chapel, surrounded by farmers and servants, villagers and landed gentry. He could not hide his exhaustion nor his impatience for the ghastly ritual to be over.

His sons stood beside him, and whoever made that arrangement chose well. Rockford was marrying for their sakes, after all. They could suffer through the ceremony too. William was neatly washed and combed, in new clothes, but Rockford knew better.

"If you lay one grubby paw on me," he whispered to the bright-eyed boy, "on my white satin knee smalls, my white brocade waistcoat, my white shirt, or my white neck-cloth, I swear I will throw you in the dungeon."

"We do not have a dungeon, Papa," William said with a giggle, which earned both of them a frown from the vicar.

Then Miss Aminta Bourke was walking down the aisle. She wore a gown of green velvet, with gold ribbons nicely delineating her still-girlish figure. More gold ribbons were braided through her hair, along with a few pink rosebuds, likely from his own forcing houses. Sweet innocence personified, she would win the hearts of all the local swains, Rockford judged, and win their parents' approval with the generous dowry he meant to provide. He smiled at her, and she blushed and missed her footing. He might have to be more generous.

Mrs. Henning came next, Alissa, his bride. Her sons walked at either side, but Rockford barely noticed them. She looked magnificent. Her gown was a milky watered silk, almost gray, he noted, and made note of her defiance. But it was touched with dark green whorls, as if she had dipped her paintbrush in a cloud. The classic styling was impressive, but not as impressive as the Rockford emerald. A large stone surrounded by pearls, it hung on a heavy gold chain between the widow's breasts. Impressive, indeed, and the jewel was nice, too.

Her hair was not in its usual neat gathering of braids at the back of her neck, but was wound into a coronet on top of her head, held there by a circlet of pearls, with a few long, honey-colored tresses allowed to frame her high cheekbones and trail down her graceful neck.

She was paler than he would have liked, but Rockford doubted his own complexion could stand comparison with a sheet right now.

At least she would not shame him by stumbling or swooning. No one could fault her elegant bearing or doubt that Rockford's wife was a true lady, despite her birth. As his countess she could take her place in London society, if not among the highest sticklers, then certainly in Prinny's circle.

Lud, he could imagine the stir she would cause. The newspapers were already poking fun at Rockford's country widow, but the rakes and reprobates of the regent's crowd would be panting at her feet. They would chase after her because she was Rockford's wife and she was pretty, but mostly because she appeared to be that rarest of creatures, a chaste woman, and thus a challenge to the hardened gamesters. The situation would not arise. The Carleton House set would not have a chance. The betting books would not be full of wagers on the identity of Lady R's first lover. Not this time.

No, children belonged in the country, and their mother belonged with them.

The gossip columns would double their gibes when she did not appear, thinking he already regretted the misalliance. Rockford did not regret it one bit. He did not even care that Prinny and his advisers were upset at the loss of the Ziftsweig alliance, or that he had married without royal approval, out of court circles. He'd smooth things over when he returned to town, losing yet another high-stakes game to the prince on purpose. He'd made the right decision.

Had Mrs. Henning? With a new wardrobe and the proper backing, she could have reentered the marriage mart and chosen herself a likable chap. But she did not have either the clothes or the connections, so he stopped feeling guilty that she had no choice. He had not taken advantage of her need, Rockford assured himself as she approached the altar;

he had rescued her.

So she would not have a grand passion. She had had it with Henning, it seemed. Now she would have money, protection, and security, a much better bargain in the earl's eyes. What he would have, however, was another wife, the last thing he wanted.

Well, this one was not going to cause a scandal or the least ripple in his well ordered life. She was not going to run off and wound his pride, or die in childbed. She was certainly not going to wound his feelings. How could she, when he felt nothing for her beyond a vague sense of possession and a more definite warming of his blood? The unwarranted heat could be cooled at any other fountain of feminine charm without the least emotional involvement. He felt none now, even as he repeated the vicar's words of love, honor, and fidelity, and he meant to keep it that way.

This was a business contract, as he had made clear. Mrs. Henning knew to expect nothing more than his considerable worldly possessions, so she could not be disappointed. She could have repeated her own vows with a shade more conviction, though, he thought. And she could have selected a fancier ring than the gold filigree band young Rothmore handed him. She was a countess, his wife, by thunder. She ought to look the part. He'd have to buy her another ring when he reached London. A matching emerald, perhaps, to the stone that nestled so damned invitingly in her cleavage that if he were not a master of control he might embarrass her, himself, and the entire congregation. No, he was not going to get involved.

So he gave her the merest brush of the lips that could still be called a kiss, then turned to accept the vicar's congratulations, a quick peck on the cheek from his weeping sister-in-law, and grins from all the boys.

There, it was done.

There, she had done it. Alissa Bourke Henning had just become Alissa Rothmore, Countess Rockford. Her knees were not knocking, her hands were not shaking as she accepted the best wishes of her neighbors. After all, they were her friends, and seemed genuinely happy for her.

She had not been the least bit anxious about the ceremony. She knew she had never looked better, knew her father would have been proud, and her former husband would have been relieved that she and his sons were so well provided for. William would have wanted her to be happy, so she tried to smile for her guests, and for his memory. Rockford wore his usual dark, detached visage, and he frowned when he placed his ring on her finger. If he had second thoughts, Alissa thought, it was too late now, and his own fault for rushing into this scrambled affair. Well, neither of them could worry over spilled milk, not with the wedding breakfast still to come.

The reception did not worry her either, although she had never attended so large an affair, much less managed one. Claymore had, and had everything in hand. The music was lively, the food was tasty and plentiful, the champagne was kept flowing, the servants were attentive to every need. The Misses MacElroy were treated as respectfully as Sir Humbers, the earl's financial adviser and man of affairs who had come from London with the settlement papers.

The solicitor was in as much of a hurry as Rockford usually was, insisting the new Lady Rockford — Gracious, that was her name now, wasn't it? — sign the documents so he could return to town and another client. Alissa had time only between the receiving line and the toasts to scan the pages, but the terms seemed far more generous than she had imagined. She'd have to thank Rockford later, when they were in private. One more thing to discuss meant one more delay of bedtime . . . and the marriage bed.

She had another dance with the squire's son, rather than think about later. To put off the inevitable, she would have danced with the devil himself, and did.

"You did an excellent job with the wedding," Rockford told her when they came together in the set. "Everyone seems to be enjoying himself. Or herself." He scowled at a spotty-faced youth who was holding Amy too close in the figure of the dance. "I commend you."

"Claymore deserves more credit than I, my lord, ah, Rockford." She could not call her husband Rock, although it suited his strength and his solid essence. "But I am glad you approve."

"What, were you worried that I'd be too high in the instep to rub shoulders with the local folk?"

She was. She'd been relieved to see him shaking hands with the apothecary and dancing once with the vicar's wife. Of course, his perfect manners would permit nothing less, but she had placed a pair of stuffed chairs at the head of the room, so he might sit like a feudal lord, away from the commoners — like her. The Misses MacElroy were happily ensconced there now. They deserved the best seats, Alissa decided, after working so hard this past sennight. And Rockford seemed content to engage his tenants in conversation after his dance with her and one with Amy. He listened to the men's concerns and flirted with their wives and daughters.

Yes, Alissa thought, her liege was holding court. He needed only an ermine-trimmed robe, a crown, and a jewel-studded goblet of wine in his hand. She thought she might try to paint his portrait like that, as a historical allegory with period dress. Her mind balked at the codpiece, though, or tight hose. He was commanding enough in his formal attire now, anyway, she quickly told herself, fanning her suddenly warm cheeks. And his white satin inexpressibles were tight enough that she could see — No, she would *not* think about Rockford's clothes, or Rockford in or out of them. She had hours yet before she had to face that hurdle.

All too soon for her peace of mind, however, the guests started departing. The farmers had to be up at dawn; the villagers did not wish to travel in the dark. The boys, who had consumed enough cake and punch for an entire battalion, were being led off by Claymore and their footman. For once Alissa was glad their upset digestions and disturbed sleep would be someone else's problem.

Although, if one of the children needed her . . . No, that would only delay the moment of reckoning. Alissa did not think she could survive another day of dread. Not that she was precisely dreading the coming intimacy with her elegant new husband, but he was a stranger, and a practiced lover. What if she did not please him? The license and the settlement papers were already signed, thank goodness.

But what if he was as cold and unyielding as he was now, refusing to grant the children another quarter hour of the party? She would have let them stay up all night, rather than face her doom — her groom.

Alissa sighed at her own cowardice. This was not like Fred Nivens's assault, nor Sir George's repulsive offer. Rockford was a gentleman, and he was her husband.

Nevertheless, she fled up the stairs when the last guest left, saying she had to hear the boys' prayers before they went to bed. She would have woken them up if they were asleep. She could only stay so long, though, and the hour was still not very late. It was not yet time to retire, unless she wished to give her husband the wildly wrong impression that she was impatient for his attention, so she went back to the gold parlor.

He was there, staring into the fireplace. The flames cast a reddish glow onto his dark countenance, almost a demonic reflection, if one wanted to frighten oneself. Alissa was already doing a good enough job at it. She took a calming breath and said, "The boys wish to see you."

He turned to look at her. "What for?"

"Why, for you to wish them good night, of course."

There was no "of course." Rockford's father had never bidden him sleep well. He shrugged. It was an easy enough wish to grant. "I will meet you here, after."

Alissa let out her breath. It was an order, but he had not said to wait in her bedroom. So he meant to talk, to get to know her, to come to an understanding of her wants and needs, as she had to learn about him. That was the way it should be, the way a marriage between strangers had to begin if they were to be comfortable together. Rockford was not an insensitive clod after all, then. Alissa felt her clenched muscles begin to relax.

The servants were still bustling about, cleaning up. She told them to finish in the morning; they had worked hard enough today.

Upstairs, Rockford was at a loss. "Good night" seemed inadequate, but he had nothing else to say, so he lightly touched the cheek of William Henning, who was nearly asleep.

"Night, Papa Rock," the boy murmured, before turning over. Rockford felt the name made him sound like something from a fairy tale: ". . . And the papa rock rolled all the way down the hill." Lord.

Will had been three when his father died, so was not as sensitive about using "Papa" as his brother was. To Mrs. Henning's older boy, he was still "sir." Kendall now said, "I am glad you are going to look after my mother, sir."

184

"And I am glad you will protect her when I cannot be here," Rockford replied, winning him a rare smile.

His own William was still awake, and still sticky from the piece of iced cake he had smuggled into his bed. "Night, Papa. Thank you for finding us a new mother."

Rockford had worried about his heir, that the sickly child might have overexerted himself at the party or eaten the wrong foods. The earl glanced uncertainly at all the bottles on the bedside table, but Rothmore appeared fine. In fact, he looked better than when he'd been with Lord and Lady Chudleigh, less like a starved owl. He put his book down and said, "Good night, Father. You have an excellent library."

"Thank you. What about Mrs. Henning, ah, the countess?"

"Oh, she likes it too."

Which seemed to be high encomium from Hugo.

Rockford congratulated himself on handling fatherhood so well. Now if only he could breeze as easily through this first night of matrimony.

While Alissa was waiting she thought of the sheer nightgown laid out on her bed upstairs, the vases of flowers the giggling maids had carried in, the extra candles they had placed around the large bedchamber, the bottle of wine. The picture of Rock Hill was there too, just a quick sketch, really, all she'd had time for, but she could do a better one if the earl seemed interested. She also thought of all the topics they could discuss, to put off going upstairs.

When the earl returned, his neckcloth was hanging loose, his shirt collar was open, and his jacket was off. A lock of dark hair had fallen across his forehead, and a faint shadow of new beard limned his square jaw. Oh, my. Alissa licked her suddenly dry lips. Perhaps they need not discuss a pension for the gardener right now.

Rockford had a glass of brandy in one hand, and she wondered how many drinks he'd had that day. Who could keep count between the toasts and the supper and the punch? She had no way of telling if he was in his altitudes, for he wore his habitual unsmiling expression, like a pagan god carved from marble. For that matter, she did not know if Rockford was a maudlin drunk or mean, if he grew silly or sleepy. If she had to guess, she would wager her new husband held his liquor as well as he rode a horse. The Earl of Rockford was not one to make a fool or a spectacle of himself. Even now, in his undress, he was elegant, in control. And masculine. Very masculine.

Alissa wished she had something to drink now too, but he did not offer. She licked her lips again. When he scowled at her, she hurried into speech. "I am glad we have this chance to speak, my lord."

His frown deepened. "We are married. Do you think you could cease handing me the title with every breath?"

Alissa ran her tongue over her lips to try to call him Rock, or Rockford.

"And stop that!"

Perhaps he was drunk after all. "Yes, well, we, ah, have a great deal to discuss, uh, Robert." She smiled at him. "Will that do?"

He had not taken his eyes off her mouth. He raised his glass to his own lips and took a long swallow, then nodded.

Alissa took a deep breath and began again. "For instance —"

His eyes had moved to her expanded chest, and he growled.

Nervous enough to start with, Alissa was nearly in a panic, but then she started to grow angry. She could not be the only one trying to make something of the marriage. He could be civil, at least. Otherwise she would lock that bedroom door, marriage license or not. Rockford had conjugal rights, but she had more self-respect than to put up with a besotted brute. The servants would talk and the whole village would know the wedding night was a failure. They would shake their heads and ask what else one could expect from such a mingle-mangle of a marriage.

"For instance, what?" he asked when she started to get up from the love seat before she started to cry.

She sat back. "We need to talk about the boundary dispute between Mr. Tavistock and Ned Danvers. And hiring an underbutler for Claymore. The wall hangings in the master suite need replacing and I do not know your preferences. The miller wishes to put up a new building, and the boys need a tutor, especially Hugo."

Only the last seemed to catch his attention. "I thought the boy was bookish. What, did his grandparents merely let him loose in the library without instruction? Confound it, they taught him to add and subtract, didn't they?"

"Of course, but —" She did not get to finish, to tell him that Hugo was so far advanced in his studies that neither she nor the vicar could teach him anything. She did not even know what books to order.

"Well, find one to bring him up to par. As for the rest, I am certain you are capable of handling everything. I have every confidence you can manage while I am gone."

"Gone?"

Chapter Thirteen

"Yes. I have matters that need attending. You knew I was a busy man. That was why I took another wife."

"Yes, but . . ."

Lud, if he did not get out of here soon, he'd pull the pins out of her rose-scented, honey-colored hair just to see how long it was, and if it could be as silky as he thought. If she smiled, he'd have her out of that revealing gown and on the floor in front of the fireplace before she could say his name again. Robert. He let the sound echo in his mind, like a sweet, unfamiliar song. If she licked those lush lips of hers once more, he would not bother with the hair or the gown. He'd lift her skirts right where she sat and bury himself in her softness.

And then where would he be? In the arms of a woman who had married him for his money but who wanted words of love. They always did, before, during, and after lovemaking. There would be tears and recriminations and bitter words, and she'd take a lover to spite him.

Besides, once a female knew the power she had over a man, how her perfume could drive him mad, how the sway of her hips could make his watching eyes cross, then she would make his life hell.

Better he left now.

"You cannot simply leave!"

He raised his eyebrow. Was she trying to tighten that sexual noose already? "I thought we had this discussion earlier."

"We have discussed nothing! Not where we would live, certainly not that we would live apart!"

"And yet you signed the papers, Countess, making you a wealthy woman. You have no cause for complaint."

"The money is to replace courtesy, then? Loyalty? Affection?"

It was to replace carping conversations like this. "Ours was, and will remain, a marriage of convenience. Those were the terms upon which we agreed."

"Your notion of convenience, it seems, does not reconcile with mine."

"Ah, but my name is the one that signs the checks."

She inhaled sharply at his bluntness. Her cheeks were flushed, her fists were clenched, and the gold flecks in her green eyes were flashing like lightning in the forest. She looked superb to him, and his arms ached to hold her, to smooth away the hurt. He might as well wear a ring through his nose for her to lead him by.

So Rockford kissed his new wife on the forehead, repeated that he had every confidence in her, and that Claymore could get a message to him at any time. Then he left. Not just the room, but the house, the village, the shire.

He left, on their wedding night!

Alissa sat in the parlor long after the fire had burned down. She did not wish to face that bedroom, the countess's chamber, more than ever. The flowers, the sheer nightgown — the travesty of her marriage!

She did not feel the cold. What was a chill after the winter in her soul? Her hopes for the future, the dreams she had not dared speak aloud, even to herself, were all turned to shards of ice, piercing her heart. Rockford was gone, and she felt more alone and abandoned than when her first husband had died. At least William Henning had not been in such a hurry to leave!

She tried to convince herself that she was no worse off now than she was then. She had no hopes of happiness then. She had none now.

What she had, in the morning, was a stiff neck from sitting up all night. She also had wealth. With it came the servants' pity, her sons' confusion, Rockford's sons' disappointment, and a few I-told-you-so nods from the neighbors.

Alissa decided she would play by the earl's rules. He dealt the cards, he held the bank, but she was still in the game. So she became the Countess of Rockford, all on her own.

She took over the books and the land management. She consulted bankers, the tenant farmers who knew the area best, architects and engineers, but she herself made the decisions of where to invest the earl's money, which improvements to make first. With Claymore beside her she started renovating the house, the grounds, and everyone's wardrobes. She hired local men to teach the boys archery and fishing and shooting, but sent to London for instructors in dancing and deportment for Aminta. She turned Hugo loose in the lending library when he had exhausted Rock Hill's collection, until she could find a tutor who knew more than young Viscount Rothmore.

Even with winter approaching, a lot could be accomplished on the farms. Manures and minerals could be spread, and late crops could be sown to nourish the soil, according to the latest farm journals. Alissa also went to livestock auctions, buying prime bulls for stud, fresh blood to strengthen the herds. She purchased seeds; she ordered the newest equipment. She hired men who were out of work and set them to clearing fields for added productivity, and to draining swamps to avoid spring floods.

Alissa also looked into starting cottage industries, such as pottery, stonemasonry, or brickworks, so the people could be independent of the land — and of their absentee lord.

That was the first two weeks.

The third week she started inviting ladies from the vicinity to tea. Some had raised their noses at her before; some had never known she existed. None refused her invitations, nor her pleas to help start a free school in the village, and a place where orphans could be taught a trade, rather than languishing in the poorhouses.

She had put the emerald pendant and the matching engagement ring back in the vault, keeping only the gold filigree wedding band on her finger. The matrons seemed to approve, noting that she was not flaunting her new wealth and elevated position. They decided among themselves that Lady Rockford was a mature, modest, capable sort, not flighty like the earl's previous wives. Alissa Henning was not as beautiful, of course, and without the centuries of blood and breeding, but she might turn out to be a better asset to the community than those young ladies who spent all their time in London. She was a good mother, too, not only to her own children but also to the heir and the spare, who obviously adored her. That mattered to these women of Leicester.

While she had the ladies' attention, Alissa made sure to introduce Aminta, who impressed the women with her sweet smile and demure manner. If mention of her sister's new dowry found itself stirred into the rumor mill, so be it. Soon the Rock Hill ladies were accepting invitations to the leading houses of local society, where Aminta met a wider circle of possible suitors than Squire's spotted son, the blacksmith's nephew, the butcher's delivery boy. She was the countess's sister now, and could look much higher, although there was no rush to marry her off. Rockford could not complain of Amy's continued presence at his residence, Alissa decided, if he recalled her existence at all. If not for her sister, Alissa would have to hire a companion or else take her meals alone and travel to social engagements by herself.

The boys kept her company when she visited the tenant farms and the horse fairs, but they had their own pursuits, their own interests, and she did not want them to grow up knowing only women's company. Hugo was not as enthusiastic about the sporting lessons, but he happily went off on walks and collecting excursions, finding plants he had only studied in books. His grandparents had seldom permitted him the outdoors, much less physical exertion. Alissa insisted that he take a groom or a footman with him, if not her own sensible Kendall, to make sure he did not injure or exhaust himself. Hugo was the heir; protecting him was half the reason Rockford had wedded her.

The other half was falling out of trees and into fountains, ransacking the pantry, and ruining the gardens by taking Rosie, the pig, on her daily constitutional. When he was not up to some mischief or other, Billy was filling an unused stall in the stable with things that slithered or slimed or swam or stung. Alissa was terrified of half of them, but she wisely let Billy have his menagerie. She knew he'd keep the creatures in his pockets, otherwise. Like his father, Billy knew what he wanted.

Alissa was getting almost everything she wanted: a good upbringing for her sons, a chance at a good match for her sister, a good name for herself. And she had a good cry both times one of Rockford's impersonal correspondences arrived from London, from his new secretary.

Then his sister came home.

Lady Eleanor was as astonished to find Alissa in the house as Alissa was to see her new in-law.

"You and Rockford are married?" the earl's sister asked, amazed that her high-toned brother would take a common-born wife.

"You are not?" Alissa asked in return.

Eleanor was dark like Robert, with his

thick brows and straight hair, but she had a different nose, one seen on some of their ancestors' portraits. It looked better on the dead relatives. She was tall and thin and sat erect, every inch a lady, except for that bare spot on her finger.

She followed Alissa's glance, then said, "No, Arkenstall and I found we would not suit after all."

After a month or so together? Alissa raised her brow the way she had seen Rockford do it. "I . . . see."

"No, I do not suppose you do." The two women had not been precisely friends, due to the disparity in their stations, but that raised eyebrow told Eleanor that Mrs. Henning had come into her own. Eleanor realized that she was no longer mistress here, and could not assume a welcome in the countess's home. She owed her brother's unexpected bride a better explanation. "I was blind," she started. "Love does that, you know," she added with a bitter laugh. "I did not see what Arkenstall was doing until too late. I never knew he was actually stealing from the estate until we were well on our way to Ireland —"

"I thought you were going to Scotland."

"Oh, that was just to throw people off the scent, if anyone bothered to pursue us. I knew Rockford would not, but Arkenstall wanted to take no chances, and it was far more romantic to be plotting intrigue.

Rockford would never have given permission for me to wed a bailiff, of course, which was why we were eloping."

"Of course not."

Something in Alissa's tone warned the older woman that she had overstepped the line. "Oh, your father was a bailiff, wasn't he?"

"And my husband. My first husband."

"Yes, well, I decided that I could wed one too. After all, I was nearing forty, with no other prospects in sight. And I thought I loved him, fool that I was. But I was not a thief! He was clever, Arkenstall was. He had me convinced Rock Hill was suffering a bad year, that the revenues were off. He said things would turn around in the spring and we could rehire the laborers, make the repairs. I swear to you I never knew he was embezzling money until he bragged about it, when we were well on our way. I never looked at the ledgers. That was Arkenstall's job, or Rockford's, if he ever bothered to look."

"I believe you. But how did you think you would live if Rockford did not give his blessings?"

"Oh, I thought he would come around once the deed was done. What was it to him whom I married, anyway? If he would not take Arkenstall back, I reasoned, then we could have led a decent life on my dowry, which was considerable."

"Was?"

"How could I ask my brother to release the money, when Arkenstall had stolen from him?"

"I can see where that would be a problem."

"I was still going to go through with the wedding, for I was already ruined and he said he had done it for love of me, to give me the life I was used to. You would think that at my age I would know better than to trust a silver-tongued devil, but perhaps I believed him just because I was an old spinster, and no one else was going to love me. Oh, I could have found a man to marry me anytime these last years, but I decided I would rather stay unwed than have a husband bought with my dowry. I was content here, until Arkenstall showed me what I had been missing."

Alissa could well understand the other woman's feelings. She handed over a handkerchief.

Lady Eleanor blew her distinctive nose before continuing. "Yes, well, then I discovered that he had not only robbed from the estate, but he had taken items belonging to Rockford besides, antiques, heirlooms, small items he could pawn. I found a case full of them while I was looking for one of my misplaced bags at an inn. There was no jewelry that I could see. Is it all accounted for?"

Alissa twirled the ring on her finger. "Claymore would have known if something was missing from the vault."

"Good, because I could not search all Arkenstall's bags. But I realized then what he was up to, why he had taken me away."

"How dreadful."

"Uglier still to realize that he never cared for me, only for what he could get. We had a terrible row. He did not want me to leave."

"He could never get your dowry then."

"Oh, he had to know Rockford would not release my portion to a thief. Anyone who has the least acquaintance with Rockford would know his moral inflexibility."

"Arkenstall must have cared for you, then, to have wanted you to stay." Because the other woman sounded so forlorn, she added, "For that matter, he must have held you in affection or he would not have taken you along or planned an elopement. Surely he could have traveled faster on his own."

Lady Eleanor shrugged. "Perhaps. Or perhaps he needed the coach. Or else he had yet another plan, like ransoming me back to Rockford." She sipped at the glass of sherry Alissa poured for her. "More likely he did not wish me to leave because I knew his plans and he feared I would tell the authorities. He claimed I was an accomplice, that I would hang alongside him, or be deported. I

199

did not want to spend another minute in his company, much less voyage to Botany Bay with him."

"So what did you do?" Alissa refilled Lady Eleanor's glass and took a swallow from her own, leaning forward. The story was almost as good as one of Aminta's novels from the lending library.

"I wrote to Squire Winslow, telling him which port Arkenstall planned to sail from. We were going to travel a bit until the dust settled."

"You did not write to your brother?"

Lady Eleanor made no comment. They both knew Rockford would not have come, if he bothered to read the letter. He would have washed his hands of his errant sister, with that same moral inflexibility. "The squire is my godfather, you know."

Alissa had not known that. Winslow was the magistrate, though. "And he rescued you from Arkenstall?"

"There was no rescue. I foolishly told Arkenstall what I had done, so he took an earlier ship. He was well out of reach when Squire Winslow arrived. Squire came home with me in the coach. Rockford's coach." She shook her head. "Quite a sad ending for an adventure, isn't it?"

Aminta's stories never ended so poorly. "At least you had an adventure. What shall you do now?"

"I thought to live here quietly. Rockford never comes, and old Claymore would not care that I am a ruined woman. He's known me from birth, too. But now . . . I do not know. My presence will reflect poorly on you. It could even destroy your sister's chances. I'd leave, but I have no funds left. I did retrieve a few items that belong to Rockford by hiding them in my own luggage, but if I sell them, then indeed I am a thief."

There was no arguing Lady Eleanor's estimation. Everything Alissa was working for would be destroyed by the scandal that was merely a rumor now — and she had enough money to send her sister-in-law away into safe anonymity. For that matter, the rent was paid through the new year on her old cottage. But this was Rockford's sister, and she was supposed to be looking out for his family, wasn't she?

"Could you be breeding?" she asked.

Eleanor stared into her glass. "No. I bled on the way home."

"Excellent. Then you are not ruined. You are a heroine, and so we shall tell everyone."

Lady Eleanor laughed in disbelief. "I should have known you were a ninny. Who else would take on my brother?"

"A practical woman with a family to protect. Here is what we shall say: You realized Arkenstall was up to no good and went after him in the family coach, with your maid for companion. You are not a young miss, so that is unexceptional. Foolish, perhaps, but not shocking. The maid came down with the influenza, so you left her behind, still bravely giving pursuit. When you located the dastard you sent for Squire, who arrived too late to arrest him but, with your help, retrieved the family heirlooms."

Lady Eleanor considered the fabrication. "But where have I been? Too much time has passed."

"Why, you have been recovering from the influenza yourself. At . . . surely you have an old school friend in the north or someone who would vouch for your presence?"

"I do have an old aunt who lives in Wales. She never comes to town anyway. It might just work."

"It will work. It has to."

"You are very good, Countess. I knew I did the right thing by sending William to you."

"Thank you. He will be anxious to see you, as will Hugo."

"Rothmore is here too? The Chudleighs always said he would never survive the journey."

"I believe they felt he could get better care here, now. He is not as strong as I would wish, but he is thriving. He has something of your look, you know. The nose, I think."

"Poor boy."

They both laughed. Then Eleanor said,

"You have indeed wrought miracles. Maybe you can manage this one too, making me respectable again."

With Claymore's help, they planted the tale on the local grapevine. Few believed the story, but if that was what the countess wanted them to think, then that was what they would, rather than lose her good graces.

None of the local hostesses had to worry about entertaining a stumbling, if not fallen, woman in their homes. Lady Eleanor refused all invitations. She would not accompany Alissa to the village or to the outlying farms. She would not join the boys on their excursions. She would not even take meals with the others. She just kept to her room or took long rides to who knew where.

Alissa was worried enough that she thought of writing to Rockford, but Eleanor had begged her not to tell him she was back, swearing that she would do it herself, in time. No correspondence waited to be sent, however. Claymore suggested the letter might have been mailed from the village on Lady Eleanor's walks, but Alissa doubted her sister-in-law went there, with all the whispers.

The secretary would read the letter either way, so Alissa kept her own counsel. Lady Eleanor was still recovering from the influenza, she told anyone who was impolite enough to ask.

Alissa knew it was far more likely that the

woman was recovering from a broken heart and shattered pride.

She could sympathize with both.

Chapter Fourteen

Alissa was starting to paint again. Sketches, actually, for she had few hours to sit in the attic room she had claimed for a studio. At night, when she and Aminta were not invited to dinner or an informal dance or a musical program at one of the neighbors' houses, she had the time, but the light was not good enough. So she drew, and planned in her head the paintings she would create, perhaps in the winter, when there was not as much to be done out-of-doors.

She also thought about hiring an instructor to teach her the art of oil painting. She had never had the funds for lessons or materials before. Now she did, and some of the subjects she wished to capture would do better in the heavier medium. Watercolors, with their light and airy feel, could not lend the heroic quality she wished in the portraits she wanted to paint. She had pads full of quick studies of the four boys, each so different, but she wanted to paint them together in one large portrait, a family. And her sister was so dear to her, so perfect in her youthful beauty, that Alissa wanted a large portrait of Amy as she was now, to keep for when she moved away to start a family of her own. Watercolors seemed too ephemeral to her, for such a lasting tribute.

After a few attempts, she did not feel she could convey the solidity, the sheer weight of Rock Hill itself in her usual softly flowing landscape style. Her efforts were good renderings and pretty, with the leaves turning colors, but Rock Hill was not pretty. It was massive and permanent, looming down over its holdings like a dragon guarding its hoard of treasures. Whenever she was out, visiting tenants or on collecting expeditions with the boys, she stopped to study her new home, viewing it from every angle, in all kinds of light, to plan the perfect painting.

She wrote letters in her mind too, picking just the right words to express her thoughts, the right tone to transmit her feelings. She would tell Rockford about his sister and how she was grieving for her lost love. Alissa could not be certain from the few conversations she'd had with Eleanor whether the lady was madder at being betrayed, or sadder at being alone. Even if Rockford had no insight to his sister's heart, his forgiveness might help Eleanor forgive her own blunderings.

Alissa wanted to tell him what fine boys he

had. Hugo was teaching Kendall German, from Rockford's own schoolboy texts, and he had made her take the potions and elixirs away from his bedside. He was far healthier now, but she thought he also wanted more room for books. Oh, and she had to make note for Rockford that Hugo was a dab hand at croquet, although he did not fare well at cricket.

As for Billy — she supposed she could call him William in her letters to his father — he had not broken anything in the last week, if one discounted the window of the apothecary, which was not his fault. They all needed more cricket practice, it seemed.

Rockford ought to know how happy her own boys were here, how Kendall was getting to play like a real boy instead of worrying over adult concerns. And her Willy was getting more confident away from her presence. With Billy's fearless example, how could he not spread his wings?

Aminta had more poise now, too, she told Rockford in the letter she composed, and did not blush half as easily. She still preferred the company of the vicar's niece and Alissa, but she was making new friends, learning how to go on in local society. The matrons all complimented the countess on her sister's pretty manners. Alissa thought he would want to know.

He ought to be informed about the plans

for Rock Hill, too. Did he have color preferences for the servants' new livery, and did he think a small weaving shed would cause unrest, as the new machinery was doing in the north?

She described everything in her mental letters: the tutor she had dismissed because he was a worse cricketeer than Hugo or Billy and did not bathe, to boot, the nervous young suitors bringing posies to Aminta, the new hat she had bought after Billy used her old one for a fishing creel, Claymore's new spectacles.

She told him, too, about her dreams, how the boys needed a father, and she needed a husband. They could have a good marriage, she believed and wanted to convince him, if he were willing to try, willing to meet her halfway. They could be partners, she was sure, not distant associates bound only by a scrap of paper and a set of rules he had created out of cobwebs. She told him she was lonely. She asked him to come home.

She never wrote the letters, of course, never sent him a word.

Some of the neighbors were not sure of the etiquette surrounding bride gifts. There had not been much of a wedding, and did not seem to be much of a marriage. They could not throw dinners and balls in Alissa's honor, not without the earl, so most simply accepted the countess and ignored her circumstances.

One neighbor had other ideas of what was proper.

"Can't deny me the right to apologize, can you?" Sir George Ganyon asked, after he had been refused twice. This time Alissa had been passing in the hall, in plain sight, so she had to nod to Claymore to admit the baronet.

"We will take tea in the gold parlor," she told the butler. "Please ask my sister and Lady Eleanor to join us." Claymore understood the unspoken plea, but could not help his mistress.

"Lady Eleanor has been out since before breakfast, my lady," the butler informed her, "and the young miss is at the vicarage helping to arrange the flowers we sent for Sunday's services."

"Of course," she said, now wishing she had made some excuse to Sir George, rather than suffer his company alone. If she did not hear his apology now, however, she would only have to do it another time, or wonder if he would accost her on the high street of the village, or at some social gathering. He did not attend the tame neighborhood entertainments she did, preferring the pub or card parties or men-only hunt gatherings, so she had escaped his company since the wedding. She had not missed it.

"I know just the thing," she told Claymore.

"The boys can join us for tea. They need to polish their company manners." Seeing the baronet's would teach them how not to behave, she hoped. He was already drooling, a trickle of saliva sliding from the corner of his mouth.

He laughed now. "Oh, they are too busy in the stableyard. I bought you a wedding present, I did, to show no hard feelings. I didn't know which way the wind blew, that was all, you and the earl. One of my hounds got out of the pen a while ago and came back breeding. I brought the pups over, so your pups can pick one."

"My . . . pups? You brought my sons a dog?"

"Well, I brought all four of 'em, actually. You've got four boys now, don't you? I meant one for each. Fine wedding present, what?"

"But I do not like dogs. I told you that."

He shrugged. What did a woman know about such things? "A boy has to have a dog if he is to grow up right."

A whole herd of hounds had not done much for Sir George. "No. I will not have dogs around the place. You will have to take them away."

He shrugged again. "They'll have to be drowned then, of course. Mongrel pups are useless, you know. You can be the one to tell your brats."

Into the awful silence that followed that

dire statement, Claymore said, "I will bring the tea, madam."

Alissa sank onto her chair, stunned and stymied. Dogs. Four dogs. An entire pack of slavering beasts. Who were right now leaping all over her children, licking them, wriggling their way into little boys' hearts. Who would be killed if she said no.

Heavens, she could see the reproach in the boys' eyes now. Kendall would understand, she supposed. He always had, when she explained her reasoning that they could not afford a new ball, that he had to do chores instead of playing. Willy would likely cry, although he was past baby tears, most often. Hugo might not care as much, although he would adore having a four-footed companion on his collecting trips. But Billy — always so sure of himself and ready for anything — if ever there was a boy made for a dog, it was Billy. He would be inconsolable.

"You should have asked me first," was all she said to her gloating guest.

"Tried. You were never home. Or home to me," Sir George said with a sly, sideways look.

Well, the dogs could stay in the stable for now, until she could have a kennel built, somewhere far from the house so she did not have to see or hear the creatures. Jake would have to assign one of his grooms to train the pups, but she would make sure the boys knew the animals were their responsibility. She was having nothing to do with them, and she was not taking men away from important, necessary duties to devote hours to the care of curs. Maybe the boys would get tired of all the effort involved and she could get rid of the dogs soon. Meanwhile, she would make it clear that one growl, one nip, and they were gone. She was not having her sons or Rockford's savaged by wild animals. As the dogs had come from Sir George's kennels, their manners were entirely suspect.

Claymore wheeled in the tea cart and stayed as long as he could, arranging the plates and cups on the table near Alissa. "Is there anything else, madam?" he asked.

"No, but do stay close in case we need anything."

Claymore peered at Sir George through his new spectacles, noting the muddied boots and dirty fingernails. "I shall be right outside, my lady."

While Alissa poured the tea, the baronet watched her hungrily, so she offered him a slice of poppy-seed cake. The sooner he ate, she hoped, the sooner he would leave. He did not seem to have food in mind, for he waved the plate aside. "See? No hard feelings. You made the better bargain, eh? I couldn't see what the earl was so riled about when he came by, but now I do." He swiped at his damp mouth with the back of his wrist, still devouring her with his eyes. "Out of those dreary gray rags you used to wear, you're more woman than I thought. Almost a lady of fashion, with that new way of fixing your hair. Almost a lady."

Alissa wondered if she should call for Claymore.

Sir George was going on: "Rockford always did have an eye for women. They say the Austrian princess he's dancing attendance on is a diamond of the first water. Foreign, of course."

"Sir, you forget yourself, and you forget I am a married woman."

"Seems to me Rockford is the one who forgets, eh?"

Alissa rearranged the slices of cake. She did not attempt a bite herself, knowing the crumbs would stick in her throat. Her marriage was a sham, but it was hers to belittle. She put the cake knife down before she was tempted to slice more than the poppy seeds. "I believe the earl asked you to give Rock Hill a wide margin."

Sir George pretended to look around, peering up through his overgrown eyebrows. "I don't see him. Do you?"

She saw a bully and a boor. "I think you ought to leave now, Sir George. Your tea has grown cold anyway, and I am developing a headache."

"So you are not quite the lady, eh, despite

the fancy feathers? A real lady treats a guest better than that. Rock Hill used to be known for hospitality, in the last earl's time. You never even offered me a drink. Not that codswallop in a cup, but a real drink."

He took a tarnished silver flask out of his pocket and poured a jot into his tea, then slurped it. "That's better."

Better than what? Arsenic? Not in her book. Alissa watched him drink, watched the liquid trail down his chin and onto his already soiled shirtfront. When he set the cup down, she said, "If you are done, I shall ask Claymore to see you out."

"That blind old stick? What is he going to do, pick me up and toss me through the door, eh? No, I'll have my say before I go. It's an honest offer, anyway."

"An offer? Of what? You have given the boys your unwanted mongrels. That is enough."

"What, did you forget my last proposal? Asked for your hand, I did, and that brat aimed a pistol at me! No, I thought to offer you a slip on the shoulder, now that you're married again."

She got up. If he would not leave, she would. "I shall return the tea tray to the kitchen. Good day."

He ignored her, and rudely stayed seated. "But I saw that wouldn't serve. I wouldn't mind taking you to my bed, by Jove, even if you are Rockford's leavings. He left, heh? But it wouldn't serve. I need a son. A legitimate son, so I need a wife of my own. So here I am, come to make a proper offer for the girl."

Alissa sank back down, setting the tray none too gently back on the table. The cups rattled and the sugar cubes spilled from their dish. "The girl?"

"Your sister, Amy, unless you have another. The devil knows I don't mean Rockford's sister. I ain't fool enough to take on that shrew. Besides, she's too old. Eleanor's what, nearing forty? I want sons, not a dried up prune who's forever telling a fellow to change his linen and mind his manners. And Miss Prunes and Prisms skipped down that primrose path fast enough, didn't she?"

"Lady Eleanor is above reproach."

This time Sir George did not bother to pour the liquor into his teacup. He drank straight from the flask. "No, it has to be the chit. She's got no birth to speak of, not even your dead husband's connections, but her being Rockford's sister-in-law makes a difference. So does the dowry I hear he's settling on her."

"Am I hearing you correctly? You are asking permission to address my sister? My seventeen-year-old sister?"

"Exactly. It's not such a bad deal for her, either. The gal ought to be a widow before too long, not that I intend to cock up my toes anytime soon. She might still be young enough to snabble herself another husband, the way you did."

His demise could not come soon enough. "I am sorry," she said, without the least regret, "but I would never countenance such a match. The disparity in ages and interests would be enough, if I thought you were remotely suited to be her husband. I do not."

"Hoity-toity. No matter. I already wrote to Rockford. He's the chit's guardian now, isn't he?"

He was, according to those papers she had signed. The solicitor had said they were necessary to protect the underage minors. But did that mean Rockford could marry Aminta off without a by-your-leave? Alissa never thought she would be happy that the earl never read his mail.

"He would not give permission," she said with conviction.

"Why not? He's paying to get rid of the chit, isn't he? Must mean he wants her off his hands. It's not as if she's a prime filly on the marriage mart, not from your stables."

"Aminta will never agree. Even with Rockford's permission, she cannot be forced into marriage, not in this day and age."

He snorted. "There'll always be priests ready to look the other way when the bride argues. A special license, a few bribes, a dram of laudanum in her wine — it's easily done. Or else I could snatch her up one day and hold her overnight. That cottage still sits empty. She'd be ruined. She'd have to marry me, even you'd agree, because no one else would take her. Half of the folks around here already believe the whole of Rock Hill is full of light-skirts."

"Nonsense. No one will think Aminta is anything but an innocent."

"They thought Lady Eleanor was untouched too. Now they know different. No, they'll think little Amy's making a creampot marriage, just like her sister."

"She is just a girl! Surely you can find another woman to wed? London is full of women looking for a mate. Any mate."

"What, I should go to town during hunt season? Preposterous."

"There must be any number of females right in this vicinity. You could advertise for a new housekeeper, and marry her."

"No, I decided I want the girl."

"Well, you cannot have my sister. She is not for sale. Not for any price to a man like you. She is not one of your unwanted mongrels to be tossed to the first person willing to take them. She is my sister, and she will marry the gentleman of her choice when she is ready. A gentleman, do you understand? If you *can* understand the meaning of the word. Now leave my house and do not return."

Sir George's face turned purple and his beady eyes narrowed. "What, a baronet is not good enough for your kin now that you're a countess?" He got to his feet, looming over Alissa's chair, spittle dampening her cheeks. "You might have the title, missy, but you are nothing but a whore, selling your favors to the highest bidder. Only the winning bid didn't want to keep you, it looks like. So you are nothing. And nothing stands in my way, do you hear?"

He took a step closer, then grabbed for Alissa's shoulders before she could stand up. He shook her, snapping her head against the chair frame. Alissa knew Claymore could not move fast enough to come to her aid, but she screamed anyway. Meanwhile her hands scrabbled at the table in front of her, seeking the knife, but came up with the sugar tongs instead. She raked them down his cheek, leaving bloody gashes. He cursed and slapped her, then pressed his hand to his face and headed for the door. He knocked poor Claymore down on the way, then turned and said, "This is not over. Not by half."

Alissa and Claymore shared a brandy. He was devastated that he'd allowed such a thing to happen to his mistress. She was distraught. Great heavens, what was she going to do now? She knew she had made an enemy for life, a brutal, unscrupulous enemy at that, who was sure to seek revenge. She would never be safe. Her sister would never be safe, or the boys. She thought of Amy, so used to walking to the village on her own. The boys were always out and about, especially Hugo. She could not keep them at her side constantly, or under guard. She could not make Rock Hill the fortress it once was, no matter how many men she hired.

She would never have a moment's peace, wondering if Sir George was waiting outside the gates, in the gardens, at a neighbor's house when they went to visit. The man was disordered, not merely disgusting. What was she going to do? How could she protect her family?

And then Alissa remembered. She was not a weak woman, cottage-bound and at the baronet's mercy. She was a countess. She had power.

She had . . . a husband.

Chapter Fifteen

What good was having a husband if he was not there to protect you? Alissa had married Rockford, in part, to be safe from Sir George. Well, she was not safe, and Rockford's money had placed Aminta in danger now too. It was his duty, his obligation to defend them against insult and harm. Heaven knew he did little enough else, other than paying the bills, which his new secretary handled anyway.

"We are going to London," she announced to her sons a few days later when she found them in the stable block. Rockford was not going to come to her. Therefore she would go to him.

She did not want to frighten the boys with her fears of Sir George, other than what they had seen, but she was not about to let them ramble unguarded either. Extra footmen and armed grooms accompanied them to lessons and on rides, to their disgust. She was happy when it rained today and they were kept inside — with the dratted dogs. Now they refused to leave Rock Hill and their new pets to travel to the city, despite promises of the Royal Menagerie, the Circus, Hyde Park, the maze at Richmond, and frozen ices at Gunters. No puppies, no ponies, no miles of countryside? No, they would not go.

Not even to see their father? Only Hugo hesitated, tempted by London's museums and galleries, Alissa realized, not the chance to visit with Rockford.

Billy said, "Papa ought to come here, where we live."

Alissa might have agreed, but Rockford was not coming, and they could not stay without his protection. Of course, the children would go if she ordered it, she knew. They would have no choice, being children. But those looks. Willy had tears in his eyes; Kendall was sadly resigned. They had had so little in their lives; now she would take away this pleasure. Hugo peered at her through his glasses, as if trying to figure out the workings of the universe, or why his adored step-mother was suddenly acting so cruelly. He had never had a real pet of his own, his grandparents having decided that anything with fur or feathers was too dangerous for the sickly boy. Now he rubbed his hand over a small velvety head over and over.

Billy, though, clutched his pup to his chest and declared, "I will not go and I will run away if you make me. And I will puke the whole carriage ride anyway. So there."

So the puppies were coming to London. They were small, Alissa had to admit, and cute in a purely babyish way. They looked harmless enough, with tiny teeth and clumsy gaits. Half hound and half some terrier or other, they were brown and white and gold, with a few black patches. Two had mustaches, one had long silky ears, one had a short tail. Otherwise, Alissa could not tell them apart, although the children knew instantly which dog was which, and whose.

They had named them for playing cards, for which Alissa glared at Jake, teaching her boys to gamble. Hugo, being the eldest, had picked first. His dog was Ace. Kendall's was King.

"But not King George; otherwise he'd be named for a Bedlamite," Kendall confided. "Or Sir George Ganyon. He might have given us the dogs, but I don't want mine having his name. He's just King."

Willy had chosen the only female, Queenie. And Billy had Jack, the knave, the pup who kept escaping from the box and wetting the floor. It figured.

Not even Alissa could have drowned the little animals, not the way they slept in the boys' laps or followed at their feet or tried to suckle at their fingers. They were only babies, these would-be hounds from hell. She would not touch them, ride in the carriage with them, or permit them inside the inns where the family would stay. She would not feed them or exercise them or learn which name was which, but the dogs could come.

The ponies would come too, so Billy could ride partway, rather than be confined to the carriage. Alissa drew the line at the pig or the donkey, though. Now Jake had to come along to be in charge of the menagerie, and Claymore would too, of course. Alissa could not face the city or her husband without the old butler's support. Extra grooms, the boys' valet, a maid for her and her sister . . .

Aminta did not wish to go to London either. It was too big, too noisy, too crowded, she had heard from the vicar's niece. And she did not know anyone.

"You will make new friends," Alissa urged, "and have new gowns from the finest dressmakers. You'll have parties to go to every night, and different entertainments every day."

"No one in London is going to invite a plain Miss Bourke to their balls, Lissie. I do not belong there."

"No one is going to reject the Earl of Rockford's ward, believe me. Perhaps we will not be invited to Almack's, but I hear that is no great loss."

"But I like the country, Lissie."

"Nonsense, you do not know anything else," Alissa said from her superior experience, having gone once to London, after her marriage to William Henning. They had visited his father's mansion to ask the duke's blessing. Alissa had been terrified, with good cause. From the cold, bare antechamber where they'd told her to wait, she could hear the angry shouts. They had left without the blessing, and without seeing the sights William had promised. "You have to give London a try, Amy. Then you can decide if you like it or not. Besides, I need you to come with me. I am frightened of going, too." But not as afraid as she was of staying.

Alissa had done so much for her sister; how could Amy refuse? She nodded, and drove off to the vicarage in the donkey cart — with an armed groom sitting in the wagon bed — to consult her friend about clothes and manners.

Lady Eleanor was harder to convince, once Alissa had tracked her sister-in-law down in the kitchens. Eleanor had heard about Sir George's visit, and was ready to go at him with her horsewhip.

"But he would still be here," Alissa said, taking a seat and pouring herself a glass of cider from the stoneware jug. "Madder than ever. Besides, I believe he will already carry scars from the sugar tongs."

"I still cannot believe you fought the scum off with a serving utensil. Not that he did not deserve that and more, but I still say good show, Countess. My brother would be proud. And you are right to go to him. But not with me. I would only ruin your welcome from him, for one thing, and with the *ton*, for another."

Alissa could not speak for her husband. She doubted her own welcome, much less Lady Eleanor's. She did say, "Fustian. You are a heroine in the neighborhood. The beau monde will greet you with applause."

"Laughter, more like. I had several Seasons in town, ages ago, it seems. I was even engaged once, did you know?"

"I heard something about that. It ended abruptly, I understand."

"Oh, yes, you might call it abrupt. The engagement ended right at the church doors. My fiancé did not arrive for the wedding."

"But why? Do you know?"

"Because I found my betrothed on the balcony with another woman the week before the wedding. Ours was one of those advantageous matches that united lands and wealth and titles. We knew each other forever, so I thought we would rub along well together. I had no wish to marry a philanderer, though, so I told him what I would do if I found him unfaithful after the wedding. He decided my dowry was not worth the family jewels."

"The family . . . ? Oh, I see. What did you do then?"

"I came home, rather than become the

laughingstock of London. I have been here ever since, except for the recent —"

"Visit to your aunt in Wales," Alissa said for the benefit of the scullery maid who had entered the kitchen.

Lady Eleanor laughed. "Jaunt. And here I intend to stay. If people choose to believe your Banbury tale, they will still remember the last scandal, that I was jilted. That will hurt your chances of being accepted, and your sister's chances."

"I refuse to believe that. You are an adult woman now, not the same young girl left at the altar, and you are the sister to an influential man. Hiding here only magnifies your shame, and gives the gossips more room for speculation. Besides, I need you to help with my sister's presentation. You know the ways of the *ton,* having lived among them, and can be a great asset. You must come, and hold your head high."

"And deflect some of Rockford's anger that you are bringing the children to London without his permission?"

Alissa grinned at her sister-in-law's knowing look and raised her glass of cider in a toast. "Precisely."

Rockford came home that morning with a headache and a mouth that felt like low tide. Her royal princess was getting to be a royal pain in his arse. With no hopes of getting his wedding ring on her fat finger, Princess Helga had grown more demanding, less conciliatory. He doubted England would ever get a treaty with her wealthy brother, but he was her designated escort, so he had to keep trying. Now he was trying to find his bed before he fell on his face.

For a moment he thought he had come to the wrong house, one under attack by howling Hottentots. The black and white marble tiles in the entryway looked familiar, but that was all. The hall was littered with running children and barking dogs and shouting women and baggage. Baggage, hell! The prince regent took less luggage when he moved the court to Brighton. Footmen in livery Rockford did not recognize were carrying in more trunks, dodging dogs whose breed he did not recognize either. A puddle spread from one corner and an odor came from another, whose source he refused to contemplate. One of the dogs was chewing on a flower from the vase on the floor. The priceless Etruscan vase had not been on the floor when he saw it last, Rockford would have sworn, nor did it have that piece missing from its handle.

His aching head exploded with pain from the noise and motion and general chaos. He closed his eyes briefly, hoping the scene would change when he reopened them. It did. Now two creatures were jumping on his leg. One was yet another mongrel puppy, trying to chew the tassel off his boots. The other was his younger son William, trying to get his attention.

Hell.

"Quiet!" he bellowed into the bedlam that was his erstwhile elegant abode. The shout reverberated in his brain like a billiard ball wearing spurs, but it was effective. Everyone turned to look at him, even the dogs. "Where is Bancroft?" he asked the room at large, seeking his butler.

"He gave in his resignation an hour ago," Claymore answered from the floor, where he was on his hands and knees, trying to find his spectacles. One of the pups had his wig in its mouth and was shredding it all over the Turkey runner in the hall. "But I am here, my lord."

Oh, and that was supposed to reassure the earl? He was supposed to host a formal dinner for the Austrian delegation that very evening, with no butler. He yelled for Upton, his new secretary. When that man stepped forward, blotting at his forehead with a handkerchief, Rockford asked, "Did you know about this?" He waved his hand around, but there was no doubt what he meant by *this*.

"Um, only yesterday, my lord."

"And you did not tell me?"

"You did not come home last night, my lord, and you told me never to bother you when you were with —"

"Out! Get out!"

Aminta grabbed for Willy's hand and made a dash for the door, but Rockford thundered, "Not you. Upton." He made a quick survey of the hall. The footmen had disappeared as fast as the now former secretary. "The rest of you wait here. That includes you, Claymore. No one is staying, so you do not need to see about the unpacking. All of you will remain in this hall while I have a short" — he emphasized *short* — "talk with Lady Rockford." His eyes fixed on her like lightning headed for a tree. "In the library. Meanwhile, the rest of you will not touch anything. You will not go into any of the other rooms. You will control those animals, and you will clean up this mess. You will not leave the house, you will not scream like banshees, and you will not climb the banister. Get down, William. You will not read the mail on the post tray, you will not stare out the windows at the neighbors, and you will not feed those creatures from the comfit dish, Will. You will not touch the paintings and you will not —"

"Jupiter," a youthful voice whispered. "Moses only handed down ten commandments."

"Yes," Lady Eleanor whispered back, but not half as softly, "but that was because he was not an earl."

Rockford turned at the familiar voice and

noticed his sister for the first time. He raised his eyebrow. She raised hers. "Later, sister," was all he said. She bobbed her head in acknowledgment.

He returned his attention to Alissa. "Madam?"

She preceded him out of the room, glancing back to see Claymore smiling encouragement and Eleanor giving her a wink. She raised her head, lest Rockford see her chin trembling. She paused, not knowing which direction to take. The hall was almost as large as the entry to Rock Hill, with doors and numerous corridors leading from it, and a grand marble staircase straight ahead.

"To the left," he said, pointing the way.

Hugo would be thrilled, Alissa thought when she saw the two-story library. If he got to stay. Rockford headed toward a huge oak desk and stood behind it, leaving her the smaller facing seat, as if she were interviewing for a position, which she was, in a way. Alissa smoothed her skirts, which were creased from traveling. Rockford rubbed his eyes. He looked tired and his neckcloth was askew, but she had no sympathy for him. He should have been home to receive her message, home to make them welcome. Home to sleep in his own bed.

"Well?" he said.

"Very, thank you," she replied. "Although the trip was arduous."

"You know deuced well what I meant, Countess. What in thunderation is that circus doing in my hallway?"

Waiting to be shown rooms, Alissa thought, but did not say. "The dogs were a gift from Sir George," she told him, in preface to her prepared speech. "A wedding gift."

"He couldn't send silver candlesticks like everyone else?"

"They were for the boys."

"The boys did not get married; we did."

Ah, so he did remember the wedding. That was a good sign, Alissa thought, ready to continue.

Before she could, he asked, "And you felt you had to trot the whole herd of them to London to . . . show me?"

"Not precisely. And the dogs did not trot. They rode in the second coach. The ponies trotted."

"You are telling me you brought the boys, their dogs and ponies, along with Claymore, who should have been pensioned off in my boyhood. Oh, and my sister, back from her foray into deceit and depravity. Lud, did you leave anyone home?"

"Sir George, bleeding."

There was Ganyon's name again. Rockford pinched the bridge of his nose between fingers, wishing for a cup of coffee. With a dash of arsenic.

"Did you kill him?" he asked, deciding to

ask *why* later. "Did you come to town to hire a lawyer? Ah, perhaps you are on your way out of the country and you came to say fare-well?"

There was a hopeful note to his last question that Alissa could not like. She merely said, "No. He lives."

"Very well. Then mayhap, Countess, you would be so good as to tell me why in hell you are here in my house when I left you in the country?"

"Because you left me in the country."

"You are making no sense."

Alissa supposed she was not, to a man like him. "I had many sound, logical reasons for coming."

"Yes?"

She gathered her defenses, all the reasons she had planned to give him. "The children need a father, someone who could have told them they had to leave the animals behind."

"Which they would not have had to do, if they had remained where they belonged. And they have done fine all these years. You need to be firmer; that is all."

Spoken like someone who had never denied a determined five-year-old anything. She sniffed and said, "Amy and I needed new wardrobes."

"You could have sent for the finest mo-distes. They would have moved their shops to Rock Hill, for your patronage."

"I could not find proper tutors for the boys. Most did not wish to travel so far for an interview without a guaranteed position. Chances of finding the best man are better in London."

"What could be so difficult about hiring a tutor? Hugo is too weak to go to school, and you feel your sons are too young, so what does it matter if they are behind in their studies?"

Behind? She ignored his willful misconception. "I wished to give my sister wider experience of society, the opportunity to meet people."

"Eligible bachelors, you mean. You would have done better to wait for the spring Season. Few people are still in town now. Besides, I doubt you will ever be able to give that chit town bronze, not when she jumps at shadows."

Ready, as always, to come to her family's defense, Alissa said, "She jumped at your shouting."

He brushed that aside. "Furthermore, if you are encouraging her to dream of a grand match, you are doing the girl a disservice. She is still the daughter of a bailiff."

"As I was."

He tipped his head. "Your point, madam. Go on."

"Amy will do fine, with your sponsorship. I was hoping, too, to see her and my sons accepted by my late husband's family."

"Hysmith? I told you the new duke is as stiff-rumped as the last. His late wife was worse."

"But the boys are his nephews, nevertheless. He should meet them." He looked dubious of the honor to be bestowed on the duke, so Alissa hurried on: "And I thought to restore your sister's reputation."

"Impossible."

"No, it is not. The country folk have accepted her as a heroine, chasing after Arkenstall to retrieve your belongings." The rude sound he made told her what he thought of the neighbors and their notions of truth. "Lady Eleanor cannot be allowed to hide away at Rock Hill for the rest of her life."

"It is what she chose."

"Out of embarrassment. Then she chose another disastrous course with Arkenstall. She is not happy, and will not be until she confronts her past. Here in London."

"I will speak with her myself."

"She brought back the Rembrandt." Alissa had given up thoughts of doing portraits in oils after seeing the small picture of an old woman with a jug.

"Did she, by Jove?"

He smiled, the first smile Alissa had seen on him since she arrived. She thought it unfortunate that he cared more for the painting's return than his sister's — or his wife's. "It is hanging at Rock Hill."

"Where it belongs. Where all of you belong." He could not hide a yawn. "You still have not given me one good reason why you came to town. Or what any of this has to do with Sir George Ganyon."

"He wishes to marry Amy."

Rockford was suddenly wide awake. "That loose screw? I would never give my blessings, so you did not have to batten on my doorstep. Or didn't you trust me?"

"I trusted you. It is the baronet I do not trust. He threatened to force my sister to wed him if he was not granted permission."

Rockford decided he would get a more accurate story from Claymore before they left. "No one threatens my family. I thought I had made that plain to Ganyon, but it was not plain enough, I see. I will handle it, so now that you have said your piece you can go home. I cannot imagine what you were thinking, bringing the boys and the dogs to the city. Here. Why, Rothmore House hosts one of the finest collections of antiquities in all of England." He raised a small white figurine, an exquisite many-armed goddess carved out of a single piece of ivory. "I cannot have children playing among such priceless treasures."

Alissa admired the delicate work of art, but said, "Your children are priceless, too."

"Yes, well, the little goblins — the little gems, that is — cannot stay here. As I said, I am hosting an important reception tonight. The prince regent himself might attend. If you leave soon, I might be able to restore Rothmore House in time."

Alissa was not budging. "I cannot put those children back in the carriages so soon. The journey was wearying enough as it was. Furthermore, your neighbors saw us arrive. What would they think if you pack us off to an inn or hide us away? They will think you are ashamed of your children, that is what, ashamed of your wife. It was just such behavior that led Sir George to think I might be receptive to his advances."

He clutched the figurine in his hand. "You never mentioned that part, by Jupiter."

"Well, it is true. Your leaving left me open to insult. And there is more."

He opened his fist and traced the curves of the ivory goddess with his fingers. "I was afraid of that."

Alissa could not come out and say that she wanted to make a real marriage out of this convenient travesty, that she wanted them to become partners, friends, lovers. That she missed the pleasures of the marriage bed, the comfort of a man's warm body next to hers. What she said was, "I do not wish ours to be a marriage in name only."

Rockford's fingers stopped caressing the

sculpture. That was not in his plan, not at all. "You agreed —"

She raised her chin. "I want a daughter."

The ivory goddess hit the desk.

Chapter Sixteen

"Hell," he cursed, then begged her pardon. Or that of the many-armed goddess now in many pieces. Bedding his wife was not only not part of his plan, but it was not part of his life. He did not want to be involved with a woman. Any woman. The Austrian princess was business, not pleasure, he told himself. No emotions were involved. No unruly passions were raised, at least not his. The princess was known to toss the occasional knickknack.

His former marriages had accounted for some of the most unpleasant intervals of Rockford's life, years filled with tears and shouts and sulks and scenes, especially when his wives were increasing. And those women he had wed were ladies. Heaven knew what Mrs. Henning, his new countess, would subject him to. She was already off to a good start, if her aim was to destroy his home, his career, and his peace of mind.

"Dash it," he said, "how could you want another infant when you have enough children to satisfy the maternal instincts of a queen bee? And if your sister is not young enough to count as a daughter, go adopt one. I am certain there are any number of moppets languishing in orphanages. Or I could have my secretary put an advertisement in the paper, if I still had a secretary, that is, for a family with extras. I'd think people would be glad to see a daughter go to a good home. Plaguey nuisances, girls. Just look at my sister."

"No."

He carefully swept the fragments of the goddess into a pile on his desk while he wondered how the nondescript nobody he'd married had turned into a woman of such strong convictions. He had admired her pluck, but independence was better at a distance. Now she was staring straight at him, daring him to disagree, as if they were equals.

"You owe me a baby. Nothing was ever said about not honoring the marriage vows. That is part of what marriage means to me."

Equals, hell. The female was far better at this than he was. He had to try, though. "I do not recall the vicar telling us to go forth and multiply. Did I miss that part?"

"Marriage is a sacred rite for the begetting of children."

"Oh, no, it is not. Marriage makes offspring legitimate. It does not demand them."

"You never said you felt that way."

"And you never said you wanted more children."

"I never had the chance. I would have on our wedding night, when we consummated the marriage."

"Confound it, I could not force myself on a woman who hardly knew me. I thought that would offend you."

She stared at her hands laced in her lap. "I am a widow, Robert, not a virgin."

There was his name again. Lud, last time he'd repeated it to himself to see if the unfamiliar syllables had any effect. They had not, not giving him the slightest inclination to leap across his desk, the way he did now. Unseemly, that's what it was. Beneath his dignity.

He had to get her out of here. Out of the country would be better, but —

"Very well, you can stay for a day or two. Until I have straightened out the mess with Sir George. I cannot travel to Rock Hill at this moment, but a letter should suffice. I'll make sure the maggot knows what will happen if he steps over the line."

"And the other?"

"The tutor? I will make inquiries at my clubs, send a message to my college. I am certain —"

"*Not* the tutor."

Damned persistent female. "I will think about it," he muttered.

"See that you do, Robert. I will not return to the country otherwise."

He stood up. "I have the right to send you where I will."

She stood up and faced him across the desk. "And I have the right to a marriage. I mean to have one."

"But if those children damage one —"

There were two crashes from the hallway. One sounded like the Etruscan vase; the other might have been the Chinese urn cane holder. Or Claymore tripping over a dog.

Bloody hell.

He was a rake, Alissa thought later, dressing for dinner in her finest gown, with jewels Claymore had insisted she bring. Why would he not leap at the chance to share her bed? She was a willing woman, rightfully his. Could he be one of those men who did not like women? He disliked females in general, she thought, but not in that way, from all she had heard. And if he suffered some physical impairment, what was he doing out all night with the Austrian princess? Playing at charades? No, Rockford was a thoroughly virile man. He simply did not think Alissa was worthy of his attentions. She fussed over her toilette far longer than usual, to prove him wrong.

Both her sister and his had refused to attend the dinner party. Eleanor claimed they were always dull affairs, while Amy swore she'd go off in spasms if she had to sit with visiting royalty. Rather than letting them escape entirely, and leaving her entirely on her own, Alissa insisted they both accompany the boys down to the drawing room while sherry was served before dinner. They would not have to stay, she told Amy and Eleanor, but the guests had to see that Rockford was not embarrassed by their presence, was not hiding them from view.

Eleanor had rudiments of German, and so could speak to one of the princess's ladies in waiting. The archduke's privy councillor had some English, so complimented Alissa on her beautiful home, of which she had seen almost nothing, and her handsome children, shepherded by Aminta. As always, Alissa was gratified at the praise to her boys and smiled at the Austrian count, until she saw Rockford scowling at Hugo.

"Excuse me, Herr Minsch," she said. "My husband needs me."

He needed her to go home, and take her blasted brood with her. "What is the boy doing, bothering the Austrian prince?" He spoke for her ears only, keeping a careful smile on his face for the rest of the company.

Alissa glanced in Hugo's direction. "The last I heard, although I could not understand much of the conversation, of course, they were discussing Euclidean geometry."

"His Highness does not speak English."

"No matter. Hugo is quite fluent in German, including several dialects. Also French, Italian, and Spanish, although he believes his pronunciation might need polishing, since he has heard so little of it spoken. There is Latin and Greek, naturally. Romany, from when a band of Gypsies passed through near his grandparents' home. He has a smattering of Russian, now that we found him an alphabet primer, and I believe he located a Norwegian textbook in your library. I have no doubt he will have mastered it soon," she said, pride in her voice. "Of course, the proper tutor would help."

Rockford was no longer listening. "In my library? That is, Hugo? I mean Rothmore?"

"Naturally. He is your son. I am sorry to say he seems to have inherited your ancestors' nose along with your skill at languages. Did you notice his resemblance to Lady Eleanor?"

The Ziftsweig prince was smiling, patting the boy on the shoulder. By Jove, Rockford thought, perhaps Hugo was his son after all.

The dinner went well, considering that the hostess could converse with only one of the guests, and that haltingly. Smiles seemed to suffice, especially after Claymore served a magnificent meal. Her dinner partners were more interested in the food than conversation after that.

Afterward, the Austrian ladies gathered at one side of the long Adams parlor, pointedly ignoring Alissa, following Princess Helga's example. Alissa kept her smile fixed, her spine straight, and took a seat at the pianoforte. She had never played such a superb instrument, and had not owned one of her own since before her marriage, but had kept her skills honed by playing at the vicar's house and for local assemblies. She was no virtuoso, but did not embarrass herself either. When the men returned, they nodded approvingly and went on conversing over state matters while she played softly. Her husband, the most handsome man there, did not smile.

Rockford was stunned. His son. His wife. The congratulations of everyone except her highness. He had never made so many miscalculations in his life. He could not wait for the guests to leave so he could go upstairs — and quiz Hugo on his studies. No wonder Alissa could not find him a proper tutor. And the boy did not seem sickly either. The young viscount had withstood a hearty clap on the back from the archduke in farewell.

His son.

His blue superfine coat almost burst its seams as his chest expanded. His heir.

His wife.

Alissa was managing superbly, his little country mouse, without speaking a word. She played well, without drawing attention to herself, and looked finer than any of the other women present. She wore the Rothmore rubies as if she were royalty, and the frowning princess were a mere overweight Teuton in a tiara.

His wife. Rockford could not get over it. His first wife, the one who was born and bred to be the perfect political hostess, had found such dinners too tedious to endure. As soon as she became pregnant, having done her duty, she'd fled back to her parents' home. To have the child with her mother nearby, she had said. To reunite with her lover, he still believed.

Instead of helping his career, as he had expected, his second wife much preferred her own literary salons, where the men wore their hair longer than the women, and they all pretended to understand the latest poetry that never rhymed.

He had had no expectations of Mrs. Henning at all. Had never conceived of her in this room, in this house, in this company, yet here she was, shining like the purest moonbeam on a cloudless night. She was wearing his rubies, his ring, and a clinging silk gown that left nothing to a man's imagination, except how he was going to get her out of it.

Rockford could not go visit his son in the nursery whenever the guests left. He had a previous commitment, and was half-aroused at the idea. The other half was outraged that he was being so manipulated by an encroaching female, and by his own body. He was no youth to surrender to ungoverned lust, by George. He just hurried the Austrians out of the house an hour early, that was all.

On her wedding night — her wedding to Rockford, that is, for she was already carrying Kendall on her wedding to Henning — Alissa had spent agonizing ages preparing for his arrival, selecting the nightgown and the flowers, having everything in her bedchamber laid out just so. Now she did not care, she was so angry. She did not care if her hair was left unbraided or the fire went out. She did not care if he came at all, the overbearing ape.

He came, naturally, while she was swiping the brush through her hair with quick, angry motions. He watched from the connecting door a minute, until she became aware of his presence in the mirror of her dressing table. Alissa did not care that her sheer gown was backlit by candles, nor that the view caused her husband to take a sharp breath. She did not even care that he was wearing nothing, it appeared, but a paisley silk robe and chest hair.

She glared at him and kept brushing. "How dare you?"

To say Rockford was confused would be an overstatement. His body was crying in disappointment. His brain was sighing in relief. He could go back to his own room, she would leave, he would be his own man. Without getting to touch that waterfall of soft brown curls. "Damn it. I thought this was a command appearance. Decide what you want, woman, once and for all."

"How dare you countermand my orders to bed the dogs in the stables?"

"That's what this tempest is about, who sleeps in the boys' beds, not who sleeps in yours?" His blood raced south.

"I do not like the animals near my sons. They could carry disease or vermin. I specifically said the creatures have to stay in the stables."

He shrugged, unconsciously letting the lapels of his dressing gown fall open more. "The dogs appear healthy enough. And I thought that a better arrangement than having the boys run back and forth to the mews. This is London, not the country. If you recall, the country is not entirely safe either. London is worse."

"Heavens, I never thought Sir George would come after my sons."

Rockford damned his tongue. "Of course he would not, not at Rothmore House. But there might be other villains or vagrants about. With luck one of the pups will turn out to be a watchdog to warn if anyone comes near the nursery."

Alissa never thought of a dog as protection, only as predator. Perhaps Rockford was right. "Still, you should have consulted me."

"You told me you wanted a father for the boys. When they asked, I made a paternal decision. The scamps did not tell me you had already refused, and I saw nothing wrong with having the dogs in the nursery, as long as they are confined until they are more convincingly housebroken. I had a dog sleep at the foot of my bed until I went to school."

"You did not have a mother."

"That does not mean I was raised by wolves."

One might gather otherwise from his manners. Still, he had not meant to circumvent her authority. And he was here, looking like Lucifer himself in the firelight. "Would you care for a glass of wine?" she asked in conciliation.

Lud, no. Rockford was befuddled enough at the sight of his wife with hair trailing down past her narrow waist, almost hiding her glorious breasts. A drink and he was liable to start baying at the moon. "No, thank you. I have had enough spirits tonight."

Alissa could have used something to calm her disordered nerves, but she did not wish to drink while he did not. He was just standing there, half leaning against the door frame, bare legs crossed at the ankles. The dratted man never lost his poise, while she was almost shaking in anticipation. And he was not making things easier for her, either, not talking, not smiling, just staring at her hair. "I'll just put this into a braid and —"

"No! That is, don't take the time."

Oh. Alissa set down the brush. Now he was in a hurry, after weeks of marriage? She was eager too, she had to admit to herself. She had not missed the pleasures of lovemaking until she met Rockford, but now she felt her skin warm in expectation. Now she would have a real marriage; now she could begin to win her husband's affection. Love was not guaranteed to follow lovemaking, of course, but it was a start. She did not think she had any other way of getting close to this handsome, worldly stranger she had wed.

Still, he had not moved from the doorway. She licked her lips in that nervous habit she had. "Shall I, ah, leave the candles burning?"

That got him stirring. He crossed the room, dousing the flames. He would have put the fire out, too, if he had the time. The only way he was going to get through this with his soul intact, Rockford told himself, was to hurry, not breathing in the scent of her, all flowers and ready woman, and in the dark. He closed his eyes so he did not have to see her tongue brush those soft lips so innocently, so suggestively. He put his hands in his robe's pockets so he would not reach out for the rippling silk of her hair.

He tripped over her slippers.

"Are you sure about the candles?" she called from one side of the bed.

He was sure about nothing, except that he should not be here. He did not want to want anything as much as he wanted this woman. That way lay disaster. But she wanted a daughter. Ah, life did require sacrifices, did it not? He climbed onto the bed, on the opposite side.

Her hand reached out for him. A small, chill hand touched the skin of his chest, where his robe was open. The fire in his blood would warm it instantly. He could not help himself. He reached out his own hand to spread her hair across the pillow, then to touch the skin of her cheek, her neck, her bare shoulder. Just to make sure she was ready, he lied to himself. His hand moved lower, to her velvet-skinned breast. Hers untied the sash of his robe.

He groaned.

She sighed.

He kissed the top of her head, breathing in the perfume she wore, rubbing his lips against the softness of her hair. She kissed his neck, his shoulder, his earlobe.

Oh, Lord, Rockford prayed, don't let him embarrass himself like a schoolboy! He ran his trembling hand down the silky length of her nightgown, then raised the fabric up toward her waist.

"Shall I . . ..?" she asked.

He kissed her mouth, to quiet her. Control was taking all of his concentration; he did not need conversation. That was a mistake. Fire raced between them, urgency, hunger, need. If he did not bury himself in her soon he would die, Rockford knew, and she would never have her daughter, only a limp rag that used to be an earl. He slipped his hand between her thighs. She was ready, thank the gods of fertility. He rose above her and joined their bodies.

And she whispered his name. "Robert."

He'd almost been afraid she would call him by her dead husband's name. This was worse. His body responded to her siren's call. Once, twice; he sheathed himself a third time, and was lost.

No, he was still breathing, barely. He raised himself on his arms, kissed his wife on the forehead, and got off the bed, pulling his robe closed before she could see signs of life in his letter opener. "Good night, Countess. Sleep well."

Sleep well? Alissa stared at the ceiling. How could she sleep when every inch of her body was on fire, when she wanted to launch herself off the bed, knock him to the floor, and demand Rockford satisfy the cravings he had aroused?

At least now she knew why his wives had left him.

251

Chapter Seventeen

That Austrian princess must have very different prerequisites for a lover, Alissa thought as she washed. And so must all those other women who had labeled Rockford a rake. How else would he have gained a reputation for his beautiful mistresses, his myriad affairs? Surely his title went only so far toward dazzling the ladies of the *ton*. Like a book's title, if the pages were blotted, boring, or blank, people ought to stop buying it.

Unless the problem was Alissa herself. Perhaps Rockford was simply not attracted to her. He could have forced himself to a perfunctory performance, simply to get the deed done. No. He had been ready, and definitely able, if not entirely willing. Alissa had hardly been able to admire her magnificent wedding present before it was spent, but like everything else about Rockford, it was impressive.

She sighed as she went back to her cold bed. Here she had been fearing comparisons with her late husband's memory. This . . .

this lightning bolt of an encounter was nothing like the tenderness she'd known with William Henning, nothing like the mutual pleasure they had shared for hours.

It was nothing to build a marriage on, either.

Alissa spent the next day getting her family settled in their new surroundings. The first thing she did was have Rockford's fragile treasures moved onto higher shelves or to his private office or his bedroom suite, both of which were off-limits to the boys and the dogs. He could break them for himself, there, like the ivory goddess.

After that she sent Claymore to placement agencies about tutors and a new secretary for Rockford, and Jake to indoor riding academies about the ponies. She met the housekeeper and the emigré chef, whose aid she immediately enlisted for practicing Hugo's French, for a raise in salary. She consulted the maids about which shops to patronize, and the guidebooks about seeing the sights. She assigned footmen to accompany the boys, footmen to escort Lady Eleanor, footmen to guard her sister. One footman she promoted to kennel master.

She got the key to the gated park across the street, where the boys had to be taught to play in limited areas and the pups had to be taught to follow on a lead. She gave a handsome tip to the groundskeeper there, in advance of the destruction they were bound to commit, despite the lectures and lessons.

She helped Aminta reassess her wardrobe, and helped her sister-in-law send letters to former acquaintances and correspondents, some of whom were now matrons of social importance. She oversaw the unpacking, the menus, and the children's schedules, without ever seeing her husband.

And she primped.

She washed her hair, she bathed in perfumed oils, she put cucumbers on her eyes and crushed strawberries on her cheeks. She changed her evening gown two times, her jewelry three, and her mind every ten minutes. Did she want him to come to her room tonight at all? Was she brave enough to go to his chamber if he did not?

He did not join them for dinner. According to Claymore, Rockford had left in the morning, and left no direction or time of his return. Now Alissa had to decide if she should wait up for him and, if so, where, and wearing what.

She was trying to decide hours later, when he was still not home. She was acting like a mooncalf, she told herself, and went to her own room with a book for company. She did make sure her hair was loose around her face and her night rail was loose around her shoulders.

Just when she was about to extinguish her candle, he came.

He came. And then he kissed her forehead and left.

All Alissa had in return for her day's efforts was another restless, unfulfilled sleep, and a wet spot.

Rockford did not come to her bed the next night. He did not even come home. Alissa knew because she stayed up, listening. Heaven knew where he did sleep, but it was not at Rothmore House. She was not happy with that fact, but not unhappy to get a good night's sleep. Besides, she had not found what she was looking for yet. She could not very well seek it out at the lending library where Hugo had spent an hour that morning, but she guessed Rockford would own the book. Unfortunately, she was too busy to search the extensive library, and too well surrounded with staff and family. Claymore might know its place in the collection, but she could never get up the courage to ask.

So she rose before dawn and crept down the stairs before the first servants were about. She tiptoed into the library — and gasped when she almost stumbled over a puppy. Hugo was asleep in one of the leather chairs, a book in his lap. Alissa had to pet the dog before it barked and woke the boy and the entire household. She gingerly patted its head, then snatched her hand back when the creature tried to bite her. It tried to lick, she had to admit, but she was taking no chances. The dog tucked its nose between its paws and went back to sleep.

Alissa wished she had a blanket to cover Hugo. She made a note that one should be kept in the library at all times, and the fire left burning. Of course, Hugo should not be out of the nursery, but exploring the library would have been too much of a temptation for Rockford's scholarly son. Like her, the boy had been too busy to spend much time here.

She gently removed his spectacles before they fell, and started to take the book from his lap when she noticed the title. "Why, you little devil." Now she would have to hire a librarian to remove unsuitable works from the shelves. They would have to go into Rockford's rooms too, along with his antiquities, but this one went first. She had what she'd come for.

Rockford was pleased with himself when he got home that evening. He had bedded his new wife twice now, and gone on his way intact, not bending to her will. He spent his days out of the house, and one of the nights, to prove to himself that he could keep away from her, that his well-ordered life could not be disrupted by a contrary countess. She might be under his roof, but she was not under his skin.

The entryway looked different, the parlor emptier. "What, have we been burgled?" He tried to joke with Claymore, who did not smile.

The old butler was not amused, likely showing his displeasure at Rockford's long absence. "Some of the breakables have been relocated for safekeeping, my lord."

"The brats are not staying, dash it! There is no need to rearrange my house." It was still his house, by George! "Where is Lady Rockford? I will get this matter settled once and for all."

"My lady is not at home. None of the ladies are at home," he added, in case the earl wished to shout at his sister again or bring the young miss to tears.

"What do you mean, not at home? It is eight o'clock at night." Alissa knew no one in town that he had heard of, and had no connections if one discounted the priggish Duke of Hysmith. Rockford doubted the stiff-rumped peer would acknowledge Alissa's existence, much less invite a former, unwanted sister-in-law to dinner. As for his own sister, they had made peace, but he doubted she'd show her face out in public until knowing if the recent scandal had been squelched.

Deuce take it, a wife ought to be waiting when her spouse returned. That was the way it was supposed to be, wasn't it?

"We did wait dinner last night," the butler offered, disturbing Rockford's mutterings.

So that was it. She — and Claymore, if he read the old man aright — were in a miff because he had not come home last night. Well, Lady Rockford would just have to learn that it was the wife who waited, not the husband, by Jupiter. Or else she could take herself and the traveling circus back to Rock Hill. Heaven knew he would not miss her. In fact, he would miss the Etruscan vase, the ivory goddess, the carved walking stick, and his former secretary more. So there.

She ought to have sense enough to stay here, however, he thought, at least until his groom returned with a reply from Sir George. The message had been clear: Leave the county or name his seconds. Until Rockford heard a reply, one way or the other, Alissa and her sister would do better at Rothmore House, indoors, under guard.

"Where the devil did they go, anyway?" he asked, thinking that he might have to go find them, to act as protection.

Claymore adjusted a fern in a brass planter on the Chippendale table in the hall. It was ugly, but unbreakable. "The countess is attending the opera this evening."

"In my box?" Rockford had been intending to use it, as soon as he changed his clothes.

"Where else should the Countess of

Rockford sit but in the Rockford box?"

Which Claymore would have directed her to. The butler might have been with the family for ages, but that did not entitle him to sarcasm. "Do you know, old man, I think you might be happier in the country after all."

Claymore took the hint, cleared his throat, and said, "My lady took Lord Rothmore and Master Kendall, besides the ladies. It was to be their first night out in London, my lord, a special occasion. The countess had never seen an opera performed. Nor had the children, of course."

Rockford caught the censorious note in his butler's voice again. Claymore obviously thought he should be dancing attendance on the woman, showing her about town, introducing her to his friends, taking her to her first opera. Sitting in her pocket. No, he would not.

He could change into formal attire and go now, just to make sure she had enough attendants, of course. He could go, sit at her side in the dark, place his arm around her shoulders. . . . No, he would not. Be damned if he would chase after his own wife. He had to start as he meant to go on. In addition, Alissa belonged in the country, not glittering amid the haut monde. He'd married a sensible, honest countrywoman, dash it. London would turn her into another spoiled, selfish she-witch. Then he would find himself leg-shackled to another man's mistress. No, he would not, not this time.

None of Rockford's alternative choices for the evening's entertainment appealed to him, though. Neither his clubs nor the gaming dens, a rout at Lady Bushnell's nor a bachelor party at one of the high-class brothels sounded inviting to him. Not as inviting as his wife's warm body. Botheration.

His sitting room was cluttered with objets d'art, and the library was too warm, with blankets piled on his favorite chair for some reason. The formal drawing rooms were . . . too formal, and too quiet with no one playing the pianoforte. He supposed he should look over his correspondence, now that he had no secretary, but it could wait. What time did the opera end anyway?

Then he heard noises from the upper levels, shouts, screams, the clash of swords. Aha! Just what he needed, murder, mayhem, a masked intruder to beat off! He grabbed up a sword stick from the Chinese urn in the hall and raced up the marble stairs, two steps at a time — in time to be bowled over by a rusty suit of armor bumping its way down.

He caught himself on the stair rail, thank goodness, but the armor did not. It bounced right into the Chippendale table, sending the brass-potted fern to the floor in a hail of dirt and greenery, then smashed into the antique Chinese urn that was used to hold canes and umbrellas.

Whatever blasphemy he shouted sent one footman, two little boys, and three puppies scrambling away. The fourth puppy cowered at Rockford's feet, so he picked it up. "Not your fault, little fellow," he tried to soothe the shivering pup, which promptly wet his shirtfront.

After a bath, Rockford went up to the nursery, thinking to demand apologies and issue warnings. Instead he saw the two youngest boys, the Williams, enjoying warm milk and raspberry tarts. His favorites. And he'd missed supper. So he stayed on in the playroom, taking on all comers at marbles, feeding crumbs to the puppies, listening to his son's endless chatter and Alissa's son's shy replies, reading tales of derring-do. He kept them up long past their bedtime, and enjoyed himself more than he had at any of the balls he'd attended that month.

He was waiting in her room when Alissa came home, in his loose robe, but with slippers on his feet. He rose from the chaise when she came in.

"I am sorry, my lord, but it has been an exhausting day." And she did not want another sleepless night filled with unfulfillment. She did not wish another of her husband's visits, either, not until he had time to read the book.

He sat down again, when she sat at the dressing table to remove her jewelry. She wore the sapphires tonight, he saw, with a blue gown. "I, ah, thought we might talk a bit. We need to set some rules for the house, for while you are here."

She started to take the pins out of her hair, wondering how she was to get out of her dress without the maid he must have dismissed for the night. "That would be good. I have a few rules of my own, too."

"I know, I kept the boys up too late." Claymore must have squealed on him. The disloyal old retainer was definitely going back to the country.

"No, I mean that you must be a father to them. You cannot disappear for two days. They simply do not understand and think you are angry at them, that you do not want them here."

Well, he did not. But he nodded.

"You have to spend time with them," she went on. "Get to know them. Take them places. I cannot show them Tattersall's and Gentleman Jackson's. For that matter, I cannot guide them through sights I have never seen for myself. Besides, I do not share all of their interests." Going to the Royal Menagerie had to be worse than having dogs in the house. "Yet I cannot entrust them to mere servants. They need a father. That was part of our arrangement."

That was fair, Rockford thought. And not terribly hard, for the few days they would remain in London. His schedule was not too busy for an outing or two. He'd enjoyed the little boys, and wanted to get to know his heir better anyway. "Any other rules you might wish to discuss, Countess?"

Alissa blushed, and hoped he could not see it by the candlelight. What she wanted was not precisely a rule, an edict handed down, but was something no woman should have to ask for. She could not come out and say the words, not to this dark-haired man lounging in her bedroom as if he owned it. Which, of course, he did. Instead she said, "I think we need to know each other better, too. I was wrong asking you to come to my bed while we are still strangers."

"What about the daughter you hope to have? It is possible you have conceived already, but not likely."

"We have time. I am not too old to bear more children."

Her age was perfect for him, one of the reasons he had married her. No flighty girl, no withered crone. "Then you don't want . . . ?" He eyed the bed longingly.

"Not tonight. What were the rules you wished to discuss?"

He sighed for lost causes. Rules? Oh, yes.

"I would like to know where you are. Finding you gone had me worried, despite Claymore's reassurances. I do not want you traipsing off without proper escort, not until the messenger gets back from Sir George, at any rate."

She stopped to consider. "What do you deem proper escort? Yourself?"

Why not? Devil take it, wagers were already being placed in the betting books about who would be her cicisbeo, her gallant. No one dared to suggest a lover for her, not yet. That would come tomorrow, after they had filled their eyes with her tonight in the low-necked blue gown, without male companion. Damn, he would not have his wife's name being bandied about. "Yes. I will escort you to a few social outings while you are in town. My secretary, when I hire one, can help decide which entertainments we should attend."

"Thank you." She looked at him inquiringly, then yawned. She was politely waiting for him to finish and leave.

He was not ready to go yet. "About the boys. I cannot have them hanging from the chandeliers, teaching the dogs to fetch using my walking sticks, ransacking the attics, playing with —"

"You will have to tell them yourself, Robert. I am too tired to remember. And you are their father."

He was her husband, too, damn it, Rockford cursed to himself, for all the good it was going to do him tonight. There she was brushing her hair, and he could not even offer to do it for her lest he forget himself and wrap strands around his fingers, rub it against his cheek, kiss the nape of her neck, nibble on her earlobes.

He wished her a good night, knowing he was going to have a deuced uncomfortable one.

After another bath, a cold one this time, he climbed into his huge bed. And found a book under his pillow. His valet would not have placed it there. Not even Claymore would have dared. No, only his wife, his modest, virtuous wife, would have placed the *Kama Sutra* from his own library under his pillow.

His countess thought he needed lessons in lovemaking besides in how to be a father?

He laughed. It was that or cry.

Chapter Eighteen

Rockford was still smiling when he heard the soft tap on the door connecting his room to Alissa's. "Changed your mind, Countess?" he asked when he opened the door. The grin spread to his groin, seeing her with her hair unbound.

Heavens, Alissa thought, if anything could make her rethink her decision to sleep alone it was the sight of Rockford smiling. His teeth were even and white, and now his mouth was softened with humor. His dark eyes sparkled, and that rare dimple showed in his cheek. His hair, damp from washing, hung down on his forehead, and his robe was loosely belted, leaving more of his chest showing. "Yes. I mean no. That is, I need your assistance with my gown. I cannot reach the fastenings on my own, and I do not want to disturb any of the maids."

"You are a countess, madam. You may disturb anyone you want." She sure as Hades disturbed him. He urged her further into the room, though, before she could change her mind about that too. He still held the book in one hand and, before setting it down on the bed to work on the complicated closures, he looked at it and said, "You are a surprising woman, you know."

Alissa did not try to pretend that she knew nothing of the small volume, that some lusty leprechaun had placed it on his pillow. "I thought . . ."

He could well imagine what she thought, by Jupiter. He might have blushed, were he fifteen years younger. "I do not like surprises."

"No, I would not guess that you did."

He had turned her around and made short work of the ties and hooks that held her gown together.

"You are very good at that," Alissa said, thinking of his former wives, his recent lovers.

He was still thinking of the book. He nodded to where it lay on his drawn-down bed. "I am good at a great many things."

"Oh. I do like surprises."

And his skill as a lover would be one? Rockford could not decide whether to be offended or amused. He decided to prove her wrong, now that his manly pride was pricked. He began to massage the muscles of her neck and back that he had just uncovered.

Alissa stepped away and turned to face him, holding the front of her gown up with her hands. "But not tonight. It is very late, and I have early interviews with prospective tutors in the morning. I hope to pay a call on Hysmith in the afternoon, if his grace will see me."

"You are still determined to confront the duke, although you need neither his financial assistance nor the social entrée he and his late wife could have supplied?"

"He is still my late husband's family, my sons' uncle. Why, his sons are their first cousins and they have never met. Willy and Kendall should know their kin."

"My William and Rothmore are their step-brothers now. Is that not kin enough?"

"What, are you worried that I will bring more Henning boys into your home? They should be young men now, I believe. Besides, if what you say about Hysmith is true, I doubt he will let his sons be in the same room with such lesser mortals as my children and me. Still, the duke's recognition and reconciliation is something William would have striven for, for his sons, had he outlived his father. A closer connection to Hysmith will make the boys' lives easier. It is not what I might wish, but it is the way of the world."

Rockford thought she was underestimating him — again. His influence was all her sons needed, but the country countess was too unfamiliar with polite society to know that. He feared she would be disappointed with her meeting with the duke, but did not think that would dissuade the stubborn wench from going. She was like a bulldog when it came to her sons . . . and like a fractious colt when it came to him. He tried once more: "Shall I unlace your corset too?"

She was halfway to her own bedroom before he could raise his hands.

How many baths could one man take in a day?

Alissa found the ideal tutor — two of them. Mr. Lucius Canover was a scholarly young man of good breeding who had decided not to accept a university position, because instructors were not permitted to marry. At twenty-one, he wanted a family of his own someday, and was saving money to be able to support a wife by giving private lessons. His earnings had suffered a setback when his sixteen-year-old brother, Lawrence, broke his arm in a fall while rock climbing. Destined for the army, Lawrence was not bookish, but mad for sports and outdoor activities, now somewhat curtailed by his injury. He could not return to military school near Oxford, nor their crowded home in Lancashire, but had landed in London, on the doorstep of his brother's one-room flat. They needed rooms, board, and income. Lucius needed a library for his Russian translations; Lawrence needed activity to keep him from boredom until his arm healed.

Alissa hired them both. The scholar had excellent references; the would-be soldier had captained his school's cricket team. Both had fine manners and pleasant looks, knew London, and liked dogs.

She was delighted, and thought Rockford would be also, if he thought about it at all. Despite their conversation of the night before, he had not made an appearance that day, had not spoken to the children nor left word of his whereabouts. So much for him becoming a father and a husband.

Alissa made Lady Eleanor walk with them all across the square to Henning House, home of Morton Henning, the widowed Duke of Hysmith, her former brother-in-law.

"I do not think that is a good idea, Countess," Eleanor tried to tell her.

"Nonsense. You cannot hide in your bedroom here. You will never be anything but a curiosity in London, the subject of rumor and innuendo, if you are not seen out and about, at your normal activities."

"Calling on the Duke of Hysmith is not one of my normal activities."

Nor was it Alissa's either. The closest she had ever come to even meeting a duke was sitting in a cold room, waiting for William to be disowned. "No matter. You are the daughter and sister of an earl. I am wed to one. We are not mushrooms sprouting on his doorstep."

Hysmith's butler must have thought they were. He wrinkled his long nose as if they smelled of the gutters, instead of the neatly groomed park grounds where the children and dogs now romped, supervised by Amy and the Canovers, with two grooms watching. He tried to shut the door in Alissa's face. "His grace is not at home."

Alissa had been anticipating this day for too long to leave without a fight. "Very well, we shall wait for him here." She gestured toward the park, where it appeared that the puppies had discovered squirrels. "I'll just fetch the boys and the dogs, inside, shall I?"

"I believe his grace has just arrived home. If you will wait in the parlor, I will inform him of your call."

The duke deigned to see Alissa and her sister-in-law, not the children. The women were shown into a room furnished in the Chinese style, with red-lacquered cabinets and fire-breathing dragons everywhere.

One of them rose as they entered. His grace raised his quizzing glass and slowly inspected Alissa, giving Lady Eleanor a more perfunctory survey. Alissa was glad she had worn the Rothmore pearls and a new peach-colored gown, although she doubted her fashion sense had anything to do with the duke's curling lip. The man could give Rockford lessons in being toplofty, she decided, and Rockford was an expert.

Alissa tried not to be as obvious in her observation. Hysmith was much older than William, so he must have well over forty years in his dish, she estimated. He looked it, with fine lines starting to spread across his features. His waist must be spreading also, for she heard the telltale creaks of a corset when he made her the slightest of bows. His sandy hair was thinning, more gray than brown, and his eyes had slight pouches under them. With a twinge of sorrow, she noted a family resemblance to her late husband's good looks, and something of Kendall's gravity. The duke was a handsome man still, in a dignified way, but in his prime he must have been as attractive as William Henning, with fine blue eyes and a well-built physique. He was neither as tall nor as broad-shouldered as Lord Rockford, but he did possess that same air of confident authority, of power that did not need words to impress.

"Thank you for seeing me, your grace," she said, making a low curtsy, then holding out her hand. The duke did not take it, so she swept her arm toward her companion as if that were her intention all along. "And may I present my sister-in-law, Lady Eleanor Rothmore?"

"We have met," he said briefly, with another minuscule bow.

Lady Eleanor's curtsy was shallower, if possible. Alissa looked at her companion in dismay. Eleanor might have mentioned that animosity already existed between the two families.

Eleanor lifted a shoulder. "I warned you this was not a good idea."

They were already at the duke's house. Alissa had to try. "As you must know, your grace, I have brought your nephews to London. I should like to introduce them to you as well."

"Why?"

"Because they are kin. Your remaining brother lives in Yorkshire, so my sons have never met any of their cousins, neither of their uncles. They are Hennings, however, part of your family."

"No."

"Of course they are. I would not change their name to Rothmore, even if my new husband wished it. They are William's sons."

"William's name was stricken from the family Bible when he made such a misalliance. Whatever whelps you spawned are nothing to me. Luckily my late wife blessed me with two healthy lads, and my second brother has three boys in Yorkshire, so your sons will never figure in the Hysmith succession. Cousins, you say? I do not wish my sons to be tainted with that bad blood."

Alissa could feel her anger rising. "They share your blood."

"My father sired any number of bastard

Hennings. They share my blood also, and I have as little to do with them."

She gasped, going as pale as the pearls at her neck. "Are you suggesting my sons are baseborn?"

"Your first was born before nine months had passed, I have heard. Who can say? No, I do not wish to meet your brats, nor, if my sons were not at Oxford, would I permit them to associate with such low company. I mean my eldest son for Parliament, not your tawdry parlor."

Alissa rose to her feet. Rockford had warned her. Now she had seen for herself. "You need not worry, your grace. I do not wish my sons to be associated with such a mean-spirited, bad-mannered churl. I am certain any sons you raised will be equally as obnoxious. Good day. Come, Eleanor."

But Lady Eleanor could not resist a parting comment: "You always were a self-centered coward, Morton. I see you have not improved with age. You are as pigheaded as ever, only now there is less hair on your thick skull."

The duke's face turned red. "You dare to speak, madam?" he roared. "You used to be an outrageous chit, and now look at you, an outrageous old maid. If half the rumors I hear are true, you did not hold your scruples so high after all. Morality could not keep you warm after all these years, could it, my lady?"

Eleanor's nostrils flared. "If I were a man I would call you out."

"If you were a man I would throw you out."

Alissa's head was swiveling between these two nobly born combatants. Just how well did they know each other, after all? A sick feeling in the pit of her stomach told her that it was a poor idea, indeed, to bring Lady Eleanor to Henning House.

Eleanor was saying, "That would be just like you to throw us out, to turn your back on your own brother's wife and children, your own responsibilities. You never were one to face up to your duties, were you?"

Like showing up for his own wedding, Alissa very much feared. Oh, Heavens, she prayed, let her get Eleanor out of here without bloodshed!

"I . . . I?" his grace sputtered. "You never knew your place in the world, never accepted a woman's role. It is just like you to stick your oversize nose in affairs you do not understand. Well, I will not have my family name dragged through the muck and mire you have made of your reputation, not even by association. Two scandals in one family are enough."

He turned on Alissa then. "The actions I was forced to take twenty years ago might have created a stir" — Lady Eleanor made a rude noise — "but so did yours with that hasty wedding to William before he was dry behind the ears. I will not have my dirty linen aired again, and I will not have more scandal touching the House of Hysmith, do you hear? So you can take your questionable brood, your disreputable sister-in-law and, yes, your hole-in-corner marriage to Rockford, and leave my home. If I were not a gentleman, I would not have admitted you in the first place."

Alissa was pulling Eleanor's arm toward the door. "I will go, and gladly," she said, "but you, sir, are no gentleman."

"Hah! What does a jade like you know of gentlemen? No gentleman marries a woman of your sort."

"Your brother did," a deep voice said from the doorway, "and I did. Are you calling me less than a gentleman or my wife less than a lady?" Rockford's tones were quiet, measured, but dangerous. They all recognized the threat in his dark look.

Alissa had never been so happy to see the earl. She could not imagine what he was doing there, but his solid presence gave her confidence and his defense of her warmed her heart. She took a step closer to his side and raised her chin. "There is nothing dishonorable about my sons' birth, your grace, my valiant sister-in-law" — whose arm she still clutched, lest Eleanor throw something at the duke — "or my marriage."

Rockford merely asked, "Do you disagree with my countess, Hysmith?"

"Stubble it, Rockford," the duke replied. "You are not about to call me out, not if you ever want to see any of your womenfolk accepted in society, which is doubtful in itself. I am not fool enough to accept your challenge, not over past issues, not over present inconveniences."

"I should have killed you when I had the chance."

"What, when your sister and I decided we would not suit?"

Eleanor did throw something. She tossed her gloves at the duke's head, but missed. "Not suit? Is that what you call leaving me at the altar?"

Hysmith ignored her outburst, speaking only to Rockford. "You were nothing but a boy."

"And you did not accept my challenge then either."

"What, kill a youth? You could not have been more than fifteen. My sons are older than that now." The duke picked up Lady Eleanor's gloves and slapped them down on an end table. "I would have needed to flee the country. Your title would have gone to some distant cousin."

"It might not have gone that way. You did not give me the chance, leaving for Scotland the way you did."

"My family deemed that the proper course. Now I make the decisions about what is fitting for the dukedom."

"And my family does not meet your lofty standards?" Rockford's voice dripped venom.

"Come, Robert," Alissa said, transferring her arm to Rockford's, to tug him out of the room before more violence ensued. "You were right. My sons have a father now. They do not need an uncle."

She might have been trying to move a boulder.

"Hysmith?" Rockford's glare could have pierced an elephant's hide, or a duke's.

"What, do you think I believe that moonshine about Lady Eleanor chasing down a thief and then succumbing to influenza at your aunt's house in Wales? That is just the kind of thing the ridiculous female would do, go haring off across the country without thinking of the consequences, but she was seen leaving with the bailiff, you know, so that won't wash."

Alissa was ready to throw her own gloves at the duke, and her reticule too. "She went along to lull his suspicions until the magistrate came. With her maid for chaperon," she hastily added.

He ignored her, looking only at Rockford, as if to judge whether he should put more distance between them. "As for the tale you told in the clubs about your marriage being based on a long understanding, waiting for Mrs. Henning's mourning period to come to an end, I say balderdash. You have been married, what? Less than a month, and you were here in London the entire time. You did not even have a honeymoon, or wait for your so-called sick sister to return from Wales for the nuptials you had a year to plan. When the grieving widow finally did arrive in town, what did you do? You spent the night with your foreign mistress!"

Now Alissa wanted to toss something at her husband instead of at the duke. She'd suspected Rockford's whereabouts, but did not need this insufferable prig to give reality to her fears by saying it aloud.

Hysmith was not finished. "You barely acknowledge your wife's existence, Rockford. Why should I?"

"You go too far," Rockford said, and then he did, in fact, throw something: his fist. "There," he said after hauling the duke up from the floor by his neckcloth. "I have been wanting to do that for almost twenty years."

Lady Eleanor stepped over, balled her fingers into a fist, and struck Hysmith on the other side of his jaw. "So have I."

The duke looked at Alissa. She shook her head. "I have not been waiting nearly so long, only since your brother died and you did not respond to my letter. You are not worth soiling my gloves, your grace." She raised her chin and walked out of the room, not caring if her husband followed her across the square to Rothmore House or not.

How could she be angry at Hysmith? He was only speaking the truth. Rockford did not respect her. He did not even bother to fulfill his promise of being discreet. She was a fool to think she could make something of this marriage, and a fool to think she and her family could be accepted into Rockford's circles. Most of all, she was a fool to come to London. The city was full of soot and snobs and spoiled dreams.

"Claymore, start packing."

Chapter Nineteen

There ought to be a rule: People should mind their own business, keep their opinions to themselves. When the Earl of Rockford needed anyone's advice, blast it, he would ask for it!

Who did Hysmith think he was, anyway? His title was higher, he was older, he was a respected member of Parliament, and he had been, it was said, a faithful husband and a good father. So?

So he was right.

Rockford knew there was talk of his wife around the clubs. Once she had been seen at the opera in his box, the town bucks had been quick to speculate about the latest jewel, and they were not speaking of the Rothmore sapphires she wore, either. His absence did leave Alissa open to conjecture and her reputation subject to slander. His sister's presence fueled the gossip. His continued relationship with Princess Helga fanned the flames.

Rockford hated to admit it, but the Duke

of Hysmith was right. Confound it, he should have hit him harder.

It was a conundrum and a quandary. No one was going to show respect for his countess until he did himself, and somehow, he found, he cared that Alissa be treated as the lady she was. Of course, none of this would have mattered if the blasted female had stayed in the country where she belonged — and where she was assaulted by bumpkins instead of Bond Street beaux. Damn!

He never wanted another wife, but now he had one. He never wanted to be personally involved with Alissa Henning; now he was. He never wanted to want her, and now he was counting the minutes until she kissed the children good-night and it was his turn. Somehow she seemed to have acquired another boy, somewhat older and with his arm in a sling. He would not demand an explanation, not until tomorrow. Tonight he had to make her forget about the duke's words. He had just the method in mind, too.

When he heard noises in the adjoining chamber Rockford went to open the door, but found it locked. There it was, the conjugal key. Blast, he knew he should never have bedded the female! Sex gave women power, and they grabbed it with both hands. Make a man jump through hoops like a trick dog, then give him a reward. If he did not please you, turn the key, lock him out, make him pant for the promised treat. Bedroom blackmail, that was what it was.

The Earl of Rockford was not going to pay. He was not going to grovel outside any woman's door. The world was filled with females eager to share his favors. Just because he was not interested in any of them did not matter. He had not been interested in this one either, at first.

He turned and tried to decide what to do with his evening, now that his plans had been knocked to flinders. Then he recalled the duke's words. Deuce take it, she was his wife. He went back and knocked on the door.

She did not answer.

"Alissa, open the door. I am your husband."

"And I am packing."

"What do you mean, packing?" he asked through the still-closed panel.

"I mean I am filling my trunks. I am going home to Rock Hill, just as you wanted me to do."

He heard the sound of something — shoes, perhaps — being thrown into a case. "Well, you cannot."

"I came without your say-so. I can leave without your permission." More thumps and thuds.

"No, you cannot return to Rock Hill. Sir

George Ganyon is no longer at home at Fairmont."

"Good. That is all the more reason why I should leave. I will be safe from his unwanted advances and . . . anyone else's."

He ignored the last. "You misunderstand. He did not leave because I threatened to have him drawn and quartered. He never got my message. The groom came back late last night. He said Sir George's man would not tell where the baronet had gone, but the villagers say he tore off in a rush, with Fred Nivens driving his coach."

"Good riddance to both of them, then." The sounds indicated she had gone back to her packing.

"No. You are not safe until we know where they are."

"Nonsense. He would not —"

"We both know he might. Lud, the man must be unhinged to think we would let him court Aminta. But think of her, Alissa, and her danger."

There were no more noises from the countess's room for a moment. Then she said, "Very well. I will not go yet. But how will I know when it is safe for us to leave?"

"I hired Bow Street to find him. That is where I was this morning, interviewing Runners, giving them his description and Fred's. Then I came to find you at the duke's house, to make sure you had ample escort and protection."

"I was only across the square," she said with a sniff. "But did you really care enough to come after us?"

"Yes." Damn it, was that groveling? "Now open the blasted door. I am getting tired of speaking to a plank of wood."

The key turned and the door opened. Alissa stood holding the knob, but she did not step aside to let him enter. She had tears on her cheeks and reddened eyes. Of course. Tears were the grease that oiled the blasted lock women used to get their way. He sighed and handed over his handkerchief. Instead of weeping on his shirtfront, though, sobbing until he promised her the moon, Alissa merely dabbed at her eyes, said, "Thank you, good night," and handed back his handkerchief. She started to close the door.

"Wait! May I please come in?" Now *that* was groveling indeed. Rockford did not care. She needed comforting. He needed to hold her.

"No. I need my rest. It has been a difficult day."

He was having a difficult night. "I, ah, read the book." He had, a long time ago, so that was no lie.

"I am sure Princess Helga will be delighted. Perhaps you will get your silly treaty signed after all."

He winced at the mention of the Austrian

heiress, and wished he had knocked out a few of Hysmith's teeth while he was there. "Devil take it, we had an agreement."

"No, my lord, we had rules. Your rules, re-member? I was not to notice your activities, and you were not to embarrass me. You broke the rules and broke your marriage vows, but you shall not break my heart. Like your sister and Hysmith, I will not love a man who is unfaithful."

"Dash it, leave Eleanor and the duke out of this. They would have killed each other years ago, if they had managed to tie the knot. Who is talking about love, anyway? I am talking about —" He realized his error immediately. He could hear the conjugal lock's tumblers clicking shut. "That is —"

"I know what you are talking about, and I will not share my bed with a man who does not share my values. I am not a light-skirt, Rockford, selling my favors for your money and title, no matter what you, Hysmith, or all of London thinks."

"I never thought that."

"But it never mattered to you that ev-eryone else might. You heard the duke: No one respects me because you do not. You married beneath you, outside your charmed circle, and you intend to keep me there, an outsider, a nobody. How can I give myself to a man who has so little regard for me and my feelings?"

To hell with the *Kama Sutra*, Rockford cursed. There really ought to be a guidebook explaining a female's mind. Of course, the man who could write the manual had not been born yet, and likely never would be. He stroked his chin, thinking. The first thing he thought was that he had wasted another shave. The second was that he had a great many fences to mend before he'd see the inside of Alissa's bedroom.

"Would you like to spend the evening with me tomorrow?" he offered. "The regent is holding a small musicale." There. If he brought her to court, the gossip ought to be stifled; she ought to be satisfied; then he could — finally — be satisfied.

"Thank you, but I promised the boys and Aminta that I would take them to Astley's Amphitheatre to see the trick riding tomorrow night if we stayed in town."

"Surely the new tutor can escort them. With extra grooms, of course."

"I promised." She looked at him in disappointment, not for missing Prinny's affair, he thought, but because he had missed the point. "I gave my word."

And Alissa Bourke Henning Rothmore kept her vows. Except the one about obeying her husband, it seemed. Rockford nodded. He thought about the elegance of the regent's entertainment, the sumptuous surroundings, the intelligent conversations. Then he thought about the raucous crowd at the circus, hundreds of shrieking, sticky schoolboys, the sickening smells of sweat and horse and cheap cologne. Damn.

"May I come with you?"

The circus was worse than he'd thought, despite having the best seats, servants of their own, and a hamper with food from his own kitchen. The loud noises and pungent odors were far more piercing than he'd remembered, the crowds far less refined. He recognized no one in the huge theater, which was a mixed blessing. If any of his acquaintances had seen him in such a place, in such company, they would have laughed out loud, but they would also have spread the tale that the Earl of Rockford was dancing attendance on his wife and family. He would rather be the butt of jokes than have his countess be grist for the rumor mill. Or quarry for the hunt. Young widows and dissatisfied wives were fair game in his world. The earl's reputation for prowess with sword or pistol, though, was worth a great deal more than a wager at White's. No one would dare his wrath, if he was shown to have an interest.

An interest? Hell, he could barely keep his hands from Alissa, so he rested one arm along the back of her seat, where he could pretend to touch her neck by accident, or brush her cheek as he shifted positions. She wore a cherry-red merino gown with only a locket for decoration, and he had to wonder whose picture graced the tiny frame. What if it were her late husband's? Deuce take it, he thought. Neither weapon nor fist was defense against a dead man's memory.

She had her hair up in the new style she had adopted, with a few softly curling tendrils covering her ears and trailing down her neck. He liked it far better than the severe coiled braids she used to wear, but not half as well as seeing her long hair loose, billowing around her shoulders, across a pillow, where he could breathe in the sweet floral scent of it.

The scent of the circusgoers was a far cry from milady's perfume. Rockford was tempted to bring his handkerchief to his nose, but none of the others in his box seemed to notice the noxious odors or the deafening noise.

Some of the language from the nearby row seats was not suitable for Alissa's ears, much less for the children's, so Rockford deemed it lucky that not even Hugo could translate the thick cockney dialect. Some of the cheers and whistles were more for the women riders' legs than for their equestrian abilities. He noted that Aminta kept her eyes averted from the female performers' scant outfits; the new boy — Rockford had still not discovered why the tutor's brother was part of their party —

did not. He almost fell out of his seat trying to lean closer, until his brother thumped him on the ear.

William declared that he had to try riding his pony bareback, standing up; Kendall told him he would break his neck, and another argument ensued. William spilled his lemonade, of course. On Rockford's boots, of course.

The riders did the same tricks at least twenty times, the music was drowned out by the crowd, and the costumes were tawdry. The clowns were barely funny, until one compared them to the lords and ladies Rockford should have been rubbing shoulders with this evening. Then they were laughable, indeed.

Hugo was fascinated by the jugglers, Kendall was determined to teach the puppies some of the dog tricks, and Aminta was so embarrassed by the display of feminine limbs that she sat looking away from the show rings, chatting with the tutor instead of watching the circus. William ate everything in sight, so the other boys declared they would not ride home with him lest he cast up his accounts, which meant Rockford would have to sit with him, up by the driver, out in the cold drizzle. The tutor's brother pinched one of the orange sellers' bottoms.

Will Henning fell asleep in Rockford's lap midway through the second act, giving the earl a cramp in his leg. He did not dare move in case he awakened the child, who slept with his mouth open, drooling.

All in all, it was a dreadful, degrading, horrible experience — and the most fun Rockford had had in years. Seeing the circus for the first time through a boy's eyes was a unique delight. Seeing Alissa rejoice in the children's excitement was another pleasure, but seeing the looks of approval she kept casting his way, that was paradise. Her green eyes sparkled and she laughed as much at the boys' antics as she did at the performers'.

When she looked at him, though, her wide smile made him feel as if he had conjured the entire circus just for her. Here was something he could provide, something that had been missing in her hand-to-mouth existence, something he could do to please her. Other women might desire jewels and clothes and carriages; his wife wanted to see the children — his sons as well as her own — happy. And he wanted to make her happy. A lot.

He was not eager to please her merely so she would unlock that dratted door, he told himself. This was not about sex. He simply wished to see her happy.

Now that was the most amazing feat of the evening, Rockford marveled. Not the daredevil riding upside down under his horse's belly, not the tightrope walker on stilts, but discovering that he really did care about his wife.

A lot.

For the first time since her marriage, Alissa was positive she had made the right decision. She had not had much selection, granted, just Rockford, Sir George, or starvation, but what a fortunate choice it had been. She had been able to give her sons so little; now they had so much. Equally important, almost, her husband could laugh!

Her sophisticated, starched-up spouse could still enjoy the simple pleasures in life, it seemed, not just the extravagances of the social world. He was finding pleasure in being a father; she could swear to it by his grins and chuckles, and the way he kept Billy from the edge of the box, and made sure Hugo did not lose his glasses, and let Kendall sip from his wineglass when he thought she was not looking. He even let Willy sleep in his lap, tenderly ruffling her younger son's hair.

Perhaps he could grow to enjoy being a husband.

He was very good at it, she decided, when he tried. Tonight Rockford had smoothed their way, handling everything from their seats to their refreshments to the number of carriages it took to transport such a large group. He even improved the language of the spectators in the next box, with a glare of disapproval and a soft, "There are children and ladies present."

He thought she was a lady. Alissa smiled, unfortunately just when a young man in a spotted neckcloth was looking her way from his seat below them. The fellow blew her a kiss and tossed her a flower, which Rockford caught and threw back, shaking his head. No, she was not available for flirtation, that movement told the brash young man; she was his wife, not a doxy.

What a relief it was to Alissa to have someone else in charge for once, to have someone looking out for her after so long. As pleasant and easygoing as he was, William Henning would never have noticed her discomfort, would not have been able to discourage such forward behavior with a glance.

William would not have turned her insides to mush with one of those rare dimpled smiles, either. She could barely remember when she felt such a thrill go through her as when Rockford's hand touched the bare skin of her neck.

He smiled. He knew. But he felt the quick touch of fire too, she thought, for he pulled his hand away, scorched.

Then an orange-girl slapped Lawrence Canover and they all laughed, but Rockford looked her way first, to make sure she saw the humor. She had missed that, too, the joy of having someone to laugh with.

They could have a marriage, she swore, a real marriage, with sharing and caring and laughter and, yes, love. She knew it would be all too easy to give her heart to this man who carried her son so gently, who warmed her blood with a smile.

They *could* have a marriage. Starting tonight.

Billy's stomach was understandably upset and he had to be comforted. Neither the footman nor the nursery maid nor Mr. Lucius Canover would do, only Alissa. She sat by his bed until he fell asleep.

Hugo and Kendall had to be dissuaded from gathering dishes from the kitchen to see if they could juggle them. The puppies were exuberant after being penned in all night, and so was Willy, wide-awake after his nap in Rockford's arms. He had to hear about all he'd missed, especially the grand finale, and begged Alissa to take him back tomorrow, to see it for himself. Someday, she promised, hopeful that the future could only get better.

Although she had refused to go with them, Lady Eleanor insisted that Alissa tell her about the evening over a cup of tea. Alissa agreed, feeling sympathy with her bored, lonely sister-in-law. None of her London acquaintances had responded to Eleanor's notes, and no invitations had been delivered. She had to be dissuaded from returning to

Rock Hill in the morning.

"Stay a few more days," Alissa urged. "I know we did not fare well with the duke" — which was an understatement of epic proportions — "but I have not given up on our chances of being accepted. Not by the highest sticklers, but your brother did offer to introduce me to the regent, and who knows what could happen then."

"The fat old lecher could make you an indecent proposal, Rockford would call him out, and we would all have to flee to the country. I merely wish to move the inevitable outcome forward."

"Don't be a goose. The prince is married."

"Now who is being a goose?" Lady Eleanor countered, but she did agree to stay on in town for the rest of the week, at least.

Finally Alissa's time was her own, but she needed a bath.

By the time she was ready for bed — and ready for her husband in a new nightgown that was not nearly warm enough for an October night unless a body lay next to her — she had talked herself out of it. Her cold feet had nothing to do with the flimsy, feathered slippers she wore.

Rockford had not said anything about the Austrian princess. He had looked at Alissa with lust and a little affection this night, she thought, but what if, tomorrow, he went back to being a married bachelor? What if, tomorrow, he remembered that he'd only wed to provide his sons a mother? She paced her room. She moved a figurine on the mantel. She chewed her lip almost bloody.

Then she unlocked the connecting door. Her husband was too proud to ask again, she'd wager, so the stalemate could last forever unless she made the first concession. The click of the key sounded loud to her ears, but he did not come dashing through the opening as she'd hoped. She stepped in. He did not greet her with one eyebrow raised, as she'd feared.

No, he was sprawled across his bed, half-undressed, fast asleep. One night of being a father had exhausted him. She found a blanket to cover him, brushed a lock of black hair out of his eyes the same as she had done for Billy, and went back to her own room, smiling. The arrogant earl was human after all.

He snored.

Chapter Twenty

The next morning Alissa found herself alone in the house except for the servants. Mr. Canover had taken Hugo to Hatchard's to purchase more books for his studies, and Aminta, Lady Eleanor, and a maid had gone along to find the latest novels. The other boys had left earlier with Jake and the ponies for riding lessons at the indoor ring. Alissa had no idea where her husband was, to her disappointment, disapproval, and dismay when Claymore handed her a visitor's card.

She did not know any Lady Winchwood and did not know if she should be received and, if so, in the small morning room where Alissa sat or the formal parlor. The problem was resolved by the lady herself, trotting along in Claymore's wake before Alissa could ask his advice.

With rouged cheeks, red hair that rivaled a summer sunset, and a gown much too daring for one of her advanced years and too tight for one of her poundage, Lady Winchwood was definitely not someone Alissa should entertain, she decided, not unless she wished her reputation tarnished more.

Then Claymore announced, "Baroness Winchwood, my lady, formerly Mrs. Battersby, formerly Lady Jasper Nunn, formerly Lady Regina Rothmore, his lordship's aunt from Wales."

"He really has an aunt from Wales? That is, welcome to Rothmore House, ah, Lady Winchwood. What a pleasant surprise."

"I'll wager it is," the old lady replied, after telling Claymore to bring the claret. "The good stuff, mind, that my father put down." She dropped herself onto a high-backed chair and kicked her slippers off. "What, did you think you spun me up out of moonbeams, just to save Eleanor's name?"

"I . . . I was not certain."

"Well, I do exist, and you can thank your stars that there is still life in these old bones. I have come to pull your chestnuts out of the fire."

Heavens, with this painted old tart on their side, they were embers. "Ah, how did you know we were in trouble?" Alissa asked, positive that Eleanor had said the old aunt never left Wales, never corresponded with anyone in London.

"Claymore wrote me, of course. Good man, Claymore. I have tried to get him to go off to Wales with me any number of times."

"As your . . . butler?"

"Do not be impertinent, girl. You need me."

At Alissa's doubting look, Lady Winchwood went "humph" and said, "I might not look it, but I do know my way around the *ton*. I gave up on the whole lot of them ages ago. Nothing but a flock of sheep, with a few old goats thrown in. Still, I won't sit back and see my family disgraced."

Alissa sat up straighter, ready to defend her birth and breeding, and the hurried wedding. "There is nothing to be ashamed of."

"Pull in your claws, missy. I ain't speaking of you. It's Eleanor. Always did have an odd kick to her gallop, my niece, but this time she's gone too far."

"She did come back, however. With the Rembrandt," Alissa added out of loyalty to her sister-in-law.

"Landed on her feet, thanks to you, Claymore says, but not entirely. My coming to check on the poor girl's health will make your tale of the influenza and her recuperation at my house more believable. Who is going to challenge my word to my face?"

Since her face sported the same nose as Lady Eleanor, no one. "That might do, Lady Winchwood. Thank you."

"Oh, call me Aunt Reggie. Everyone does. You're part of the family now, and one of the best parts, according to Claymore."

Alissa felt herself blush. "I never —"

"Of course you did. Taking in Eleanor after she blotted her copybook so badly decent folks would have cut her dead, and taking charge of my grand-nephews. Claymore says you brought the pair of them to London with you."

"Yes, along with my two sons. They get along well. Do you not approve? Hugo does not seem to have taken any ill effects from the journey or the air."

"I think it's an excellent idea. Can't abide those women who leave their babies in the country for some other female to raise. Unnatural, it is."

"Do you have children of your own, then?" Alissa asked.

"No, to my regrets. My first husband died too soon, my second was too incompetent, and Winchwood was too old. Then I was."

"I am sorry." Alissa felt that covered everything, the lack of children, the demise of so many husbands, the need for hair dye and face paint.

Lady Winchwood shrugged, jiggling a formidable chest. "I haven't found another man I liked half so well since Winchwood or I'd be married again. Not that I didn't try out a few, or have other offers, mind, but I have money and the dower house and friends aplenty. Who needs another husband when a female of my age can do whatever she wants anyway, with anyone she chooses? I would have loved a lapful of babes, but had to settle for being an aunt instead. Luckily all my husbands came from big, fertile families. The little boys are best. You can send them to the kitchens to snabble snacks, and they always know the best gossip and where the key to the liquor cabinet hangs."

Oh, dear. Rockford was going to have to lay down some rules for his relative, if the outrageous widow was going to reside with them.

She was going on: "And they don't set up a caterwaul afterward, when you win their pennies at cards. Eleanor once kicked up such a fuss over a hand that she accused me of cheating."

Alissa would not put anything past Rockford's aunt Reggie. "Had you? Cheated, that is?"

"How else are they going to learn not to trust the dealer?"

"What about Rockford?"

Lady Winchwood swallowed half the glass of wine Claymore brought, then held her glass out for more. When the butler left, she said, "Oh, that one never did trust a soul. Rock had to play by his rules or not at all. Not that he was not a good boy, just that he knew who he was and what was expected of his name from the day he was born. The boy takes himself too seriously, I always said. You'll bring him around, though."

"Robert is a man now, not a boy."

"Robert, is it? Humph. Ain't been married long, have you? They are all boys at heart. They want what they want, on the instant, and they'll do anything to get it. They'll do more to keep it, especially if another boy has his eye on it, and that goes for horses and women as well as toy soldiers and make-believe mountains. Little boys, every one of them, which ain't to say they can't be taught. You'll see."

Maybe Lady Winchwood was wiser than she looked, or maybe Alissa just hoped she was right.

She was right about helping. Aunt Reggie made Alissa write out a hundred notes, it seemed, then send out a squad of footmen to deliver them. In no time at all, responses were flying back like birds to the roost. Invitations, welcome messages, a few matrons in person arrived at Rothmore House. As soon as Amy and Eleanor returned, Aunt Reggie enlisted them in the cause too, dragging all three of the younger women off to pay calls on everyone who had answered her notes, and a few who had not.

Lady Eleanor was on her best behavior, under threat of having to go live with Aunt Reggie otherwise. She even managed to cough a few times, to corroborate the story of her illness. There were a few flared nostrils, but no one turned their backs on her.

After all, she was no young miss whose indiscretions made her unsuitable for marriage to their sons. A woman so firmly on the shelf could be forgiven a slight sidestep from the moral path.

Aminta was so quiet and demure, the dowagers all labeled her a prettily behaved girl. That she was actually petrified into silence was of little account. After all, she *was* a young miss. Her birth was not what they might want for their own sons, but the dowry Aunt Reggie whispered in their ears would be ideal for a nephew or younger grandson.

Alissa was the one truly on trial, though, and she knew it. Over her hundredth cup of tea, it seemed, she smiled and quietly diverted talk from her marriage onto her children. Instead of speaking of Rockford, she spoke of his sons. When quizzed, she admitted to having given painting lessons, and opened her locket to reveal a miniature of her boys. Aunt Reggie's friends all wanted portraits done, some of husbands, some of children, one of her lover. Alissa also confessed to entertaining the entire Ziftsweig delegation, without knowing a word of German. She smiled, the matrons smiled, Aunt Reggie grinned.

Alissa passed the test.

Invitations started to arrive at Rothmore House that very afternoon, for all the ladies. There were balls and breakfasts, dance parties for young ladies, card parties for the older ones. Rides to Kensington, drives to Richmond. One dowager was having an opera singer at her house; another was having a cellist. Everyone wanted to entertain the new countess before the Christmas holidays when most of the polite world left town, not to return until springtime. Some of the invitations were to house parties and hunt balls. A few ladies who were staying in London planned elaborate dinners, festive routs with fireworks to celebrate the new year. Alissa could not accept, not knowing Rockford's plans.

Aunt Reggie did insist she accept the invitations to Almack's, the exclusive assembly rooms. "It took a lot of tea drinking to get those vouchers," she claimed. "And without them you are still Alissa Henning, bailiff's daughter, poor widow. Nobody. Once you are accepted by the jackaninnies who run Almack's, though, you are one of them. Countess of Rockford, a lady with a capital L. Your sister and my niece get in on your coattails. No doors will be shut, no ugly rumors will take root and grow. You will accept those vouchers, by George, or I will wash my hands of the whole pack of you."

Lady Eleanor refused. Almack's was nothing but a marriage mart, she claimed, and she was resigned — no, determined — to staying unwed.

"Well, I ain't," Aunt Reggie declared. "I intend to look over the crop of widowers and old bachelors, and I suggest you do the same. You can't be hanging on your brother's arm the rest of your life, nor cluttering up Alissa's house."

Alissa protested. Her sister-in-law would always have a home with them, for as long as she wished.

"That's all right and tight, missy, but look ahead. Is Hugo going to want to clothe, house, and feed an old auntie? Does Eleanor have an independent income? No, she counts on Rock to pay her bills. Hah. Besides, even if Eleanor ain't husband hunting, she needs to show her pretty face" — bless an aunt's prejudiced view — "to put an end to the gossip once and for all."

Aminta had to go too.

Aunt Reggie was adamant. "What, hide away in the nursery? Here is the opportunity of a lifetime, girl, and you will go, no matter how your knees knock together. Asides, you're not looking to snare a title. No use having lofty ambitions; the dowry ain't all that rich. Why do you think your sister swallowed all that tea? So you could have choices, that's what. You'll go, and you'll smile. That's enough. Oh, and you'll have to wear white, of course. Eleanor, I think yellow or red, something bright so they know you ain't trying to fade into the woodwork. As for you, Countess, make sure you wear the

Rothmore rubies. Anyone who doesn't know who you are today, will after Wednesday."

Lady Winchwood, in fact, had them go to a dressmaker that very afternoon, before dinner at one of her friends' houses, then a piano recital, a card party, and a poetry reading that evening. "Rockford can pay the extra charge so new gowns can be ready on time," she said. "What else is his money good for?"

Rockford was managing to spend his money with no help from his aunt. He had decided early that morning to go with the boys to their riding lesson at the indoor ring. The ponies he had selected were well schooled, but they were not used to London traffic, all the noises and commotion, and Jake and the grooms might not be vigilant enough on the way to the livery stable. Besides, all the boys had talked about on the way home last night was how they were going to stand on their ponies' backs, how they were going to practice leaping on and off.

Lud, dissuading them from trying to break their necks was the very devil. Rockford had to promise them wooden boats to sail on the Serpentine if they listened to Jake's instructions.

He didn't like Jake's tutelage. No, William's feet were too far forward. Will's back was not straight enough. Kendall was clutching the reins in a death grip. The tutor's brother, on one of the livery stable's horses, rode too fast, as if he were joining the cavalry eventually instead of a rifle unit.

Jake threw up his hands. "My schooling was good enough for you, b'gad. If you don't like it now, you can take over teachin' the sprouts. I've enough to do without arguin' over every step and every turn. The lads will never be ready for the jumps if you have your way."

Jumps? The infant who slept in his arms last night was going to go over jumps? Not on his life.

After the lesson, they stopped in at Tattersall's. If the tutor's brother was going to help bear-lead the younger boys, he needed a better horse. By this time they were all thirsty, so Rockford took them to Gunter's for ices and pastries. The sweets completely ruined their appetite for lunch, of course, so they went shopping for the boats instead of returning to Rothmore House. Wooden puzzles would be fine for a rainy day, the skittles at Rothmore House were ancient, and none of them had ever seen such finely painted metal crusaders. Rockford bought them all, and an extra boat for Hugo, too. They naturally had to try them out in Hyde Park, and William fell into the Serpentine only once.

If they went home to change his clothes —

and Rockford's, ruined fishing Will out of the water — questions would be asked. Like what kind of father was he, anyway, letting his son get wet on a cold autumn day? It seemed easier to purchase the boy new, ready-made clothes. The children's haber-dasher had a dandy stock of boys' hats, just like Rockford's beaver, only smaller, so he bought a beaver dam–ful, it seemed.

They looked so fine, matching Rothmores and Hennings and one Canover on the strut, that old ladies smiled and older gentlemen nodded approvingly. Young ladies sighed: They wanted a father just like that for their future sons. Younger gentlemen rushed to White's Club to lay down bets on Rockford's transformation and how long it would last, and on how many of the lads were his bastards.

Since the only thing waiting at home was lessons for the boys and secretaries to inter-view for the earl, they decided on extending their excursion, once they had eaten meat pies and chestnuts from street vendors, and hot buns and raspberry tarts from the bakery they passed.

They had to save the Tower Menagerie for when Hugo was along, the younger boys in-sisted, and the new steam-engine exhibit for when the elder Mr. Canover could explain the workings in detail, his brother suggested, not trusting Lord Rockford's scientific erudition. The art museum was deemed too dull, the cathedrals were voted too much like history lessons, but the waxwork gallery was the unanimous choice. Dead people, gory scenes, mayhem re-created — what more could a boy ask?

What more could a gentleman ask than such a successful day with his new family? A successful night with his new bride, that was what.

Unfortunately, Alissa was not at home when Rockford brought the tired, dirty children home. Fortunately, the nursemaid, the tutor, and Claymore knew how to get them bathed and ready for bed, for Rockford hadn't the least idea. Nor did he have the least idea where his wife might be, not with his indefatigable aunt in town. Aunt Reggie was as likely to have the women at a balloon ascension as at an assembly hall, as long as there were men handy. Lud, he did not want Alissa meeting all the bucks and beaux in town, not without him at her side.

He searched through his cards of invitation for the night, deciding to stop in at a few of the offered entertainments in hopes of finding his family, but he found only trouble. The Hafkesprinke heiress was furious. He was supposed to have driven her in the park that afternoon. To make up for his dereliction, Rockford had to escort her hefty highness to a number of parties, where he could not often leave her side, since she needed him to translate all the insincere compliments and overheard gossip. Since much of the talk concerned his wife and aunt and sister, who had been there earlier, he did not repeat it. That meant he had to make up stories about the other guests.

Later, courtesy demanded he escort the plump princess back to her hotel. And up to her room. And pour her a last glass of spirits. And . . . and he did not feel like it. The gossip would not have stopped him from accepting the blatant invitation, nor would his marriage vows. Three-quarters of the husbands he knew, and half the wives, kept lovers on the side. No, it was Alissa's image dancing in his mind that made him refuse Princess Helga. He did not want to hurt Alissa's chances of being accepted, he told himself. He did not want to hurt her feelings, he added to his mental reasoning. Hell, he reluctantly admitted, he did not want to sleep with any other woman!

Now there was a novel idea to end a day of new experiences: the Earl of Rockford was going to be a faithful husband. For a while, anyway. He was certain this peculiar attraction to his own, unremarkable wife would soon wear off. Alissa would return to the country and they would live independent lives, just as he had planned. The uncomfortable feeling in the pit of his stomach must be from the odd assortment of food he had eaten today. It could not be from the notion of Alissa taking a lover.

She wouldn't, his countess. If there was a woman on earth who was to be trusted, he would wager on Alissa. The problem was, no woman could be trusted. Well, she would not stray from her marriage bed, not while he was keeping her satisfied there. Rockford intended to keep her satisfied indeed, and to the devil with his former ideas about keeping this a passionless union. To the devil with that book, too. Had she even read it? Her blushes suggested not. Confound it, he knew enough ways to pleasure a woman without becoming a contortionist!

So first he would tell her that he was finished with the princess. No, a gentleman did not discuss his affairs with a lady. He never apologized or explained his actions, either. He might try to become a good husband; he was not going to become a lapdog. Alissa was intelligent. She would figure it out when he spent the nights in her bed instead of out on the town.

Then he would show her what a good lover he could be.

No, first he would crawl through the keyhole of her door if he could not get Claymore to find him a key.

Crawling was not necessary. The door was unlocked. His privates rejoiced by standing to attention and leading the march into her room. By the light of a lamp left burning, Rockford could see that Alissa was asleep, looking far younger than usual with her light brown hair in a long braid atop the blankets, like cream in coffee. Her soft cheek was flushed with sleep and her eyelids showed the faintest of blue lines. Had he thought she was unremarkable, merely passably pretty? She was beautiful, except he couldn't see those glorious green eyes.

He bent to kiss her awake, like a sleeping princess — no, not that princess, by Harry! — when he noticed another brown-haired head on the pillow.

Damn. The littlest Henning was in his bed. Willy was in Alissa's bed, actually, but the brat was in Rockford's place, for certain. Not for long. The earl gathered up the sleeping child and headed out of the countess's chamber.

"Papa? Is that you?" Willy woke up and asked.

Rockford kept going, up the stairs to the nursery. He was not sure if Willy meant him or Henning, so he said, "Yes, it is your new father, and you are much too old to be sleeping in your mother's bed, young man."

"But I was afraid, Papa Rock."

"Silly gosling, there is nothing to be afraid of in Rothmore House. You must have had a bad dream."

"Will you stay with me until I fall asleep, to make sure?"

So the earl sat in the rocking chair in the nursery, Willy in his arms wrapped in a blanket. He rocked and he rocked, waiting for the boy to fall asleep so he could put him in his bed, then go put himself in Alissa's. Willy, wide-awake, told him all about the dead people, the one hanging by a rope, and the man with the dagger in his heart, and . . .

Perhaps the wax museum was not the right place to take the children after all.

Chapter Twenty-one

Almack's. Every maiden's dream. Every man's nightmare.

"I do not see why I have to go to that rubbishing place," Rockford complained to his aunt.

"Why, to lend your wife countenance, of course," Lady Winchwood replied, adjusting the feathers that graced her turban, along with a strand of pearls and a large sapphire.

It was a wonder the old girl could lift her head, Rockford thought as he made minor adjustments to his own apparel, the formal satin knee breeches demanded by the patronesses, the elegant dark coat and pristine white linens demanded by current fashion. "One dance, that is all." He could manage one country dance with his wife. It would be the first chance he'd get close to her, his aunt had kept her so busy. Alissa got in so late at night, she fell instantly asleep, and he had not the heart to awaken her. He'd been a faithful husband for almost a week now, and he wondered if she even noticed. Another week would kill him. Or he'd kill his aunt.

Aunt Reggie nodded, disordering his hair with an ostrich feather. "And one with Eleanor, of course, to show your faith and brotherly affection, lest anyone think you hold her to blame for your bailiff's chicanery."

Well, he did. Eleanor should have kept a better eye on things, and a wiser head on her shoulders. Still, that was water under the bridge. He could dance with his sister if Aunt Reggie deemed it necessary.

"And one with dear little Aminta, too. You would not wish any of the young bucks to think our darling Amy is unprotected, would you?"

"I should think my presence there would discourage anyone from getting forward with her."

"No, it must be a dance. You know, like male wolves leaving scent to mark their territory."

What did Aunt Reggie know about wolves? In a moment, Rockford would — No, he was a gentleman. He gritted his teeth.

"And I would not mind a turn about the floor with the handsomest gentleman in town," his aunt said, batting her darkened eyelashes.

"I doubt Prinny will attend."

She swatted his arm with her fan. "Four

dances, then you can disappear into the card room until we are ready to leave. I know the stakes are not what you are used to, but the money goes to a worthy cause."

"I did not know the winnings went to charity."

"Charity? Who said anything about that? I meant establishing your wife in society, seeing your sister's reputation restored."

Rockford reluctantly agreed to what promised to be the dullest night of his life. Staying home and playing skittles with the boys sounded more inviting. Hell, visiting the tooth drawer sounded more inviting.

Then he saw his ladies. Amy looked like a fragile spun-glass ornament in her white lace and frills. She could have borrowed a bit of rouge from his aunt to give color to her cheeks, but she was a beauty, if one admired that delicate sweetness. Eleanor was more Amazon than angel, her formidable figure showing to advantage in gold satin, with pearls woven through her dark hair. She had a militant glitter in her eyes, daring anyone to cast aspersions on her or on her sister-in-law, giving her a regal look, an air of substance that far overshadowed mere prettiness.

Alissa outshone them all. She'd outshine every woman at the deuced assembly, he thought, once he caught his breath.

She was wearing his rubies, nestled between her breasts. Oh, and she had on a new gown, too, he eventually noticed. Ivory velvet, it was, with a lace overskirt. A simple ribbon that matched the rubies held her hair back. Lud, he wanted to pull that ribbon away to see her hair flow down her back. He wanted —

He'd better stay in the ballroom to keep an eye on the rakes and reprobates.

Alissa almost stumbled down the steps of Rothmore House when she saw her husband waiting at the bottom. He was magnificent, and he was watching her with the look of a hungry lion. She was glad she had not listened to Aunt Reggie's opinion about her gown, not when he so obviously appreciated this one. Tonight, she vowed, tonight she would go to his room if he did not come to hers. She just had to get through this foolish ritual of Almack's; then she could concentrate on being a wife and a mother again, not on being the proper countess.

They were well received by the patronesses at the door, then took a row of seats along the edge of the dance floor. Soon Aunt Reggie was surrounded by her cronies, and a few very young gentlemen, pushed by their hopeful mothers, no doubt, came to stutter requests for a dance with Miss Aminta Bourke. No one else approached until Aunt Reggie hissed at Rockford to stop frowning. His dark scowl was frightening off any would-be partners for Eleanor or Alissa.

The ridge between his eyes deepened further, but then it was time for the first dance and he forgot his animosity toward anyone who dared look at his wife. She was his. She would not look at any other man, not his countess, not this lady. She smiled when they came together in the steps of the dance, smiled just to be in his arms. He smiled too, thinking of later, when she would be in his embrace from her head to her toes. That kiss she had bestowed on his cheek when they left the carriage, thanking him for the flowers he — or Claymore — had sent to each of the ladies had been a promise. Later.

Heads nodded knowingly to see the looks pass between the newlyweds.

"You could heat your morning chocolate by that look in Rockford's eyes," one old lady whispered loudly enough to be heard across the room.

Her companion merely fanned her suddenly hot cheeks.

He danced with Eleanor, keeping his smile firmly in place while Alissa partnered one of the high-ranking Austrians who had attended their dinner party. Then he danced with Aminta, who was looking paler, if possible.

"Smile, sweetings," he told her. "You will have every beau in the room calling on me in the morning to ask permission to pay their addresses. I'll refuse them all, until you tell me which one you prefer. All right?"

Amy managed a tremulous smile and went off with her next dance partner a bit more readily.

"Thank you," Alissa murmured. "For being so good to her. She will gain her confidence, I am certain."

Rockford was not as positive, noting how Amy kept her eyes on her feet instead of young Althorpe, and spoke not a word. His aunt, on the other hand, stepped on his feet during their dance, and never stopped talking.

"You see? I was right. The gels are a success, all of them. Now get off to the card room before you scare away any eligible gentlemen. I might join you in a bit, myself."

What, let his aunt fleece the dowagers at Almack's? That would go a far way to seeing them barred from society altogether. "No, I would feel better if you stayed to make introductions and such. Miss Bourke is not comfortable with so many strangers about, you know." In fact, she seemed near panic to him, but there was nothing more he could do to help.

Aunt Reggie clucked her tongue. "They won't be strangers long, I wager. Prettily behaved girl, and with your blunt behind her, we'll fire her off in no time."

"Not too soon," he warned. "I am in no hurry to see her go."

"You won't have the choice, Rock. Look at

the bantlings signing her dance card."

He looked at the older men ogling his wife, and decided he'd better take himself off to the card room while he still had a shred of his famous sangfroid left.

After Rockford left the ballroom, the evening turned flat for Alissa. Few new people approached her, and no one asked her to dance. Eleanor sat beside her, also partnerless, looking mutinous, as if she too would rather play for pennies than sit on the sidelines. Alissa frowned Rockford's sister into staying put. Then she noticed that the crowd of matrons around Aunt Reggie had thinned, and two of Amy's partners excused themselves before their promised dances. One claimed his mother was ill; the other said he had mistakenly promised the quadrille twice. Amy's next partner did not bother coming to offer an excuse. He simply did not come near them at all.

"Something is wrong," Lady Eleanor whispered to Alissa when the nearby wallflowers and their mothers got up and moved to other seats. "I'll go find Rockford."

"What, and leave me here facing all the stares?" Something was definitely amiss, for Alissa could feel all the malevolent gazes focused on her party, like a family of rabbits surrounded by a pack of wild dogs. She shuddered. "Send a footman."

Aunt Reggie got there first. Two spots of

rouge on her cheeks were all that remained of her color, and she looked far older than her years. Even her ostrich plumes were drooping forlornly as she sank into the now-vacant seat beside Alissa. "Someone is talking," she reported. "Saying the most awful things about us."

Alissa patted her hand. "Like what, Aunt Reggie?"

"They are saying that Eleanor is no better than she should be, that she ran off with a common thief."

"There was nothing common about Arkenstall," Eleanor declared, snapping the spokes of her fan.

"And . . . and that you, Alissa, dear, are less than a lady. That you trapped William Henning into marriage by getting with child, and then you did it again with Rockford, conveniently 'losing' the babe after he wed you. That's why he left you in the country, they are saying."

Alissa gasped. "Nothing like that ever happened. How could anyone say so?"

Aunt Reggie had to uncap her vinaigrette to go on. "There's more. The rumors are that our sweet Amy is for sale to the highest bidder, with or without a wedding ring. That Rockford is giving such a handsome dowry because he cannot promise her maidenhood."

Already as white as her gown, Amy silently

slumped back in her seat in a dead faint.

Alissa pried the vinaigrette from Lady Winchwood's trembling fingers. "How dare these awful people believe such vicious lies? And who could hate us so much that they would start them?"

"I think I know." Eleanor jumped to her feet, ready to do battle. She strode straight across the dance floor, not caring how many dance patterns she disrupted. She went right up to her quarry, where he was leaning against a pillar watching the activities, and poked him in the chest with the broken edges of her fan. "You maggot."

The Duke of Hysmith bowed. "Good evening to you, too, Lady Eleanor. I see you are your usual charming self."

Eleanor was so angry she could only hiss, "Bastard."

The duke polished his snuffbox against his sleeve. "I assure you my mother was a most circumspect lady, unlike others I could name."

She drew her arm back to slap him, but Hysmith caught her hand. "Remember where you are, my lady. You do not want to create a scene here, on top of all your other troubles."

"My troubles are thanks to you, Hysmith. No one else. But did you have to destroy Alissa and that sweet, innocent child, just to get back at Rockford and me?"

"I? You think I started the vile slander? Your low estimation of my character truly hurts more than any slap could."

"You did not start the rumors?"

"No. Come. They are starting a waltz."

"What? You are asking me to dance? Now?"

"No, I am telling you that you have to dance now, if you ever hope to lift your head in London again. Dancing with me might be a hardship, for which I apologize, but it is the only way you are going to scrape through this."

"You have a high opinion of your social credit, then."

"I have a higher title and deeper pockets than any man here. That is all that matters. Now smile, damn you, and act as if we are old friends."

Old friends? She'd threatened to emasculate him, and he'd left her standing at the altar. Just this week he had called her a strumpet, and she'd left a barely faded bruise on his chin. Cats and mice made better friends.

Yet the duke had stood against the tide of opinion to waltz with her, and he was an excellent dancer besides, and just the right height for Eleanor. She actually felt feminine in his sturdy clasp, so dredging forth a smile was not as hard as she had imagined, especially when she glimpsed the open mouths of the tattlemongers along the edges of the room. There she was, the outcast spinster, in the arms of the most eligible, most respectable man in all of London, waltzing. She laughed outright, bringing an answering smile to Hysmith's lips.

He twirled her in a dizzying circle. "I suppose it is fairly amusing, the two of us dancing in the sea of scandal again after all those years."

"No, that's not why I am laughing, although the astonished looks on the faces of the starched-up biddies who rule this place as if it were their own private island of morality are almost worth the cost. What's so funny, your grace, is that those petty despots in diamonds and lace never granted me permission to waltz!"

He laughed with her, their appreciation for the absurd foibles of society matching as well as their dance steps. Eleanor regretted the end of the music, but not that attention had been diverted from Alissa and poor Amy, who was recovered from her swoon, but now appeared near tears.

The duke returned Eleanor to her companions and said he would fetch Rockford for them. Equally amazed at his kindness as everyone else in the room, Alissa managed a heartfelt thank-you before he left. Perhaps there was a little of William Henning's sweetness in his elder brother after all.

★ ★ ★

Rockford was not as bored as he'd expected to be. At first he was busy accepting congratulations on his wedding — and on his choice of bride. Whoever thought he would be proud of a wife? A horse, naturally, but a wife?

Then, as the well-wishers faded away and most of the card players claimed they had to go perform duty dances, he was left with a half-deaf retired general for companion. Instead of listening to old General Cathcart refighting the India campaign, Rockford congratulated himself on his new secretary. Now here was a fellow who understood life-and-death matters. The new secretary had instantly recognized the importance of the message from Bow Street, and had sent a footman with it to Almack's. While the general droned on, Rockford planned his wife's seduction tonight, and Sir George Ganyon's destruction tomorrow. The baronet was in London, it seemed, staying in rooms at the Albany.

Rockford did not intend to leave his wife's bed too early in the morning, and he did not intend to leave that pond scum in England past noon. The future was looking bright, except for the large shadow that the Duke of Hysmith was casting across the deal table.

"If you are here to call me out for that blow to your chin," Rockford said, "you are wasting your time. Make an appointment with my new secretary and I will meet you at Gentleman Jackson's Boxing Parlor."

The duke leaned over — his corset creaking slightly — and whispered in Rockford's ear. He need not have bothered, for the general was too deaf to hear, and everyone else in the place knew the rumors.

"Bloody hell!" Rockford cursed, loudly enough to make the general frown.

"But we won the battle, I said," he said.

Rockford ignored him. "Ganyon."

"No, not a canyon. I told you, it was a mountain pass that day."

Rockford pushed away from the table, threw down his useless cards and a few coins, and headed toward the ballroom.

The duke kept pace with him. "You know who would slander your family this way, and he is still alive?"

"Not for long."

They had to go through the area set aside for refreshments before they reached the dance floor, and there he was. Speak of the devil; Sir George Ganyon was speaking to a fop in a puce waistcoat with shirt points so high he looked like a horse with blinkers on. The baronet was pouring spirits from a flask into the insipid punch served at Almack's, and laughing at something his companion said. He touched his cheek, where a row of half-healed scars ran the length of his face.

"This? Oh, I tried to pick up a wildcat, don't you know," he said with a wink and a snicker.

"That was no cat!" Rockford roared. "That was my wi—" He caught himself before he could plunge Alissa's name into another sordid story. "My sugar tongs, by Jupiter!" He shoved the tittering fop aside in his haste to get his hands around Sir George's chicken-wattle neck.

The duke stopped Rockford by grabbing his arm, and almost earned himself another livid bruise. "Think, man," he urged. "You can't kill him here. This is Almack's, confound it. Ladies present."

All the women had fled the refreshments room, shrieking. The gentlemen kept their distance, but some were placing bets on the forthcoming confrontation, whatever form it took. No one doubted, from Rockford's expression, that some kind of challenge was about to be issued.

"If he spread those lies, I will stand your second," the duke said, "but not here."

"I will not face that cur on the field of honor," Rockford swore, struggling to shake off Hysmith's grasp. "For that would give him the courtesy due a gentleman."

Sir George was grinning, a trickle of punch dribbling down his chin. He knew he was safe here in the cradle of civility. He also knew he had already had his revenge. He might be scarred for life, but that Henning bitch and her sister were ruined. And Rockford was stuck with both of them forever — and that shrewish sister of his, too. He laughed.

That drunken cackle was too much for Rockford. No one laughed in his face, especially not a midden worm in soiled linen, with three parallel claw marks down his cheek. He lunged, but Sir George sidestepped, holding up his glass of punch in salute.

Rockford was almost beyond reason now, but the duke managed to hold him back. "You cannot hit him here, by all that's holy!" his grace said. "Think of your wife, her sister and yours, man. They will be the butt of more gossip, not less."

Rockford thought of his gentle wife, his shy little sister-in-law, his freethinking sibling. Then he picked up the punch bowl and threw it at Sir George's head.

The patronesses were lined up by the door. "I am sorry, my lord," Sally Jersey said, "but you and your party will have to leave. Your vouchers have been recalled, at least until spring. We cannot have this kind of scene at Almack's, we who are supposed to be the shining stars of the social galaxy. We do have rules, you know."

Chapter Twenty-two

Rules? Rockford did not even know what game they were playing anymore.

He had neither committed murder nor issued an illegal challenge. Granted, Ganyon had slithered off before Rockford could do either of his first choices, but he had defended his wife's honor, a gentleman's right and duty.

Now he was barred from a place he never wished to visit, and a bedroom he wished very much to visit.

"How could you?" Alissa cried, guarding the door to her bedroom like Saint Peter at heaven's gate.

"How could I?" he shouted in frustration. "How could I not?"

"But at Almack's, of all places. You heard the ladies. Now we shall never be accepted!"

"Deuce take it, Alissa, a month ago you did not give a rap about Almack's or that other useless twaddle."

"A month ago I was not a countess. Now I am, and I do care about ruining your good name. I want to be worthy of my husband, not be a burden. I've already landed you with an entire family of castoffs. That's enough. I will not have you throwing fists and punch bowls at every insult. You will be thrown out of your clubs and the diplomatic corps and every respectable house." She sniffled. "I am going home."

"You cannot."

"Why?"

He had not thought that far, just that he did not want her to leave London. "Because, ah, because we do not know where Sir George is. The Runners lost his trail in the dark, and he was already gone from the Albany when they got there."

"It does not matter where he is. The damage is done. If he wishes to make further mischief he need only send letters. People here are willing to believe whatever pig slop is tossed their way."

"Not everyone. Hysmith stood by us."

"He stood by your sister for some reason. Perhaps he felt guilty for not standing by her at the altar all those years ago. He would have let me and Amy be tarred and feathered, though, right there at Almack's. And he has shown no interest whatsoever in meeting his nephews. So I am going home. The boys will have their ponies and their lessons and the dogs to run with. Amy will be happier, too. She hates it here, and I will never get her to go out in public again, not after to-night. One of the reasons I came to town in the first place was to find her a gentleman to wed, but the only man she met in London whom she talks to is the boys' tutor. So coming to the city did not get my sons recognized by their father's family, did not find a husband for my sister, and did not even keep Sir George Ganyon from bothering us."

"But you also wanted to conceive a daughter," the earl said, grasping for reasons to keep her here.

She had also wanted a marriage, but not at such a high price. Rockford could get killed in a duel, or get set upon some dark night. She would not put it past Sir George to hire thugs to satisfy the hurt to his pride caused by punch dripping down his balding head. She had to leave before Rockford was injured — and before she rushed into his arms begging him to go home with them. He would hate that, and hate her for causing him such bother in their marriage of convenience. Alissa could not bear the thought.

She shook her head. "I shall have grand-daughters someday."

Rockford hated to see her giving up on London, and on him, he feared. Where was the backbone he admired? Where was that courage that let her face down a duke? He could not let his brave Alissa scurry back to her mousehole, chastened and afraid. "No. I will not have you giving up yet. The *ton*'s opinion is as bendable as a reed, and I have yet to call on my resources. Tomorrow afternoon we will visit the regent. Prinny is not universally admired, but his influence is not to be discounted. My associates at the foreign office will stand firm too. And Aunt Reggie promised to call on Lady Bessborough and Princess Lieven, who were absent from Almack's tonight. We'll have royalty on our side, a cabinet minister or two, and a duke, if Hysmith does not back down. One punch-sodden baronet cannot stand against us."

Alissa was wavering, Rockford could tell. He pushed his advantage: "Besides, I promised Hugo a visit to the Kew Botanical Gardens. I have a friend who is a member and can get us passes. The boys have yet to see the Menagerie or the Tower of London or a balloon ascension or the maze at Richmond or —"

"All right," she said with a laugh. "You have convinced me. We will stay, but only for a few days more."

With such a great deal of ground to cover, Rockford had to start now. He bent to kiss his wife's satiny cheek — he did not trust himself further — and said he'd be off. "To my clubs, Alissa. Not to another party or ball." Not to Princess Helga, he tried to tell her without coming out and saying it, which would have broken all of his own private injunctions against petticoat governance. "Reputations are made at White's and Boodle's, not ladies' drawing rooms. You'll see. Sleep well, my dear. Tomorrow will be a busy day for both of us."

Tomorrow he would show her what an influential earl could do, what a good father he could be. Tomorrow night, he vowed, he would show her what she'd be missing if she left.

The clubs were full of talk, naturally, after the incident at Almack's. Interestingly, the Duke of Hysmith was before Rockford in defending Eleanor's actions and his former sister-in-law's character. She had been a true and loving wife to his brother William, his grace stated, and was a devoted mother to his nephews.

Rockford raised his brow, but gladly bought his grace a drink. Then he proceeded to blacken Sir George's name, implying that no gently bred female was safe from his foul grasp, no lady's name protected from his filth. Why, the bad-breathed baronet might pick on Lord Winstanley's daughter next, for her habit of disappearing at the various balls, or Sir Vivian's wife, who was used to riding unaccompanied in the park. If some dastard was intent on ruining a woman's reputation, the earl warned, no one was above reproach. Since neither of his examples was, in fact, innocent of misdeed, the message was well received. A gentlemen's agreement was silently reached. Silence would be maintained.

So Rockford's wife's good name would be restored, among the men, anyway. Lady Eleanor was once more considered an eccentric — nothing was going to change anyone's mind about that, not even Rockford's or the duke's minds — but nothing worse.

As for Miss Aminta Bourke, why, one look at the chit ought to prove her innocence. If it did not, Rockford vowed to darken the daylights of any man offering her an improper proposal. Not only was he not in a hurry to see the girl married off, but he intended to make a prospective bridegroom wait six months at least, to guarantee that Miss Bourke was sure of her choice. Fathers with marriageable daughters nodded their approval. Fathers with needy sons to settle were disappointed.

It was a good night's work, Rockford thought as he made his way home a few hours and a few clubs later. It was not the work he would have chosen, of course, but it was a start. By tomorrow night Ganyon would be found and dispensed with, and Lady Rockford would be firmly established in her rightful place, in the *ton* and in Lord Rockford's bed. Hallelujah!

★ ★ ★

The next day's rainy weather was not going to stop Rockford or the boys. He trudged along the botanical garden's damp paths with his heir, listening with pride to young Rothmore's learned conversation with the head groundskeeper. The other boys followed with the tutor, getting a quick lesson in horticulture, besides wet and muddy. Aminta had come along too, claiming a need to identify various species for when she became a governess.

"You are not going into service, dash it!"

Amy cringed at Lord Rockford's shout and stepped closer to Mr. Canover, but she raised her chin and looked at him with those clear green eyes, reminding the earl all too much of his stubborn wife. "I am not going to attend any more balls whose only purpose is to match a girl's dowry to some dunderhead who cannot earn his own living, when the other guests are not shredding someone's reputation. I am not on the marriage mart, my lord. And that is final."

Lud, Rockford felt old. Aminta was seventeen. What did she know about final? Rockford left his wife's sister with the tutor and the younger boys to watch his heir exclaim over some never-seen species or other. He brushed the drizzle off his beaver hat and tried to show a bit of enthusiasm for the greenery that all looked alike to his eyes.

When the rain came harder, and when William stuffed a flower in his pocket, they left, in a hurry. Rockford left a generous donation, in case the plant was some rare, exotic bloom. Devil take it, first they were exiled from Almack's, now they were in danger of being banned from the botanical gardens!

The Tower Menagerie had to be a safer bet — except for the giraffes William wanted to pet, and the lions in barred cages all too climbable for his simian son. Mr. Canover seemed unperturbed, but Rockford was in a sweat by the time they left the dank enclosure to go back out in the rain.

The boys would not believe the balloon ascension was canceled until they saw for themselves. Kendall picked up a fallen rope and struck up a conversation with one of the workers, who was kind enough to demonstrate the gas valves and the struts, and let the boys climb in the gondola.

By then they were thoroughly wet and filthy, and Rockford was too, from lifting the smaller boys in and out. He bought them all hot spiced cider, then had an idea so perfect, it ought to be in a gilt frame. "You, my lad," he said to Hugo, "are about to start learning the duties of an earl, which include paying morning calls in the early afternoon." He sent the younger boys and Aminta home in a hired hackney with Mr. Canover and his brother, while he followed Hugo up into his own carriage. "Lady Thurgood's house, Jake," he ordered. "Russell Square."

Elizabeth, Lady Thurgood, was one of the most fashionable hostesses in town. She was not as strict in her notions of propriety as the Almack's set, which made invitations to her parties even more coveted. Where she led, others would follow. The beautiful baroness had exquisite taste, a wealthy husband, and a generous nature. She had also been Hugo's mother's best friend, bridesmaid at Rockford's first wedding.

Lady Thurgood adored Hugo, as Rockford had hoped she would. She wept over the embarrassed boy, then embarrassed him worse by folding him against her breasts. Worst of all, she sent for her eight-year-old daughter to come meet the earl's son. The little girl had freckles and spectacles and carroty braids, but she batted her pale eyelashes at Hugo like a courtesan. Lud, Rockford thought, they must be born knowing how to flirt.

Lady Thurgood sent the youngsters to her conservatory, once she learned of Viscount Rothmore's interest in botany. Then she asked Rockford what she could do to help. He left with an invitation for Alissa and himself to share the Thurgood theater box that evening. Hugo left with a better understanding of what it meant to be a gentleman of privilege — and prospects.

Rockford was not finished. He took Hugo to Covent Garden to buy flowers for the ladies, including Lady Thurgood and her little girl, another important lesson for the boy.

Finally they went home, in time for Rockford to change his clothes for a visit to Carleton House to present his wife to Prince George.

The regent was at his most charming, his most gracious, and his most accommodating. After all, Rockford was one of the profligate prince's most forgiving lenders. To show his support, Prinny insisted on taking Rockford's new countess for a turn in the park in his coach, now, at the fashionable hour. Let everyone see that Lady Rockford was a favorite of the Crown; then let them try to exclude her from their midst.

Rockford decided to ride alongside the prince's open carriage, in case his hedonistic highness became too accommodating.

So the polite world saw the scandal-plagued countess courted by royalty, while her obviously besotted husband glowered jealously at her side. That night they saw her embraced by Lady Thurgood, and her box visited by two Almack's patronesses, six high-ranking members of Parliament, and countless gentlemen . . . while her husband glowered jealously at her side.

Who was that lying Sir George Ganyon chap anyway, and why was he invited anywhere? He never would be again, that was for certain. Why, everyone could see this was a love match, a bit unconventional, perhaps, but not beyond the pale. Lady Rockford would do well in her new role.

And Lady Rockford would do well in her husband's arms that night, the earl vowed to himself.

"Oh, my," Alissa said, halfway between a purr and a sigh. "I see you really did read that book."

Rockford stopped what he was doing, eliciting a mewl of complaint, and laughed. "No, I am writing a book of my own, dedicated to you." His fingers went back to inscribing desire from her head to her toes, with exclamation points at the sensitive spot behind her knees, the ticklish area under her ribs, the tips of her breasts, and the tops of her thighs. He explored every crease, every fold, every texture, like a cartographer mapping new worlds. His long, heated kisses were complete volumes, and Alissa was lost in the literature of his lovemaking.

"But aren't you going to . . . you know?" she asked.

Rockford laughed again, a rumble that vibrated against her bare skin. "You can bet the Rothmore rubies that I am going to . . . you know. But not yet, Countess. Tonight is for you, first."

First? She was already on fire, the kindling laid by his request to join her this evening, then fanned by his undressing her, taking her hair out of its nighttime braid and spreading the long length of it across the pillow. The blaze took hold when he lay beside her, flesh against flesh. He was all muscle and strength, yet tender and gentle, understanding just where to touch her to send the flames higher, first with his knowing fingers, then with his kisses and his tongue. He kept moving, though, shifting his interest, changing the rhythms, exploring and worshiping a different part of her body before allowing the fire to consume her.

The whole while he kept murmuring sweet words of love, words that were more arousing, even, than his kisses. Alissa almost believed them. Goodness, she thought she might believe anything the man said to her now, and she desperately wanted to believe he wanted her. Half the words might be true. Maybe a quarter of them. Oh, let him mean one or two endearments, she prayed while he stirred a conflagration in her blood. If she had not fallen completely and hopelessly in love with Rockford when he and Hugo carried in armfuls of flowers, grinning together like schoolboys, she did now. She was irredeemably in love and desperate to tell her translator husband in a language she thought he would understand.

"Now, Robert. Come to me now."

"Not yet, my love." He took her higher and higher, until she almost feared falling off the ladder he was building for her to climb, rung by rung by rung. Then came the moment when nothing existed except him, his hand, his mouth, his warm, damp skin against hers, all one sensation, all one fire. One all-consuming pyre.

"Oh, Robert." There was nothing else to say as she slowly drifted down from the heights. "Oh, Robert."

He held her and softly kissed her cheek, then pulled away, brushing at the dampness that he found there. "What's this, my love? Tears? Did I skip a page?" he teased, knowing full well she had found pleasure.

"They are tears of happiness, Robert. It had been so long, I thought I would never feel this way again. And I don't think I ever felt so . . . so . . ."

"Not even with . . . ?" He dared to hope, hating the idea of William Henning in his bed.

She shook her head, no. "That was different. This was . . ." She had no words to describe it, but Rockford understood.

He'd never felt such intense urgency before either. He'd never had to hold himself back, at such effort, never with either of his wives, never with any of his mistresses. But seeing Alissa lost in passion, feeling her shudders, knowing he was the world's greatest lover, at that moment, with this one woman he desired above all others . . . why, that was almost ecstasy enough.

Almost.

Rockford was going to expire soon if he could not find his own release in Alissa's welcoming warmth. Either that or he would impregnate her sheets.

He kissed her again, then said, "If chapter one brings forth tears, I cannot wait to see the result of chapter two."

This time her body responded instantly to his touch and she arched against him, moaning his name.

"Yes, my love," he said between gasps, rising above her. "Now." Their bodies, slick with perspiration, slid against each other. "Now. I need to be inside you now or surely I am going to die."

He was going to die.

"Mama." Kendall's voice followed a hesitant scratch on the bedroom door. "Hugo is sick. I think you had better come."

Chapter Twenty-three

"He's going to die. I know it."

"Do not be ridiculous," Alissa told her husband, wringing out another damp cloth to place over Hugo's forehead. "Our son is not going to die. I will not let him."

"You could not keep your husband from dying," Rockford insisted, staring down at the slight, still form of his eldest boy, his heir.

"Hugo has a mere recurring congestion and fever. My husband had a sore throat that turned putrid, and his lungs filled. And you called in the best Harley Street physician, one who has trained in Edinburgh. We had naught but the local sawbones, who physicked cows when he was not trimming hair. You have a shelf full of medications, while we had only willow bark tea and leeches."

"Lud, you won't let them bleed the boy, will you?"

"Of course not. I stopped when I saw how the letting was weakening my husband, instead of causing healthier blood to flow. Who knows but the leeches contributed to his death. Hugo is not nearly as sick."

"His grandparents warned me Hugo could go off at any time."

"His grandparents were fools who kept the poor boy on a short leash because it suited them. You saw how he has thrived since coming to us. And you must stop speaking like that. He can hear you."

Rockford shook his head. "The doctor said Hugo was out of his mind with the fever."

"I do not believe that. He squeezed my hand when I told him how much I love him, and he asked for his puppy before we gave him that last dose of medicine. It is the laudanum that is keeping him asleep, not the fever. Your physician thinks rest is the best thing for him, and fluid. Now hold him up while I see if I can get him to sip the barley water."

Rockford despaired when more got on his sleeve than down the boy's throat. "It is all my fault."

"What, that he is too sleepy to drink? We will try again in a few minutes."

"No, that he is so ill, that I did not let you take him back to the country when you wanted."

"What, in a cold and drafty carriage, stopping at indifferent inns? That would have been dreadful for him if he were coming down with an ague or something. And what would I have done with him without you to send for the physicians, to stir the kitchens to prepare invalid food, to keep the other children away before they also took ill?"

"But I dragged him all over town today in the cold rain, never once thinking that he might take a chill. I should have remembered how weak he is."

"Hugo is *not* weak. All children suffer contagions and disease. It is part of childhood. Even you and Eleanor must have had the measles or the sniffles when you were children. It happens."

He could not recall being sick, never so ill that he was kept drugged and confined. "I should have taken better care of him. I am his father, by heaven. I should not have let this happen to him."

"And how would you have stopped it? I ask. Despite your high opinion of your own value, you are only his father, not God. And you saw him when you got back with all those flowers. He was beaming as never before. He told us all that this had been the best day of his entire life."

"But it could be his last!"

She almost threw the bowl of water at Rockford. "Leave at once if you feel that way. I will not have Hugo hearing your doomsaying. He might think it true."

Rockford would not go. Alissa was capable and loving, but Hugo was his son, for all the good he could do. He took the damp cloth from her hand and swabbed at Hugo's face the way he had seen her do. "Still, I should have waited for better weather to take him to the gardens."

"And disappointed him past bearing? Stop blaming yourself, Robert. Blame me for bringing him to London, then. Or blame me for threatening to take him away before you had a chance to make up for all the years you did not have together. If you must feel guilty over something, feel remorse that you did not give him a hundred such wonderful days filled with his favorite things, including his father's attention. Feel sorry for yourself that you missed your brilliant child's early years. But rejoice in how many more glorious times you will have with Hugo, as soon as he is back on his feet. You will be a magnificent father, my lord, once you realize you do not have to accomplish everything in a day or a week."

"I am not a patient man."

"But you can be." Her blush told him she was remembering their own time together that night. "And you will be."

He had no choice but to be patient for his wife and his son, but how was he to get through the wait?

By staying at Hugo's bedside through the night and the next morning. If Alissa thought Hugo could hear him, Rockford would tell the boy to be strong, that they both had so much to learn, that he would try to be a better father than his own absent, uncaring sire had been. Just in case Hugo was bored with the repetition, the earl spoke his words in every language he thought the boy knew, and some he did not yet. Things he had never said to anyone, ever, were important to say now, lest he never get the chance. He would think about telling some of them to his wife later.

Finally Alissa made him go to sleep, so that he could relieve her in the afternoon for a much-needed rest of her own. After that they took turns at the bedside, pouring lemonade and honeyed tea and barley water and beef broth into Hugo when he was awake, cooling him with damp cloths when the fever climbed higher.

Rockford rigged a coal brazier and a tent of sheets to make steam when the physician thought the moist air would help keep Hugo's lungs clear. He saw the anguish on Alissa's face when the doctor said that, wondering if such a simple thing might have saved her husband.

But then, had Henning lived, she would not be here with him, Rockford thought, jealous again of a dead man. She would not be helping with his son, and helping him keep from going mad with worry. She never complained, never let the maids or the physician's nurses take over the sickroom, believing that Hugo should see a familiar face whenever he awoke, hers or his father's. She never fretted about her appearance or her comfort as she sat in the chair at Hugo's bedside, her brown hair curling around her face from the humid air in the room. She never looked more beautiful, or more appealing . . . for the brief moments he saw her as they changed shifts every couple of hours.

Alissa spent whatever time she could spare with the other boys and Amy, who had been banned from the sickroom. She also spent a few minutes praying each time she reached her bed, before falling into an exhausted sleep. Despite her assurances to Rockford, she was concerned about Hugo. He was not getting worse, but neither was he improving, so she prayed for his recovery. And for her husband. If anything happened to the boy, Rockford would never forgive himself. He would go back to being the coldhearted man she first met, the one who armored his heart in ice to keep from being wounded. He would blame himself, and then he would blame her, even if he never said so.

All he had wanted was a mother for his sons so he did not have to worry over them. She was already a failure by his standards, to say nothing of how many of his rules she had broken by coming to town, by demanding his protection and his fidelity and his lovemaking. Now he was so worried over Hugo that Alissa barely existed for him. He spoke only to the boy, in languages she could not understand. With his silence to her, she had to stop believing those tender words he'd whispered in her ear, no matter how much she wanted them to be true. Everyone knew a man would perjure his soul for sex. Oh, she understood Rockford was attracted to her, possessive of her. He'd sent a Bow Street Runner to Rock Hill to watch for Sir George Ganyon's return, hadn't he? But did Rockford feel more for her? Did he feel enough to build a relationship? He did not say and she could not ask. Those were rules of his that she would not dare break.

Alissa prayed, for all of them.

Mr. Canover and his brother did their best to keep the other boys from fretting or getting underfoot. They took them and the pups to the nearby park, kept up the riding instruction, and visited historical, educational sites, after formal lessons in the nursery schoolroom.

Aminta refused to pay morning calls with Aunt Reggie or to go shopping with Lady Eleanor, so she helped with the children, as she had always done. She'd much rather visit the Tower of London than another highborn hostess, and she had more clothes than she'd possessed in all of the years of her life combined. Claymore made sure the young miss had a maid in attendance when she went out, for her reputation, and Jake made sure a strong groom accompanied her, for her protection.

Aunt Reggie stopped arguing, seeing that the girl was not comfortable out in society and did not shine there. She would find a nice, quiet young man to marry in her own time, the older woman conceded.

If left to her own devices, Lady Eleanor would never marry. Just look at the last man she had chosen, a bailiff and a thief! Before that, she had done something so awful that a duke broke half the tenets of polite society to jilt her. Lady Winchwood, with her three husbands, could not be satisfied to leave it at that. No, she was a firm believer in the institution of marriage for everyone, especially females without income or residences of their own.

"No, you cannot stay home," she told Eleanor. "People will think you are hiding. We have accomplished too much this past week to let it all go for naught now. Your reputation wears the thinnest layer of respectability, so you cannot afford to let it tarnish in storage. We have to represent Alissa, too, so no one forgets that she is acting just as she ought. Let them know how she and Rockford are caring for poor Hugo."

"No one will believe Rockford is sitting at

a child's bedside," Lady Eleanor responded. "I have a hard time believing it myself."

"If they can believe you went chasing after Arkenstall to recover your brother's artwork, they can believe anything, even the truth. Now put on something pretty, for we are going to a ball. I have a good mind to look over the gentlemen myself. No sense in letting an opportunity like this slip."

So Lady Eleanor Rothmore once again entered the social world, with more trepidation, but also more success. Lady Thurgood, especially, befriended her, eager for news of Hugo, whom she had selected as a future son-in-law. When other matrons came by the seats Aunt Regina had claimed, happy to discuss their own children's illnesses, Eleanor was wise enough to hide her complete uninterest in the topic. A few of Rockford's diplomatic cronies practiced their diplomacy by asking her to dance, or to stroll about the perimeters of the ballroom. Lady Eleanor was not precisely a middle-aged belle, but neither was she a faded wallflower, not in burnt-orange silk. Having seen that her charge was occupied enough, Lady Winchwood had found some elderly gentlemen to play cards with. If she could not coax a proposal out of one of the old dears, she could at least relieve them of a few pounds.

Two more dances, Eleanor decided, then she would collect her aunt and go home. Her head hurt from the weight of the jeweled turban Aunt Reggie had insisted she wear; her feet hurt from the too-small shoes selected to make her seem less of an Amazon; her mouth hurt from maintaining the artificial smile. She had done enough to keep her own reputation intact, and Alissa's shining from all the praise of her devotion to Rockford and his son.

She accepted Viscount Montmorency as a partner for the next set, a reed-thin gentleman of sixty summers. Eleanor asked to visit the refreshments room instead of taking her place in the Scottish reel, for if she was not too old to be kicking up her heels, and her sore toes, with the schoolroom chits making their come-outs, Lord Montmorency certainly was. Eleanor could imagine the gossip if her partner keeled over during their dance.

The viscount handed her a glass of champagne and proceeded to bore her with tales of his aches and his ailments. No wonder the man had never married, Eleanor thought as she idly surveyed the room over the rim of her glass; he wanted a nursemaid, not a wife.

Then her eye caught a familiar figure. The Duke of Hysmith nodded to her as he continued to chat with Lady Hargreave, a widow reputed to be in need of a wealthy husband to pull her and her gambling debts out of River Tick. Eleanor wondered if Hysmith knew the gossip, and if he cared to be viewed as a banker instead of a beau.

He must have, for he left the widow's side as soon as the orchestra stopped playing, to walk in Eleanor's direction. No, she was in front of the champagne table, Eleanor told herself, that was all.

"I think the waltz is next," his grace said, holding out his arm. "My dance, I believe, Lady Eleanor."

It was no such thing, but she could not say so in front of Lord Montmorency, so she tipped her head slightly — any more and the blasted turban would have slipped over her ear — and placed her hand on his well-cut coatsleeve.

Silently they walked to the ballroom and took their places when the music began. Silently they danced, knowing that every eye in the place was on them. When a duke danced with an earl's daughter, no matter their ages, people took note. When a widowed noble waltzed with the woman he had condemned to spinsterhood, a slightly shady spinster at that, the rumormongers started salivating.

Finally Eleanor asked, "Why?"

He did not miss a step. "Because you are the right height for me and won't bore me with tedious small talk."

She raised the Rothmore eyebrow. "Not out of kindness or sympathy, like at Almack's?"

"Humph. I could have sent flowers. Besides, the tongues would have tattled more if I had ignored you."

She waited for another few turns, enjoying the feel of his solid, only slightly overweight body guiding hers. "Why do you come to these affairs, Duke, if you find the talk as boring as I do?"

"Have you never been lonely?" he asked.

Oh, she had been lonely. "Of course. That's why I fell for — That is, I would never have come to London with Alissa otherwise."

"So you are looking for a husband?"

"Heavens, I never said that! What, at my age?"

"Your aunt Winchwood never gives up."

Eleanor did not wish to discuss her marital prospects, nor her aunt's. "No, I am merely in town to support my brother and his new wife, to relieve the tedium of the countryside, you understand. Adventures are few and far between at home," she lied, regretting her last not-so-grand adventure more every day. "But what of you, your grace? Are you looking for a new wife?"

He smiled then, a pleasant smile, Eleanor thought, if a bit rueful. "A rich man does not have to go looking, you know. The prospects keep cropping up like toadstools. A wealthy man can find hopeful ladies falling off their horses in the park, dropping their handkerchiefs in the streets, swooning into his arms at balls."

"I do not swoon."

"Were we speaking of you, my lady?"

Eleanor coughed, and hoped he did not notice the color tingeing her warm cheeks. "Of course not."

He noticed, and suggested they walk a bit on the balcony when the dance ended, to cool off.

"Are you not promised for the next dance?" Eleanor asked.

He simply tucked her arm in his elbow and headed toward the glass doors at the far end of the ballroom. He stopped a waiter to relieve the fellow of two glasses of wine before they reached the balcony, where Chinese lanterns had been strung to light the way. "Is it too cold?" Hysmith asked, ready to turn back.

"We cannot stay long, not without damaging your reputation too, but anything is better than that overheated ballroom," she said, sipping at her wine as she leaned against the balustrade. "And tonight one can see the stars for once. I have missed that, in the city."

Hysmith leaned too, or as far as his corset permitted. He watched her instead of the sky. "You are still a devilishly handsome woman, Lady Eleanor. I always thought so. Still do."

Compliments, from the duke? "How kind, your grace."

He sighed. "You used to call me Morton."

"We used to be engaged."

He sighed again, more heavily. "I do not suppose you can ever forgive me for that, can you? I would like to be your friend, if you could."

Hysmith, her friend? That would be harder to believe than Rockford's reformation. She started to shake her head, having to reach up to adjust the dratted turban, but then asked, "Why?"

"Why do I wish to be your friend? I always liked you, for one thing, right from the cradle, I suppose." Which was when and where they had been affianced. "I liked how you always spoke your mind and never suffered fools easily."

"Then why did you not marry me?"

"Because you always spoke your mind, and never suffered fools easily, I suppose. I was a great gawk as a youth, wasn't I?"

"You were charming. I thought . . ."

"Yes?"

"Nothing." She finished the wine in her glass and wrapped her arms about herself. The cold was starting to seep through the thin fabric of her gown, but she did not wish to go inside yet. Hysmith was easy to talk to now, in the dark, staring up at the stars. "You did not believe my threats to, ah, dismember you, did you?"

"Of course not. Although you might have

tried. I would not have put that past you, even now."

"Then I suppose I will never understand how you could have been so cruel."

"Cruel?" He was honestly surprised. "I was saving you from marrying a man you disliked. Your parents would have forced you to go through with the ceremony, no matter what you said."

"But I never disliked you."

"You did not trust me, which came to the same thing."

"How could I trust you? You flirted with every girl in town. You kept opera dancers and actresses. I knew about that little house in Kensington."

He stepped closer, putting his arm around her shoulders. "For warmth," he said when she started. Then he asked, "Do you think Lady Rockford can ever trust your brother? He was seeing that Austrian princess even after their marriage."

"I do not know. I cannot speak for Alissa, but she seems to have a more forgiving nature, thank goodness. I would always wonder, and worry."

"That's what I meant. I was just a youth, sowing my wild oats during our engagement. I intended to be a faithful husband, to respect the vows I spoke before God and my family. But you would never have believed that. You would have doubted every word I said, every move I made, thinking I was a hardened philanderer. That was no basis for a marriage, but you would have been forced to it, I knew. So I left, giving us both time to mature. I never took another mistress for the next year, never had even a casual fling with a willing barmaid, you know, to prove to you that I could be true to my vows. I wrote to tell you, but my letters came back unopened."

"I never knew what they said."

"How could you, stubborn wench, without reading them? I did try to visit, but was turned away on your orders. Eventually I realized you would never relent. I had the succession to ensure, my family to appease. So I took the bride they selected for me. And I was a faithful husband to her, for all the years we had. They were good years, too, for she was a fine woman, and a beloved friend."

"I am sorry." Eleanor was sorry Hysmith's wife had died, sorry she had been too obstinate to read his letters, sorry for the mess she had made of her entire life.

"So am I," the duke said, turning her to face him so he could look into her eyes. "So am I, my love."

His love?

Chapter Twenty-four

The entire house was in a state of impending doom.

Rockford had never known such despair as he suffered that week, and, already exhausted, Alissa could only weep as her worst fears came true.

Billy had come down with the same illness as Hugo.

The physician declined to repeat his first visit. The nursemaid quit. Two footmen disappeared without bothering to give notice. Aunt Reggie took to her bed, and Claymore took to drinking Rockford's brandy.

Young Rothmore, Billy to his stepfamily, William to his father, the spawn of Satan to nearly everyone else, refused to stay in bed. He would not take his medicine, would not keep his covers on, would not eat invalid food. He spit up and sat up and would not shut up, all day, all night.

He wanted his new mother, then he wanted his old nanny. He wanted his father, his aunt, and the mother he had never known. He wanted his puppy, and all the other boys' puppies. He wanted to go home, out to the park, or back to the circus. He was hot, he was cold.

He was having the time of his life.

No one else was.

Alissa was run ragged, trying to see to both sick boys and the rest of her household, while Rockford did his best to assist her. His best was playing chess with Hugo, who was much improved. His worst was shouting at Billy to act like a proper young gentleman instead of a monkey, at which his son started sobbing hysterically, until Rockford promised to buy him a monkey. The earl shouted at everyone else then, because he had no intention of honoring such a promise and was furious he had lied to his own flesh and blood. His new secretary resigned.

The Henning boys, who might have been able to help entertain Billy, were not permitted in the room, lest they be stricken. Likewise Aminta and Mr. Lucius Canover, who had to stay healthy to look after Willy and Kendall. Mr. Lawrence Canover was being sent back to his school outside Oxford despite his broken arm. If he was able to pinch the housemaids' bottoms, Rockford reasoned, he was fit enough for his studies. He was to be put aboard a hired coach in two days, before the earl broke his other arm for tormenting the servants.

Lady Eleanor offered to help, for a price. She had developed a sudden interest in her wardrobe, without the wherewithal to make the needed improvements. The earl had never really spoken to her about her part in Arkenstall's thievery, and she had never mentioned the allowance that was stopped when she ran off or her dower money that was never paid out. Alissa had simply added Lady Eleanor's expenses to her own accounts, but Lady Rockford was not going shopping these days. Nor was she going out in public, to need new clothes. Eleanor was.

She hated to ask her brother for money now, when her foolishness had already cost him so much, but she had no choice. He might come out ahead in the long run, anyway, if this investment paid off. "I'll sit with Hugo in the afternoons while Alissa rests, Rock, if you will let me set up an account at Madame Monique's."

"Hell, if you'll sit with Billy — that is, William — for an hour a day, I'll buy you the shop."

Lady Eleanor threatened to tie her younger nephew to the bedpost and read to him from the fashion journals unless he stayed in bed, and Billy had no reason to doubt this aunt who had run away adventuring. Why, there was nothing his aunt Eleanor wouldn't do, including showing him how to load a pistol and how to spit raisins across the room.

They had a great time cutting Rockford's cravats into new sails for Billy's wooden boat, too, and using Alissa's charcoal pencils to draw a lovely mural on the wall.

Kendall and Willy were not having half so much fun. Four untrained dogs were a lot of work, for one thing, and so were four ponies to exercise and groom. They could not go sightseeing, having to wait for the others, but still had to do their lessons. Even when they did get to go out, Mr. Canover seemed much more interested in conversing with Aunt Amy than with the boys. And Willy missed his mother.

One rainy afternoon when the boys were supposed to be working at their sums they grew too bored to keep at it without Mr. Canover's supervision. Aminta and the tutor were in the library, supposedly looking at his research papers. He'd likely forget all about their assignment anyway, the way he recently did when Aunt Amy was around. Their mother was playing jackstraws with Hugo and Billy.

"Do you think she likes them better'n us?" Willy asked, putting down his chalk and shoving his practice slate to the side.

Kendall did not have to ask who *they* were. He did have to consider his answer for a minute. "No, I don't think so," he eventually decided. "Not really. They're just sick, and she doesn't want them to die, like Papa."

Willy barely recalled the man who had sired him, or his illness. "Papa Rock likes them better."

"Well, he is their father, their real father, not pretend like he is to us. And Hugo's the heir. Noblemen put a lot of stock in that, Jake says. Like keeping track of a racehorse's pedigree."

"He yelled at me to get out of the nursery. And to leave Mama alone so she could rest." Willy crumpled up the page of his mathematics assignment and threw it across the floor. "I was just going to show her my new tooth."

"You should have heard what he said to me the night I came to get Mama when Hugo got so sick. She would have washed my mouth out with soap for half of it. Mama didn't even yell at him."

"And Aunt Eleanor is never home anymore, except to play with Billy in the morning."

"She's not really our aunt anyway."

"Aunt Reggie cheats at cards."

"I know, but she says a gentleman never squeals."

"It's a good thing she's not our real aunt either." Willy had to take the paper out of a puppy's mouth. He found a ball and started throwing it for the dogs.

They took turns tossing the ball until the little dogs decided they'd rather wrestle among themselves, leaving the boys out of that game, too.

Willy stayed sitting on the floor, rolling the ball between his knees. "I want to go home, Ken."

Kendall was staring out the window, where cold rain poured down on the nearby park. "What, to that old cottage? It's not ours anymore, and I don't care if we ever go back to it."

"No, to Rock Hill. Mama said that is our home now. No one yelled at us there, and Mama had time to tell stories."

"But Mama has to stay here, to take care of everybody."

Willy started kicking at the leg of his desk. One of the puppies came over and started chewing on his stocking. Another started gnawing on the chair leg. "The dogs could play outside at Rock Hill without having to be on leashes."

Kendall rescued his brother's chalk from another dog. "Jake built a run, just for them."

"And we could play outside at Rock Hill without having to tell anyone but Claymore."

"Claymore has to stay here, too. You heard Mama say she could not manage without him."

"But she took away the earl's decanters. I saw her do it."

Kendall shook his head. "Claymore would

never leave here. He has the key to the wine cellar, and he likes being butler with all those footmen to boss around. He likes going to his pub to tell the other butlers that Prince George himself sent a set of toy soldiers."

"To Hugo and Billy," Willy added morosely.

Kendall went on, explaining why two young boys could not simply decide to go home. "Rock Hill is almost empty now. Mrs. Cabot is away visiting her sister, and Cook went to Bath on holiday, so there's no one but the grooms and gardeners to take care of the place. They'd never let us stay there on our own."

They both thought about that for a while.

Kendall opened a book of maps, pointing to the north of England. " 'Sides, it's too far away."

"But I don't like it here. And I miss Rosie."

"And the donkey," Kendall added.

"No one would miss us," Willy said with a quaver in his voice. "Not even our own mama."

"Don't you start sniveling, now," his older brother warned. "Rockford says only babies cry, and silly girls."

"I bet Papa Ro—" Willy thought better of that and changed it to "Rockford would be happy if we left."

Kendall nodded. "Then he wouldn't have

to pay extra. Mama said we must not be a burden on the earl, remember? That's why she went to the duke, so he'd pay for our lessons."

"Do you think he'd want us?"

"The duke? He hates us worst of all. Remember how Mama cried after she visited his house?"

"And Pa— Rockford called him a jackass."

"Aunt Eleanor says he's not so bad anymore."

"But she liked Mr. Arkenstall."

That ended all consideration of Henning House as a refuge.

Willy was not satisfied. "But we're only in the way here. Everyone thinks so, even Claymore. It wasn't my fault the dogs got in the kitchen and ate all the breakfast sausages. I only wanted one."

"But we have nowhere to go, Willy. We have no relatives of our own."

"We have cousins. Mama said so. Why, the duke must be old now. When he dies, our oldest cousin will be his grace. Maybe he'll pay for our school so Mama won't have to work so hard taking care of Hugo and Billy."

Kendall considered the notion. "I bet the duke's sons have big allowances."

"And I wager they keep them, too, 'cause they never play cards with Aunt Reggie. And Mama did say she wanted us to get to know our own kin, remember? When Hugo and

Billy are well enough we might go home finally, so we'll never get another chance to meet them."

Kendall turned the page of his map book. "But they are not in London. They go to school at Oxford, don't they?"

And wasn't that right where Mr. Canover's brother was going in a hired carriage?

The day the tutor's brother was leaving, Lady Rockford took an early breakfast with her sons.

"Can't you play with us, just this one morning?" Willy asked when she hurried through her chocolate and toast, after an all-night stint in the sickroom.

Alissa was exhausted from another bout of Billy's antics. She never saw her sister or her husband, spent mere minutes with her sons, and rarely slept in her own bed. She had constant headaches and was losing weight from such irregular, hurried meals.

"You know she cannot, Will." The earl had entered the breakfast parlor to have a cup of coffee. He was exhausted and irritable too, after losing a chess match to Hugo. He had nothing to look forward to but more humiliation and more time in the nursery instead of at his usual pastimes. The pastime he would have made a habit, visiting his wife's bedchamber, was out of the question while she looked so worn and weary. She was seldom there, besides. So he was frustrated, beyond fatigue, and feeling guilty that his sons were so demanding. The last thing Alissa needed was more claims on her time. "Your mother needs her rest, William. Now stop being a complainer, when you are the healthy one."

Alissa set down her cup. "Willy was not complaining, Robert. He merely wishes my company after so long a time."

"He is a big boy now. You baby him."

"I do not promise him pet monkeys!"

Rockford knew he was in the wrong but could not admit it, not in front of the Henning boys and Claymore. "William was sick."

"Not that sick. What would you do if he were truly ill? Promise him a unicorn with a golden antler?"

"I will speak to William. He is a reasonable lad." He ignored the snort from his butler. "He'll understand we cannot have simians in the city."

"So he will expect one when I take him home to the country? That makes me the ogre for refusing him, my lord. What a joyous homecoming that will be after an arduous journey, as trips with your son always are."

"What, are you blaming the child for suffering motion sickness? Perhaps you think it his fault that he came down with this disease?"

"If he had listened, like my sons, and not sneaked into the sickroom every chance he could, he might have been spared."

"I suppose that is my fault too?"

"Oh, stubble it, Rockford. I suppose I should not use such cant terms, but I am too tired to care. The boys are recovering and that is all that matters. I shall not argue with you. In fact, why do you not go for a ride? You need to get out, and I am certain your horses need the exercise. Hugo is content with his books and Billy is finally asleep, with one of the maids at his bedside. I intend to rest myself while Willy and Ken are at lessons. Perhaps we can all take tea together this afternoon, or go to the park?"

Rockford leaped at the chance to get out of the house. He kissed his wife's cheek, not daring more in front of the children and the butler, and left, giving the Henning boys a cursory nod.

Alissa touched the top of Kendall's head and rubbed her hand across Willy's cheek. "I'll see you later. Be good."

Instead of going to her bedroom, Alissa decided to peek in on Billy, just to be sure. The maid was in tears, the chamber pot was in pieces, and Billy was in his altogether, dancing on top of the bed.

"Stop that this instant!" Alissa yelled, stamping her foot for emphasis. "You will not act like a barbarian in my house, and that is

369

final, do you hear? I have had enough. The servants have had enough. More than enough. I have given up my sleep, deprived my children of my attention and my husband of my — Never mind, but you, sir, are a spoiled, impossible little brat. And that will stop."

"My papa won't let you send me away."

"Your father would be the first to pack your bags! Why, in any other household you would be birched for such behavior. If your father knew anything of young boys he would have seen to the matter, instead of letting you run all of us ragged. If Mr. Canover were not such a mild gentleman, I would ask him to spank you soundly."

That got Billy's attention. "You wouldn't ask Jake, would you? He's got arms like tree trunks."

"I will think about it. Meantime, you will clean up this mess. And you will entertain yourself for the morning. Heaven knows you have books and toys aplenty. No one is going to come in here until midday, no one at all, no puppy, no Aunt Eleanor to encourage your naughtiness, no one. So you can cry and throw things to your heart's content, but you shall not rule this house. No more. If you carry on, if you refuse your nuncheon, refuse your medicine or your bath, then you shall have no more stories, no more games with your father, no more special treats from the kitchen. You will sit here alone until kingdom come, or Jake. Do you understand?"

"Huzzah, madam," the maid cheered, until Alissa glared her out of the room.

"Do you understand?" she repeated.

Billy nodded, tears in his eyes. Alissa had to harden her heart to keep from scooping him into her arms. He would never learn that way. "Good. I shall see you this afternoon, dressed and fed and rested, ready to join us downstairs for tea if you have no fever."

"Will my monkey be there?"

Alissa went to her room, satisfied that Billy would be a better man, and that she would survive his boyhood. She thought she would rest for an hour or two, then join her own sons at their riding lesson and perhaps take them to Gunter's. The poor boys had been left in the care of Mr. Canover long enough. As soon as her head hit the pillow, however, she fell into a deep, long sleep.

Mr. Canover, when he returned from seeing his brother off, could not find his charges. Claymore said the earl had gone riding, so the tutor assumed Lord Rockford had taken the Henning boys along with him. He sought out Miss Bourke for a pleasant conversation in the schoolroom, during which very few words were spoken.

Finding Billy's door locked, with the footman on duty outside refusing entrance,

Lady Eleanor happily took herself off to the shops. She was accompanied by Aunt Reggie, who was restored to good health by the thought of matchmaking again.

Lord Rockford came back from his ride invigorated and ready to take on his younger son. When he heard about Alissa's edict, he was relieved enough to take on his elder son at chess again. He won, but not easily.

Alissa was still sleeping, and the boys must be at lessons, he assumed, so he stayed to have his midday meal with Hugo. Then he took a well-deserved nap while Hugo dozed off.

They both awakened feeling more the thing, and hungry. "Tea in the drawing room, my boy," Rockford announced, carefully watching Hugo on the stairs lest his steps were unsteady. He sent a footman up to the nursery to fetch the Henning boys.

Mr. Canover came down. "I thought the boys were with you, my lord, out riding. I have not seen them since after breakfast."

"Damn, they must have gone into the countess's room after all, when I specifically told them not to bother her."

Aminta said no one had answered at the countess's chamber when she knocked.

Rockford went up and stepped through the adjoining door, only to find Alissa sprawled on her bed, in her gown, fast asleep.

He backed out and tried Billy's room, but

his youngest son was also sleeping. So were the puppies, in the nursery. He sent footmen to the stable mews, to the garden, to the park across the street. Lady Eleanor and Aunt Reggie returned, without the boys. Claymore shook his head, and Aminta started crying.

There was nothing for the earl to do but awaken Alissa and ask where her boys had gone.

"Gone?"

Chapter Twenty-five

"You've lost my children?"

"I did not lose them. I never had them. I thought they were here in the schoolroom, or with you."

"After you barked at them to leave me alone? They would not dare." Alissa was hurriedly pinning up her hair again, after splashing her face with the cool water from the jug on her nightstand. "And they are good boys, anyway."

"Unlike my son, you mean? At least he never ran off."

"Hah. How do you think I acquired him?"

"By marrying me, that is how. Now stop acting like a fishwife and tell me where they would go, so I can fetch them back before it grows dark."

Alissa ran to the window. The autumn sun was already lowering. "But I don't know. Do you think Sir George has them?"

"What would Ganyon want with your sons?"

"To hold them for ransom? Or for revenge?

I don't know. You said yourself that he was deranged."

Rockford had already sent a message to Bow Street, but he did not want to worry Alissa worse. "Someone would have seen him. No one noticed the boys talking to anyone or getting into a carriage."

"Not even Claymore? He always knows where everyone is."

"Claymore was, ah, replenishing the wine supplies from the cellar."

"You mean he was drunk, while my babies were being abducted?"

"They were not abducted! Stop working yourself into a frenzy. They must have gone visiting or something."

"Are the dogs here?"

He hated to say it, but he had to tell her that yes, the puppies were all accounted for. The boys were not merely out walking their pets, forgetting the time. Their ponies were in their stalls, and Jake had not seen the Henning boys since before breakfast.

"Then they have been kidnapped. I knew I should never have brought them to this evil place!"

He put his hands on her shoulders and gently squeezed them, staring into the depths of her worried green eyes. "Alissa, please do not do this. We will find the boys." Then he would have them shipped to the antipodes. "I promise."

She rested her cheek briefly on his chest, borrowing his strength. "But you promised Billy a monkey too."

Lud, he regretted that ridiculous vow, almost as much as he regretted snapping at the Henning boys this morning. They had only wished to spend time with their mother, and he could not fault them for that. Heaven knew he wanted to lock the bedroom door and listen to her calling his name at the height of her passion for the next twenty-four hours. Or the next twenty-four days. Twenty-four years might satisfy the craving he felt for this woman he had married so conveniently.

He had to put such thoughts out of his mind, or as far away as they would go, with her in his arms. "Come, we will check the cellars and attics and gardens again. We'll go ask all the servants and the neighbors, the stables and the crossing sweeps. They cannot simply have disappeared off the face of the earth. This is London, where nothing goes unnoticed. Someone is bound to have an idea where they could have gone."

When the search proved futile, the family gathered again in the morning room. Blame flew like arrows in a Robin Hood tale.

Claymore was ready to retire. He was too old for his position, he claimed. His eyesight was too poor if he could miss the boys leaving the house.

"The old fool wouldn't miss half of what

went on if he stopped looking at the bottom of the glass," Rockford muttered while Alissa reassured the butler that he was not responsible, that he was, in fact, invaluable.

"I could have been more helpful, I suppose," Lady Eleanor admitted. "I never thought they would like to go to Bond Street with me."

Silent in the air was the notion that she could have gone elsewhere for once, somewhere young boys might enjoy, but Rockford's scowl said enough.

"I did not notice you offering to take them riding with you this morning," Lady Eleanor answered her brother's frown with scorn of her own. She saw no reason why she should bear the entire brunt of the guilt by neglect.

Lady Winchwood clutched her glass of restorative in both shaking hands. "I shouldn't have taken their last pennies. Then they might have kept playing cards with me, and not been so restless."

"You stole their allowance money?" Rockford poured himself a glass of wine, and one for Alissa. Dash it, how far could the boys get with no money? Kendall was too intelligent and thoughtful a lad to go off without fares or money for food. Which meant they might have been abducted after all. He set the glass down, deciding that he needed all of his senses unimpaired, and said, "Aunt Reggie, they are small boys. You should find yourself a new husband if you want to cheat someone."

"This is no time for sarcasm, my boy," she answered, taking up his discarded glass. It was the perfect time, it seemed, for getting castaway.

"Don't blame Aunt Reggie," Aminta wailed. "I should have been watching them. That's all you've ever asked of me, Lissie, and you have given me so much."

Mr. Canover handed Miss Bourke his handkerchief. "No, it was my job to supervise the children." He stood and addressed Lord Rockford. "I shall hand in my resignation in the morning, my lord. I will understand if you do not feel you can supply references, for I have failed in my duties."

He had, and he was lucky Rockford was not a vindictive man or Canover would be out on the street before he could tender that resignation. The earl was about to nod his acceptance of the tutor's departure when Aminta wailed louder.

"You cannot let him leave, Lissie. Don't let Rockford make Lucius go. He is the only man I will ever love."

Claymore dropped the plate of biscuits he was handing around. Alissa was speechless, while Lady Winchwood set down her wineglass — Rockford's wineglass — long enough to clap her hands.

"You love the tutor?" Rockford drew out

his quizzing glass to inspect his sons' teacher, for perhaps the first time. He could not remember noticing the fellow much before, except the time Canover had patently admired Alissa's bosom, or was that the randy younger brother? Now he saw a slight young man with a weak chin, not quite compensated for by heavy eyeglasses and hair that was longer than fashion dictated. His coat was of quality fabric, but frayed at the cuffs, and his cravat was neatly if inelegantly tied. His complexion was pasty, as if he did not see the light of day too often — or he had something to feel guilty about. Rockford did not think that something was merely dereliction of his duties, not the way sweet, innocent Amy was blushing. Good grief, the tutor could end up being his brother-in-law!

Alissa had the same thought, and was not well pleased. Lucius Canover was an unassuming, intelligent, pleasant man, but she had wanted something more for her sister than a poor scholar, and Amy had not yet begun to test the waters of the matrimonial sea. "We shall speak of that later, and of Mr. Canover's resignation. Now we have to consider the children. Mr. Canover, do you think they might have gone off with your brother?"

"Why would they do such a thing? And why would Lawrence allow it? He was going to stay with some friends instead of the dormitory." He gave a guilty look toward Lord

Rockford, for letting him think Lawrence was going back to his studies, which were so close to the end of the term his attendance was useless. "The boys would have been decidedly *de trop*."

Rockford could well imagine what the young Romeo had in mind, which was why he had written to the headmaster of his school, to be on the watch for young Canover.

The tutor was going on, lest anyone think his brother might have resorted to holding the boys for ransom, rather than return to his studies. "Furthermore, I placed the hamper of food from the kitchen in the coach myself. I certainly would have noticed the lads then." He shook his head. "No one was inside but my brother."

"I was not doubting your sibling, Mr. Canover. It was just a thought," Alissa said. Now she had no others.

Lady Eleanor did. She jumped up and said, "I know where they could have gone. I'd be willing to wager they went to Henning House to see the duke."

"How much would you bet?" Aunt Reggie wanted to know.

But Rockford asked, "Why would you think that?"

Alissa added, "You know he refused to acknowledge them."

Eleanor was not quite sure why the boys

might have gone there, but it seemed a reasonable assumption to her anyway. Hysmith was such a calm, capable fellow, she thought he could help. His sons were grown, so he had ample knowledge of boyish pranks. And it was a good excuse to call on him.

"Come, Aunt Reggie," she said, dragging her aunt out of the room before anyone could stop her. "We will go ask if his grace knows anything about the boys."

Alissa was thinking. "I did tell them that I wished they could meet their father's brother. Perhaps they did go there."

Rockford doubted it. They had been gone too long. "Hysmith would have sent them home with a flea in their ear. He would not have kept them, not without sending word to us. No one could be that cruel."

"But where else could they be?"

Rockford did not know. He was ready to fly off into the night, as soon as he knew which direction to take. His horse was saddled, his pistol was packed, but he could do nothing until one of his messengers came back saying the children had been sighted somewhere. He had never known such frustration.

Alissa was weeping, besides, blaming herself for ignoring her sons' needs. Her muffled cries tore at Rockford's heart until he wanted to rip it out and hand it to her. The blasted thing was doing him no good, anyway. Neither would it have brought her sons back, though.

Damn, it was all his fault.

Hugo thought it was his, for being such a bother and a weakling and a bad brother to the Hennings, requiring so much of their mother's time. They couldn't go places because of him, had not seen half the sights, waiting for him to recover. He could understand their boredom and their upset, but he had no idea where they would have gone.

"Unless they went back to Rock Hill," he suggested. "They liked it there, knowing all the villagers and the tenants and the children," he added with a wistful tone that did not go unheard by his father.

"We will return there soon. You'll get to make friends in the neighborhood too." Rockford sent another rider to Rock Hill, although he doubted the boys would have set out for there without funds. He would have someone check the toll roads heading in that direction, anyway, in case a drayman or a delivery driver picked them up. In fact, Rockford decided, he would go himself, rather than spend the rest of the night sitting at home doing nothing but worrying.

"Here," Alissa said, handing him her locket, opened to show facing miniature portraits of her sons. "You can show this to people, to ask if they have seen Kendall or Willy."

"Excellent." And better that it was not a picture of her dead husband that she wore constantly next to her heart. "I'll stop off at Bow Street first to show the picture, but I'll leave the rest of my route with Jake, so you can find me if they come home before I do, or if Eleanor learns anything at the duke's. Otherwise, I will return as soon as I have news. Try not to worry, my dear. I know that is easier said than done, but we will have them back soon."

Alissa did not want him to go. How could she get through the night without his comfort, his confidence? She knew she had to stay behind, but her sons were out in the dark, in an unfamiliar city. And her sister was crying in the tutor's arms. "Aminta, please go to check the attics again. Mr. Canover, you and Claymore can search the cellars. Perhaps they found an old priest's hole or something and are trapped behind the walls. They have to be here." Or else she would lose her mind. "I'll wait here until Lady Eleanor returns, making more sketches of the boys to show around tomorrow." Her voice caught on a sob. "In case they are not found before."

She had time for a lot of portraits before her sister-in-law came home. In fact, she was so impatient she began to wonder if the Duke of Hysmith was swallowing up her family, person by person. If Lady Eleanor did not return soon, Alissa decided, she would send Mr. Canover. If he disappeared . . . Well, a sister could hope.

"Deuce take it, woman, do you never have a care for your reputation?" The duke hauled Eleanor into his book room before any of the servants saw her. His disapproving butler had let her in, of course, but the man valued his position too highly to carry tales. "Coming alone to an unmarried man's home at night is tantamount to declaring your lack of morals, if not your lack of sense."

Eleanor was looking around. She particularly admired the painting hanging over Hysmith's desk of him on a dark horse. Rockford's masterpieces were all well and good, but here was art a person could truly enjoy. The horse looked good too.

When his grace finished his ranting, she made little of his concerns. "My recently acquired good name is safe," she said, "because Aunt Reggie is outside in the coach. She had a shade too much restorative, I assume, although what she hoped to restore by downing half a decanter of Rockford's best brandy I cannot imagine. That is not to the point. Your fusty old rules do not apply in the face of such an emergency. Your nephews have gone missing."

"And so have your wits. My brother's sons are in Yorkshire, precisely where they belong.

I had a letter yesterday."

"My wits gone begging? You must have lost your understanding when your hair fell out. Do not be obtuse. You know I mean your brother William's children. They are not at home. Have you seen them?"

The duke reached a hand up to make sure the long strands of hair still covered his bald spot before he said, "I believe I saw your stepnephews in the park once with a pack of dogs. Mongrels."

"The puppies might be. The Henning boys are not. They are fine children, which you could see for yourself if you were not so pigheaded."

"Pigheaded, is it? What do you call yourself, rushing off on some fool's mission that can see you ostracized from polite society again? A messenger could have sufficed."

"I call myself a concerned relative, despite having no blood relation to the Henning children, unlike some others I could mention, who will not get off their fat —"

"Very well. You have come to ask. Lady Rockford's sons are not here. They have never been here, and, with luck, they shall never be here in the future. Now may I show you to the door?"

Eleanor was not ready to leave. "Why do you dislike them so much, without knowing them?"

"I do not dislike them. I simply choose not

to accept anything to do with my unfortunate brother, who broke our mother's heart, or the woman who trapped him into the marriage that caused such a rift in my family. I should think you would feel the same, since the wench snared your brother, too."

"Wench? Snared? You make it sound as though my brother — or yours — is a rabbit, caught unawares. I cannot speak for Henning, of course, but Rockford is top over tails for Alissa, although I doubt if he is entirely aware of the depth of his current state. Why, anyone seeing them together could recognize a love match, and a well-deserved one, I swear. Lady Rockford is everything I would wish for in a wife for my brother, unlike those ninnies he married before. She cares for people, Duke, she truly cares. How many highborn ladies with perfect reputations can you say the same about?"

"Not many," he was forced to admit. Most fashionable females, and a lot of men, cared for nothing but their own pleasure.

"Dashed few, I'd wager. Why, Alissa has worn herself out tending to Rockford's sick sons. Who knows what would have become of Hugo without her devotion. And Billy . . . Well, someone would have strangled the little blighter by now if not for her. And she has worked wonders on my brother. She might even make him human one of these days. Your brother might have married beneath him — I never knew William Henning, so cannot say — but my brother the earl wed far above him, and I thank God for that."

"Very well, you have convinced me. Lady Rockford is a paragon. Where have you looked?"

"For the boys?"

"Of course for the boys. That's what you came for, is it not, to enlist my aid in finding the little devils?"

"I never thought . . . That is, thank you. And I am sure Rockford will thank you, and Alissa will also, of course."

The duke touched his jaw, where Rockford had left such a bruise. "I am not doing this for Rockford, nor for his lady."

"Well, the boys will thank —"

"Now who is being obtuse?"

Chapter Twenty-six

"I am afraid you will have to be more specific." And Eleanor was afraid to get her hopes up.

The duke was uncomfortable, despite not wearing a corset tonight. He had not been expecting to go out so his coat was left unbuttoned, making room for his more than plentiful dinner. He tried to hold in his less than flat stomach, then gave up and took a deep breath. "Dash it, Eleanor, it is you I'd be helping. The boys are . . . well, boys. They are always getting up to some prank or other, no matter that it gives their parents palpitations. They'll be waiting at home now, mark my words, looking as innocent as cherubs. Which is not to say we don't have to go looking."

"We?"

She was back to that. The duke tugged at his cravat. "Rockford won't have much experience with the sprigs. Stands to reason. He hasn't been their father all that long. Have to be firm with them, don't you know."

"We?" she repeated, tapping her foot impatiently.

He cleared his throat. The dratted female was worse than a dog with a bone. She was never going to give this one up. "Don't like to see you worried, you know. Always been, ah, fond of you."

"But ours was an arranged match. We were promised from the cradle, nearly."

The knot of his neckcloth came undone from his pulling. "Bother, now if anyone sees me, they'll think that we . . . that I . . ."

Eleanor would not think about what anyone would think. She had enough trouble thinking about her nephews, instead of how very welcoming his grace appeared now that he was not so stiff and starched. She wondered what it would feel like to rest her head on the soft middle of him, like a pillow. She wondered if he would mind that her own attributes were not all they had been when she was a girl, nor in the same place. "Wasn't it? Wasn't it an arranged match?"

"Neither one of us had to go through with the engagement. Nothing formalized until then, you know. The parents would have been disappointed, but nothing more. I asked you, recall, if you truly wanted to marry me, or if your family was pushing you into the match. You said it was your choice. That I was your choice."

Having a formal betrothal, with announcements in the newspapers and balls in their honor, had not kept him from missing their wedding day, so Eleanor supposed he could have refused their parents' projected union, just as she could have turned down his proposal. "You really wanted to marry me?"

"I did not want a wife who accepted me for my prospects or to please her family. I wanted a willing bride, not a woman who disliked me and distrusted me, and who would be miserable in the marriage."

Eleanor ignored most of his statement, to pick out the important parts. "I did not dislike you. I was afraid."

"You? Bah. You have never been afraid of anything in your life."

She stared at the painting of him as a young man, a dashing, devil-may-care youth. "I was afraid you would love one of your inamoratas, not me."

"What a rare mess we made of things, eh?" He came closer and took her hand in his, patting it. "I could not recall a single one of their names, they mattered so little. I never forgot about you."

Eleanor turned to face him, studying the changes time had wrought on his still-handsome face. "And I never stopped missing you."

"What about that bailiff fellow?"

"I already forgot his name. What about your wife?"

"Claudia was a good woman. Why, she never once threatened to leave me singing soprano. Never hit me a blow Gentleman Jackson would applaud. Never had me making a spectacle of myself at Almack's. She was not you, Ellie, my girl."

"I am no longer a girl, Morton."

He smiled. "You always were my girl."

"And now?"

He studied their joined hands, then brought hers up toward his mouth. "I am a creature of habit, not a here-and-thereian. I have always loved you, you know."

"And?"

"And I suppose I will love you forever."

Lord Rockford was having a lot less luck than his sister. Bow Street had no news of the Hennings or Sir George. The coaching inns recalled no boys who matched the locket portraits, although one ostler did remember seeing a youth in the coach Rockford had hired for Canover's brother. The young man had used the necessary, then ordered an ale, and a second. He drank them both, then left.

Most of the stable hands were abed this late in the evening and were no help, no matter how much the earl was willing to pay for information. No message waited for him at any of his stops, telling him the children had come home, and now he had exhausted all of his possibilities and his horse, too.

They would have received a ransom note by now if foul play was involved, he thought. He calculated how much money he could get his hands on immediately, just in case, how much he might have to borrow from the bank until he could sell off some investments. He loathed the idea of paying a felon to return what should not have been taken, rewarding knavery, but he'd do whatever he had to, for Alissa. He hated to go home to tell her of his failure, so he stopped for an ale himself, thinking.

If they were not abducted from the middle of Mayfair, which he truly doubted, then the boys had to be somewhere nearby. He thought of shy little Will and grave Kendall, lost in London, and had a hard time swallowing past the lump in his throat. They had backbone, though, he consoled himself, just like their mother. Their father must have had bottom, too, to break all of society's rules to wed against his family's wishes. To wed Alissa, Rockford's countess.

The man's sacrifice was worth it, Rockford decided, although Henning might have felt otherwise, disinherited and possibly dying for lack of proper medical assistance. But Alissa was worth five of any woman Henning's parents might have chosen for him. Lud knew she was worth more than both of Rockford's deceased wives combined. Oh, not in the monies and the lands they brought to the marriage, but in everything else that counted. Those first two matches of his had been safe, expected, practical, suitable, laudable — and disastrous.

Rockford had not intended to sacrifice anything by wedding Mrs. Henning, certainly not his social standing. A wife took her status from her husband, and his was secure enough. Besides, his countess belonged in the beau monde. She was a true gentlewoman, a lady. One had only to speak with her to know she would be a jeweled ornament of polite society, if she cared to join those hallowed ranks. He would not lose a single invitation on her account.

He had not had to give up the approval of anyone who mattered to him, for few people did. He had no one to answer to, no parent to be disappointed. His sister did not count, for her opinions would always be colored — and discredited — by her own conduct. So what had he sacrificed by marriage to the impoverished neighboring widow?

A mistress he did not want in the first place and a diplomatic career that he did not enjoy or respect.

The peace and quiet of his formally elegant but formerly lifeless residence.

And his soul.

He was a changed man, the earl acknowledged, without the distress the acknowledgment or the change should have caused. He who had vowed never to put himself under a woman's thumb was so firmly in Alissa's grasp that he no longer bothered to squirm. Before, his own convenience was all. Now all he wanted was to please his wife. And pleasure her. And be with her, be part of her world, part of her.

Was this love, the kind of love Henning felt for Alissa? Rockford had no idea, never having experienced that tender emotion, not since suffering calf-love in his school days for the French teacher's willing wife. If love meant having his pulse pound at the sight of her, racing from his head to his heart to his — No, that was lust. He could recognize that affliction easily enough. Having his guts gather into knots when a woman was near, though, and when she was not near, but merely in his thoughts, that was something unfamiliar to him. Why, just the womanly scent of her or the sound of her voice sent him reeling. The recollection of that one memorable night made him break out in a sweat.

Having any woman on his mind for more than a week was a new experience, but Alissa was in his thoughts constantly, which meant that his mental state was as chaotic as his house had become, as disordered as his wardrobe, and as unruly as his arousals — no, that was lust again — as unruly as his children.

He thought that might just be love, although why those old troubadours felt it was so marvelous he could not understand. He was wretched. His wife might be growing comfortable with him, perhaps even fond of him, and she had certainly enjoyed his love-making, but that did not mean she ached to be with him, not the way he wanted her more than his next breath. Or was that lust, still? No. He would move mountains for Alissa. Big ones. With a small shovel. That had to be love.

Rockford had no idea what Alissa thought of him. Likely as nothing more than a way out of poverty, a protector and a provider, with a little bed sport thrown in as a bonus. Botheration.

He had one more glass of ale before he had to go tell her he could not find her sons. Move mountains? Hell, he could not even move her boys home.

As he sipped his ale, putting off the dreaded task, he tried to cheer himself with the notion that maybe this turmoil he was suffering was temporary, a mere infatuation, as he'd occasionally felt for a new mistress at first. It would fade quickly, especially if Alissa did not return his regard. Regard, hell. He'd likely become a drunken sot if she could not love him.

He set the glass down. He was the Earl of Rockford, not some puling poet. This romantic nonsense would not last. Soon enough he could go back to enjoying other females and his well-ordered, reasonable existence.

Or else he would love her forever.

"These will be an enormous help, ma'am," the Bow Street inspector said after he paged through the stack of portraits Lady Rockford had done of her sons while she waited for someone to bring them back. There were pencil drawings, charcoal sketches, even a colored pastel picture so the searchers could recognize the missing children's skin tones. Inwardly the Runner groaned, for this meant he'd have to go back to all of his usual sources of information, and his feet were already aching from the afternoon's hunt for a hint of the Henning boys' whereabouts.

His lordship was paying more than enough for a few blisters. The Runner and his fellow Red Breasts were tripping over each other to earn the generous wages the earl was paying, and to win the promised reward. Now the officer could see why the earl was being so openhanded. Lord Rockford was wealthy enough, to judge from the town house that was as big as the block the man from Bow Street lived on. Furthermore, the earl's new wife, the mother of the missing boys, was worth every shilling Rockford had to lay out. As pleasant as she was pretty, she even invited her unexpected and unequal guest to join her in the parlor, and then to have a seat. He lowered his old bones into the soft chair with a sigh of pleasure, at which the countess rang for refreshments, for him, who was nothing but an arthritic old thief-taker near to retirement. Then she offered to do a sketch of him while they waited for the tea.

Not many other ladies would treat a Runner as well, so he did not mention the tears that were falling on his portrait. He said, "I'll bring the pictures of the boys back to Bow Street so the other chaps can take a look and then show them around. We'll have every innkeeper and street vendor on the alert, and every cutpurse and criminal too. We'll get your sons back."

"Thank you. I know you are trying."

"Those gallows-baits will likely be bringing you every half-starved wharf rat, street urchin from the Rookeries, or filthy chimney sweep they can find, come morning. As if you couldn't recognize your own sons, or might want to add a few of the ragamuffins. It's the reward, of course."

Alissa nodded, dropping another tear onto the drawing page. "I'll tell the kitchens to be prepared. At least we can feed those children." She had to stop to blow her nose, thinking of her own boys going hungry somewhere. Then she tore the sheet off her pad and handed the Runner his portrait.

"That's me, to the life! Why, you even got that scar when Two-fingered Harry bit my ear."

"I'm sorry it is a bit waterstained, but your wife might like it anyway."

"She's been gone these many years, may she rest in peace."

"I'm sorry. But perhaps a lady friend . . ."

The officer shook his head. "No, but my sons might like it, so they can show their own sons what their old grandfather looked like. You see, I have boys too. They're all grown now, but they'll always be boys in my mind. I can see you feel the same way. But don't worry, my lady. We'll keep looking, even if it takes forever."

When the Runner left, and no word had come from either Rockford or Lady Eleanor, Alissa had nothing to do, no occupation to keep her busy. She could not keep her thoughts from dwelling on the dire fates her sons might face, and on why her husband had not returned. He had to know she was on tenterhooks, anxious for news. So where was he, and what if he ran afoul of some of the scoundrels the Runner had mentioned? Or what if he decided that her sons were not so important after all, and had stopped his search?

Rather than fill her head with one disastrous scene after another, Alissa decided to go up to the nursery to check on her other sons.

She told Aminta, "Hugo will ruin his eyesight worse, reading all day and night. Billy was sleeping during tea, so now he must be wondering where everyone has gone."

Billy knew where everyone was, he said, once Alissa apologized for neglecting him and gathered him and a blanket onto her lap in the rocking chair. He knew because he was watching from the window all day, except when he was sleeping, of course. The servants chased each other through the gated garden, and Papa rode off up the street at a gallop, and that funny old man limped away down the street to hire a hackney, and Aunt Eleanor pulled Aunt Reggie into the carriage just to drive around the square, and Willy and Ken climbed into the boot of the coach taking Mr. Canover's brother Lawrence back to Oxford because he pinched the maid's bottom.

"Why do you think he did that?"

"They left after breakfast, with Mr. Lawrence Canover?" Now it was dark, and they had been gone so long. Alissa was horrified, but she was relieved, too. The boys had not been kidnapped, not stolen away from her by white slavers or Gypsies or Sir George Ganyon. They'd gone on their own, but Lawrence would look after them once he discovered their presence, unless he became distracted by some tavern wench.

Alissa was relieved, too, now that she knew where Willy and Ken were going. The only reason that she could think of for their flight to Oxford was that they might be trying to find their Henning cousins there, likely because she had spoken so often of the importance of family. Their own family, Rockford, Amy, and herself, had all been too busy for the boys.

Billy wiggled closer. "Why are you crying? The maid Lawrence pinched wasn't crying. She laughed. Mr. Claymore was the one who got mad and told Papa."

"No, dear, I am not weeping over the maid or Mr. Canover. But why did you not tell me about Willy and Ken going away? You had to know they were not supposed to leave the house on their own without permission."

"You mean I should have peached on them like Mr. Claymore did to Lawrence?" He jumped off her lap and stood in his nightshirt, fists clenched, offended that she would think so poorly of his honor.

"But they could be in danger or lost. They must be hungry."

He could not decide if that changed the rules about tattling. Then he remembered that it had not been his decision to make anyway. "But you locked me in here and told me I couldn't talk to anyone, remember?"

The morning seemed an eternity away to

Alissa, but she did recall leaving Billy on his own. "Yes, and I am so sorry I did. Can you forgive me?"

Billy came closer to her rocking chair, rubbing his bare feet together until she leaned over and wrapped the blanket around him again, then pulled him back to her side. "I s'pose," he answered. "Are you mad at me again?"

"No, I am not mad at you. At Willy and Ken, maybe, for worrying me so."

"But you still love them?"

"I will always love them."

"And me?" he asked with hope in his voice.

"I will always love you too, and Hugo. Forever. Do you still love me?"

He threw his arms around her neck and kissed her cheek, a loud, wet kiss. "I will love you forever too. What about Papa?"

"Oh, he will love you forever also."

"No, I mean do you love him? For forever?"

Chapter Twenty-seven

How long was forever?

Alissa was halfway to loving her husband until her dying breath, if not beyond. Now that Robert had shown a father's affection for her boys and a lover's attention to herself, she was almost ready to give her heart entirely into his keeping, as she had her life.

Almost.

If he wanted it.

Rockford had made no secret of the fact that he wished no emotional attachments whatsoever. Of course, Alissa knew that not even the Earl of Rockford could control where his passions led, but she had no doubt he would try. How hard he would try was the question. If he never grew to love her, never let his own feelings get tangled in Cupid's net, then he would never be the rock she needed to anchor her own love. Forever would be only until he took his next mistress.

Meantime, she had to find her sons.

She tucked Billy back in his bed and kissed

him good night, happy to note that his skin felt cool, his fever entirely gone. "I will not be here tomorrow night unless the boys return before then, so here is another kiss to hold you until I come home."

She did the same to Hugo, to his embarrassment. He too felt cool, so she could leave Rockford's boys with the tutor without worrying about either of them. She could not, however, go away and not worry about leaving her sister behind, with the tutor.

"Shouldn't we wait for morning?" Aminta asked as she watched Alissa throw a nightgown and a hairbrush and a fresh gown into a satchel.

"The hired carriage has too long a start for us to ever think of catching up to them before Oxford, despite Rockford's best team, but I do not wish to lose the boys at the university. If their cousins do not take them in, heaven alone knows what will become of them, or how they will get home. I have to be there as soon as possible." Alissa packed her late husband's pistol, too, just in case. Two women traveling alone at night, in a coach with a crest on the door, were an easy target. She took off her jewelry, except for her wedding ring.

Seeing the pistol, Aminta paled. "We ought to wait for Rockford, at least."

"No, he might stay out all night looking. Claymore can tell him where we are headed and he can meet us in Oxford if he wishes. Although it might be better for the boys if he does not encounter them so soon."

Aminta lost more color. "He will be very angry, won't he?"

"You are right." Alissa took out the flannel nightgown and traded it for a nearly transparent silk peignoir set that Aunt Reggie had given her as a wedding present. "If this does not take Rockford's mind off thrashing the boys, nothing will."

Now color flooded her sister's cheeks as Amy left to pack a valise for herself.

Claymore also urged the countess to wait for dawn or the earl, whichever came first, and she heeded him as little as she had Aminta. She had to go. They had to understand nothing else mattered but her sons.

Shortly after they left, Lady Eleanor and Aunt Reggie came home, with the duke as escort. Aunt Reggie called for a celebratory brandy on hearing that the boys were located, if not recovered. Lady Eleanor insisted she had to chase after Alissa. The countess could not be allowed to journey through the night with no one but her young sister for company and old Jake on the driver's box.

The duke, naturally, could not let Eleanor go on her own. Besides, the Henning boys were most likely going to see his own sons, according to Claymore's interpretation of Lady Rockford's best guess. His grace had to be there to make sure Rockford did not wreak havoc on any Hennings for this misadventure. They would take his phaeton, which would be much faster. With the moon out and unobscured by clouds, they ought to catch up with Lady Rockford well before she reached the university town. Especially, Lady Eleanor claimed, since she could spell his grace at the ribbons.

An unwed female and a widower duke driving through the night in an open carriage? Aunt Reggie swooned again.

As soon as the duke left to fetch his rig, Claymore whispered, "Will you not reconsider, my lady? Or take a maid along? Think of your reputation." He whispered in case there were any servants left who did not know about all these comings and goings. Perhaps the scullery maid did not know by now that Lady Eleanor had gone off to visit the duke. Claymore did not hold out much hope of being heeded, for none of the butler's admonitions had ever carried any weight with the earl's sister. Loyal Claymore had been whispering until he was hoarse the day she carried out her elopement with Arkenstall. He could have saved his breath now, too.

"Too late," Eleanor called back as she ran up the steps to gather what she might need for a short stay from home. "When Aunt Reggie awakened in the coach outside

Henning House, she set up a screeching that alerted the entire neighborhood. At least a score of servants, and one retired general brandishing his saber, raced into the house. At the time I was not precisely dressed to deliver my urgent message about the boys."

"Heavens!" Claymore declared.

Lady Eleanor smiled. "Yes, it was."

Lord Rockford came home a brief time later. The air in the hallway of his town house turned smoky with curses. He kicked at the ugly umbrella stand that replaced his prize Oriental urn, succeeding in ruining his new boots, if not relieving some of his frustration. "Damn it, could no one wait for me? The boys are my wards, aren't they? By Jupiter, Alissa is my wife, and I should have gone instead. She took her sister? The one who weeps at a raised voice? What kind of protection is that, I ask?"

"Duke Hysmith left shortly after," Claymore said, trying to be reassuring.

"Hah! He left my sister at the altar once. Heaven knows where he will leave her this time."

"I, ah, believe His Grace and Lady Eleanor have an understanding."

"No one understands my sister, and that is a fact."

Rockford called for his curricle. A horse would be faster, of course, but his best mount was fatigued now. The curricle pair were tireless beasts who could travel long distances before they needed to be changed for fresh horses. Rockford only hoped he had as much stamina, after so many sleepless nights.

He left in a swirl of dust, the capes of his greatcoat fluttering behind, trying to decide which route Alissa would have taken, where she would stop first for a change of horse. His sister and the duke could drive to Gretna Green for all he cared.

The Bow Street Runner was not pleased either. This was work for professionals, not frenzied mothers and autocratic guardians. They did not need the reward money. He did. So he hailed a hackney after speaking to Claymore, and set off after the earl and his lady.

Rockford was paying expenses, after all.

Mr. Canover was torn. He was the one at fault for letting the Henning boys escape Rothmore House, and for letting them stay missing so long that catching up to them would take a day, at least. He should be the one to go after them, to bring them back. He yearned to follow Lady Rockford and her sister — he yearned for Miss Bourke all the time, in fact — but he could not leave the other boys.

What if the Henning children had met with

trouble along the way? Gads, what if Lawrence had met up with other choice spirits on his drive back? For all Mr. Canover knew, Lawrence would bribe the driver to let him take the reins, or he'd find a doxy to dally with. He might even decide not to return to his school at all, eluding the driver Lord Rockford had instructed to see that Lawrence arrived there. Who could know what would happen to the little boys if any of those dread possibilities occurred? And who knew what Lord Rockford would do to Canover's brother then? For certain the tutor would lose his position, and any chance he might have had to win Miss Bourke's hand in marriage.

He had to go after her. After them. The Rothmore boys were no longer ill, and they would be sleeping through the night. Tomorrow . . . tomorrow he'd promised the viscount another visit to the lending library if Hugo was well enough, and he had promised young Billy a return to the Tower Menagerie if the weather was clement.

Before Mr. Canover could agonize over his conflicting duties and desires, the boys came hurtling down the stairwell, Billy sliding down the banister and Hugo bumping along with a valise, the four puppies yipping and swarming at his feet. They were dressed in their overcoats and hats, gloves and woolen mufflers.

"We are going after Willy and Ken," Billy announced. "They are our brothers now and we will not be left behind."

"We have decided," Hugo added, standing as tall as he could, trying to raise one imperious eyebrow as he'd seen his father do so often. Then he had to adjust his slipping spectacles. "And no one can stop us."

"Of course we can," Mr. Canover and Claymore said at once.

Aunt Reggie said, "We can lock you in your room."

Hugo held up the key. "No, you cannot. Besides, we looked. We can climb out the window, go across the railing, then over the rooftop, and find the drain spout. Billy knows how to slide down one of those."

Aunt Reggie swayed on her feet. Claymore did not bother to try to steady her this time. He had to sit down, his head in his hands, at the idea of the heir, with his poor eyesight and fragile constitution, climbing over roofs and down gutter pipes. "I am too old for this. I helped raise Master Robert and Lady Eleanor. That was hard enough. I told the countess I should not have come to London, and now she will see that I was right."

Mr. Canover ignored the butler's muttering to try to reason with his charges. "You cannot have put your excellent mind to this problem, Rothmore. How do you intend to get to Oxford? Walk? You know the grooms will not take a coach out of your father's carriage house without his say-so, or Mr. Claymore's, at the very least."

"We shall hire a hackney at the corner to take us to the nearest coaching inn. I have studied the schedules and routes."

"But how shall you pay for it?" Aunt Reggie asked, miraculously recovered since no one was paying the least attention to her. She knew she had won most of the boys' allowance money.

"My grandparents sent me away with a parting gift," Hugo answered. "They did not wish to be bothered having to remember me at Christmas or the New Year or my birthday in January. I would not gamble with that money."

"And I know where Aunt Lissie — our mother — keeps the peppermint drops," Billy chimed in, holding up a paper sack, "so I won't get sick. Hugo says I can sit up with the driver if I feel like casting up my accounts. I won't fall off, either."

"And the dogs will be a great help in finding Willy and Kendall," Hugo added. "They are scent hounds, you know."

"And they miss everyone, too," Billy said.

Hugo nodded. "They don't want to stay here when everyone else is gone."

Two of the pups were shredding the glove of Kendall's that Hugo had thought to bring, to start them on a hunt. A third mongrel was chewing the fringe off the hall Turkey runner, and the last one was leaping on Billy, trying to get the peppermints.

Mr. Canover wanted to go after his lost love — but like this? If it was the only way he could leave in good conscience, and the only way these two scapegrace boys would be safe, then yes. "Very well. I will take you to Oxford. It might be an educational opportunity at that. You can see the college your father attended, and so might aspire to those lofty towers of erudition and academia yourself."

"What does he mean?" Billy asked his brother.

"He means we can go."

So they left, after packing hampers with food and medicines and more warm clothes than Wellington's army possessed, and hot bricks and warm cider. They took the carriage Lady Eleanor had left behind, but with extra grooms and guards.

Claymore stared after the departing coach, shaking his gray head. "His lordship will dismiss me for certain after this," he said with a sigh. "He'll make me retire to some dreadful little cottage in the country, where I shall raise roses." He sighed again. "Roses make me sneeze."

Aunt Reggie's turban had fallen off, leaving the gray roots showing in her dyed red hair. She looked at Claymore, then at the street where everyone had gone. "What say you, old man; shall we follow them?"

"Follow? Us?"

"That's right. Why should we miss all the fun?"

"But your health . . . ?"

"Pshaw. You could not kill me with a stick. A little of my nephew's brandy will have me right as rain in no time."

"But your reputation, my lady."

"It's my niece's reputation that is at stake here, and that sweet little Miss Bourke's. Besides, after three husbands and more years in my dish than I care to count, I am not going to start worrying over what people will say if they see me with a butler. Gammon. I have lived too long for that, and so have you, old friend. Come on now, fetch the brandy and blankets and some hot bricks, unless you're intending to keep me warm through the night."

They started out on the journey right after Lady Winchwood waved her vinaigrette under Claymore's nose.

No one in the neighborhood could miss all the commotion at Rothmore House. Draperies twitched and faces appeared at windows as coach after curricle after hired conveyance was packed and driven off. It must have something to do with the missing boys, the observers speculated as they took another tour of the gated garden in the square, hoping for more activity.

Some of the servants wagered on the children's return, while some bet on Lady Eleanor's chances of landing the duke this time around. A few put their money on Regina, Lady Winchwood, to snabble her fourth husband.

One observer was not interested in butlers or tutors or missing brats. He was interested in revenge. All doors had been shut to Sir George Ganyon. He could not go to his clubs, where he was a laughingstock, thrown out of Almack's with punch and a floating flower dripping down him. Everyone knew he had grievously offended Rockford and had left his rooms at the Albany to avoid a challenge.

A man could survive many labels: miser, womanizer, fool, drunk. He could not live among his fellows as a coward. Ganyon was considered lily-livered for not meeting Rockford, although everyone acknowledged that a duel with the earl, pistols or swords, illegal or not, was as good as a death sentence. The baronet was also deemed a cur for his suspected assault on Rockford's wife, although she had been neither wife nor peeress when he committed the offense. He'd compounded his sins by slandering the countess, and was now considered a danger to gentlewomen everywhere. No gentleman would give his daughter's hand to a craven brute, no cit would want his daughter wearing Ganyon's tarnished title. So Sir George would have no heir, no sons to help on the estate, no housekeeper, and no bed-mate for the winter — if he dared return to his home in the country. He might, if Rockford stayed in the city, as was his wont.

No one in London would acknowledge Sir George any longer, although they could not help recognize the scars from the sugar tongs put on his cheek by that Henning bitch. Rather than sitting in the mean rooms he'd rented, the baronet had been sitting in his coach across the street from Rothmore House. He'd been watching the house, waiting for a chance to get back at the earl and his wife for all the trouble they had caused him.

"What do you think is happening that they're all leaving?" his driver asked. Fred Nivens had a broken nose, three missing teeth, and a jaw that would never shut right again, thanks to the earl. He also had a thirst for revenge. He was all for burning down Rothmore House and everyone inside. Only now there was no one left inside except the servants. There was no fun in that.

"They must have figured out where the brats got to."

"Who cares?"

Sir George did. He wished he had found

the urchins first. According to the rumors in the pubs, the earl would have paid anything to get them back, and the jumped-up countess would have been repaid when they were sold as chimney sweeps or cabin boys. Ganyon could have had the money and the satisfaction at the same time.

He took another swig from the flask he held, then wiped his mouth on his sleeve. If he had the brats, he could have offered Alissa a trade: the sprigs for the sister. That would have been an interesting choice to hand the jade who had rejected his proposal, his proposition, and his honorable offer to take the sister off her hands. Sir George licked his fleshy lips, imagining the wench's suffering if faced with that dilemma.

Without the Henning boys, though, Sir George had nothing, not even a chance to get even . . . unless he followed them.

Chapter Twenty-eight

In another carriage, in the meantime, the reasons for the cavalcade leaving London were on their way back.

The journey had started out fine for the Henning boys. No one saw them slip from the kitchen door with a bundle of food, and no one saw Kendall boost his little brother into the luggage boot of the hired coach. Lawrence Canover had few belongings, so they had ample room. Having stayed up half the night, worrying and planning, both fell asleep as the carriage left town and took the northwest road. While his brother slept on, Kendall peeked out at the first stop, then got down to find a likely groom to carry a note to their mother. The groom drove a hard bargain, though, to carry the message, and the boys were left with little food and less money.

They were cold, besides. And bored. And cramped, now that they were fully awake. And Willy needed to relieve himself. "I miss Mama," he said.

"So do I."

"Do you think she got our message yet?"

"I don't know. That rider had a mean smile. Maybe he took the letter and ripped it up."

"She'll worry, when she remembers to look for us."

"She might cry."

Tears formed in Willy's green eyes. Kendall pretended it was too dark to see, and the noise of the wheels was too loud to hear his brother's sniffles.

At the next stop, which seemed like ages later, Kendall heard the driver tell Lawrence that they were almost halfway to Oxford. Only halfway? Their jug of cider was gone, and their last apple. And Willy had to relieve himself. But what if the driver was in a hurry and left without them while they were in the bushes?

"We'd better talk to Lawrence."

So they walked into the inn, Kendall holding on to the back of Willy's collar. Young Mr. Canover was sitting at a table there, counting out the coins the earl had given him — into the hands of a serving girl who could have used her ample bosom for a shelf. Instead she was using it as a deposit bank, stuffing the coins down the front of her gown. Lawrence's eyes followed every ha'penny piece.

"Hallo, Lawrence," Kendall called when they were halfway through the room. "We decided that we want to go home."

Lawrence dragged his eyes away from the vault he fully expected to visit before his driver finished his meal. When he caught sight of the boys, he leaped to his feet, dropping the rest of his purse. "He'll kill me!" was all he said, head swiveling from side to side in search of the earl, or a back way out of the inn.

"Not if you take us home," Willy offered.

Then Lawrence cursed like the army trooper he aspired to become, after he became a rake and a womanizer. The serving girl, laughing, went off with his money. "Come find me when you tuck your little brothers in their beds tonight. Although the older one might be ready for a little —"

Lawrence hauled the boys out of the inn. Tonight? They were not staying another minute, if he had his way. Unfortunately, the hired driver did not see the need to rush back to London.

"I got my orders, I do. I take you straight to your school in Oxford, with no side trips; that's what the governor said. And what he's payin' me for. I ain't takin' you nowheres else, nor the kiddies, neither."

"But they are the earl's sons! He'll want them back."

"Thought you called 'em Hennings."

Lawrence almost pulled the hair out of his head. "Lord Rockford married their mother.

They are his. I swear it!"

"Like you swore you was just askin' that trollop for another glass of ale?"

"But we can't leave them here. The earl will have my head on a plate as is, if my brother does not shoot me first. And Lady Rockford will be distraught. You don't want any countess going into a decline, do you?"

Willy was eating an apple tart. Kendall was watching anxiously. The driver scratched his head. "Well, I suppose we can take 'em along to Oxford. Then I can drive the bantlings back to town tonight. Goin' there anyway, I am."

That was the best Lawrence could do. After a humiliating conversation with the barmaid, he got his money back, enough to bribe the driver to let the boys meet their cousins. They had come all this way, he told the jarvey, and it would be a shame for them to leave without seeing the duke's sons.

Earl's sons, duke's sons, it was all the same to the driver, but he waited while Lawrence explained to his headmaster about the need to find two university scholars to take charge of their young cousins. The headmaster saw prospective students and sought the earl's favor, if not the duke's, so he sent a note to a colleague of his. Within minutes, it seemed, the Duke of Hysmith's sons appeared: Magnus, the Marquis of Henfield, the heir, and Lord Bertram Henning, the spare.

Both of the young men had their father's somewhat stocky build, but neither had his superior air. In fact, they thought their little cousins were game 'uns, full of pluck. They remembered their uncle William, who had been an idol to them when they were no older than Will, and were prepared to befriend his children.

Lawrence happily surrendered the Henning boys into their cousins' care, who instantly decided that the lads could not be entrusted to a mere hired coachman. They would accompany Lady Rockford's sons back to London — and get a look at their estranged aunt, besides. Their father would not be pleased with the families' mingling, nor would he approve their absence from school, but he'd never find out, they told themselves. The little Hennings would never cry rope on their magnificent new cousins, and the driver would only report to Rockford. They were safe.

And they were on their way to London, where one of their friends kept a handy flat and an openhanded opera dancer.

Alissa could not get Jake to drive any faster. Then, when he did, one of the wheels hit a rut, and they had to crawl to the nearest inn to have the wheel straightened. The wheelwright had to be awakened and offered a generous bonus to work at night. The moon was covered now, with rain on the way. The temperature was dropping too, so the precipitation might fall as sleet, Jake warned. They might not be able to go on tonight.

Alissa could not, would not accept that. She would hire postilions to carry lanterns. She would hire a horse to ride. She would walk to Oxford if need be. Jake shook his head and told her he would talk to her after supper, after the wheel was repaired.

The food was well prepared and ample, the inn's best in honor of their titled guest, but Alissa could not eat. How could she, when her boys might be hungry? She had never been apart from them for an entire day before, much less a night. She kept going to the window of the private parlor Jake had taken for her and Aminta's use, wiping her hand across the fogged glass, trying to see out into the dark night.

Amy had hardly eaten all day and was hungry, so she sampled the innkeeper's wife's cooking: the pigeon pie and the turbot in oyster sauce, the loin chops and the steamed pudding. Then she excused herself to use the necessary at the rear of the building.

She never returned.

Alissa thought Amy was back when the parlor door opened, but it was only the innkeeper's wife with a tray of tea and biscuits. Alissa thanked the woman, then asked her to see if Amy needed assistance.

Amy was not using the convenience, had not gone upstairs to lie down, had not joined Jake in the taproom, had certainly not gone for a walk in the steady rain that was now falling. She was gone. Vanished. Like the boys.

Rockford pushed his horses nearly to their limit. He stopped at every tollbooth, and knew he was mere minutes behind his wife. He should have passed her by now, though, he calculated, trying to see through the rain. The roads were getting muddy, the visibility next to nothing, until it was growing unsafe to continue. His clothes were already sodden in the open curricle despite his caped riding coat, with shards of frozen rain finding their way down his back. She had to be somewhere just ahead. He urged his tired horses onward.

At the next toll, the keeper told him that only one carriage had passed by the last hour, a shabby rig that held a man and a woman inside. Their surly, broken-nosed driver had asked about the nearest inns.

Rockford did not care about some battered coachman's manners, only that his wife had not passed this way. She must have taken shelter somewhere earlier, for he would have seen a mired coach. He was glad — and surprised — that Alissa had sense enough to cease her mad dash through the night and the rain. Jake and Aminta must have insisted, he thought, for Alissa would ordinarily have killed herself, the horses, and anyone coming between her and her sons.

Rockford stayed at the tollbooth, contemplating his choices. He could press on toward Oxford, where the boys must have arrived and must have found shelter either with Lawrence Canover or the duke's sons. Or he could backtrack and spend the night in some cozy inn, with a warm fire, warmed punch, and his warming wife.

He turned the horses back toward London so fast their hooves kicked up a tidal wave of mud and muck. The toll taker cursed until Rockford threw him a coin.

The duke did not bother making inquiries. He was wet and tired, and far too old for this kind of derring-do, racing about the kingdom in an open phaeton. His arms ached from holding the ribbons of his high-bred pair — but he'd be hanged before he let Lady Eleanor take them. She was just as wet and cold as he was, his grace knew, the hot bricks from the last stop long gone useless, but she only complained about his driving, not the conditions. He pressed on, rather than let the lady find him lacking in manly fortitude. She said the Henning children were in Oxford visiting his heirs, so he was going to drive her to Oxford, by Hades.

His sons were not in their dormitories, however, not in Oxford at all. They had gone back to London with some country cousins after supper, Henfield's roommate reported after a bit of intimidation on the duke's part. They could be halfway there by now, or holed up at some tavern to wait out the weather. He could have passed them on the road if his eye had been on the other vehicles, instead of on his passenger. Blast.

His grace had a choice similar to Rockford's. He could stay in Oxford for the night, where he was well known at every decent hotel. His companion would be duly noted, and grist for the rumor mills by morning, whether they took separate chambers or not. Lady Eleanor was traveling alone with him, at night, contrary to all the dictates of polite society. Or he could head back the way they had come, finding a smaller, out-of-the-way inn where no one knew either of them, and continue the afternoon's conversation in private.

"You always were a cow-handed driver," Eleanor shouted as she clutched the seat rail beside her with one hand and her hat with the other.

Rockford recognized his carriage in the inn yard of the third hostelry he tried. He almost did not recognize the distraught woman who threw herself into his arms as soon as he entered the private parlor the landlord directed him to.

"I knew you would come!" she cried. Her eyes were red and puffy, and her hair hung down in damp curls. Her russet traveling gown was sadly rumpled, and her hems were muddied. He thought she looked beautiful. She felt beautiful pressed against him too, so he forgot the cold and the wet and the mud. He could not forget that she'd left London without him, though. He set her aside to take a hot rum toddy from the innkeeper.

As soon as the man was gone, he said, "If you knew I would come, dash it, why the devil didn't you wait for me? Didn't you trust me to keep my word that I would look after all of you? Or did you think I was dallying with some Austrian countess?" He'd been trying to honor his marriage vows, and her lack of confidence in him rankled.

Alissa was shredding her handkerchief. "No, no, I never thought —"

"Precisely. Here I have had to worry about you for hours, besides the children. You should have stayed in town while I went to fetch the boys. You would have, if you had any faith in me."

"I had to go. They are my sons."

"Mine now, too. Those were your rules."

"And my sister."

"Your sister?"

So Alissa had to tell him that Aminta was

gone. That the coach was not repaired yet. That the innkeeper predicted the roads would be impassable come morning if the rain kept up. That a scarred man had been seen stepping out of a carriage, but he never came inside the inn.

"Bloody hell. Ganyon. That gatesman said another coach had gone through an hour before me. At least we know which direction he took. I'll set out as soon as they can find me a horse to ride. The curricle would get bogged down before I reached that toll-booth."

"I am coming too. Amy needs me."

"Absolutely not. It is too dangerous for you to ride, much less confront Sir George and his driver, who I suspect is Fred Nivens."

Alissa shuddered. "All the more reason for me to go."

"No! Amy is my sister now too, and it is my job to protect her and you and the children, do you hear? Mine, and no one else's."

The duke walked in then. "Sorry to steal your thunder, old chap, but I have come to lend assistance."

Rockford set down his drink and looked past Hysmith to see his sister, resembling something the cat would have left outside on the doorstep. "You brought my sister? I'll strangle you this time, for sure."

Eleanor giggled, a very strange, girlish

sound to come from the earl's spinster sister. "If you kill him, he won't be able to make an honest woman out of me."

The duke harrumphed a few times, then held his hand out for Rockford to shake. Alissa hugged Lady Eleanor, while the earl told his second-time brother-in-law-to-be about Aminta's disappearance. The boys would have to wait.

"If that dastard is desperate enough to make off with an innocent female," the duke said, "then you need help. There are two of them, you say? You might think those are good odds, but you still need someone to watch your back."

Rockford nodded reluctantly and left to find the innkeeper to see about horses. Before he reached the door, he nearly tripped over Mr. Canover, who was carrying Billy. The boy's complexion was as green as rotten cabbage. He smelled like it, too. Hugo trailed slowly at the tutor's side. Four young hounds barked and bayed and bounded at their feet, sliding on the polished wood floor.

"Bloody hell!" Rockford yelled. "You brought my sons — my poor, sickly sons — out in a storm? This time you won't be merely dismissed; you'll be decapitated!"

"No, Father," Hugo said, trying to stand tall despite his weariness. "Mr. Canover did not take us. He came with us, for we were going to come help find Kendall and Willy on our own. With the dogs."

"Hugo was as bossy as you, Papa," Billy added proudly, now from Alissa's arms.

By this time everyone was in the entry of the inn.

The duke raised his quizzing glass as if to examine a new species of insect. "Your heir, Rockford, I presume?"

Hugo squared his shoulders and made a proper bow. "Viscount Rothmore, sir, at your service." Then he collapsed. Luckily the innkeeper caught him before Hugo's head hit the inn's registry desk. Two of the innkeeper's sons were trying to gather the dogs before they destroyed the furnishings.

The innkeeper's wife, trying to figure where she was to put so many high-toned guests, and who shared which bedroom, took over. She took Billy from Alissa's arms as if he were a kitten, and said, "Here, now, I'll take care of the wee ones. I've had seven of my own, I have, so I know all about youngsters and what ails them. My boys will take the pups out to the stable. You folks worry about finding the young miss."

"The young miss?" Canover yelped, looking around frantically. "You've lost Amy?" He turned accusing eyes on Rockford. "You'll answer to me for that, my lord."

Rockford groaned. Just what he needed, an overweight duke and a moonstruck tutor.

And his aunt. Lady Winchwood predictably

swooned when she heard Amy was missing. Claymore staggered, but caught her. Then he had to lower her to the floor. He sank down beside her, gasping. "Sorry, my lord."

The duke's lips twitched, until Lady Eleanor poked her elbow into his ribs. "Well, Rockford, what is our plan?"

"To kill those bastards, of course."

"Not so fast, my lord," the Bow Street Runner said, limping into the inn, brushing rainwater off his shoulders. "This is a criminal matter now, and as such has to be handled by the courts."

"The courts can handle what's left after I find Ganyon and his bully. Can you ride?" When the Runner nodded, Rockford gestured toward the tutor. "See if you can locate a map of the area. Hysmith, you check with the stables about horses. Claymore, ask about nearby inns. I'll see what weapons are available." He told the innkeeper, "We'll need hot drinks and blankets, too, whatever you can spare. We'll meet back here in half an hour."

Alissa helped him gather an arsenal from the various coaches and the inn, besides the personal pistols he and the duke carried. She handed him Henning's old pistol, but he made her keep it, just in case.

Then he opened his arms. "I need to hold you, just for a moment."

But the moment continued. Alissa pressed herself to him as if she might never have the chance again, and he kissed her as if he were drowning and her breath were the only air keeping him alive. Her arms wrapped around his damp shoulders and his hands kneaded her back, then her waist, then her derriere. She reached under his coat to touch his chest, separated from her fingers only by the thin fabric of his shirt. He reached under the neckline of her gown to touch her breast, separated from his fingers by nothing. He groaned. She whimpered. He used his tongue to echo the thrust he ached for; she answered by pressing her hips against his hardness. He whimpered. She groaned.

His hand reached down to lift her skirts. "Now. I need you now."

"Now?" Her hands fell away and she stepped back, straightening her bodice. Her face was flushed and her breath came in short gasps. "Now? You want to make love now? My sister has been abducted, my sons are missing in the night. Your sons are upstairs, ill, and your sister is facing possible disgrace. You are riding off to face ruthless, barbaric ruffians with a ragtag group of rescuers. And everyone is meeting here, in this very room, in less than fifteen minutes."

"So . . . ? The door has a lock."

Chapter Twenty-nine

As soon as the men left, Eleanor and Alissa put their heads together. The rain was tapering off and the boys were fast asleep, with the innkeeper's wife and two of her capable daughters looking on. Aunt Reggie and Claymore were sipping hot buttered rum in the private parlor.

The two women were agreed: they were not going to wait behind like poor helpless peahens, flapping their wings and squawking. The only question was whether to take the duke's phaeton or the earl's curricle. Eleanor decided on her brother's vehicle. If she wrecked the rig, her brother could only disown her again, while the duke could change his mind about marrying her. Besides, if they did overturn, the phaeton was higher off the ground and thus more dangerous. The curricle's bench also held more room for Aminta, which the gentlemen, in their haste to be off, had not considered. Amy would be best off in a closed vehicle, but Eleanor was not as skilled at four-in-hand and the

Rothmore carriage was not yet repaired. Eleanor borrowed the landlady's oilskins while Alissa packed more blankets and more jugs of hot tea wrapped in cloth. She also packed William Henning's pistol.

Coming from the other direction, the coach with the Henning boys and the Hysmith heirs was having a slow time of it. The rain had been falling hard, with icy gusts, and the coachman was thinking about looking for a place to spend the rest of the night. He drove past one inn that was nothing more than a hedge tavern with a few rooms, likely used by the barmaids and their customers. He deemed it unfit for a duke's sons, or an earl's. From inside his carriage, though, came shouts and thumps.

"Stop!"

"That's Aunt Amy! And Sir George has got her!"

"We have to go back!"

He pulled up. The youngsters were shouting to the duke's sons about their aunt and their neighbor and sugar tongs and the wicked groom and everyone getting thrown out of Almack's.

"Whoa, there," Lord Henfield said. "You say the young lady has been taken against her will?"

"She would never go off with Sir George otherwise. He is mean and he drools."

"He smells and he spits."

"He made Mama cry."

"A veritable ogre." The young men looked at each other and grinned, then clapped Kendall on his back and rubbed Will's head. "Good show, cousins! You chaps are top of the trees, leading us on a fine adventure, rescuing a damsel in distress!"

His brother asked, "Is she pretty? We do need a maiden fair, you know. No fun saving a girl who looks like the hind end of a horse."

Kendall nodded, but Willy said, "Aunt Amy is almost as pretty as Mama, who is the most beautiful woman in all of England. Our other father used to say so, didn't he, Ken?"

The duke's younger son asked, "What could be better than rescuing the second-prettiest girl in all of England? Driver, turn around."

This was the last time the coachman ever worked for the swells, he swore, but he turned the carriage and drove into the yard of the dilapidated inn. *The Yellow Duck*, the roughly lettered sign read, lit by one swaying lantern. No one came out to get the horses, but his passengers tumbled out into the yard, arguing. Hysmith's sons wanted the younger boys to stay outside, but Will and Kendall would have none of that. Henfield hauled Willy up, to toss him back into the carriage, and Lord Bertram grabbed Kendall's collar.

Rockford galloped up to the carriage and drew his horse to a rearing halt, his pistol in his hand.

Hysmith kicked his horse between the earl and the boys.

"Get out of the way, Duke. Those bastards have my sons."

"Yes, but regrettably, those bastards are my sons. If anyone shoots them, it will be I."

The little boys were tossed into the coach, with firm orders to stay there, or else.

"Or else what, Papa Rock?"

"Or else you'll have to ride in the carriage with Billy on the way home."

Rockford decided he and the duke should wait outside until the rest of their group caught up, so they could surround the building. The Runner had definite ideas about apprehending villains, ideas that he had made plain did not include shooting on sight. The earl wanted this done right, with an end to Sir George and his hireling, without a messy trial where poor Amy might have to testify.

Meantime, Hysmith's boys, who could not be recognized by Sir George or Fred Nivens, were sent inside to reconnoiter, to see where Amy was being held and how many other men might be involved. They were to come back outside immediately, to check their horses, supposedly, and to give a report.

Ah, but they were young and full of

swagger, to say nothing of the contents of the flasks they carried. They saw a pretty little miss struggling in the arms of a brute, right there in the common room of a smoke-filled pub, while five or six men looked on, laughing and wagering on the outcome. One old woman with hair the same color as the yellow duck on the inn's sign was watching in disgust, but she made no effort to help the girl.

The broken-nosed man holding the girl was trying to drag her toward the stairs, while the scar-faced man negotiated with the innkeeper.

"I don't want no trouble in my place, you hear?" the aproned landlord said, holding his hand out for additional fees.

Aminta was sobbing, flailing her hands ineffectively at her captor, who had her clasped about the waist.

The duke's sons looked at the girl, looked at each other, shouted, "Tallyho," and leaped at Fred Nivens. He fell back against one of the tables, still grasping Amy with one hand. His other suddenly held a knife. Two of the pub's patrons decided to leave after all, and the innkeeper hefted a club to swing. Amy shrieked.

Sir George held a pistol on Henfield, who held Amy's other arm and was trying to wrench her from Fred Nivens. "Let go of her, boy," the baronet said. "This is none of your affair."

"It is mine, however." Lord Rockford spoke from the doorway, his dueling pistol fixed on the center of Sir George's oily forehead.

"Damn. I should have known you'd stick your long nose into my business again." Ganyon started to lower his weapon as Rockford said, "Yes, you should have. Put down the gun and I might let you live long enough to stand trial."

Just then Mr. Canover rushed into the room. Seeing Amy in the arms of a young man, he took up a boxer's stance and advanced on Henfield. The innkeeper hit him over the head with his club. Aminta screamed louder. Fred held the knife to her throat. "Ke' back" he grunted through his mangled jaw. Young Henfield backed away, his hands in the air. His brother picked up a chair. The duke raised his pistol. Mr. Canover groaned.

"Stop in the name of the Crown!" came from the entry as the Runner hobbled in the front door. The landlord and the blonde ran out the back. The Bow Street man held no gun or knife, only a short baton. "Put down your weapons," he ordered.

Sir George laughed, spittle dripping from his fat, fleshy lip. "Why should I? So you can drag me off to prison? No, I have something Rockford wants. He'll let me go, if he wants to see the girl's pretty little face unmarked by Fred's knife. Though why I should leave her untouched when I bear the scars of that bitch he married —"

Lord Bertram Henning threw the chair. Fred ducked and Aminta wisely collapsed atop Mr. Canover, out of the groom's hold. Fred turned to swipe his knife at Bertie but a shot rang out. The knife dropped, then Fred dropped, clutching his head, from which blood poured onto the debris-strewn floor. Bertie kicked the knife into the corner.

"Thank you," the duke said to Rockford, who tossed aside his now-empty pistol. "He's not much, but I am fond of him."

Now the duke and Sir George held the only loaded weapons. Hysmith had his fixed on the baronet, but Sir George could not decide on his target. Hysmith's heir? The girl? Rockford himself?

"What's it to be, Ganyon?" Rockford asked, his hands held loosely at his sides, ready to fasten around the dastard's neck as soon as he got the chance. "You will never get out of here, you know. There are too many of us, and only one ball in your pistol. If you put it down, I will give you the chance to face me, alone. No weapons but fists. If you win, you go free."

"No. That is not justice," the Runner protested. He addressed Sir George. "I arrest you in the name of —"

But Ganyon had found his target.

"Hell and damnation," Rockford cursed as

both his wife and his sister came into the room.

The duke swore too, until he looked out the window. "It's your curricle, Rockford, thank goodness. Seems to be in one piece." He pulled Eleanor behind him.

While he'd been looking out, Ganyon took aim at Alissa, who was too far from Rockford for the earl to shield. He cursed again, then inched toward the corner where Fred's knife lay, trying to distract Ganyon's attention.

The ploy did not work. Sir George never took his beady eyes off Alissa, or his gun's muzzle.

"Well, well. If it isn't the countess herself," he said. "Come to pour tea, have you? Where are your furs and the Rothmore rubies? I'm not important enough to dress for, eh? I was not good enough for you, was I? And not good enough for your simpering little sister. She'd never have borne me healthy sons anyway, that one, always weeping and going off in swoons. No, you would have suited me fine, my fancy lady, better'n you suit Rockford, who's used to highfliers." He licked his fleshy lips, his eyes glittering with a madman's intensity. "I am thinking that if I cannot have you, Rockford shouldn't either."

Alissa slowly drew her late husband's pistol out of the folds of her cloak. She calmly faced Sir George and said, "You have threatened my family once too often, sir. I cannot let you do so again."

"No!" Rockford shouted. Ganyon was beyond reasoning, beyond any rules of civilized behavior. Rockford could not stand by and watch the Bedlamite and Alissa kill each other. It would kill him, he knew. The children needed her. He needed her. "No!" he shouted again, launching himself into the air, intending to knock Alissa to the ground. Shots rang out. So many shots he could not count, except for the one that creased his scalp, from Ganyon's weapon, and the one that went cleanly through his arm, from Alissa's.

The duke's ball hit Sir George in the chest. Lady Eleanor's hit him below the waist. The coach driver's blunderbuss peppered him with shot from head to toe, and the Runner's tiny pistol, hidden in his boot, sent a bullet right between the baronet's beady eyes.

Aminta sobbed, and Mr. Canover and Bertie both cast up their accounts. The Runner put manacles on Fred, then threw a cloth over Sir George. "Don't suppose anyone is going to miss this one. Trial would have been a waste of time."

Alissa was ripping up her petticoat to stanch the blood dripping down Rockford's cheek. Tears were falling down her own face. "Can you ever forgive me?" she cried.

"For shooting me?" he asked. "Of course. For not believing in me enough to let me rescue your sister, dash it, Alissa, never. You should have stayed behind in safety. When in this lifetime are you going to trust me?"

"I do trust you, Robert, I swear I do. You had already rescued Aminta when I arrived. And the boys too. It was you I was trying to keep safe; can't you see that?"

He could, despite the odd tear in his own eye.

There ought to be a rule, Rockford decided. When a man was shot, then jounced along in a curricle — driven by his own skitter-witted sister, no less — then poked and prodded by a country sawbones, he ought to be allowed to recover in the comfort of his wife's arms. It had been so long since Rockford had known the sweet softness of his countess's embrace, heard her murmur his name in ecstasy, that he thought he might go as mad as Sir George — hell, as mad as King George.

It was not to be.

As soon as the surgeon declared that he would live, unless the wound turned putrid, his skull was concussed, or a fever developed, a veritable parade passed through the earl's room. At least he was sharing the inn's best chamber with his wife.

Rockford took great satisfaction in knowing that the Duke of Hysmith was sharing quarters with his sons, while Eleanor roomed with

Aminta. Canover had a pallet in the younger boys' room, and the Runner was guarding the wounded Fred in a storeroom. Rockford did not inquire as to Aunt Reggie's sleeping arrangements. He felt that not knowing where his aunt and his butler slept might hasten his recuperation.

First to enter were his sons, all four of them, looking as worried as lost chicks. For a moment he took pride in knowing that they really cared about him and his well-being, until Billy — he had given up days ago, it seemed, on calling the hellion William — asked, "Are you going to beat us, Papa?"

"Cousin Bertie said you would."

"Aunt Eleanor said you should."

"Mama said you could."

Alissa squeezed his right hand, on the arm that was bandaged, from the side of his bed.

Beat these little boys? The angels with Alissa's green eyes, his brilliant heir with his sister's nose? Billy with the courage of a lion and the brains of a slab of bacon? No, not even Billy. He shook his head. "I shall not take a switch to you this time. My arm is too sore where your mother shot it. But you have to swear you will never leave the house without permission again, is that under-stood?"

Four heads nodded.

"There is more. As punishment for your misbehavior, the dogs will be returned to

Rock Hill. London is no place for such un-governed animals."

Tears filled at least one pair of eyes. One chin quivered, and one head bowed in stoic resignation. Alissa started to go to the boys, to comfort them although she knew they deserved some form of punishment, but Rockford held her back.

"Of course," he continued, "we shall all be joining them shortly, as soon as we can pack and conclude some business in town."

All the boys, and Alissa, cheered. Rockford held up his free left hand, the one that had not been wounded. "However, I will demand everyone follows the rules. There must be no ball tossing in the orangery, no swimming in the ornamental fountain. Schoolwork must be completed before play. The armory is off-limits, as is my office and —"

"Yes, Father," Hugo interrupted before he could go on. "We shall be good, we swear." He leaned over the bed and kissed Rockford's cheek. "I am glad you are not hurt too badly."

Kendall came next. "And thank you for coming to find us, sir. We are sorry to have caused so much trouble." He thought about shaking Rockford's hand, then kissed his cheek too.

He held up Willy, so the little boy could pat the earl's face and say, "And thank you for saving Mama, Papa Rock."

Billy clambered up on the bed and tried to look under the bandage on Rockford's brow. "I love you too, Papa," he said.

At Alissa's nod, they all scampered for the door, relieved to be let off so easily. Too easily, Rockford decided. "Halt. One thing more. In light of all the disobedience and rash behavior" — he fixed his dark eyes on Billy — "including talk of climbing down rainspouts and across roofs, there will be no monkey."

"Well done, my lord," Alissa whispered as the boys left.

Next to arrive at his sickroom door were Aminta and Mr. Canover, come to inquire about his health and, not coincidentally, ask his permission for their betrothal. Since the chit had sat across Canover's lap on the ride back to the inn and had not left his side since, it appeared there was no other choice. Rockford looked at Alissa first, though, to see her nod. "Very well, you have my blessings if you are certain, Amy, that you will not mind living on the meager wages a scholar can earn."

"Not a scholar, a schoolmaster," Amy said. "If you will still give us the dowry you promised, Lucius and I intend to open an academy of our own. One is needed near Rock Hill, and I have always wished to teach."

"We could pay you back in a few years, I

calculate," the tutor offered.

"That will not be necessary. The dowry is for you and your children, Amy. Building your school is my responsibility, especially since it will serve my dependents' children and my sons."

"And daughters," Alissa added.

He smiled. "And daughters."

Aunt Reggie and Claymore scratched on the door as soon as the lovebirds left, cooing about Latin lessons and geography globes.

Claymore cleared his throat. "I regret to inform your lordship that I shall be leaving your service, as soon as you have recovered sufficiently. I am accepting Lady Winchwood's offer to accompany her to Wales."

"But I thought you wished to retire from butlering, Claymore?" Alissa asked.

"Oh, I do and I am. That was not the offer I accepted, my lady."

Rockford had to reach for the glass of restorative by his bedside, to avoid laughing at his wife's wide-eyed look. "We wish you well. Both of you. Both of us."

When they left, he turned to Alissa, his eyes smiling up at her. "Lud, a tutor for a brother-in-law, a butler for an uncle. What next?"

A duke in the family, that was what. By now Rockford was growing weary. Not of his wound, but of all the company. He wanted to be alone with his wife, by Jupiter.

"Yes, yes," he told Hysmith before the duke had a chance to pay his formal addresses. "Take her and get out. I wish to spend my last breath with my countess. But," he told his sister, "there will be no Gretna Green elopements, do you understand? I shall not have my wife and my sons embarrassed by your behavior."

Lady Eleanor sniffed. "I intend to do the thing up right. St. George's, Hanover Square, for everyone and his uncle — even Claymore — to see."

"Lud, St. George's again?" Rockford turned to the duke. "If you leave her there again, Hysmith, this time I will come after you with my horsewhip, I swear."

"If he leaves me there again, brother," Lady Eleanor said, "I shall go after him with my pistol."

The duke simply put his arm around his lady and started to lead her out of the room. Rockford called them back. "What about your nephews, Duke?"

"They are Lady Eleanor's nephews."

"Not good enough. They are my sons." He could feel Alissa's hand tighten around his.

The duke nodded. "And my brother William's sons. Give over, Rock. I have already accepted the countess's invitation to Rock Hill for the Christmas holidays, along with my sons. My other brother and his children are used to spending their yuletide at Hysmith Hall, so perhaps he will venture to your place too, to meet his nephews."

While Rockford contemplated how many bothersome guests he'd be burdened with, the duke stepped toward Alissa and took her hand. He bowed over it and raised it to his lips. "My brother was no fool," was all he said. "I was, and my father." Before he left, Eleanor at his side, he added, "Oh, and I understand you are starting a school. Half the expense is mine, for my nephews' education. The William Henning Academy, what say?"

When Alissa's tears of happiness were dry, and no one else seemed about to enter the room — Hell, Rockford thought, the only one left was old Jake from the stable — Alissa went behind the screen and changed into her night rail, a scrap of ivory lace and ribbons that hid nothing, not even her intentions.

One of those pistol balls must have pierced his lungs, for all the breath left his body. "Dash it, woman, you wear that now?" he said with a gasp. "I have not slept in days, I have been shot by my own wife, drenched to the skin, racked with worry, and badgered by every mooncalf in the county."

Alissa smiled.

"So . . . ?"

Chapter Thirty

Rockford rose to the occasion. Twice. Rosy with lovemaking, his satiated wife rested her head on his uninjured shoulder, her hair in disarray on his chest. He pulled the covers higher over her satin skin, then tenderly combed his fingers through the soft brown locks, marveling that he had ever thought this woman ordinary, or a mere convenience. His Alissa was about as convenient as a hurricane, but as necessary as sunlight itself. The marvel was that she was his.

"You do love me, don't you, Lady Rockford?" he asked, kissing each of her closed eyelids in turn. "You did not just say so in a moment's heat?"

"A moment?" Their lovemaking had lasted through the night. Sleepily she murmured, "I love you, Lord Rockford, as much as you love me."

He could not let her sleep, not yet. "How do you know?"

"I know because you leaped in front of

flying gunshots to save my life, as I would do for yours."

"I would have had no life without you, my love. I never realized I was only half a man until I almost lost you."

She frowned and opened her eyes to look into his dark ones. "You would have had four sons to raise."

"Without you? I would leap in front of a firing squad, by heaven, not just a madman's pistol."

She shivered to think of Ganyon, and then to think of her sons, all four of them, alone. "Promise you will never do such a foolish thing again."

"Only if you are never in danger. Promise me you will never confront a lunatic with a weapon again. I think I lost a year of my life."

Alissa could not promise, not if it meant saving her Robert's life. Instead she said, "But we might have made a new life to-night."

"The daughter you want?"

Alissa stared at him by the dimming firelight. "Do you not want her too?"

He placed his hand on the softness of her belly. "If she has your green eyes and half your courage, I shall adore her. And spoil her unmercifully. With any luck she will not ask for a giraffe."

"But if she has your brown eyes and twice your pride?"

"Lud, she'd be another Eleanor. And I will still love her to distraction because she will be yours and mine, a child born of this miracle we have made."

Alissa sighed in contentment and started to drift off to sleep. Then her eyes snapped open. "What if we have another boy?"

She could see his smile by the light of the dying fire as he said, "Well, then, we shall just have to keep trying, won't we?"

"You won't mind?"

"Another boy or the trying?" He placed butterfly kisses on her cheeks and her ears and her neck. "Shall I show you how much I mind?"

"Now?"

"Well, I believe we have only reached chapter two of the pillow book I was composing."

Wide awake now, she gasped in pleasure as his kisses reached her breasts. "I thought you must be at chapter five at least by now."

"Oh, no. I am a slow writer. So slow that I have had to make a rule."

Alissa smiled, reaching out to caress him in return. "I am sure you did."

"Are you making light of me, wife?"

She took the weight of him in her hand. "Never, my husband. Your rules are always, ah . . ." She gave up searching for the right word, as his kisses trailed lower, searching for her pleasure.

"Yes, well, I have decided that this particular book shall go on forever."

"That . . . is your rule?"

He joined with her then and sighed in contentment. "Yes, my beloved." His lips again on hers, he whispered, "You see, I never intend to write . . ."

THE END

About the Author

The author of more than two dozen Regency romances, **Barbara Metzger** is the proud recipient of a RITA and two *Romantic Times* Career Achievement Awards for Regencies. When not writing Regencies or reading them, she paints, gardens, volunteers at the local library, and goes beachcombing on the beautiful Long Island shore with her little dog, Hero. She loves to hear from her readers, care of Signet or through her Web site, www.BarbaraMetzger.com.

2